Clouds of Darkness

By Jeffrey Caminsky:
    The Referee's Survival Guide
    All Fathers Are Giants (ed.)
    The Sonnets of William Shakespeare (ed.)
    The Guardians of Peace series:
        The Sirens of Space
        The Star Dancers
        Clouds of Darkness

Coming soon:
        The Guardians of Peace

Clouds of Darkness

A Novel

Jeffrey Caminsky

NEW ALEXANDRIA PRESS
LIVONIA

Published by New Alexandria Press
PO Box 530516
Livonia, Michigan 48153
www.newalexandriapress.com

Hardcover Edition:
ISBN-10: 1-60915-003-1
ISBN-13: 978-1-60915-003-7

Softcover Edition:
ISBN-10: 1-60915-002-3
ISBN-13: 978-1-60915-002-0

Quantity discounts are available on bulk purchases of this book Special books or book excerpts can also be made available to fit specific needs. For information, please contact sales@newalexandriapress.com or send written inquiries to New Alexandria Press, PO Box 530516, Livonia, Michigan 48153.

Printed in the United States of America
First Printing March 2011

10 9 8 7 6 5 4 3 2 1
First Edition

2010916929

To Alana, and the grandchildren of the world....

Author's Note

THE HISTORICAL CONTEXT OF THE ensuing chapters promises to remain a source of debate as well as a window into the human soul, and interested readers can find information about the era from a variety of sources. Unfortunately, as noted in previous volumes of this story, most of these sources are not yet in print.

To aid readers curious about the years to come, as a prelude to the first two volumes of this work, the Author managed to convince a reluctant Publisher to share some passages providing information and insight about what the Future may hold in store for our descendants. These were culled from the award-winning works of preeminent historians from a few different eras. Excerpts were planned for subsequent volumes as well, but these and similar works were unavailable as time came to send this book to the printer. Instead, the reader will find an excerpt from a charming but little-known anthology of Crutchtan myths and legends, taken from the original translations published shortly after the end of the conflict portrayed in the story. The Author's hope is that the passage cited provides some small insight into the relationship among some of the characters in the story—albeit, perhaps not as effectively as the historical texts might have allowed.

Apparently, it seems that printing material taken from texts of the future is a bit trickier than one might suppose. The ensuing problems appear to have disrupted the Publisher's present-day printing schedules, as well as occasioning some minor dislocations in a few literary databases of the future. For this, as well as for an inexcusable inattentiveness in neglecting to set time parameters in the search for helpful "cover blubs" to insert on the back of the book, the Author takes full responsibility, and offers his heartfelt apology for any ensuing confusion.

As for the confusion that is simply a part of early 21st Century life, with no proven link to any dislocation in the continuum of time and space that defines our observable Universe, the Author continues to deny any active complicity.

Excerpted from Munshi, Trans, *Legends of the g'Khruushtani*, (New Alexandria, cc:145-7678; 2565 OE; 429 Is):

As nights grew cold and damp with the coming of Winter, village fires warmed the darkness like love warms the lonely heart. But mysteries grow in the forest like flowers beneath the sun, and one long Winter's night, far from the embers of Life that warmed the hearts and souls of the villagers, a spark of Death rose from the depths of the forest, spreading gloom and despair as it consumed valley and highland like a wildfire. And thus the coming of the Sheregal saw days become dark with fear, like the night that frightens the innocent child.

From their huts the villagers could see the eyes of animals in the darkness, glowing wildly in the soft light of their fires. But the eyes of the Sheregal were not the dull eyes of serene incomprehension, but the cunning eyes of evil. These Evil Ones, waking from their long slumber on that Longest Night, were soon thirsting for the blood of infants and howling wildly in the wind. And for many years, the villagers huddled in fear through the night, while their men went to stalk and slay the Evil Ones by day.

Yet it came that among the Sheregal there arose a Beast with the mind of a wizard and the soul of a demon, whose laughter filled the night and as his treachery haunted the day. For unlike the animals of the forest this Beast knew no fear, and he stalked the land like a hunter...

IT IS 2555.

For three years, interstellar war has raged across half the known galaxy, leaving one side exhausted and desperate, and the other impatient for victory.

THE PLAYERS

Terrans

Captain Jeremy Ashton, *captain of the Morning Star*
Lt.Cmdr. J. Peterson Atley, *staff aide to Admiral Weatherlee*
Christopher Barnes, *a native of Planet Isis*
Benjamin Brewster, *editor-in-chief, United Media Network*
Lt. Jerry Burdick, *CSO officer*
Captain Tom Chandler, *a starship captain*
Admiral Porter Clay, *commander of the Terran Fleet*
Yeoman Chief Gregory Connors, *senior yeoman on Starship d'Artagnan*
Roscoe Cook, *a native of Planet Isis*
Ens. Alan Danley, *ship's navigator on Starship d'Artagnan*
Lt. Kirkland Dexter, *systems officer on Starship d'Artagnan*
Ens. Charles Finley, *junior officer on Starship Morning Star*
Captain Brian Fitzgerald, *captain of the Magellan*
Yeoman Chief Francis Flanagan, *senior yeoman on Starship Morning Star*
Lt. Thomas Gerlach, *weapons officer on Starship d'Artagnan*
Commodore Matthew Grissom, *a Terran wing commander*
Lt. Hal Hansen, *a Terran soldier*
E. Emerson Hollenback, *senior senator from Earth*
Commander James Jefferson, *commanding officer, Liberty Base 223*
Commodore Jefferson McKinley Jones, *a Terran wing commander,*
Duncan Heathcoate, *president of the Terran League*
Lt. Mary Mathison, *radio officer on Starship d'Artagnan*
Admiral Peter Medwick, *Terran command staff*
Irene McGinnis, *Chancellor of Isis*
George McKenzie, *Isitian Minister of Defense*
Lt.Cmdr. Janet Mendelson, *helmsman and executive officer on Starship d'Artagnan*
Nicholas Schiller, *chief of staff to the President*
William Schroeder, *a native of Planet Isis*
Tom Sullivan, *crewman on Starship d'Artagnan*
Lt. Cmdr. Bruce Van Horn, *chief engineer on Starship d'Artagnan*
Yeoman Chief Kevin Ward, *senior yeoman, Liberty Base 223*
Admiral Winthrop Weatherlee, *Terran command staff*
Lt. Cmdr. Pauline Wiggins, *new commander, Liberty Base 223*
Admiral Miriam Wright, *Terran command staff*
Suzie Yang, *a journalist*

Crutchtans

Ad'Dranaka, *commander, Convoy of Hope*
bra'Lendt, *a monitor*
dra'Khranda, *family retainer for Dralanvengi clan*
Dra'Lengish, *Imperial Chief of Tactics*
Dra'Tanglos, *First Assistant of Tactics, nephew of Dra'Lengish*
fa'Shenali, *a young subaltern*
fo'Rendish, *a monitor*
Ga'Glish, *Lord Commander of the Crutchtan Empire*
Ga'Glishek, *Imperial Governor of Gr'Shuna. father of Ga'Glish*
Gal'Shenga, *Imperial First Minister, brother of Ga'Glishek and uncle of Ga'Glish,*
Glishenda, *mate of Ga'Glishek and mother of Ga'Glish*
Gor'Faradan, *a pilot*
Khla'Chenga, *High Commander of the Greloosh Region*
Ja'Rend XCVI, *Imperator of the Crutchtan Empire*
La'Gralokh, *an aide to Ga'Glish*
La'Shendra, *commander, Frusenite Eminence*
lash'Hanna, *a menial*
ls'Shen, *a soldier*
Segusha, *mate of ts'Segu*
Shl'Glisen, *a young boy*
Shl'Lanasha, *a widowed soldier, father of Shl'Glisen*
Sra'Chenga, *an aide to Ga'Glish*
ts'Segu, *an itinerant freight-hauler*
Va'Nazze, *Chief of Protocol to the Lord Commander*

Other Members of the Consortium

Drubid, *a Glincian ambassador*
Fralama, *Official Confidante for the Glincian Embassy*
Jarah, *a Glincian ambassador*
Lenorsa, *First Deputy Director, Glincian Ministry of State Security*
Remohla, *a Glincian ambassador*

A SELECT GAZETTEER
OF OBSCURE HEAVENLY BODIES

Athena, *a Terran planet*

Balarium, *seat of the Grand Alliance of the Consortium*

Ceres, *a Terran planet*

The Crutchtan Cloud, *a vast natural formation of rocks, gases, and precious elements*

Demeter, *third most populous Terran planet*

Denlubi Vortex, *a large interstellar eddy near the Great Bend.*

Dibishi Transverse, *a clearing near the Frusenite Eminence*

Earth, *former capital of the Terran League, most populous Terran planet*

Frusenite Eminence, *a jetty hiding a small cul-de-sac in the Crutchtan Cloud*

Gaea, *a Terran planet*

The Great Divide, *the Crutchtan name for the Neutral Zone*

g'Khruushte, *ancestral home and capital of the Crutchtan Empire; also, Crutchan Empire*

gla'Shenzhi-Khu'ukhtari, *a star just east of Gr'Shuna, shrouded by the Crutchtan Cloud*

The Great Bend, *the eastern terminus of the Crutchtan Cloud*

Gr'Shuna, *a Crutchtan planet and regional capital*

Gutterman's Gap, *a narrow passage to Isis through the Nakahashi Storms*

Ishtar, *Terra's easternmost planet*

The Ishtari Belt, *a formation of rocks, gases, and precious elements near Ishtar*

Isis, *Terra's westernmost planet*

Khu'ukhana Rift, *a narrow passage through the Crutchtan Cloud*

The Lesser Bend, *a bend in the Crutcthan Cloud just east of Gr'Shuna*

Ling'tari, *a star just east of Gr'Shuna*

Ling'tari Crescent, *a shallow clearing in the Great Cloud near Ling'tari*

Looking Glass, *colloquial name of Star Base 102*

Mullinberry's Star, *the star dominating the Demeter system*

The Nakahashi Storms, *a large and intense formation of gases and rocks east of Isis*

New Babylon, *capital of the Terran League, second most populous Terran planet*

Pirate's Alley, *a dangerous stretch of space from the Ishtari Belt to Demeter*

Shunite Prominence, *a bulge in the Crutchtan Cloud near Gr'Shuna*

Trillinary Rille, *a mineral-rich gaseous deposit along the Glincian border*

Zarathustra, *one of two inhabited Terran planets west of Earth*

Major Battles (and their Crutchtan names)

Denlubi

Geroulanashi, (*Grulanashi Binary*)

Girshoona, (*Gr'Shuna*)

Greloosh, (*Gr'Lusshe*)

Lashuni

Lagrush

Fralenga

Clouds of Darkness

Child of Mine, will you remember me?
Child of Mine, will you remember me?
Through cruel skies
I am bound away,
And if I ne'er return
Will you remember me?

Crutchtan Song of Farewell

Blow, blow thou winter wind
Thou art not so unkind
As Man's ingratitude....

Shakespeare, *As You Like It*, III, vii

Chapter 1

THE WAR WAS GOING BADLY, but War was an alien thing, never meant to go well for the *g'Khruushtani.*

On a great ship a few units away from the line of battle, as he had done each day for nearly two cycles, the Imperator's Supreme Lord Commander sifted through reports from each of the divisions under his direction. The Imperial Flagship enjoyed all the comforts of a modern haven. On a nearby table, Ga'Glish had the most sumptuous meal prepared with the finest sauces that the Flagship's culinary staff could devise. Bright murals danced across the walls, and an intricate tapestry of richest velvet cushioned the feet of all who approached his chambers. Yet amid the trappings of wealth and civilization, Ga'Glish found himself wishing for the simplicity he had known as a child. Alone with his thoughts and his work, he sat facing a table littered with charts and graphs. His mind ached for rest, for he had not slept in two days. The latest Terran offensive threatened to shatter their crumbling defenses. Along the entire front the Terrans advanced relentlessly, showing as little fear of death as of the *g'Khruushtani.*

This was the third such push in the past month. Each time, the Terrans pushed forward along a broad line of battle, intent on ripping holes in their enemy's battle lines. Each time, they pushed the Forces of His Worthiness to the brink of disaster, stretching the *g'Khruushtani* defenses to their limit and beyond. And each time, the longnoses had been driven back, more by the force of sheer desperation than anything else.

But the strain was exacting its price. The Empire's reserves were depleted, their ships falling like the petals of dayflowers. For the thousandth time since the war began, Ga'Glish sensed that all was lost, that the end was drawing near.

A great sadness swelled within his breast, a sadness he could share with no one. Ga'Glish rose and strode to the viewing panel on the west wall of his cabin, looking toward skies now under enemy control. The stars burned in the blackness like distant embers, their silence tormenting him with unanswered questions, mocking his small efforts to change the tide of Fortune. In his heart self-hatred burned with a royal flame.

Why did the Terrans not press their advantage, he wondered, his jaw locked in anger. Instead, the longnoses toyed with him, prolonging the agony of the *g'Khruushtani* ordeal. It was obvious that the barbarians had the power to obliterate anything in their path, yet they advanced cautiously, tentatively, as if fearing that the smallest misstep would change the currents of reality. They clung to the edge of the Great Cloud like children to their mother's leg, though the *g'Khruushtani* had yet to find the strength to contain them in open skies. There, the hated Terran warships could form vast, charging phalanxes, powerful enough to shatter anything rising against them. And they had not yet unleashed their most potent force, the most evil weapon Terra possessed within her ranks and the one that Ga'Glish had given them so freely, like an innocent girl on her wedding night.

Though hailed as a hero in all corners of the Empire, Ga'Glish took no pride in anything he had done since the outbreak of hostilities. In the earliest days of the conflict he had squandered what he now knew was their best chance for victory. Without thinking, he had condemned his people to war with a foe as merciless as it was bloodthirsty. No matter how heroic they seemed to others, his efforts only postponed the wickedness looming in the emptiness of space.

He had come to hate himself for saving the ugly, vile creature that he now realized would prove the destruction of all he knew and loved. Killing the monster had been within his grasp. He chanced, on the eve of war, to have the monster at his mercy, and Fate had handed him the power to destroy the Evil One upon his own barest whim. It would have saved his people oceans of grief and suffering, and he could blame none but himself, and his naive sense of honor, for sparing both the Beast and his ghastly ship. It was the Terrans' proudest engine of death, one which they had used but sparingly in the past cycle-and-a-half, as if sensing its importance and taking pains to preserve it for the conflict's final phase.

Those who saw the monster's ship and lived to tell spoke little of the grace and artistry of he who commanded it. They told instead of the fire in its wings, and the terror it brought in its wake. It would appear from the emptiness just when the battle seemed about to turn in favor of the *g'Khruushtani*, destroying all hope of victory and sending the Forces of His Worthiness into panic and despair. As for the Beast himself, he was the One feared throughout the Empire. His mere presence brought death and destruction to all that the Imperator's subjects held dear. But to the longnoses—and to those who would gladly die to kill him—he was simply the One Called *Khu'ukh.*

Ga'Glish struck his fist against the wall. The pain only inflamed his anger. Again and again he pounded the wall, until his bloodied hand ached from the pain. Looking out onto the distant skies, hatred flaming in his soul, he vowed that he would see the longnoses driven from *g'Khruushtani* skies.

And he vowed to see the destruction of the One Called *Khu'ukh*, or to die in the attempt.

* * *

A FEW DAYS later, a slightly built youth walked nervously down the great hall of the Imperial Flagship. The wide, arching hallway reminded him of the grand palaces of the capital, and the aroma of morningsong blossoms filled his nostrils with the smells of spring, and his mind with memories of better days. He was a Small One, of common birth and low station, and so approached the Lord Commander's quarters with trepidation. Ga'Glish was, after all, nephew to the First Minister and, if gossipmongers told the truth, a stern and demanding superior. Yet the last two cycles had seen changes sweeping through the Empire as never before. Even one such as he, without pedigree or connections, could be summoned to serve His Worthiness at levels unimaginable under the Old Regime. A dozen days earlier he had graduated with top honors from the newly constituted command school on the Planet *Zha'Rabi*. Now, he was about to meet the Lord Commander in person.

Laying his baggage sack on the floor, fa'Shenali of *g'Khruushte* paused to read a sign hanging on the wall. The directions here were as ponderous and indecipherable as the lectures of most of his professors, he thought. Anyone without advanced study in the science of cartography would find the labyrinth as impenetrable as the *Zha'Rabine* jungles.

"Subaltern fa'Shenali?"

Shenali turned his head to see one a little older than himself, clad in the purple sash and golden armbands of the Imperial Guardsmen. The Guardsman's markings gave him the rank of subcommander. From the officer's arrogant smirk, the young subaltern surmised that this one was a senior staff aide to Ga'Glish, and doubtless from a royal family. The lad had seen the type before, and was unimpressed. The accident of birth often left those such as the subcommander with a heaven-endowed smugness. During the course of his studies Shenali had left dozens of this young one's ilk foundering in his wake.

"I am fa'Shenali," he replied with a bow.

"I am Va'Nazze, Chief of Protocol to the Lord Commander. His Lordship has asked me to escort you to his chambers."

"He expected me to become lost, then? Hardly a vote of confidence."

Va'Nazze smiled, but Shenali felt no humor in the words, nor warmth in the subcommander's heart.

"The Flagship can be rather confusing, especially for newcomers. Follow me, please. The Lord Commander is waiting."

Shenali followed Va'Nazze down the vast corridor, through the Engine Room Bypass, finally coming to a hallway marked "Command Center." Soon they neared a large, semicircular doorway. Beyond the door, the young man could see hundreds of officers and soldiers, each scurrying madly from station to station.

"What is he like?" asked Shenali.

"I beg your pardon."

"The Lord Commander—what is he like?"

Va'Nazze chuckled acerbically, taking no pains to mask the contempt he felt for the commoner now standing before the corridors of power.

"You shall know soon enough."

"I have heard— "

"His ways are not for you to judge, Small One," Va'Nazze said sharply, through a mirthless smile. "Your role is not to question, but to serve."

Resentment burned, then simmered in the subaltern's heart, and the grandness of the Flagship soon passed unnoticed before his eyes. The two men walked the rest of the way in silence.

* * *

THE LORD COMMANDER'S chambers were the grandest the youth had ever seen, with carpets as plush as bedpillows, and artworks and other relics of grandeur surpassed only by the private collections of royalty. The two sat on cushions as soft as air, and Shenali paid attention less to the regal furnishings than to the gruffness of his superior's voice.

"You are not at all what I expected."

Ga'Glish looked sternly at the newcomer.

"I am sorry, Lord Commander," Shenali said, struggling to master his instinct to melt into nothingness. He was surprised when the Lord Commander started chuckling good-naturedly.

"No, it is I who must be sorry, One Called fa'Shenali, for my words did not convey my meaning. But you must admit that you do not look the part of a staff officer."

The youth looked at himself: the markings on his armband showed his lowly rank of Subaltern. His white sash showed his inexperience and lack of permanent assignment. Not stylish, perhaps, but military dress made him uncomfortable.

"I fail to see— "

"You look rather like a shop clerk in a bookstore," Ga'Glish smiled, humor radiating from his eyes like the warming sun of morning. "Hardly the sort to set the green blood of the g'*Khruushtani* to boiling."

"If you are displeased, my Lord— "

"We can get you properly attired," Ga'Glish interrupted, silencing the young man with a wave of his hand, "for all the good it will do. Besides, I requested you myself, Subaltern, and not because of your pedestrian appearance."

Shenali looked at the Lord Commander warily.

"I sense your disquiet," Ga'Glish said, with a regal blandness. "But remember that I am of Gal'Shenga's blood. And for good or ill, I share much of the First Minister's contempt for polite society. You will find many without pedigree in my service, fa'Shenali. And you will find that like my uncle, I reward ability, rather than rank."

"I am grateful, Lord Commander."

"I prefer my officers to express gratitude through their work, One Called fa'Shenali. And I am afraid that your task will be among the most difficult of any on this ship."

As Shenali kept guard on his thoughts, panic started to grow inside him. Ga'Glish rose from the floor and walked toward the far entrance to the drawing room, toward the large situation room beyond. Turning to see that his new subaltern was still seated, he beckoned for the young man to follow.

"Here."

As Shenali neared his side, Ga'Glish gestured grandly, the sweep of his arm encompassing the entire command hub, his lordly speech honed by dint of frequent repetition.

"This is where the fate of our people will be decided. It will be determined by all of us, fa'Shenali of *g'Khruushte,* by our dedication and resolve. And it will require a willingness to endure all manner of privation to defeat the dark tide that threatens us."

"Yes, my Lord." The young man felt a wave of strong emotion flooding his mind as his Lord Commander spoke. Like others before him, he was becoming one with the task before them, willing to give his life and his soul freely for his people and his Imperator.

"We must know our enemy, Subaltern. We must know how the longnoses think and breathe, how they love and how they reason—if we deign to call it reason."

"Yes, my Lord."

"I have assigned analysts to study all the Terran commanders, fa'Shenali, in the belief that if we cannot yet match Terran power, we can still out-think them."

"Yes, my Lord."

Ga'Glish turned to face his new staff aide. Shenali could see the fire and determination in his commander's eyes. Such a fire would soon burn within himself just as brightly.

"I hear that you were the brightest student in your class, One Called fa'Shenali. A student with a gift for sensing enemy movements and an ability to detect and exploit small changes in enemy tactics."

Shenali's heart cringed. Standing before the One on Whom All Depended, he was less confident of his abilities than at any time since his first day at the war college, when he faced the cruelties and taunts hurled at him by sons of the nobility.

"I must confess certain failings— "

Ga'Glish dismissed his remarks with a wave of his hand.

"Yes, yes—we all have our failings, Shenali," said the Lord

Commander, using the familiar form of his newest subordinate's name for the first time. "Even the Terrans have their failings."

"Some more than others, Lord Commander."

Ga'Glish chuckled darkly. When he spoke again, it was in the hushed tones of conspiracy. Yet his words carried a grim fascination, which fa'Shenali could sense as clearly as the stars burning in the blackness around them.

"Oh, yes—and you will learn that the Beast can be most elusive, Shenali. Yet of all the Terrans, his is the mind I know best, for it is the one Terran mind I have touched. He is an animal—wild and frenzied, devouring all he sees like a starving predator. Yet his mind is probing and curious, desperate in its quest to understand. We feel his power at every turn, for he, as much as the Terran death ships, dictates the course of the war. For all his barbarism, his is a stronger, more majestic mind than any I sense around me. And he is by far the most dangerous enemy we confront. He once fooled me into thinking him civilized, and his simian capacity for deceit has brought us all to the brink of disaster. If he comes again within our power, he shall not escape me a second time."

"What do you want of me, my Lord?"

The mind of Ga'Glish relaxed, as it came to focus upon more immediate concerns. "Your assignment, fa'Shenali, is to study the Beast—to study the One Called *Khu'ukh*. Follow his movements, as well as our monitors can detect, and probe whatever you can find that reveals his thoughts or his moods. You must learn to understand him—how his mind functions, how he thinks, how he will react. You must come to know him as you would your own brother, and sense his thoughts as if he were your son.

"Most importantly, you must find us a way to stop him."

"I shall do my best, my Lord."

Ga'Glish laughed without humor; the young aide could feel the bitter truth beneath his Lord Commander's words.

"Our survival may rest upon whether your best is good enough, Subaltern fa'Shenali," he said. "I shall give whatever help I can provide. Go refresh yourself, now. You will start work tomorrow. I expect the data from the Grulanashi Campaign to arrive in the next few days, and you must master what little biographical information we have on the Beast before you begin."

"Yes, my Lord."
"And fa'Shenali?"
"Lord Commander?"
"Welcome to the Flagship."
"Thank you, my Lord."

* * *

SOME DISTANCE TO the East, where the skies were still free and war had yet to come, work was proceeding feverishly.

"Rest period—cease work and relax."

As the groupleader repeated his command to the work squadron, ls'Shen of *Gr'Shuna* breathed deeply, his gasps sounding dully within his helmet. Countless stars adorned the black, airless sky overhead. Coldness pressed upon his outer covering like the specter of death, but within his pressurized clothing all was comfort, for he could adjust the temperature and air to the settings best suiting him.

"Shen— !"

The young man turned to face Shl'Lanasha, his workmate and elder. Like most men in the *Shunnite* Sector, commoner and noble alike, the two had been impressed into the service of His Worthiness. But they were lucky, if Luck still visited the troubled worlds of the *g'Khruushtani*. They were not consigned to stop the Terrans with their bodies, as little more than fuel for the war machines. They were assigned as builders—here, close to home, helping to erect the defenses that would shield their homeland, if the Barbarians succeeded in overrunning the precarious interstellar defenses of His Worthiness. Then they would be the last bastion left standing against the Terrans. But such thoughts belonged to a different time; now was the time for thoughts of rest.

Shl'Lanasha sat down on a nearby rock, and ls'Shen sat beside him. Shen could hear his comrade panting heavily over the intercom. Though the lifeless world's small mass made them stronger than if they had been walking the sands of home, they tended to compensate by overexerting themselves, and the final result was the same: exhaustion.

Shl'Lanasha smiled and motioned toward the horizon. A large, bluish star was rising in the east—or was it a star at all?

"She rises, Shen," breathed Lanash. "Like the Spring, she rises even in the midst of despair."

Ls'Shen looked again, and then he knew. It was home: it was Planet *Gr'Shuna*, nearly as distant from them now as their hopes were from thoughts of rest. But as it rose above the horizon, his heart filled with renewed hope and determination. The Terrans were strong, but the *g'Khruushtani* could be stubborn, and their cause was a just one. Though the heavens' silence echoed through eternity, the Universe could not be so cruel as to let civilization fall to the forces of barbarism.

Soon, a sharp command called them to resume their work. The defense station would be large, and its guns would be strong. If one day the war came to *Gr'Shuna*, they would be ready.

Chapter 2

"IT WAS KIND OF YOU to see me on such short notice," trilled the Glincian Ambassador. "We have much to discuss, and your diplomats do seem to relish the discussions so much more than the resolutions."

Senator E. Emerson Hollenbach smiled blandly in return and leaned back comfortably in his soft, oversized chair. The sharpness of the Glincian's beak made the effort to smile seem forced, and when Hollenbach looked into the clear, dark eyes of the Glincian, he saw nothing he could recognize as humor.

Surrounded by old, leather-bound books he'd never read, and original paintings he'd never noticed, Hollenbach's home on the outskirts of Covington was the epitome of an office expense account put to studied use. A glowing fire lent a warmth to the room that neither of the participants felt. Even the mellow coloring of the alien's downy feathers raised alarms deep inside the wily old Earther, reminding him of the bland, refined clothing of the upper crust snobs he'd come to hate in his youth on Planet Earth. They were quite alone; the Ambassador had insisted upon it. And Hollenbach was glad that there would be no other witnesses. It was the reason he insisted on having the meeting in his own den, rather than in his Senate office. It was easy enough to slip the Glincian out of his embassy; but sneaking him past the horde of reporters on Senate Hill would have been impossible.

"Diplomacy is the art of overcoming problems by talking them to death," Hollenbach agreed, sipping his wine and motioning for his guest to do the same.

"Politics is the art of possibilities," the senator continued. "I'll prattle on with the best of them, when it suits me. But if you want to have a real chat, Your Excellency, I'm willing to be as blunt as you can stand." The alien nodded, then leaned forward, speaking quietly, in tones not quite hushed, yet soft enough to be soothing.

"We have heard of your influence in certain quarters of your Government. Helping your friends overcome their problems appears to be one of your many gifts. We appreciate and admire such talents, Senator. Whatever it takes, we are interested in coming to some sort of understanding."

"I can't believe you find my Government hard to understand, Ambassador. I think our position is quite clear."

The Glincian tittered brightly. Hollenbach recognized the sound as laughter, though his instincts told him that the alien was covering a tactical retreat. Had he just been offered a bribe? He smiled inwardly; the aliens were seeming more human to him every day.

"You misunderstand me," trilled the Glincian. "Perhaps it is my clumsiness with your language. As with our hopes for all of Terra, we wish to be on amiable terms with all persons of influence. We have heard that you question our sincerity, and that your position in the councils of your people is so respected that *your* doubts are *Terra's* doubts. I would be glad to reassure you, and to answer any questions you might have about us, or our intentions."

"Why do you insist upon exploring the Crutchtan Cloud—now, of all times?" Hollenbach asked sharply, without a moment's hesitation.

"I assure you," the Ambassador replied after a short pause, speaking with a practiced precision that was not lost on his companion, "its riches are quite beyond measure. And we are quite happy to share whatever we have with our friends. Exploiting the Cloud will take time, resources, and endless patience. And with Terra so occupied with her other concerns, we only wish to begin the endeavor. The war will not last forever, my friend. Would it not be better to have the task half-done at war's end, rather than to face such an arduous task from, as you say, scratch? And who better to begin such a project than your allies—allies who, as you well know, have at once the time, the knowledge, and the resources to put at your disposal."

"You are also allies of the Crutchtans, are you not? Why should I think you have our interests at heart? Why shouldn't I conclude that you will prove to be the same sort of friends to us that you are to the Crutchtans?"

"We are members of the Consortium, it is true. But members of the Consortium have quarreled among ourselves for thousands of your years. We have been rivals of the Crutchtans since the two races first made contact, uncounted centuries ago. And we will remain rivals long after your conflict with them is past.

"But look at what we have brought to your table, as evidence of what is in our hearts. Have we not supplied you with maps, charts, and insight into Crutchtan technologies, all in technical violation of our obligations under the Charter of the Grand Alliance? We have undertaken all we dare, without risking the wrath of the Galaxy, and still you find cause to doubt us. While we take no official stand in your conflict, it is because we are forbidden by solemn treaty. Yet our actions show us to be your true allies. Surely, you cannot doubt our good intentions."

Hollenbach's gaze didn't flinch. "Why ask Terra to permit an alien presence in a zone of military occupation? Even Terra's children are not so naive. The threat from such a course should be apparent to all. Especially to a friend. Or to a true ally."

The Glincian shook his head slowly. "If I cannot convince you, then perhaps it is I who am naive," the Ambassador sighed. "We hoped merely to spare you a generation of effort. But it is not our intention to cause you to doubt us. If you do not wish our help now, you may summon it any time in the future. Friendship, after all, does not wither and die like a flower. It is more like a rock, a foundation for the future. And such a glorious future, my Terran friend, you cannot imagine."

Hollenbach listened to the Glincian outline his plan for the future—Terran outposts and colonies, helped along by Glincian traders and industry, fanning outward into the heavens. It was compelling, riveting…endless riches leading the way to a glorious future. It was enough to send the most cynical tycoon to bed with dreams of gold and power. Wealth beyond imagining, all there for the taking. And the old senator didn't believe a word of it.

* * *

"…AND EVERY TERRAN thrills at the deeds of those brave young souls, manning the front lines of Civilization."

The kindly image of the President smiled on the vidscreen, beaming his rugged good looks to every corner of Terra. His soothing presence gave voice to the thoughts and images of a nation that had little time to think about the distant terror filling the Eastern skies on both sides of the conflict.

"In the face of untold Crutchtan atrocities," Heathcoate's image continued, his eyes filling with hope, "the relentless advance of our noble Fleet is spreading hope throughout the Galaxy. On planet after planet—from Sheroni, to Lagrush, to Bala'Rundi—each new victory is adding another proud chapter to human history, in Man's struggle for decency, for Humanity, and against the alien menace.

"But as we celebrate our triumphs, we cannot help but feel the humble pangs of gratitude for those who have fallen...."

Sitting in the large, leather chair in his Senate Office, his feet propped up on his desk, Senator Hollenbach turned his gaze from the screen to his companion.

"Does he really believe all that crap?" the senator winced. "I mean—Schiller, for crying out loud...."

"He believes anything he's saying," answered Nicholas Schiller, the Presidents' Chief of Staff. "That's why he's such an effective speaker. People sense that his words come straight from his heart. Of course, I have no idea if he believes any of it after he's done talking. In fact, sometimes I suspect he doesn't even remember."

"He should have been an actor," Hollenbach chuckled darkly. "But then, all politicians are actors to some extent, don't you think, Schiller?"

Keeping his gaze fixed on the screen, Schiller was careful not to let Hollenbach know just how closely he was watching the senator's reactions.

"I hear you had a meeting with a friend," Schiller said blandly.

"News travels fast, doesn't it?" said Hollenbach, the warmth of his voice concealing the coldness in his eyes. Immediately, he resolved to have his aides sweep his home for listening devices. It was past due anyway, the Senator grunted to himself. And he didn't much like the implication of his own suspicions. If Schiller had the Senator's house bugged, the bastard likely had the whole damn planet wired.

"Not really," Schiller said blandly. "We just like to keep tabs on our friends. It helps keep them out of trouble."

"You weren't much help today," Hollenbach said, convinced that the Chief of Staff knew much more than he was saying. "I think the goonies offered me a bribe, though their ambassador could easily deny it if confronted about the matter. They want me to help scuttle opposition to the Glincian plans for exploring the Crutchtan Cloud. And they're so slick about laying on the appetizers that they'll have you drooling before you realize that what they really want is to serve you up for lunch."

Turning his gaze to study Hollenbach's reaction, Schiller found himself relieved to see genuine anger in his companion's eyes. Hollenbach's distaste for the aliens was well known; if he could be bought, then the government had already lost the chance to nip this thing. And if they were going to avoid losing in the cloakrooms what they were winning from the lizards in battle, Hollenbach was the one man in the Senate they really needed on their side. His skill as a headcounter was legendary, his instinct for the political jugular unparalleled. Schiller hated the thought of being in Hollenbach's debt yet again but, he realized, there was really no alternative. And this was the logical time to bring the old Earther on board.

"You're not the first, you know," Schiller said at last. "This was the fifth contact we've documented, all from our own party. But you're the first to report the bribe attempt." He decided against revealing who the turncoats were. Until they had proof, it wouldn't do any good. And if he was wrong about Hollenbach, he didn't want to compromise any of their informants.

"I wouldn't jump to conclusions," Hollenbach grunted. "The goonie bugger's a bit too subtle for this town. The others may have been too stupid to realize what he's up to."

"That's not likely, Emerson. The other four all changed their vote on extending the Cozzies' authorization to make trade exchanges with the birdies along the frontier, right at vote time. And wasn't that just what the goonies had been lobbying for, the entire summer long—to turn the trade runs over to our private shipping companies? With the last-minute defections, we barely managed to pull in the votes to defeat it. Now we owe a roomful of favors to a gaggle of Federalists for pulling our butts out of the fire."

Recalling the vote, Hollenbach immediately realized who the traitors were and filed the information away to use in the future. "He's a smooth talker, this *Drub'd*," he said at last. "But every now and then he overdoes it. That's what gives him away. You watch him, Schiller. Or you make damn sure someone's watching him. He's up to no damn good."

Schiller smiled blandly. He didn't want to admit that they were already watching a lot of people. And not just the Glincian ambassador.

"You're too cynical, Emerson."

"Well dammit, Schiller! I can smell it a mile off. They want that Cloud, Schiller. The goonies are salivating at the prospect. It's richer than even the Cozzies are willing to admit—I'd bet my last credit on it. And they think we're too dumb to figure out what they're up to. But playing us for suckers is one thing. Bribing our own people to stab us in the back is another."

Schiller laughed. "I'm glad you're on our side. I'd hate to have to go toe-to-toe, Emerson. Not after all we've been through, together."

"I'm not above turning a small profit myself, now and then," Hollenbach chuckled. "But I'll be damned if I dance to someone else's tune."

"What about the four turncoats? I've got the Justice Ministry looking into it, and brought in the CSO, to handle any details."

Hollenbach grimaced; Schiller could be such an amateur about some things, he thought.

"You nitwit," the senator laughed gruffly. "We've no need for such theatrics, at least not yet. Just document the contacts, make your cases…then hang onto the files. So long as things aren't out of control, there's no reason to tip our hand. No telling when all this might come in handy."

"Thanks, Emerson," Schiller smiled blandly, trying not to look smug. They were already busy gathering all the information they could, trying to identify every last traitor.

And as far as waiting until just the right moment, Schiller was already light years ahead of his erstwhile mentor. But, he mused, it didn't hurt to let the old Earther feel superior every now and then.

* * *

THE ROOM WAS filled with a flurry of excitement over the latest news from home. The perfumed scents of a Glincian slave girl wafted tantalizingly down the curved staircase. Amid all the activity, only a single aide noticed the look of concern in the Ambassador's eyes.

Taking his leave from the festivities, the young man walked over to the entranceway, continuing into the study as the Ambassador beckoned for him to follow.

"Your meeting," queried the aide. "How did it go?"

Sighing deeply, Drubid shook his head. "Not well at all," he replied. "This Terran is different from the others. He is no less motivated by self-interest, but I sense a deep malevolence toward us and our mission." He walked to the plush, velvet chair near the large, bowed window overlooking the house gardens, and sat down. Lanesel followed and stood by his side.

"He is of considerable importance," said the aide. "It was well worth the effort, Excellency."

"He would have been a prize convert to our cause," nodded Drubid. "But he was also important enough to leave alone. From now on, we must watch our every step. I only hope I haven't jeopardized all our hard work through a moment of conceit."

Bidding his aide to leave, Drubid gazed out the window at the birds feeding themselves at the nearby trough and listened to the cheerful songs of summer. This world was so much like home, he reflected. It was difficult to remember that it was an alien world, inhabited by alien beings. And simians, at that.

"Barbarians," Drubid whispered softly. "Barbarians, all." He had been among them for more than a year, and the strain was starting to wear him down. They were, without exception, crude and mannerless. But every once in a while he would meet one with a mind as crafty and subtle as any Glinci.

This portly Terran senator was a patriot, he reflected. From the deftness the Terran had shown at turning his own words against him, Drubid suspected that this one was fully capable of sensing trouble. Perhaps, he thought, caution was the best course for now. He would continue cultivating his friends in the Terran Senate, and simply bide his time. He knew that friends were fickle, and allies could shift with the changing wind. For now, the wind was a Terran wind, blowing with the force of a hurricane, obliterating all in its path. But no storm lasted forever. So long as the news from the battlefront remained good, Time was the Glincian's truest ally.

Chapter 3

D OCKING MANEUVER COMPLETE."
      "Ready to fire reverse thrusters."
      "Engage."
      The spacelorry released her hold on the trailer and started
back toward the transport, leaving a cargo of manufactured goods and
foodstuffs mated to the alien vessel. Her skipper looked out the rear
viewer, watching the Glincian vessel slip into the darkness. The alien
skies were as black as those of home, he thought, and the stars burned
just as brightly. Yet there was something eerie about being in foreign
space. And no matter what his superiors told him, he trusted the
birdies no more than his dead brother had trusted the lizards.

"Lieutenant?"

Mason McGee turned his head toward his yeoman. A single
crewman was a bit spare to be calling a crew, and he'd much rather
have been east, fighting the enemy. But he couldn't help smiling at
the thought that a bounder such as he was now wearing the blue of
a Cozzie officer, commanding a ship in the service of the Cosmic
Guard. Two ships, actually, if you counted the transport he'd
consigned to the care of his second in command. But Mason loved
sailing through space with only his wits to keep him alive. If the
transport was too big and unwieldy to give him the illusion of
freedom, at least the lorry was about the size of his old civilian ship.

"Don't be so formal, Gates. There's none to impress within earshot,
and I keep tellin ye the brass won't dare send the likes of us into
battle. There's little brass to be polishin in these parts. That I can tell
ye true."

"Sorry."

Mason laughed roguishly. "And don't go bloody apologizin all the
time. Least of all to another draftee. We're cut from the same cloth,
mind ye. Uniforms won't change the fact that we have near as much
in common with the goonie birds as we do with true blue Cozzies."

Gates grinned widely. He liked his skipper: Lt. McGee was just

about the least military of all the officers assigned to duty along

Terra's centerside flank. But that didn't change his mixed feelings

about working for the Cosmic Guard. Or his suspicion of those the

Cozzies chose for command. Perhaps in time, he'd learn to trust the

blueshirt. For now, it was enough that McGee didn't seem to take

The lorry eased toward the mother ship, and before long, Mason

mother ship would come about and ease back toward home, to load

up once more and then begin the long, slow journey all over again.

From the Trans-Terran Dispatch, 15 May 2555:

To the Editor, Trans-Terran Dispatch:

Once again, I find myself in the unenviable position of responding to

such a multitude of inaccuracies that I fear your readers will tire of

hearing my complaints. Still, given the seriousness of the topic, I feel

constrained to point out several mistakes in your account of the recent

Empire.

As your report indicates, our Senate recently endorsed the newest

Peace Proposal by a margin of 99-0. However, with due respect to

widespread belief on Planet Isis that the Crutchtan War should be

My Government's concern has been, is, and will remain the

senseless nature of the current hostilities. It is my firm belief that the

true cause of the War stems not from Crutchtan aggression, but from

This, in turn, tempts us to exploit our current advantage in military

we came upon the scene, I find it unlikely that we need look further

than our own hearts to find the real cause of the conflict.

Nothing in the history of Mankind should lead us to think that our

current dispute with an alien culture is any different than the many

on Old Earth. Money, power, and a primal urge toward dominance once gave us a world where strength, and not wisdom, settled disputes, and where the strong preyed upon the weak without remorse. In my humble opinion, our modern, 26th Century civilization differs from the past primarily by the level of violence we can inflict upon our fellow creatures, not in the level of civility we show them.

Your fine Journal has done an admirable job of portraying the agonies and barbarisms confronting the brave men of the Terran army, and the men and women who serve in the Cosmic Guard. War has always been a terrible, brutal undertaking, and will always remain so. It is a pity that you do not devote more attention to the root causes of the War—which, I believe, will be of more lasting interest to future generations, and a lasting source of shame for our Era.

IRENE N. McINNIS
Chancellor, Isitian Senate

* * *

"I'M SORRY. BLAKE, was it?"

"Burdick, sir." Lt. Commander Jerry Burdick stood stiffly at attention. The air conditioning barely dented the planet's suffocating heat, and sweat streamed down his face. The utilitarian furnishings lent an air of sterility to the spartan surroundings of the compound. Through the window, he could see that the sun was only an hour past rising. On his shoulders, his new lieutenant commander's bars gleamed brightly in the light. He'd had his doubts about this transfer, and the gruff Security Office captain was doing nothing to ease his mind. But each week brought more alien prisoners to warehouse. The Guard was running out of experienced security officers to help run their work camps.

Besides, he thought, with the transfer came a promotion. With every junior line officer competing for a limited number of positions, it would have taken forever to get his next advance in rank if he'd stayed in space. This way, he kept his career right on schedule. And he could always transfer back to space when things eased up a bit.

"Yes...Mr. Burdick."

Captain Alex Whiting rocked back in his chair and gazed harshly at the newest addition to his command staff. He did not like dealing with newcomers, especially those with little practical experience on the ground. But he had his orders. And like it or not, his new executive officer came highly recommended. He looked at this Burdick's dossier; what he saw raised his eyebrows.

"Last assignment was on Cook's ship, was it?"

"The *d'Artagnan*, yes, sir."

"Well, Mr. Burdick, duty on shore is different than duty aboard ship."

"Yes, sir."

"These lizards are wily buggers, with more of them outside the compound gate than you can shake a stick at. Work here at the mine is already months behind schedule and falling further behind at every turn. You can't turn your back on them for a minute."

"I've read my briefing papers, Captain."

"Lagrush used to be their planet, you know."

"Yes, sir."

"You can see it in their eyes. They hate us, Burdick. They'll never accept our presence here. Not until we take the fight out of them."

"Yes, sir."

"All right, report to Personnel for processing. Then you can refresh yourself in your quarters. I'll introduce you to the rest of the staff at dinner."

"Thank you, sir."

"Dismissed."

As the young man turned smartly and left the room, Alex Whiting eyed his new executive officer harshly. There was something different about this one, he thought. Something unsettling. Most likely his head was still among the stars. Still, there'd be time enough to turn him into a real CSO officer.

If he had the stomach for it, that is.

In the meantime, they had more pressing problems.

Like how to stop the raids on their foremost outposts, beyond the perimeter of the main compound.

And how to stop the renegade lizards from disrupting the work in the mines.

* * *

BIRDS CHIRPED MERRILY outside the partly opened window. Everywhere, the sweet fragrances of blossoms filled the air. With the Senate adjourned until fall, the pace of city life had slowed to an easy stroll. Far removed from the incivilities of the front, the Terran capital reveled in the warm glow of a Babylonian Summer.

Seated behind a large, oaken desk, the President's Chief of Staff sifted through the mass of reports in front of him and picked out the three or four that interested him. Leaning back in his oversized chair, staring blankly at his terminal screen, Nicholas Schiller pulled the first file, marked "Weekly Battle Manifest," and slowly scrolled the pages. Finding nothing of particular interest—reports of casualties and supplies consumed tended to make him drowsy, but as Chief of Staff he felt it his duty to scan each such report as it came in—he skimmed through the accounts of the past week's larger skirmishes, the deployment of the various fleets, and enemy ships captured, and entered his initials to show he'd read it. He was about to examine the next folder, when the intercom sounded.

"Yes, what is ?"

"Senator Hollenbach's office on line one, Mr. Schiller."

Schiller took a deep breath. He knew exactly what Hollenbach wanted, and knew that he couldn't dodge him forever. But now was simply not the time. Not with the Army pressing for another round of conscription for its ranks. And not with the rest of the Senate howling about the mounting costs of outfitting yet another generation of starships.

"Tell them I haven't finished studying the Senator's report yet. I'll get back to him personally, by the end of the week."

"Yes, Mr. Schiller."

Closing the second file, he opened a third one. This one came in a paper folder, sealed on one end, that a courier had hand-delivered to him. The middle of the front bore the dark blue Senate Seal; the red edging told at a glance that it was to be kept under lock and key. Schiller opened the folder and loaded the contents into his console to bring it to the screen. It was a report, directly from the spooks at the Intelligence Section of the CosGuard Security Office to the chairman of their oversight committee—who happened, more conveniently than coincidence would allow, to be Earth's senior senator.

Schiller chuckled as he read the title: "Security Threats Along the Periphery." Hollenbach was enough of a cynic not to trust his own mother, he thought. But as he continued reading, he wondered whether the old Earther might not have a point. The Atkvalo and Glinci were still largely unknown quantities. While the might of

Terra's Cosmic Guard could explain their interest in coexisting peacefully, trading with Terra was hardly in the interest of their erstwhile allies, the Crutchtans. Besides, though their commercial delegates presented alluring pictures to industrialists like Schiller who saw the universe largely in terms of credits and losses, they'd been less than forthcoming about sharing technologies and resources, and had placed strict limits on contacts between the races.

Schiller thought a moment. The CosGuard brass, at least the current crop, would flatly oppose any venture likely to expand the war. And he didn't really blame them. Despite glowing reports from the battle fronts, he had his own doubts about the wisdom of pressing other members of the alien alliance too aggressively, so long as the Crutch-tans remained unbeaten. But he'd learned from his days as head of Galactic Mining & Manufacturing that little was lost by examining alternatives. With the resources of the Terran Government at his disposal, they'd lose nothing by planning for contingencies. Turning to the end of the report, he signed Hollenbach's draft order, directing CSO to prepare plans for the possibility of attacks against the Atkvalo and the Glinci. He put the report back in its security folder and finally turned to the next report, the only one that really captured his interest because it touched a soft spot in his heart.

Two pages into the report, he shook his head and quickly jumped to the conclusion. Reading about the details of camp management on the occupied planets was too depressing. But the bottom line showed that Galactic Mining was making money hand over fist from the ore mines at the camps, and he was disinclined to disturb the arrangement. The CosGuard Security people seemed to be doing a fine job, so long as he didn't look too closely at the details. And if they were cutting a few too many corners, he didn't really want to know. After all, they were only working with lizards; and the lizards should feel lucky that their new rulers didn't just kill them all.

Satisfying himself that everything was running smoothly, he returned the report to its tray, and picked up the final report, another one sealed in a paper security folder. After scanning the title, he placed this last report back on top of the stack without reading it. There was no sense in creating problems prematurely he thought, rising to leave for his ten o'clock meeting with the President. And the title of the report suggested that it would be political dynamite.

Locking the door behind him, he told his secretary to keep his office locked until he returned. Except for the clattering of office machinery, and the gentle trills of the songbirds in the garden, his office fell still. And as the sun crept along its course, it soon came to shine on the folder he'd left on top of his basket.

"**THE ISITIAN CONNECTION**," read the bold print on the folder lip, though nobody was there to see it: "Residual Security Risks and Potential Solutions."

Chapter 4

"IS IT HIM?"
"There he is!"
"It's him...it *is* him!
"Commodore! Commodore—over here!"

Though she knew it was useless, Suzie Yang craned her neck, hoping for a glimpse. The noise was deafening, as each voice around her bounced off the archway back onto the crowd. Like all of her colleagues, Suzie hated being on the outside of something larger than life. She couldn't help feeling a sense of exhilaration at being part of the crowd, and like most of those present she'd never actually seen him in person. But unlike its politicians, most of Terra's military had little use for journalists and reporters, and this particular leader was the most inaccessible of the lot.

The mob surged forward like a sea of flesh, groping its way past the cordons and toward the narrow corridor where he was headed. Soon the hero of Geroulanashi—and Lashuni, and Lagrush, and Fralenga, and a host of other battles she couldn't remember and could barely pronounce—stepped past the guards and into sight for the briefest of moments. Suzie felt elbows digging into her side and head and struggled to keep her balance, having long since surrendered her dignity. The crowd surged and ebbed, pushed back by the uniformed guards of the CosGuard Security Office. Their quarry soon disappeared, heading toward whatever secret meeting had brought him to the base.

It was his first appearance at Looking Glass since the early days of the war. Like hundreds of other correspondents consigned to the media's forwardmost outpost with little to do but speculate about what was happening, Suzie sensed that something big was in the works. It was the only explanation that made any sense to her. The only reason why CosGuard would ever bring him so far from the front lines, so far away from the fighting.

Soon, the mob began to scatter. As their respective deadlines approached, the dispersing reporters found themselves looking elsewhere for something worth filing with their home office.

"GLAD YOU COULD finally make it, Commodore," said Miriam Wright, raising her voice to be heard over the crowd. Stepping past the East Mall fountain, the sweet scent of Babylonian daycress filled her nostrils. Wright briefly closed her eyes; the scent called back her Academy days, and a love long lost to time and distance. She secretly smiled at the memory and continued without losing a step.

"Of course with you arriving this late, Admiral Weatherlee will be livid."

"He usually is," laughed Roscoe Cook. "And what is it this time? He needs help deciding which socks to wear? Or maybe he's forgotten how to turn the water off in his shower? Surely, he hasn't changed his mind about my Plan? Mongoose, I mean. Or does he just need someone to explain it to him again?"

Walking along behind their two superiors, Janet Mendelson exchanged a knowing smile with Admiral Wright's junior adjutant, a young lieutenant named Schlesinger. Weatherlee wasn't CosGuard's brightest tactician, Janet thought, but few possessed his clout with Covington. Weatherlee had spent a career cultivating contacts inside and outside the service, and was never averse to using them.

"Actually," Wright continued, stiffening her pace as they neared the Tube Station, "he's been complaining about the tenor of your last few memos to Fleet Headquarters."

"Acchh—"

Wright's face turned serious. She had no intention of letting her best officer get into any more trouble with the top brass. Not if she could help it.

"Now listen to me, Commodore— "

"That pompous toad couldn't—"

"Commodore Cook!" Wright interrupted, her voice taking an imperial edge that would admit no further backtalk. "Headquarters has made the siege of Greloosh Admiral Weatherlee's project. The planet is his to take—"

"Or not, as the case may be."

"And however long it takes," she continued, undaunted, "it is not your place to second-guess him. Not in public, and certainly not in any shape, manner, or form likely to embarrass him. And I'll tell you something else,

Commodore. A little humility on your part would go a long way in smoothing a whole flock-full of ruffled feathers. Unless, of course, you'd rather spend the war listening to squawking geese, rather than fighting the enemy."

Cook snorted derisively, but the lecture had its desired effect. For the moment, it kept him quiet. Soon, the four officers arrived at the Central Tube Station. Bidding their CSO escorts to enter the car, Wright turned to the two younger officers bringing up the rear.

"Admiral Weatherlee objects to having junior officers at these command briefings, and I have a feeling that you would find this particular meeting more boring than most. Lt. Schlesinger?"

"Ma'am?"

"Why don't you escort Lt. Commander Mendelson around the base? We've made a lot of changes since the last time she and the Commodore were here, and I'm sure she'd find it all very interesting."

"Yes, ma'am."

"That's unless the Commander has something she'd rather do?"

Janet shook her head. "No, Admiral. That's fine with me." Actually, she thought, there were better ways to spend liberty time than being squired around a starbase by a post-pubescent desk jockey, but she held her tongue. The day would pass quickly enough, and she had no need to hurt the young man's feelings. Besides, she and Cook already had plans for the rest of the day. This outing would help pass the time.

Wright's voice soon faded, as she and a sullen-looking Cook entered the Tube car, leaving the two junior officers alone.

"Hungry?" Schlesinger asked eagerly. "I know a nice bistro near the G-Deck observation landing." He pointed down the corridor, toward the docks along the western rim of the base.

Janet shrugged. "Fine."

Soon, they were walking down the hallway with Janet staring sullenly ahead, making curt replies to her companion's attempts at conversation. Before long they arrived at the bistro, a small open café with a dozen or so tables surrounding a small fountain. Settling into a quiet corner, they ordered lunch. Janet ordered a small salad; her escort had lost his appetite.

"Perhaps you know," Schlesinger said at last, having exhausted topics ranging from the Babylonian climate to the engine differentials on the new model B-X21 class scouts. "I've never been able to figure it out."

"What's that?"

"Weatherlee and Cook."

"Come again?"

"They don't seem to get along very well, do they?"

"Not really."

"I suppose it all stems from the Hawkins incident."

Janet tilted her head back and smiled, then slowly shook her head.

"Actually— " she began. "No, I'm sorry. But it's only a rumor. A long dead rumor."

"Well?"

"Well...." Janet paused, reluctant to speak, yet suddenly dying to share what she knew. "My first year at the Academy I heard a story about some Eastern Fleet commodore who'd come back for a tactics seminar the previous year. You know, one of those refresher courses the Brass use as a prelude to a promotion to admiral."

Schlesinger smiled and nodded, relieved at last to get some sort of reply from his assigned date.

"At the end of his course, after he'd completed a master battle plan—you know, complete with landers, timetables, and everything?— he asked his instructors to arrange a mock battle. One of those grand simulator sessions, where you control entire fleets with the press of a button."

"I've never been much good at it."

"They're pretty tough, especially when you're doing it solo. Anyway, this commodore strode into the simulator room in the middle of class one day, unannounced, accompanied by a whole phalanx of fawning administrators and all. And he asked the professor to have his best student face off with him the next day. Right there, on the spot, in front of all those people, with one day to prepare and a whole entourage from Central Command there to cluck and chuckle at the slightest goof."

"And?"

Janet bit her tongue teasingly, then broke into a wide grin. Schlesinger thought she had the loveliest smile he had seen in months. It brightened her face until she became a different woman. All at once she seemed playful and lighthearted, rather than the cold, sexless prig he'd taken her for.

"Well, that year's Most Distinguished Senior was a midshipman named— "

"Roscoe Cook?"

Janet nodded mysteriously. "When the commodore heard he'd be battling an Isitian he couldn't help but make some boorish crack about the level of talent in that year's senior class. Cook said nothing…but when they got to the simulator the following day he took less than ten minutes to destroy the enemy fleet. And he did it six times in row— getting better each time, without repeating his tactics so much as once—until finally the commodore got sick of losing and left in a huff."

"The commodore was Weatherlee?"

Janet shrugged her shoulders. "No one ever said. Even today, Skipper's never given me a straight answer when I've asked about it. But I'd already taken it into my head to become something of an expert on the Midshipman from Isis. In many ways, my plebe year was the worst of my life, and there was something comforting about….well, I suppose that's no concern of yours. But a friend and I hacked our way into the CentCom computers and checked the records. Weatherlee was the only commodore promoted to admiral that year—and wouldn't you know it, his service record shows him attending a seminar on New Babylon the preceding spring."

Schlesinger smiled and nodded, as Janet kept chatting on and on about her commanding officer, his likes and dislikes, his moods and shortcomings, her eyes becoming distant and dreamy. Like most of those in a position to know, he had little regard for Weatherlee, or his tantrums. Insight into the minds of the top brass was often hard to come by.

But, he smiled, even more intriguing was the look he'd been given into the personal life of a CosGuard legend…and the legend's favorite first officer.

* * *

"Incoming message."

"Put in on the screen, Lieutenant."

"It's a communiqué. From the Skipper."

"Read it, then."

Mary Mathison pressed the display button on her communications console.

"He and Miss Mendelson have arrived at Looking Glass and will be staying another day or two. If they get the express couriers lined up, they should be back in a week or two."

"All right, Mathison, page Mr. Van Horn, and bring him up to date. Tell him that I plan to rendezvous with Starbase F-111 in eight days—if he concurs, that is. That should cut another day out of the Skipper's travel time."

"Shall I— ?"

"No, Mathison, don't file our flight plan yet. Not until Van Horn gives us the 'go-ahead.' He is in command, technically, at least. I don't want to step on his toes."

Mary nodded. Even if the Skipper had made clear who would really be in charge of the ship, the book said that Van Horn was third in command. If Cook didn't care a whit for protocol, it was still the polite thing to do.

"Anything else?"

Lt. Kirkland Dexter swivelled in the command chair to face the ship's radio officer.

"Skipper did want us to keep up our drilling schedule," said Dexter, his maturing tenor voice calm and even. "With all the rookies on board, I expect it would be easier on all concerned if we tried to break them in a bit first."

Mathison laughed brightly. "Good luck, Dexter. You're cutting yourself a tall order."

"Page the rest of the bridge crew. We'll recommence with the First Team at 700 Hours."

"Aye, aye."

"Helm, come about and reduce speed. We're not in any hurry. At least not for the next week or so. And certainly, not until we're done with the day's drilling."

"Aye, sir."

"And Mathison, tell Mr. Gerlach I'd like him to recheck the main keel shield before we begin the drill. I didn't like the readings I saw in the status report, and our weapons officer has been taking our vacation a little too seriously."

"Aye, aye, Lieutenant."

Dexter smiled inwardly. This would be the first drilling session he'd handled solo, and there already were a lot of noses out of joint over his elevation to executive aide. He could already taste the sweet irony of it all, and wondered how he'd ever handle all the headaches. But he remembered what the Commodore had told him about the need for even-handedness—and that whatever the temptation, revenge was never a prerogative of command.

He turned to face the forward viewer and sighed deeply. If he passed muster with the Skipper, Ensign Danley would be their third navigator since Connie McKenzie, and Connie had been the best of the lot. Good navigators were hard to come by. These days, with CosGuard stretched thinner than the Cloud itself, navigators were worth a week's liberty on Demeter. But on the *d'Artagnan*—with CosGuard's best navigator sitting in the command seat, instantly aware of the slightest imperfection—the job was just too demanding. Cook had paid the young lieutenant the biggest compliment of his life, Dexter thought, just by placing the ship in his hands. Above all else, he was determined to make the Skipper proud of him. If giving Danley a taste of life under Cook's thumb would help the ship run more smoothly, he was willing to try.

* * *

"CAPTAIN... IT'S NICE to see you again."

"Hello, Janet," Jeremy Ashton smiled and sat down across from her. His new captain's bars fairly gleamed on his epaulets. He was late, about five minutes late, but he would have bet a month's pay that he wouldn't be the last of their party to arrive.

"I see you're still waiting for.... "

"He hasn't changed much, Jeremy," Janet laughed; though she would never admit it to herself, it was the first real laugh she'd had in weeks. "Though I'm sure you got the worst of it. For all his faults, he's enough of a gentleman not to dump quite as much onto my desk as he did yours."

"There may be other reasons for that, you know."

Janet's face reddened. Jeremy could be awfully sweet, she thought, but sometimes, she wished he'd be less of a friend.

"You know, they still haven't assigned me a first officer yet. My offer's open...for as long as you want it to be."

Janet shook her head. She should have known better than to turn to a man as a confidante. He meant well, of course, but all he had to offer were solutions instead of sympathy, and it just made her feel worse. She was already resigned to what little she had, and what she would have to sacrifice to keep it. For all his good intentions, Jeremy's clumsy attempts to help merely kept the wounds from healing. In the end, she found it flattering to think that his motives might spring from something deeper than altruism. And as much as she'd hated to see him leave, she thought, they were all quite lucky his promotion came through when it did.

"Sorry," she said at last.

"It's still him, isn't it?"

"Jeremy— "

"He's no god, Janet. He's proven that to you time and again. Why do you put up with it all?"

Before Janet could answer, a familiar voice sounded from a few steps away.

"Captain Ashton, as I live and breathe!" bellowed a familiar voice from a few yards away. Reflexively, Jeremy turned to face his old commander, and for the briefest of instants, a wave of cold tension passed between them.

"You use people, Skipper."

"That's enough, Jeremy."

"You use people up, and spit them out when they no longer suit you."

Cook smiled broadly, though Jeremy still felt a measure of condescension in the commodore's voice. Cook's cocky self-assurance never bothered him before, Jeremy thought. Now, it felt like his old Skipper was making clear that he'd never quite accept the former first officer as an equal. It made Jeremy even more aware of his own limitations, and strengthened his determination to escape the shadow of the great Commodore Cook. And there would always be the lingering undercurrent of tension between them: neither was comfortable with the way they'd parted company. Jeremy could only trust that Cook wouldn't rub his nose in it.

Not that it would do Janet any good, Jeremy reflected; but at least Cook didn't have to humiliate both of them.

"Hello, Jeremy. Glad to see you managed to survive your first outing on the hotseat of a starship. Different on the other end, isn't it?"

Jeremy forced a laugh as Cook took the seat across the table, to Janet's left.

"Not as different as I'd expected. You get used to giving the orders pretty quickly. I guess on most ships, things just take over and start running themselves. Once you get them organized, that is."

"Yes," smiled Cook. "I suppose they do."

The three friends ordered dinner and were soon lost in talk about old times, and friends lost to time and folly, their past disagreements having faded like yesterday's clouds. Life had changed for them in the past cosmic year; it had changed for everyone the war had touched. But Looking Glass was a hundred parsecs from the front. For a short time, the war would be a dim memory.

* * *

From the diary of fa'Shenali:

Day 237 of the Twelfth Cycle of Ja'Rend XCVI:

I have completed the official biography of the Terran called Khu'ukh. It is a conceit that the superficial facts in our possession will lead us to understand the Terran. For example, I have discovered that "Khu'ukh" means Foodmaster Apprentice in the Terran language. Yet such facts, much prized by our Intelligence agencies, are without significance, for while the Terrans pass names from generation to generation, they have no castes to pass professions in a similar manner. The fact that one of his ancient ancestors was perhaps a Terran Foodmaster is of no importance at all, yet these are the facts from which I must draw my conclusions. Still, despite the lack of any real facts at my disposal, I will endeavor to do my best.

Ga'Glish is anxious for me to begin analyzing this Terran Foodmaster's latest campaign, the annihilation of Shra'Kenchi's fleet in the skies surrounding the Grulanashi Binary system. But if I am to understand the mind of Khu'ukh, I cannot begin in the middle. And so I have ordered data from all prior campaigns, from the earliest days of the war to the present, hoping to discover something worth finding, hidden away in the confusion of battle. Tomorrow, I will tell the Lord Commander that as he has charged me with understanding the Terran, I must do so in a way that I find comprehensible, and that I must study Khu'ukh in my own way, or not at all.

If I remain here after tomorrow, I will begin my studies in earnest. If I have misjudged my commander, I shall likely be en route to the front, instead.

* * *

```
cc:        144-3027.8
  FILE:       Log.personal.RCook
  ACCESS:     Private.RAC 74737H5A1-6
  SECURITY:   Voiceprint<<SCOOTER>>
  LOCATION:   SB 102
```
Our stay on Looking Glass ends tomorrow. Duty calls, and the war waits for no man.

I am getting so sick of death that I welcome any chance to put it out of my mind. Each day, I worry that I'll get careless, just to stop myself from killing. But I'm equally haunted by the constant reminders of the many people who all depend on me. I seem destined to spend my life destroying everything I touch and often find myself lying awake in my quarters, sweating at the pain I leave in my wake. I watch helplessly as everything I know—everyone around me, everything I hoped to be, every gift Life has given me—shatters beyond recognition. Each day I wake with the hope that it will come to an end. Yet every night, I struggle under the weight of the suffering I've caused, and the realization that tomorrow will be no different.

I learned today that the Looking Glass Personnel Office had accumulated a month's worth of my personal mail, including two-dozen letters from home, apparently waiting for my arrival. Thanks to a crackerjack rookie clerk, they shipped it all to the d'Artagnan the day after I checked in with base command. It's nice to know how well CosGuard takes care of its own.

"Computer off," sighed Cook.

"ACKNOWLEDGED."

The cabin fell dark, and the sound-proof walls insulated him from the life outside the confines of his temporary lodging. The light soon faded from his voice transcriber, and only a gentle rattle in the air duct was left to remind him of the worlds beyond the darkness that surrounded him. He'd had a long day, but alone in the blackness even the sharp words of his superiors slowly faded from his mind, and oblivion called him to rest. He drifted off to sleep, and the weight of the Universe slipped from his shoulders, his mind returning to the serenity of a boyhood on a peaceful world light years away.

The night was unusually restful. He awakened only once, to the sound of tortured voices calling from a grave of fire. As his mind dragged itself toward consciousness, he realized that the sound he'd heard was just his own screaming.

* * *

//II/COMMAND ALERT:
   cc: 144-3028.5/
   TO: CommandingOfficers-EasternFleet/
   FROM: FtAdmPorterMClay/
   SECURITY   CodeBlue/
   PREFIX: Need-to-Know,Eyes-Only/
   FLAGS: red1;red2;red3/

CSO reports a major diversion of enemy forces toward the Crutchtan Planet Greloosh. It appears that these reinforcements are being sent to help the local enemy detachment break the siege, now entering its second month. Best estimates are that the contingent will arrive sometime after 144-3200.

All ship commanders in the vicinity are advised to watch for an order of redeployment in the near future. All wing commanders shall prepare contingency plans for the rapid commitment of forces under their command to help bring the siege to a successful conclusion before the arrival of enemy reinforcements. Area commanders shall suspend all offensive initiatives, pending the conclusion of hostilities at Greloosh, to ease the redeployment of friendly forces. Defensive operations may, of course, continue.

ENCRYPT/TRANSMIT//

Chapter 5

THE NEXT DAY, COOK FOUND himself staring down a dim corridor, feeling the gentle vibrations of the small ship's engines beneath his feet. He'd looked forward to the trip to Looking Glass. It was a welcome break from the grim routine of command in wartime. But beginning the journey back to his ship he felt more worn and tired than when he'd left her, and they still had a long sail ahead of them.

Clearly, the old *Mulligan*-class escorts were not built for luxury. The narrow corridor ran the length of the ship from the air lock aft, over the engine room and past the upper crew quarters all the way to the bridge. Four feet wide, only the shortest crewmen could walk its entire forty-meter length without hunching over. The handholds along the side, installed to give the crew quicker movement along the spine when the gravity was cut, were green with tarnish. The blandness of the walls was broken only by the occasional discoloration of a past water leak. Cracking floor tiles carried the full burden of nine decades of service and two decades of neglect. The *Mulligans* were once the scourge of pirates everywhere. Now resurrected for use as couriers, they ferried Terra's military elite from one theater to another, and from the command centers eastward to the Front.

The escort's control room was a mess. Charts littered the auxiliary controls, and the pilot's station was covered with the half-eaten remnants of dinner. Eight feet across, the bridge barely had room for the two stations placed at the controls. The accumulated clutter nearly sealed the two control officers into their station seats, and stood in marked contrast to the meticulous trim her commander kept on the rest of his ship. From his vantage just aft of the entry ramp, Cook took a deep breath and smiled. His first command had been an escort, a newer and sleeker model than this one, to be sure, but an escort just the same. And his own control room would have failed the inspection of a blind old pirate, much less a Cozzie blueshirt. It was good for him to see how the rest of the fleet lived, he thought. Perspective was always healthy. And right now, he could use a hearty dose of nostalgia, as well. Looking toward the bridge, he smiled to see the small ship's two officers busily engaged in navigating the escort back toward the front, and began walking down the corridor toward the bridge.

"HEADING STEADY," THE navigator reported, checking his instruments. "Guide-beacon constant at 050; 'lights-out' beam still active."

"Roger," responded the pilot. "Holding steady as she goes."

"Hear anything from our VIP's, Steve?"

"Not a thing. Both were sacked out, last I checked. Near as I can tell, You-Know-Who got his tail rearranged by some of the Brass. Probably took the fight out of him, for a while."

"Goddamn," grinned the navigator. "Bet the lizards would be sliming down their chins to hear that. Hope he doesn't stay down like that for too long."

"His traveling companion would probably second the motion, don't you think?" The two young blueshirts laughed roguishly, and turned their attention back to their instruments.

COOK STEPPED ONTO the entry ramp and paused. In the midst of chaos, routine and training would hold even the creakiest ship together. But the pride an officer took in his command could make even the smallest ship sparkle. The evidence of this young lieutenant's promise was apparent even through the aging fixtures and superficial clutter. Though cracked, the floor tiles gleamed; even the tarnish-stained hand holds shined as if ready for inspection. Upon first coming aboard, Cook had wondered if the last bits of spit and polish were for his benefit; if so, it would not have been the first time a junior officer had gussied up his ship to impress a visitor. But the routine on board was too fixed, too well ordered, to be anything but standard. Besides, he'd picked the ship at random. No young blueshirt could have trimmed his ship this well in just a few short hours. Smiling at the memory of simpler days, he turned his attention to the two young officers at the controls.

THE NAVIGATOR SEARCHED the mass of star charts and pulled a

broad vista on the console in front of him. An intense round of calculations on the computer left him scratching his head.

"Charts say we've got shoals ahead, composition unknown. Rocks and ice, most likely. Pretty big patch, too."

"Give 'em a wide berth, don't you think?"

"Well, charts also say we just passed through the middle of binary star system—Class Double-G," replied the navigator. He looked from one side of the forward viewing window to the other, then turned his head to peer out the portside porthole.

"I sure as hell don't see any star system," continued the navigator, exhaling loudly. "So either we're lost, or the charts are fucked to high heaven again."

"Mike, don't do this to me. Not again. And not now, for God's sake!"

"Sure beats the hell out of me what we're going to do, Steve. Go round the shoals, we're likely to wind up in the middle. Plow straight ahead, and bam! And if something happens with You-Know-Who on board, it'll mean our hides. Assuming, of course, that we actually live through the encounter with that maverick herd of asteroids out there...somewhere."

"Oh, Christ— "

"Problems?" Cook stepped out from the shadows, and walked toward the small bridge. After a brief flash of panic at the prospect of having a senior line commander snooping around their bridge, relief flooded the faces of the young officers.

"Commodore Cook—!" gasped the navigator, an ensign on his first duty.

"We have a problem with the charts," the pilot interrupted. Cook gave him a quick sizing glance. The lieutenant had a lone, dark blue duty stripe on his sleeve, showing a single tour of duty on a starship; his dark brown eyes were intelligent and intense. Though obviously concerned about his ship, he showed no signs of the numbing fear that often gripped junior officers when confronting a navigation problem alone, in the vastness of space.

"Nature and extent?" Cook's commanding voice and gruff scowl immediately set the young blueshirts on the edge of their seats, concerned that the smallest mistake would become an indelible blot on their service records.

"The chart doesn't conform to the observable cosmography," the pilot replied, in his most objectively analytical tones. "Specifically, we seem to have missed a binary star system that's on the map, directly on our course line. At present we can't be certain where we are. The extent of the failure is unknown—and to be honest, Commodore, I cannot rule out human error as a contributing factor. But our orders are to maintain radio silence until the next checkpoint, so we can't call and ask for directions."

Cook moved some clutter from the auxiliary station and took a seat on the edge of the console, pretending not to notice the embarrassed glances exchanged by his young companions.

"Please..." The navigator started to rise from his station. Cook stopped him with a wave of his hand. The commodore glanced over the chart of the surrounding skies before bending over to look outside the ship through the forward window bay.

"You can't really trust charts, you know," he said absently, looking first ahead to port, then toward starboard, his brow furrowed in concentration. "At least not these charts. Actually, not the first charts of any new skies. They're usually made in a hurry by some junior mapmaker and rushed to print before anyone checks them again."

Cook stood and eased his way behind the station seats to the starboard side of the ship, where he peered through the porthole.

"Problem is," he continued, "we need accurate charts, and we need them all yesterday. That's an impossible order to fill, so don't blame the chartmaker. Just don't trust his work. Leastways, don't bet your life on it."

Cook turned and smiled wryly. "That's why the Crutchtans will always have an advantage fighting in their own skies. They've had a millennium or two to iron out the wrinkles in their maps, while we're left plodding through the heavens, hoping we don't run into anything solid along our way. It may not prove decisive, but then a strategic advantage in war is often nothing but an accumulation of little edges, all added together."

The navigator and pilot both nodded attentively. They both hoped that the Commodore would eventually get around to solving their navigation problem for them, but were too well disciplined to interrupt a senior officer in the middle of a lecture.

Especially this senior officer.

"Well then," Cook said, his mood changing from philosophical to business-like. "I think I have this little muddle figured out."

The pilot's eyes widened; his navigator's mouth opened, then closed in disbelief. Cook squinted as he looked out the forward observation window.

"Whoever scouted this sector obviously did so from that general direction," the commodore pointed ahead and to port, "coming from Cosmic West. Probably made most of his readings visually, instead of relying on instruments." He sat back down on the console.

"How do you know...," the pilot began.

"Comparing the chart with what we can see from here," Cook continued, briefly scanning the chart again, "there seems to be a marked bias toward Galactic Center, toward our starboard beam. It's variable, but definitely there. So as far as the missing star system is concerned— "

He pointed over his shoulder. "There's a single G-class star astern to starboard, another single-G ahead to port. Since Central Command has never lifted the standing order to note the location of all uncharted G-class star systems, this sort of sighting would have caught the eye of the dullest scout in the fleet. I suspect our chartmaker took a visual sighting from a few parsecs anticenter-east, mistook them for a single system, and took their mean distance for his positional reading."

"But how— "

"As far as our particular problem is concerned—and as a rule of thumb on any chart of unsettled skies, for that matter—I'd trust a hazard indicator before I'd trust the marked position of any star system. Since they rarely appear on your screens until it's too late to avoid trouble, shoals are a menace to any ship in the vicinity, and a survey scout would place the shoals properly if he did anything right at all. So I suspect that the chart's anticenter plottings are accurate enough. And if you ask my advice," Cook smiled inwardly, knowing full well that anything he said would be taken for divine truth by his two young companions, "I'd assume that the shoals are right where the map says they are, but I'd still bear a tad to port and give them a wide berth, even if it does make our route a little less direct. Twelve points over 155 should do quite nicely, I would think. Just hold the course until the shoals show on your instruments, then make whatever adjustments you need."

Both junior officers kept a stunned silence; Cook scratched his head and smiled sheepishly, trying his best not to look smug.

"Of course," he said at last, "it's not my ship, so it's not really my decision." He rose to his feet; the younger officers were too startled to move.

"Well, it's been a long day, and I won't trouble you any more. Maybe tomorrow, after we've passed the shoals, you can show me what this old escort can really do." He chuckled gently, and started toward the ramp.

The lieutenant was the first to regain his wits.

"May I escort you back to your cabin, Commodore?"

Cook shook his head as he walked. "Achh—couldn't get lost here if I tried. And I do have rather a lot on my mind. Thanks anyway."

"Thank you, Commodore."

Turning at the entrance ramp, Cook smiled wearily and nodded.

"Carry on, Mr. ....?"

"Cavanaugh, sir."

"You run a fine ship, Mr. Cavanaugh. Carry on. Call, if I can be of any help. I used to run one of these ships, you know. But that was a long time ago."

"Yes, sir. Thank you, sir."

Cook disappeared into the shadows, heading back to the interior of the ship. The two young control officers said nothing until they heard the commodore's footsteps echo past the forward hold, heading aft toward the mess room. The instant they were sure he'd gone, Cavanaugh craned his neck looking out the forward observation window while his navigator ran a quick positional check on a half-dozen nearby stars.

"My God—all a point or two off…or three or four. Every one off to starboard, just like he said.

"Looks like a damn bunch of stars to me. Can't tell one from another. Not without a map."

"All that, from one glance. Didn't even look at an instrument. Not a single fucking one."

"Mike— "

"I know – come to port— "

"Heading 155, north 12 degrees."

"Aye aye."

"Christ."

"You know, I'd heard stories...but I didn't— "

"Me neither."

* * *

LIGHTS FROM THE display monitors danced across the faces of those in the darkened room. Clicks and whirs from the computers filled the air, echoing in the tense hush. All eyes in the room turned toward the center, waiting for the order everyone knew would come.

"Give the order to attack!"

"Yes, Admiral Weatherlee."

Staring down at the star map in the center of his command center, Winthrop Weatherlee felt a rush of satisfaction. Around him, aides scurried about their business, rushing to carry out his orders. Attendants carrying stacks of briefing documents followed his every move. His assistants hovered near him, their faces glowing with eagerness to answer any question he cared to pose. Large screens showed the position and strength of all forces on both sides of the battle line, plotted on the tactical grids and sensor projections of the surrounding skies. Red lights dominated the screen, enveloping and encircling the green lights that showed the enemy force deployments. Everything was perfectly plotted and graphed. Weatherlee had personally run the last simulation a dozen times. Each time it resulted in a Terran victory. There was nothing left to chance, nothing that could go wrong.

The lizards were living on borrowed time, Weatherlee mused. They couldn't hold out forever. Watching the flashing points of light move into position, he had no doubt that this wave would succeed where the others had failed. With his ships massed into a gigantic wedge, the enemy could not possibly withstand the massive concentration of forces. And as the lizards tired, he'd need just a single chink in their defenses. The planet would fall, and he could walk on a lizard planet for the first time as a conqueror.

This time, he vowed, no blunders by his line commanders would get in the way of victory.

This time, there would be no turning back, no retreat.

This time, he smiled to himself, the lizards would finally feel the sting of a Weatherlee triumph.

* * *

The scent of blood burned the air, and screams rose like thirsty flames. Higher and higher they soared, exploding his eardrums with fire.

COOK AWOKE WITH a start, his heart pounding furiously. Panicked, he found reassurance in the gentle whine of the escort's engines. He stared into the darkness, struggling to calm himself with each breath, trying to relax with thoughts of happier times, of warm, sandy beaches, and youthful indiscretions.

As drowsiness returned, and the small ship sliced through the dark skies heading east, toward the war, Cook started fading into oblivion once more. As he drifted back to sleep he was soon roaming the woodlands of home with his dog and his grandfather, and all the wonder and innocence a seven-year old brings to life. For the first time in his life, Cook tried not to think of space. Or stars. Or wandering the Universe. Or anything he had done for the past thirty years.

Chapter 6

THREE DAYS LATER, A FLOOD of elation washed over the exhausted *g'Khruushtani* in the Command Room.

"They have broken off the attack! They have broken off the attack!"

The senior aide's outburst easily eclipsed the gentle pulsing of the chronometer and the enhancer's high-pitched whine. Across the command room, eyes turned to look at the sight, and the noise as well as the breach of etiquette soon became a source of general amusement. As the screen showed the longnoses to be in full retreat, and lights from the monitors danced across his face, Sh'Alani rapped his hands on a countertop and whistled with delight like a small child.

Khla'Chenga, High Commander of the Region and Centurion of His Worthiness, looked sternly at his deputy commander. Such displays were unseemly enough. But they were inexcusable, when the indulgence took place in front of inferiors.

"Sh'Alani," Lord Chenga of the Khlavana spoke calmly. "When you resume control over yourself, you may recall our defenders to base."

Properly chastened, Sh'Alani bowed to acknowledge his failing and returned to his station to relay the message.

Khla'Chenga turned to resume looking at the screen. He smiled to see the Terrans pulling away from the planet *Gr'Lusshe* at flank speed, beaten back by the ferocity of the planetary defenses. On all sides, battleships of the *g'Khruushtani* were pursuing the barbarians.

The High Commander knew that much of their success was due to the dullness of the Terran battle leader. Like most of his kind, the Terran was willing to sacrifice his own people to a battle of attrition, showing a plodding stubbornness in confronting the courageous *g'Khruushtani* resistance. But he thanked the heavens for the Terran *OOH-eh'thrli,* and for all the others like him. Each day brought their needed reinforcements closer; each day made the end of their ordeal more nearly within their grasp. For the longest time his people had precious few victories to sustain them through the darkness of the Terran Night. It was all he could do to restrain his own welling elation.

* * *

"AND RECONNAISSANCE— ?"

"Our scouts report nothing to confirm our fears, my Lord," said Dra'Lengish, the Chief of Tactics in the Imperial High Command. "The Terrans are simply regrouping for another battle, same as before. Nothing has changed."

Seated in front of the monitor screen, Ga'Glish rocked gently on his seating pillow. He could not refute the obvious. For all his doubts, there was nothing to render bitter their success in stopping the invaders at *Gr'Lusshe*, nothing to dim this victory that the Empire had wrested from the barbarians, a triumph that His Worthiness now held high as a shining image of the future course of the war.

"Splendid," Ga'Glish said at last. "Let us redouble our efforts to break the Terrans while they are still beyond the outer perimeter of the Basin. Perhaps a victory here will stall their other efforts."

"Yes, my Lord."

"Radio Centurion Chenga and convey our congratulations. And order the relief force to proceed with all available speed."

"Yes, my Lord."

The screen went dark, and Ga'Glish clapped his hands to activate the lights. Rising to his feet, he wondered if his Uncle Gal'Shenga, First Minister of His Worthiness and head of the Imperial Government, was not correct in calling him a sour cloud, seeking to rain whenever the sun burned too brightly. As menials dashed about the monitorium, attending to their duties, Ga'Glish strode through the exit and walked toward the control center of his ship, nodding his head as he passed his lessers and received their salutes.

Yet he knew that the siege was still not broken, and the planet could fall at any time. And whatever their scouts might report, none could refute a single, ominous fact.

Days had become weeks since last they had seen the ship of the Terran called *Khu'ukh*.

* * *

THE MURALS IN the hallway showed scenes of summer, and fa'Shenali always loved the summers of home. The gentle odors and warming sunshine had made his long walks in the woods a sanctuary, granting him a brief escape from the anguish of his childhood.

Rounding a corner, he saw Dra'Lengish and Va'Nazze standing in the corridor. High Chiefs on the Lord Commander's staff, the two were sharing a moment of intense conversation. Fa'Shenali had heard the whispers about him making the rounds of the Flagship, and considered turning to avoid them. But showing such weakness, he concluded, would only further undermine his position on the command staff. Proudly he strode forward, pausing as protocol demanded in case his superiors wished to address him.

"Subcommander—Centurion—greetings," fa'Shenali touched his hand to his breast, saluting in the time-honored manner of the *g'Khruushtani* imperial guard. Both men returned the salute with contempt.

"I trust time will improve your manners, Subaltern fa'Shenali," Dra'Lengish sneered, his patrician eyes trumpeting his disdain for the young commoner. "Or must we be ever subjected to your intrusions into the private conversations of your betters?"

"Let us not be uncharitable, Lord Lengish," Va'Nazze said, his words striking the young man like a public flogging. "Can we reasonably expect more from the bastard son of a serving wench?"

Shenali considered his words carefully. It was not proper for an inferior to answer questions addressed to another. But he had endured much in silence these last weeks, much more than protocol demanded. His heart rose to his throat, and he decided not to let the insult pass.

"When younger, I often wondered about my father," he nodded, his voice as cold as he could make it. "At times, I even imagined him to be of noble rank. But I shudder to think, Centurion Va'Nazze, that realizing my fondest childhood dreams could mean learning that we were somehow related."

Without waiting for a reply, fa'Shenali continued to the library to begin his day's work. He kept walking even after his superiors called for him to halt. He knew that his future lay in the hands of Ga'Glish, and none other. And he reasoned that his tormentors would never dare to reveal their own bigotry by bringing the matter to the attention of the Lord Commander.

* * *

Far to the west, alone in the Looking Glass situation room and pacing in front of a giant star map, Fleet Admiral Porter Clay was torn by conflicting instincts and emotions. He'd known loneliness and fear even before the war. The power to order others to die always haunted him, and he often thought that command itself was less a blessing than a curse. But his current problem tore at his conscience like no others, for he knew exactly how to solve it. From the start, he knew precisely how to accomplish the mission he'd set for Fleet Group Alpha, at the minimum cost of lives and equipment. Yet he'd shied away from it, for reasons that made him feel like a coward for the first time in his life. The reasons had little to do with the valor of battle: it was politics, pure politics. He was coming to hate himself for compromising his people for the sake of escaping the headaches that would come from making the right decision.

He stopped in front of the area that showed the battle sector near Planet Greloosh. A sea of red markers surrounded the planet, marked in green to show that it was held by the enemy. From the vantage of space, it was simple: the planet could not stand. Yet against all odds, it was holding out. Whether by some defect in Terran planning, or the enemy's animal tenacity, the planet remained in Crutchtan hands. As long as the enemy held the planet the Terran offensive would stall, for it was the only habitable planet for ten parsecs in any direction, and they had learned the lessons of their past mistakes. The First Battle of Lagrush had almost been their undoing, handing the Crutchtans a major victory in the early days of the war; if not for the arrival of Cook's missing starship at the last moment, it would have opened Terran skies to the enemy. Since then, Terra had learned not to extend their forces beyond an unbroken front. They would never give the enemy an outpost behind their own lines.

He lifted his eyes a few degrees, seeking the most recent position of the green fleet as it inched its way toward the planet.

Weatherlee's task force could not fight two battles simultaneously. They could either divert to stop the incoming enemy fleet, or they could continue the siege. They couldn't do both.

The longer he grappled with the tactical dilemma, the clearer his decision became. There was no other option; his conscience simply would not allow it. As difficult as it would be politically for himself in the halls of Central Command, the next move was as clear as the vacuum of space. He only hoped that he hadn't delayed the inevitable too long already. If he had, and all the lives lost trying to take the enemy planet proved to be in vain, he would never forgive himself.

A rush of air from behind the security screen told him that someone had just entered the room.

"Admiral Clay— "

Clay looked to see Miriam Wright coming toward him, flanked by the fleet's senior tactical advisors. He had called them together to see if they could salvage Weatherlee's pride by coming up with some new ideas for taking the planet. The approaching enemy fleet might make their efforts futile, but given the sensitivity of the alternative it was worth trying.

"All right, people," he began. The resignation in his voice told everyone present that this would be their last chance to avoid what each sensed to be inevitable. "We have less than two weeks before the enemy fleet arrives at Greloosh. "Is there any way we can help Weatherlee take the planet? Or am I left calling in our trump card?"

Everyone knew exactly what the Admiral meant. The longer they debated the tactical options, the less likely it seemed that Clay could avoid issuing the order.

* * *

A FEW DAYS later, a shuttle hatch lock opened and a slightly disheveled blueshirt stepped into the hangar deck of the Cosmic Guard's most famous ship.

"Permission to come aboard?"

"Permission granted, Captain Fitzgerald. Welcome to the d'Artagnan."

Fitz smiled at his pretty young escort, a lieutenant who, as he recalled, was a member of Cook's bridge crew. His ruddy skin crinkled around his eyes, and he wished that he'd taken the time to change into a clean uniform before leaving the Magellan. After the time spent cooped up on his own ship, he needed a change of scenery, and she was a lass after his own heart—a touch of sauce, ripe for a saucy touch. It never occurred to him that the young lady had her own views in the matter, and an entirely different opinion of him.

"Skipper's still an hour away," Mary Mathison said, as pleasantly as she could manage. "They would've been back yesterday, but they changed the rendezvous point again."

Fitz laughed roguishly.

"They had to deliver some briefing papers to him," Mary continued, a trace of haughtiness creeping into her voice. "By express courier, no less. The rest of the group is already here, now, so I guess the delay won't really mean much. I mean, the Skipper can attend long-distance, if he wants to."

Fitz nodded absently, paying less attention to what the young lieutenant was saying than how she was saying it. As they neared the officer's lounge, he reflected that the *d'Artagnan* was really little different than any of the other starships in the fleet. The flooring might be a different color, but the corridors were the same hexagons, and the walls were the same standard beige. Passing them in the hallways, the crew looked much the same, though the missies always looked better on somebody else's ship.

But being on this ship—Cook's ship—felt different. Whether it was the bearing of the crew, the jaunty pride even the lowliest crewman showed at helping to man the grandest ship in the Cosmic Guard, or something as minor as the slightly subnormal gravitation the ship kept to remind her skipper of home, he couldn't really tell. But he felt it every time he came aboard. Something about the *d'Artagnan* set it apart from the rest of the fleet.

Entering the lounge, Fitz smiled to greet many of his old comrades: Tanana; Blake; even Forestall, the group's senior wing commander. Some he'd known for years, and some he hadn't seen for ages, since shortly after the war started. But lifetimes passed quickly in war, and he had many friends he would never see again.

"Fitz—!!"

It was Chandler, his old friend from his DemCom days. Chandler looked tired, almost worn out. When Fitz looked at the others, they all had the same haggard, gaunt look. He wondered if he looked any different himself.

"You crafty old bastard! How the hell are you?"

"Same as always," Fitz shrugged. "How's life been treating you under Old Blunderbutt? Keeping your backsides safe from harm, I hope. From what we hear, the slimy bugger keeps dropping load after load. And now you groundtoads need help cleaning up the mess."

Rough laughter filled the room. The warmth of friendship was easy enough to rekindle, Fitz thought. Besides, Admiral Weatherlee was nobody's favorite commander. All along the front lines, the potshots at him were as thick as the bloodgnats on a Demetrian summer night.

"Those who're still here can't complain," said Drake. "Leastways, not so long as Winnie's in earshot."

"Well, you can all rest easy now," returned Fitz. "Cookie's a-coming to the rescue—again. But by God, seems it's bloody well getting to be a habit, don't you know."

"This time, Cookie's got his work cut out for him," said Forestall, his face turning serious. "The lizards are getting tougher every day. We lost Goddard in the last attack— "

Fitz nodded sadly. Goddard had been part of the old gang at DemCom for longer than any of them could remember, as free with his money as with his jokes. Willing to do anything for a laugh, or for one of the good old boys. Now, like so many others Fitz knew, he was gone forever.

"— and he's just the latest."

"What's the problem? I thought— "

"They're getting smarter, Fitz. We've kicked their slimy tails from the Neutral Zone half-way to the end of creation, but they're starting to pull things together."

"Cookie's never put much stock in just bulling past'em," Tanana interjected, "so you might not have a sense of how dicey things are getting. But they've started holding their forces back—pulling in their lines, shoring up their flanks."

"Most of all," continued Chandler, "now that their backs are against the wall they're starting to press the attack."

"And jumping all over us," added Forestall, "when we make the slightest mistake."

As his friends continued bringing him up to date on the enemy's strengths and tactics, Fitz felt his insides twisting into hard, tight knots. Once again, now that they were set up for the kill, the lizards were fighting like demons. And after the Terran brush with disaster early in the war, they each knew better than to take the lizards lightly. Especially when it seemed like the battle was all but won.

Surrounded by buddies from the old days, Fitz poured a cup of coffee and took a seat. Soft, soothing music sounded over the speakers, and the plush, cushioned chairs in the officers' lounge did wonders for his stern. It had been ages since he'd taken the time to sit and relax. On the *Magellan*, he found himself constantly besieged by a million things that demanded his attention. Here, on another ship, his mind could drift like a tramp schooner. He reveled in the freedom it gave him. But even here, he couldn't escape forever; soon, the war came crashing back into his brain. He found himself caught by the stories of old friends meeting death, or heroics that were passing unsung in the darkness, so far away from civilization. He wondered when it would ever end.

More to the point, he began to wonder when his own commander's magic would run out, and whether this time Cookie would have any more luck than Old Blunderbutt.

* * *

"LORD COMMANDER?"

The footfalls of a thousand souls thundered through the Flagship concourse, each proceeding toward the execution of duty. Lost in a cloud of his own concerns, Ga'Glish did not hear his Chief of Tactics calling. Soon, out of breath, Dra'Lengish had overtaken him.

"Lord Commander!" panted the Dralanvengi.

"Perhaps we should reconsider the advice of some of our junior officers," smiled Ga'Glish, pausing to wait for Dra'Lengish to recover his wind. "Perhaps the conditioning we require of our young soldiers would be of benefit to my command staff, Lengish."

"It would thin our ranks—appreciably, Lordship," the Chief of Tactics nodded between gasps, "if only through—accelerating—the mortality tables. Whether that would benefit the Empire remains an unanswered question, I suppose."

Turning to proceed toward the briefing area, Ga'Glish laughed without cheer.

"You have news?"

"Yes, Lordship. Good news, this time."

"I am listening."

"They have waited too long. The Terrans have delayed their offensive for too many days. Our relief force reports clear skies, and has made remarkable progress. Now they are but a few days away. The longnoses no longer have time to secure the planet before the arrival of Ra'Danli. They must retreat or perish."

"Your confidence is most heartwarming," Ga'Glish observed wryly. "Of course, it is easy to be confident when we are so far away from the battle, but let us not speak of trifles."

"Speaking of trifles," Dra'Lengish said; Ga'Glish sensed his Deputy's mood shift to one of disdain. "I note that our newest arrival has yet to produce anything of value. He prefers to mouth only drivel and tripe, unbecoming a staff aide to the High Command."

"Fa'Shenali has barely had chance to unpack, Lengish. Give him time. I am sure that the first time you spoke her name, your mother did not chide you for the paucity of your wit. Besides, he comes highly regarded, and he does seem to learn rather quickly."

"But he is a—a commoner," Dra'Lengish whispered. "Worse, his pedigree would offend even the rabble! Oh, Lordship, let us see reason together. This—boy, if you wish to be gracious about his appellation— "

Stopping to face Dra'Lengish, Ga'Glish held out his hand to silence his Chief of Tactics. "This is a new age, Lengish," the Lord Commander smiled wearily. "The exigencies of our era demand certain…well, concessions."

Dra'Lengish kept his face impassive, but Ga'Glish could feel the frustration welling within his subordinate's breast.

"Besides, the old Castes never did us much good. The philosophers have denounced them for eons."

"Empty-headed rubbish!" rejoined Dra'Lengish. "They gave us order. And discipline. We knew who we were and what we were. And they never were very rigid, you know. At least, not among— "

"Not among the masses. I know, Son of the Dralanvengi. But the Oligarchy itself must occasionally admit new blood, or die of its own inbreeding. And truth be known, we have been slowly dying for millennia, Lengish. We simply did not perceive it. For that perception—whatever other crimes they have committed along the way—we must thank the longnoses."

Dra'Lengish recoiled in horror. "Such talk sounds of—of treason, Lordship."

Ga'Glish watched in amusement as the color fairly drained from the eyes and gill slits of his tactical chieftain. Reformists like his uncle were long considered mad, he mused, and he was coming to doubt his own sanity, as well. Perhaps a civilization without its madmen simply lacked the energy to thrive. But he had long passed the point of caring about such things.

"Treason or not, the Terrans have made it all quite irrelevant," he replied. "For the time being, the Empire needs all her sons, from all her daughters, if we are going to survive."

"Have we really sunk so low as this?" Dra'Lengish breathed deeply; his voice quavered as he spoke. "So low as to need every harlot's son to beat back the barbarians?"

Ga'Glish patted his subordinate on the shoulder, his smile belying the fire Dra'Lengish felt in the Lord Commander's soul. "Bigotry ill becomes you, Lengish."

"But— "

"I shall hear no more of such things," Ga'Glish commanded regally. His eyes narrowied fiercely, enough to make his subordinate fear for his liberty. "I have made my decision, and so has the First Minister. We are a common People. And the Terrans are a common enemy, dedicated to our destruction. If we cannot put aside our differences now, in the face of such dangers, then we do not deserve to call ourselves civilized."

They continued down the hall, heading toward the Flagship's Grand Hall of Congregation, for the weekly assembly of Thanksgiving. To ones observing, they passed as if related by blood—Ga'Glish walking like a family lord, with proud eyes and defiant heart; his tactical chief shaking his head and pursing his lips like a sour old aunt.

* * *

"THEY'RE ASSEMBLED IN your office. The senior line officers from Task Force Alpha, I mean. One of ours has already arrived, so he's there with them."

"Who?"

"Captain Fitzgerald."

Cook shook his head as he and Dexter hurried into the hangar deck lift. They headed toward the Conning Deck, and programmed the lift control for "Express." The metal grids on the sidepanels gave a passing view of the ship's insides. A small light flashed each time they passed a different deck.

"I might have known," Cook smiled. "If any of our own people could make it here ahead of us, it would be Fitz."

"As for current status on the ship—well, aside from the new apprentice navigator...."

Cook raised his hand to interrupt. "Lieutenant," he said with a weary sigh. "I've had a long trip, and I have a lot to think about in the next few days."

Dexter looked crestfallen. "I only thought.. ."

Cook laughed, more in pity than anything else. "Don't misunderstand me. I am impressed, Mr. Dexter. You have performed admirably. I have never seen handrails glisten like that, or floor tiles sparkle so brightly. And your initiative in winning certification at the remaining two bridge stations in my absence certainly does not give me any regrets—except that since you're now eligible to command your own ship, you may be taken away from me just as you're starting to become indispensable. But you've a lot to learn about your commanding officer's quirks, as our executive officer can tell you. And you can tell Miss Mendelson and me all about it later, after I find out what we'll be up against."

Dexter's eyes bulged. "Mendelson!" he exclaimed. "Oh, Jesus! She's still— "

"Don't worry, Mr. Dexter," Cook said, looking up at the floor indicator. "She's a big girl. I'm sure she can find her way back to her room by herself."

"But we just left her— "

"As for protocol," Cook began.

The door opened, and Cook stepped out into the Conning Deck corridor. Concerned about what the Book would describe as a minor breach of manners, Dexter stared ahead dumbly, his mouth open.

"Just tell her you're sorry, and that it won't ever happen again. And pray that she's roped a redshirt into carrying all her bags. She did a lot of shopping on Looking Glass, and I'll tell you quite honestly that being her valet is no fun at all."

The elevator door closed, and Cook started down the hallway toward his office. He wondered whether the tactic of apologizing to the ship's Executive Officer would work better for Dexter than it did for himself. Without fanfare, he entered his office and strode to the seat behind his desk, ignoring the startled animation that greeted his arrival.

"As you were; everyone be seated," he began. He frowned to see that his desk had been tidied in his absence, and made a mental note to talk to his new executive aide about the pitfalls of mindless efficiency. "We don't have time to bother with introductions. Besides, I'm sure we all know everyone here.

"I've read the status reports and battle manifests on the trip over here. At least, enough of them to give me an idea of what we're up against."

"And we've got wind of some of your zingers to the brass," interrupted Chandler. "Must say you're none too complimentary of our late Leader. Not that he might not be deserving it."

Cook silenced the growing chorus of chortles with an acid smile.

"My personal opinions are not for public consumption," he said coldly. "And as far as the past is concerned, I've read enough of your own reports, Captain Chandler, to know that there's plenty of blame to go around. If all this good cheer at the change in commanders reflects the level of support Admiral Weatherlee received from his subordinates, I may have overestimated what he had to work with—and may well owe him an apology."

The entire group fell silent.

"As for where we go from here," Cook continued, "I've sent for some of my own people to help us take the planet."

"It's about time we got some help," ventured Forestall. The others nodded.

"Who's coming to help us?"

"Captain Fitzgerald is already here," Cook said, nodding toward Fitz. "Captains Ebling and McKinnon should be here in a day or two. We attack the day after they arrive."

"Three ships? Three bloody ships? The lizards have been beating our butts for nearly a month and you think— "

"Captain Forestall," Cook said, his eyebrows arching regally. "I've got troubles enough, without any that your rudeness and mouth might add to the pile. Three additional starships—plus my own—should be quite sufficient for our needs. Given our time constraints, and the enemy's tactical position, anything more would be a waste of resources. In fact, I doubt we really needed any additional help at all, but Admiral Weatherlee had already committed all his starships to the battle. I was afraid that what I have bouncing around my head might not work if the enemy realized that some of you were missing.

"Besides," Cook smiled coldly, " I didn't really want to embarrass Admiral Weatherlee, or the lot of you, any more than necessary."

"But— "

"As for our precise plan of attack...," stifling a yawn, Cook leaned back in his chair. He fought off the drowsiness that tried to intrude into his routine from time to time. Wing commanders had little enough time as it was. Weariness simply had no place on his duty schedule.

"I need to give things a bit more thought. I'll have something in writing for you by tomorrow. I trust you'll all have it mastered by the end of the day."

"But— "

"You're all free to return to your ships, or to stay on board here, as our guests. But be back here—in my office—tomorrow at 200 Hours, sharp."

"But— "

"Dismissed."

The squadron leaders filed out the door. Their shuffling feet dragged noiselessly on the carpet, and they each kept a sullen silence. Cook watched them carefully as they left. He suddenly realized that he'd worked with very few of them. From what he could see, they were hardly the sort to inspire innovation in a commanding officer. As the last of them neared the exit, he spoke again.

"Captain Fitzgerald, I'd like to speak to you."

Fitz made his apologies to his friends, and promised to meet them in the officer's lounge. When the door closed, Cook motioned for Fitz to take a seat.

"Well, Maestro," Fitz laughed, plopping onto the overstuffed guest chair to Cook's right, "looks like you've got your work cut out for you. The lizards—sorry, the Crutchtans—are giving our people fits here. And you're sure as hell not making any friends with the locals. In fact, I'd say you've taken it upon yourself to prove to the rest of the Fleet that Weatherlee can't even beat you when it comes to driving people crazy."

Cook leaned back in his chair and laughed. "Ah, Fitz, honest to a fault. You'd fail completely as a diplomat, you know."

"In this room, I think I have the market on tact cornered right now. What's on your mind?"

Cook changed the programming on the overhead speakers, filling the room with the ancient, spritely music he used to help forget his troubles. He smiled wanly as Fitz winced at the change in programming. Clasping his hands behind his head, he leaned back in his chair and closed his eyes, savoring each ebb and billow of the string section for the next several moments.

"You know these guys, Fitz," he said at last. "Tell me about them."

"Well, I— "

"And not the stuff I'll find in their service records." Cook sat up in his chair, laughing softly at his own private joke. "I mean—who's sailed with whom; who discovered what; who's gotten which medal. That's about as helpful as finding rocks in a rockpile."

"Well, if I knew— "

"I need to know what's inside them." Cook pointed to his heart. "How much can I trust them to do exactly as I say? And how much fight do they have in their bellies?"

"They're all fine officers," Fitz interjected hotly, as annoyed at having to defend his friends as at having to fight his way into the conversation. "Among the best I've served with."

"You've seen none of them in battle, though? I mean—lately."

Fitz shook his head warily. "Not since the First Battle of Lagrush. Forestall was in the next squadron over during the ambush. The others? I served with them all at DemCom. They're all first class officers. I've never had reason to think that any of them are—you know—squeamish."

Cook smirked, the same Isitian smirk that had made enemies all along the front lines. Cook's smugness was annoying enough in the past, and Fitz often got sick and tired of defending him. Now, even Fitz was reaching the end of his patience.

"Never mind, " Cook sighed. "Go join your buddies, Fitz. They're probably half drunk by now, and I'm sure you don't want to be left behind. Not this close to a battle."

"Dammit Cook! I'm not a bloody mind reader. And I don't much care for being laughed at. It might help if you told people what the hell you wanted to know, every once in a while."

Cook lifted his head to look at the ceiling. He took a deep breath and chuckled mirthlessly to himself. When he spoke at last, there was a note of sadness in his voice that Fitz recognized, one that never failed to send a shiver down his spine. He'd heard it often enough. Always just before a battle. Just before Cook sent people off to die.

"If you had to pick one of them for a mission you had just doomed to fail—one that may kill thousands, on the chance that it might save thousands more," Cook looked Fitz straight in the eye. "Which of them is most likely to come back alive? And who would bring the largest number of his people back with him?"

Fitz swallowed hard. His stomach tightened like a steel drum, and his gaze dropped to the floor. When he looked up, he saw Cook smiling the loneliest, weakest smile Fitz had ever seen.

"Not easy being a commodore these days, is it?"

Fitz said nothing; his face turned a deep crimson.

"Don't worry, Fitz," Cook said at last. "I'd never make you choose between your friends."

Chapter 7

TWO DAYS PASSED, AS THE *g'Khruushtani* battalions scoured the heavens for signs of their enemies. Each day brought news from the rest of the Empire, news of the approaching fleet, and of the parades and rallies in honor of the brave warriors at *Gr'Lusshe*. But on the third day, tension and concern seized everyone in the Monitorium.

"Screen Six shows enemy movement, Centurion."

Khla'Chenga moved to look at the brightly colored dots that disclosed the Terran positions on the motion screen. Many days had passed since the longnoses had stirred. Sh'Alani, his deputy commander, thought it likely that they were nursing their wounds until the time came for another assault. Khla'Chenga worried that the hiatus carried more sinister overtones.

"Transmit Terran movements to Tactics for analysis," the Centurion said. "I wish to know of any change in the movement patterns we have observed…and whether there is anything new for us to take into account."

"I understand," said the monitor. "You wish to know if they have changed commanders."

Khla'Chenga smiled. Though from a lowly station, this monitor had a keen mind and sharp powers of observation. "Let us hope that I am worrying like a grandmother," he patted the monitor affectionately on his shoulder. "But I am worried, nonetheless."

Leaving the monitor station, Khla'Chenga strode down the hall toward the Tactical Center. From there he would control the defense of the planet. The large room arched above and below, like the expanse in which the fighting would loom. Holographic projections would display the contours of battle. And in the center, suspended over the transparent flooring that his subordinates would share with him, was a blue globe, suspended in the darkened room, spinning in the blackness like the real *Gr'Lusshe* circled the heavens.

Technicians and assistants swarmed about the Center like summer insects, tending to the endless details that would help their commanders repel the invaders. Khla'Chenga looked at the mass of activity. Like the planet below them, the great room was crowded with refugees. Only here they were refugees from fear, and their refuge was their work, rather than the warmth of a friendly world. The Centurion felt the weight of creation pressing upon him, for the fate of all on the planet below—on the Defense Station—even in the ships that had beaten back the longnoses for the past hundred days—rested upon him. Yet in a few days it would be over: the relief force was but two days away. If they could hold out until then, he could draw his first relaxed breath in what seemed like a lifetime.

Khla'Chenga strode proudly into the Center.

"The High Commander comes," called the Tactics Controller. The command staff stopped their tasks to stand stiffly in place, a gesture of respect for the one who had replaced their darkest fears with hope and pride.

"The Terrans are shifting their line of attack," reported the Chief Monitor. "They are moving into Sector Twelve, and forming a broadened front for their assault."

"I do not like this," added Sh'Alani.

"You do not like the fact that they are moving between ourselves and our approaching relief force," Khla'Chenga said wryly, "or the fact that they are trying something different this time?"

Sh'Alani fell into an embarrassed silence. At once, Khla'Chenga felt a sense of shame. Alani's enthusiasm had proved a valuable asset during the long ordeal. The Centurion knew that it was wrong to use his rank to mock one who had performed so admirably.

"I apologize for my tactlessness," smiled Khla'Chenga. "But we must forget our likes and dislikes. We must concentrate only on living through the next few days."

"Their tactics are changing," said his deputy. "I pray that it does not mean— "

"We gain nothing by assuming the worst, Son of Gralani, except a paralyzing sense of fear," said Khla'Chenga, strengthening his voice so that all could hear. "Yet we have all known that it could well come to this, that the Terrans might one day send their best into battle against us. And if it is truly the Beast himself who now seeks our destruction, then we owe our people, and our Imperator—and everyone huddling in fear on the planet we are guarding—all the courage and daring we can muster for the struggle before us.

"We have won a great battle, just by staying alive. In two days— three, at the most—the forces of His Worthiness will arrive to break the siege and bring us the rest we have not known for ages. Surely a few days more can be as nothing, for those who have already accomplished so much."

A deafening cheer rose through from the throats of those assembled, and cries of "Victory!" soon filled the Center. Yet as they returned to their tasks, each felt the first twinge of despair start gnawing within.

They were within days of denying the longnoses the first contested planet of the war. Victory, however transitory it might prove to be, was within their grasp.

Yet each knew that the most hated Terran was out there, somewhere, looming in the blackness like death.

And each knew that the One Called *Khu'ukh* had yet to lose in battle.

* * *

"WITH ALL DUE respect, Commodore... "

"Get to the point, Forestall. I don't want to keep the Crutchtans waiting."

"Setting your people off to the side... and splitting the troop landers like that. I don't understand— "

"We went over it all at the briefing, Captain. This is not a debate, and I'm not conducting a tactics seminar."

"But— "

"If you have any questions, I'll be happy to discuss the matter afterwards. If we both live through this. And if I'm not called away as soon as it's over. Right now, I don't have the time."

"But why— "

"That is all, Captain. You have a squadron to tend to."

"Yes, sir."

"*D'Artagnan* out."

"Over and out—*sir.*"

* * *

SLOWLY, THE ENEMY forces drew closer. The Terrans advanced along a broad front, the Crutchtans moved cautiously, approaching in a single, tight formation aimed at the Terran midsection. Just beyond the solar limits of *Gr'Lusshe*, the Terran left flank raced forward and pivoted forty-five degrees, seeking to engage the Crutchtan flank at an angle to soften them for the bulk of the Terran attack. It was a maneuver that Khla'Chenga had seen before, though only in briefings and study sessions, and he countered by sending a small detachment to engage and deflect the Terran charge. But concern rippled throughout the Crutchtan defenders. Few Terran commanders dared to split their forces at the onset of battle, and the One Called *OOH-eh'thrli* lacked both the wit and the vision to begin a battle with such a maneuver. This concern soon matured into worry, as the Terrans followed their opening slant by pivoting the main body of their forces and slicing toward the besieged Crutchtan flank, isolating the Crutchtan wing and positioning the bulk of the Terran force to lunge directly toward the besieged planet. It was a thrust both daring and simple, and bore the dreaded hallmarks of Crutchta's deadliest enemy. As it became apparent that the longnoses had changed commanders for a last attempt to take the planet, a cold fear spread among the Crutchtan defenders.

"CHANDLER REPORTS THE bulk of the main Crutchtan body moving past Squadron Four to engage him."

"Already noted."

"Forestall reports enemy reinforcements moving toward our left flank."

"Commodore, a trailing enemy squadron has engaged Squadron Four. Captain Drake reports stiffening resistance."

Cook looked up from his star map. In his command room, adjacent to his office, he kept the lights dimmed, better to see the movements on the screens. As his tactical aides kept their eyes glued to their computer screens, his own eyes narrowed in fierce concentration, the monitor lights casting a soft glow across his face.

"Tell Tanana to move into position to support Chandler's squadron, and await the order to engage. I expect the fighting will be rather intense, and he'll need all the help he can get."

"Aye aye."

"In the meantime, I want to know the instant the Crutchtans begin moving their second wave into position."

"Yes, Commodore."

"And Calloway— "

"Sir?"

"Page the bridge, and tell Commander Mendelson to have the first team stand down. They shouldn't be needed for the next hour or so. Tell her not to start worrying until I show up there."

"Aye aye, sir."

KHLA'CHENGA LOOKED anxiously at the monitor screen. Grimly, he paced the Center, his eyes never moving from the center of the battle.

"Report," he commanded.

"Engagement proceeding. Detachment Six reports heavy losses."

"Detachment Five reports their lines under attack."

"Detachment Two reports their lines are holding, but the Terrans are intensifying their attack."

Khla'Chenga felt his mind under siege. *Khu'ukh* pressed upon them from every corner of the battle, giving them not a moment's reflection. Forcing himself to remain calm, he called for Sh'Alani. His voice was dispassionate and controlled, but Alani could sense the growing anxiety of his commander.

"Analysis?"

"Our reserves remain uncommitted."

"As are those of the Terrans."

"They are directing their thrust toward the middle of our forces. Perhaps a counterthrust along the peripheries... "

"Our peripheries are barely holding their own. Without reinforcements, they cannot attack. And if we commit ourselves there, the Terrans will press their central attack and overrun our main force."

"Help is less than two days away. If we can last— "

"We must first fight the Terrans to a draw. We cannot do so if our lines collapse around us."

As Sh'Alani pondered the problem, Khla'Chenga glanced again at the battle projector. *Khu'ukh* was a more daring commander than he had ever encountered, with a quick, adaptable mind and a stunning sense of timing. So far, the Terran had anticipated and countered his every movement, pressing the attack closer and more furiously with each turn of battle.

And yet with each passing moment, the Terran line was arching forward at the peripheries, leaving a bulge in the center of battle where the fighting was most intense and resistance by the *g'Khruushtani* was the fiercest.

Suddenly, it struck him; coldly, he mulled it over in his mind until he was certain. Soon a grim smile danced over his lips, and those closest to him felt their own spirits lifting with the growing hopes of their commander.

Khu'ukh could be beaten.

Now.

There!

And Khla'Chenga knew exactly how to do it. It had been so simple that it nearly escaped his notice.

"Order two squadrons of the reserves forward," he said, his voice carrying echoes of his own confidence. "The remainder shall await my order."

"And they are— "

"They are to attack," said Khla'Chenga. "Let the longnoses feel the lash of defeat. Today, let their ashes light the skies, and let the Imperator's Medallion go to the defender who destroys the One Called *Khu'ukh*.

"They are to attack! They are to push at the center of the Terran positions and not let the longnoses shake loose until the battle is won. They are to attack!"

"WHAT?"

"I said— "

"He's ordering us to do *what?*"

"We are ordered to disengage and retreat, and reestablish our lines one-hundred klicks due east of— "

"Get him on the line."

"I beg your par— "

"Get our esteemed commodore on the line, Lieutenant. Right now."

"But— "

"Don't give me 'buts' — or I'll kick yours myself. Just do it!"

As the radio officer hastily tried to raise the *d'Artagnan* on the emergency channel, Captain Chandler fumed in his command chair. Outside, just beyond the range of his visual sensors, a furious battle was raging. His tactical screens told him that his ships were starting to turn the battle. Though the toll was high on both sides, the enemy was starting to give way. If they kept up the pressure, they might well break through the enemy line, though how long it would take was anyone's guess.

But now, if this latest scheme wasn't countermanded....he just didn't want to think of the consequences. A stern voice on the communications screen jolted him back to grim reality.

"All right, Chandler, what is it? And why are you still holding your position?" It was Cook; his angry eyes told Chandler that he was in more trouble with the commodore than he was with the Crutchtans. But Chandler was hardly in a defensive mood. Having his own commander angry at him was the least of his worries.

"I wanted to confirm— " he began.

"Retreat order is confirmed," Cook said sharply. "Reestablish your position one-hundred astrokilometers due east of McGregor's Star. You may make your retreat as orderly as possible, but you are ordered to withdraw, immediately."

"But that means that Drake— "

"Immediately."

"They'll have to slug their way back, Commodore. And there's no telling— "

"You have your orders, Captain."

"Dammit, Cook! You're cutting off our own people!"

"Those are your orders, Captain."

Chandler signed off angrily, and nodded to his radio officer to relay the order to the rest of his squadron. He tried to ignore the twisting, gnarled feeling in the pit of his stomach. He knew that the battle would soon come hurling toward him in its full fury. But his own squadron would hardly know the worst of it. Already, Drake's people were in the thick of the battle. Chandler realized that if he retreated, the front around them would collapse, letting lizards pour through the breach and cutting Drake off from any help from the rest of the attack wing.

It was almost as if Cook was dooming his point squadron to a pointless death.

Chandler felt fear gnaw at his belly. All around them, the Terran battle lines were collapsing. It seemed clear that Cook had finally met his match. Either that, or the man had finally lost his mind.

* * *

A GREAT CHEER rose through the Center. All voices rose in jubilation, and many rose from their seats, breaking into a dance of celebration.

Khla'Chenga steeled himself against such outbursts. Whatever the temptation, giddiness was an indulgence they could not afford. Though relief would arrive in less than two days, the battle was far from over. Many brave *g'Khruushtani* would die defending the planet.

Yet the Centurion permitted himself a measure of inner satisfaction. Though they needed only to hold out for two days, he felt the tide of battle turning in their favor. For the first time since the early days of the war, a major victory was within their grasp. And for the first time ever, they were on the verge of humbling the great Terran commander.

"Advance through the opening," he bellowed proudly. Cheers greeted his words, and he raised his voice to make himself heard.

"Order Groups One and Three to charge forward with all available ships! We have broken through the Terran ranks. Let us not see victory slip through our fingers!"

* * *

AS THE CRUTCHTAN ships streamed forward, cutting off the forwardmost Terran positions, the Terran lines retreated, and then stabilized. Before long, as all the *g'Khruushtani* knew they would, the Terrans began their counterattack, struggling to free the longnoses trapped behind the wall of defenders. Soon, the black sky burned with the remains of ships, scattering the ashes of the dead to the heavens. Yet for all their efforts, and all their early successes, a single presence haunted the defenders like a ghost. All were aware that until their most hated enemy made his appearance, the battle would hang very much in doubt.

He appeared without warning. Soon, the ship of the One Called *Khu'ukh* was lighting the skies with its deadly fire, rallying the Terrans as in countless battles before. The blackness soon filled with the fury of war, and the Terrans began their advance once more. The Crutchtan forces fought back bravely, but all sensed the grim truth: if *Khu'ukh* forced them to turn in retreat, the battle was lost. And along the entire front, they could sense that they were slowly being forced back.

Suddenly, as chaos raged all around them, deliverance rose from the void. From out of nothing, another breach appeared in the Terran battle line, between the Terran center and left flank—an opening wide as the Beldisi gulf, summoning the *g'Khruushtani* on to triumph like a palace temptress beckoning her master.

"Why do you hesitate?" screamed Sh'Alani. "It is there—it is ours—for the taking! Only a coward would fail to attack!"

Khla'Chenga stood firmly, his back stiffening under the barrage of insults, but said nothing in reply.

"Are you blind, High Commander? We can break the back of the Terrans with one final thrust! They have spent their strength trying to reestablish their lines and rescue those we have cut off. We can isolate the Beast with all the rest of his blood-crazed animals. Once we break through and surround them, there will be no escape!"

Still, Khla'Chenga wavered. Another day and the relief force would be with them. The Terran force at *Gr'Lusshe* was strong, but even the Beast could not fight both defenders and rescuers at the same time.

Yet the thirst for vengeance burned hotly in the Centurion's breast. He had watched too many friends consumed by the death fires of bursting ships not to feel revenge kindling in his soul. And Sh'Alani was right about something else, something more important than any of the lives around him. This was their opportunity to destroy the One Called *Khu'ukh*. The Terran's life seemed charmed by the gods, but now they had the chance to avenge everything the Beast had destroyed. The wily Centurion knew that they were unlikely to get another.

Khla'Chenga rose to his full height. The weight of duty seemed a trifle compared to the many lost to the barbarians. "Give the order to attack, with full force," he cried, the cheers from his subordinates ringing in his ears. "Send all available ships toward the breach! Let us kill this Monster once and for all!"

"Enemy ships are moving into Sector Three," reported Dexter, his voice hoarse from the strain of constant use. "They're pouring everything they have into trying to close the noose around our necks."

"Mr. Gerlach, divert all available power to weaponry."

"Yes, sir."

"Miss Mathison— "

"Sir?"

"Broadcast the signal to Captain Fitzgerald. His party may now begin their advance."

"Aye, aye...*Magellan* acknowledges."

"Sound the command—all starships to the rally point; all forces stand by to attack."

"Yes, sir."

"And hang on for just a while longer, people. The worst is almost behind us."

"HIGH COMMANDER ..."

Khla'Chenga felt primal surge of bitter satisfaction. His ships were streaming into position. Soon, they would cut off any hope of retreat for the One Called *Khu'ukh*. Trapped between enemy forces, the monster could do nothing but await his own destruction.

"High Commander."

The Centurion looked at the giant monitor screen. The changing patterns of brightly colored blips showed the deadly battle unfolding. This time, there would be no escape for the Beast. The demon would squeal like a scavenger caught in the flames of a smelt mill, Khla'Chenga smiled grimly. And the embers of the monster's death fire would ignite celebrations from one end of the Empire to the other.

"*High Commander*—!" Anguish filled the voice of Sh'Alani.

Khla'Chenga looked behind him, toward the rear monitor station, only to see horror in his deputy's eyes and feel the panic in his heart.

Khla'Chenga looked—and then he saw it! What he saw drained his courage like water from a bottomless cup. As suddenly as a bolt of lightening, all hope had vanished.

All was lost : the thought kept thundering in his mind.

A small Terran force was approaching from the west, as leisurely as on a summer stroll.

All was lost.

Three starships, enough to destroy their command center and lay waste to the entire planet, were escorting a dozen Terran landing craft.

All was lost.

He knew at once. The entire battle had been a mirage. A cruel mirage. With all their strength engaging the Terrans to the east, nothing was left to stop the advance from the west. Nothing to stop them from destroying the planet, or invading it without risk. Once the few planetary defenses were obliterated, *Gr'Lusshe* would lay at the Terrans' feet.

Around the room, there was no sound but the clicking of computers. The screens showed the tide of battle swiftly changing, for what they all knew would be the last time. From the small conceit of elation, nothing was left but surrender or death.

His mind numbed and spinning, Sh'Alani wandered toward the screen showing the main battle. In the passing of a heartbeat, the Terrans had turned with vengeance upon the *g'Khruushtani*, attacking on all sides and devastating the defenders' suddenly overextended battle lines. It seemed so clear now.

Sh'Alani heard a whirring noise, a sickening noise that was quite familiar to him. Tears welling in his eyes, he spun about to see the dead body of Lord Chenga of the Khlavanal lying on floor. A bloodless hole was burned into his head; a lasergun lay beside his lifeless hand.

* * *

WITH A single exception, morale on *d'Artagnan's* bridge was nothing short of elation.

"The *Magellan* reports the destruction of enemy headquarters and the surrender of the planet," announced Mathison, beaming a smile from the radio desk. "The base didn't even put up a struggle. Captain Fitzgerald thinks the enemy brass may have fled to the planet before he arrived."

"Enemy flank is distending," said Dexter, raising his voice to be heard over the barrage of cheers.

"Chandler reports the enemy center starting to crumble," Mathison added. "Looks like we've got them on the run. And it's high time, if you ask me."

Laughter and light spirits filled the bridge. Though one of their shorter campaigns, it had been a tough battle, made all the more precarious by the Skipper's penchant for daring, and the need for pinpoint time. But the planet was now Terra's, and they were on the verge of routing the enemy once again.

"This is almost becoming routine," laughed Janet, her voice filled with the merriment of relief. She spun in her chair in celebration as the rest of the bridge crew laughed and whistled. "What do we do next?"

Cook smiled sadly, and shrugged his shoulders. "This is as far as I've thought it through," he said quietly. "From here, we make it up as we go along."

Chapter 8

YOU HAVE READ the communication?"

Seated behind an ornate table of carved stone, Jarah, First Glincian Ambassador to the High Council, nodded slowly. He did not trust this Remolah. The young aide was not his own choice for the job, and was too much given to the intrigues of the Inner Circle to warrant the trust of anyone. Remolah had come to Council on the recommendation of Drubid himself, and with a master plotter for a mentor, Remolah needed to be watched.

Constantly watched.

"Our course seems clear," Remolah whispered from across the table.

"Does it?" Jarah answered skeptically. Few things seemed clear these days to the old Ambassador. Clearest of all, he mused, was that only fools pretended to see clearly into the murkiness of the future.

"Our Terran friends seem to have matters well in hand, Ambassador. With their front collapsing around them, the Crutchtans cannot stand alone. They must sue for peace or beg for help. The time is quickly approaching for us to intercede. Drubid's report shows that matters are now under control in the Terran capital. Perhaps a well-placed overture—now, after this latest disaster—might persuade the Crutchtans— "

"Nothing will persuade the Crutchtans," retorted the older man. "The barbarians have slaughtered too many for the Crutchans to give up the fight."

"But if their cause is lost.... "

The old man looked into the clear, certain eyes of his aide. It must be comforting to know all there is to know, he smiled to himself. To be young enough to have no doubts, even if that is the surest route to disaster.

"Their cause is not lost until they lose their heart."

"They cannot afford to lose many more people or ships," Remolah replied smugly. "They will soon listen to reason."

"Even if they listen," Jarah answered, "how do you know the Terrans will do likewise?"

"Drubid has assurances— "

"And if Terran assurances mean no more than Drubid's own blandishments?"

Remolah made no answer. For the first time since his arrogant young aide arrived on Balarium, Jarah detected the smallest trace of doubt in the eyes of his young deputy.

It might not serve the Republic, Jarah smiled cynically. But for one day, it was enough to make an old man happy.

* * *

From the UMN Trans-Terran Dispatch, 14 June 2555:

COOK TAKES GRELOOSH, ROUTS ENEMY FLEET

by S.L. Yang
STARBASE 102
June 11, 2555

Commodore Roscoe Cook, in yet another daring masterstoke, has put the Cosmic Guard in firm control of the contested region of space in the vicinity of Duffington's Rift.

Called to the Duffington theater of battle a week ago, after Terra's mid-line offensive had stalled, Cook assumed command of the siege of the planet Greloosh....

PUSHING HIS breakfast plate away, Admiral Weatherlee shook his head and grimaced sourly. On the table was a stack of classified documents, printed on "eyes only" blue paper. A folder marked "Mongoose" rested on top of the stack. Seated on a plush chair, in a plush office on a well-trimmed starship well to the rear of the fighting, Weatherlee found it impossible to make peace with the most recent turn of the war. All this fuss over a grandstanding showboat without sense enough to know when to consolidate a position. It was enough to make him retch.

Gritting his teeth, he continued reading.

With an enemy relief force less than two days away, Cook launched what senior military analysts at Fleet Headquarters had called a "last ditch" effort to capture the planet before the Crutchtans arrived in sufficient numbers to break the siege. But in what these same analysts are now calling the "boldest" and "most inventive" deception of the war, Cook's main attack itself proved little more than a diversion.

"Diversion, my ass," muttered Weatherlee. "Blind luck—that damn fool has such blind luck— "

He lowered his voice to an inaudible murmur, and continued. "Asinine. Simply asinine."

Concentrating his attack on the enemy's eastern defenses, Cook drained all but the last remnants of the resistance in a short but fierce battle along a broad front. Then, puncturing his own battle line by a series of short, strategic withdrawals, he collapsed the Terran lines around him, leaving his own ship in the thick of battle and luring the last remaining enemy defenders into the fighting....

"Bloody idiot."

With the entire enemy force now locked into battle, leaving the planet virtually defenseless, Cook summoned a small contingency force, hidden in some shoals to the west of Greloosh, toward the planet. There, the attackers easily overcame the remaining Crutchtan defenses, and captured the enemy stronghold.

The fall of the planet now assured, Cook turned on the remaining defenders with his customary fury, destroying or capturing the remaining enemy contingent. This accomplished, he led the bulk of his forces eastward, advancing on the larger enemy fleet approaching the planet from the east.

Now caught between Cook's forces and the larger main body of the Terran fleet, the Crutchtans sought to withdraw toward anticenter-north, but were soon overtaken by a squadron of Cook's starships, sent ahead to slow their retreat. Forced to choose between a full engagement, and losing much of his own fleet to cover his retreat, the Crutchtan commander turned to engage Cook's smaller force, apparently reasoning that another battle would find the Terrans spent and exhausted. After a day of intense fighting, and finding their retreat blocked by the approaching Terran flotilla, the Crutchtans surrendered, having lost more than half their ships in the battle. Terran losses, by comparison, were described as "mild" or "inconsequential."

A spokesman for Fleet Admiral Porter M. Clay, asked to describe the outcome....

Admiral Weatherlee could bear it no longer. In disgust, he pressed the intercom button to summon Atley, his newest aide-de-camp. Atley was a thin young man, with a well-trimmed beard and cold blue eyes. He entered with a graceful step that would have gotten his face bloodied at any spacer's pub along the old frontier.

"Have you read this drivel?" Weatherlee demanded.

Atley nodded, his tongue clucking disapprovingly. "It's such a disgrace. That buffoon wins all the headlines, while we do all the real work. You just barely stopped all that other nonsense about diverting some attack wings away from the safety of the Cloud—as you said at the time, Admiral, that Isitian just can't understand the concept of cover. And now— "

Atley nodded toward the stack of command documents on the table. "Well, they're likely to give this harebrained Mongoose project another look. All because that showboat happened along just as the enemy's defenses were about to collapse. There's simply no justice."

"Get me a channel to Covington." Weatherlee tapped his finger on the table. "Get Admiral Weiss on the line for me. I've had about all I can stand of this. It's time for some changes in the way we do business around here."

"Yes, Admiral."

"Some serious changes."

"Oh yes, Admiral."

As the door whooshed shut, Weatherlee started doing some serious thinking, about any number of things.

Like whether it was finally time to have it out with Clay, once and for all.

And whether to take Cook up on his grand plan. The one that the damn fool insisted would win the war.

* * *

As ADMIRAL Weatherlee waited for a clear channel to Covington, wondering why Fate was often so kind to fools, two high government officials walked slowly along the marbled tiles of the Capitol's Presidential Gardens, past the summer lilies and Babylonian orchids, toward the grand fountain at the center of the grounds. Overhead, fleecy clouds skated through the sky, lending a playful grace to the pristine blue of a Babylonian summer. Generations of Terran leaders had found peace and solace in the graceful charm of Covington's loveliest courtyard. But serenity was often lost amid the turmoil of politics, and the burdens of war left little time for contemplation.

"Damn bastards! Can't trust any of them."

"Emerson...."

"I tell you, they're no better than the lizards. Worse—at least the lizards make no bones about hating us. These birds and bugs are just as slimy in their way. Mark my words, Schiller—the day will come when we'll have to take them on. And dammit, we'd better be ready."

"Emerson, you have a one-track mind."

"I believe in taking care of business."

"And I believe in taking care of first things first."

The talk continued, about the shortcomings of other races, and the shortsightedness even of their own kind. As always, the need to do something remained an unspoken thread, binding together elements as diverse as they were becoming intertwined.

* * *

FAR TO the East, the narrow aisles of a library were deserted. Their day's work long done, most of the analysts working for the Lord Commander had retired to their quarters. They were exhausted by the arduousness of the task before them and weary from despair. At one of the long, thin tables near the tactical computers a solitary figure was still at work, his thoughts as silent as the cramped chambers in which he toiled.

Fa'Shenali stared at his sketches for the hundredth time. Battling drowsiness, he tried his best to distill patterns to the movements he had charted, yet it was no use. It was like reducing poetry or music to numbers. The task was inadequate to the subject under study.

Turning aside from the latest disaster, the loss of the stronghold at *Gr'Lusshe*, he looked again at his notes from the Battle of Fralenga Rift. The battle occurred during the early days of the war, before the Terrans had begun their slow, relentless advance on the outer planets of the Shunite Sector. The Imperial Fleet had stopped the initial Terran thrust, and the clever ambush at Alagishi Cape near *la'Khryshk* had almost ended the war. But once the *g'Khruushtasni* counterattack failed, a stalemate fell over the skies, and for a time neither side could seize an advantage.

Until Fralenga, Shenali corrected himself. He looked at the sweeping lines of the Terran attack—the forceful opening thrusts, the broad lines of starships blossoming into powerful wedges that shattered the *g'Khruushtani* positions and sent hundreds of Terran ships streaming past the battle lines deep into Shunite skies, severing contact between the Empire and the doomed planet *la'Khryshk*. It was Terra's first breakthrough since the *g'Khruushtani* introduced their refitted freighters into the war as battleships. And it had been the first Terran battle commanded by the One Called *Khu'ukh*. It seemed so ordinary on paper, reduced to a few lines of frozen motion; so simple, like a profound thought ripened into an adage. But he remembered studying the battle at the war college, listening transfixed as the *g'Khruushtani* commander at the scene told them that through it all he felt as if he were fighting a Demon—one who could read his soul and counter his every move before the thoughts finished forming in his own brain.

He then looked at his chart for the Battle of Franlangi. It took place a few weeks later, led by the same *g'Khruushtani* battleleader. But the enemy commander had been a different Terran, the One Called *Dziones*. The result had been much the same: the Terrans routed the Imperial forces and forced a wholescale retreat. The lines of motion looked little different, when sketched on paper. Yet the battle had taken many days longer, with immeasurably greater casualties on both sides, and the Terrans failed to follow and destroy the defending forces. And the same *g'Khruushtani* commander who had seen *Khu'ukh* sweep away his fleet only weeks before told not of demons, but of the exhaustion of his people, fading before the relentless onslaught of superior strength. He knew that he would find it much the same with other battles. He did not know why he knew it, but it was something he could sense, like an animal reading danger in the wind.

No, thought fa'Shenali, this was not the way. He would learn nothing by studying graphs and charts: frozen lines and vectors of motion told him nothing. He had to find a way for his studies to make sense to him, but he was running out of time. Another loss like the one at *Gr'Lusshe* could prove their undoing, yet until he understood the Terran's mind, he would have nothing to offer his superiors. There had to be another way.

* * *

"WE HAVE reviewed the reports, Subaltern," said the Lord Commander, "and we have all read accounts of the battles. This is getting us nowhere."

Fa'Shenali stood rigidly before the senior commanders. The blinding lights illuminated his charts and kept him from seeing beyond the speaking area. His mind blocked thoughts of nervousness from his consciousness, but he feared that his superiors could sense his uneasiness. This was his first briefing before the command staff, and he knew how badly he was doing.

"I am sorry, my Lord."

"You have nothing to report on the Beast himself? No insights into his being? Not even any hints of the esteem shown him by his own comrades?"

"We have decoded a few intercepted enemy communications," the young Subaltern replied.

"Let us have them."

"Lord Commander, I fear that discerning its meaning lies beyond our capacity for— "

"Let us have them, Subaltern," Ga'Glish said sharply. "We shall decide the matter for ourselves."

Shenali's pride sank beneath the floor, and he started perspiring with shame. To have Ga'Glish rebuke him in such a public fashion was nearly more than his lowborn ego could tolerate. But the Small One struggled to master his emotions and continued the briefing with proud voice and a clear mind.

"We have examined all intercepted Terran messages for references to the One Called *Khu'ukh*. Unfortunately, the Terran language is as mysterious as it is colorful, and our language computers have trouble piecing meanings together. Of approximately thirty or so informal references to *Khu'ukh*, only a few share a common terminology, and they are encumbered by what our cryptologists call 'collateral contexts.' Worse, our language computers identify most of them as idioms, which defy literal translation.

"The first such reference was taken shortly after the final battle for *la'Khryshk*, following the engagement we call Fralenga Rift. The last came about twenty days ago, shortly before the Terrans began their push toward *Gr'Shuna*. The source of each is unknown, but all are believed to come from well behind enemy lines. Taken literally, the earliest reference describes *Khu'ukh* as "Yon Complete Burdenbeast-from-Planet Isis—"

Shenali could hear his audience murmur and sensed their growing confusion. In passing, he wondered if their confusion might help them understand his own, but he pressed ahead without pausing for questions.

"We also have detected several references to him as 'One-Who-Ingests-Male-Birds-Through-a-Straw....' "

Shenali felt the confusion ripen into widespread befuddlement.

"...and many descriptions comparing him to various quantities of dried nasal mucus. I have no idea what any of these references might mean," he continued, "though my impression is that they are vaguely pejorative."

"Pejorative?"

"Yes, Lord Commander, as if someone on the other side were bent on disparagement. Whether this is a uniquely Terran method of expressing affection, or indicates a measure of dissatisfaction with some aspect of *Khu'ukh's* leadership, I cannot say. But I have been wondering why the longnoses— "

"I am sorry, fa'Shenali," interrupted Ga'Glish, his voice rising from the darkness beyond the bright lights. "Perhaps we have called upon you too hastily, before your studies have had time to bear fruit."

"I regret my failure, Lord Commander." Shenali stood at attention, fully expecting to be dismissed from his post. His heart ached with disappointment, but he was too disciplined to show such weakness in his voice or thoughts.

"Return to your duties, fa'Shenali," Ga'Glish said in a peremptory tone of voice. "Perhaps you will have more for us next time."

"Yes, my Lord." Without another word, the subaltern packed his charts, and placed them into the portfolio that contained the research on his Terran subject. His ears pricked at every whispered reference of his name, and he was certain that his future would be the topic of discussion the moment he left the briefing area.

As the young officer left the room, his commander's disappointment echoed in his ears. He could hear derision in the half-heard voices of the Lord Commander's senior staff. Struggling to contain his shame, Shenali strode down the arching hallway. Fury burned inside him as his footsteps sounded down the empty corridors. This was the last time, he told himself. This would be the last time he would give the snooties on the command staff the chance to demean him or his abilities.

Chapter 9

THE IMAGE ON the vidscreen was snowy, but Admiral Clay's voice came clear as a winter's night.

"...and so now, he's changed his mind. And that's freed up channels for a go at your Operation...Goose, was it?"

"Mongoose," interjected Admiral Wright, from the screen next to Clay's. "But just who does Weatherlee think he is? That wasn't the plan, Admiral. Cook wanted ten starships, not three. And it was to be coordinated with a flank assault by Commodore Tanaka's wing. Weatherlee has him flying off by himself, with no support to speak of. And yet he expects...."

Seated in his own communications room, alone except for Janet and a few technicians and surrounded by four sterile walls, Cook found his mind wander from the conversation taking place by long-distance relay. Weatherlee was a fool, but foolishness was simply a fact of life. And no matter how Mongoose was changed or constricted, Cook was convinced of its central premise: the Crutchtans could not tolerate a major disruption to their internal security. Send a few starships into their interior, and they'd do anything to remove the threat. If nothing else, a major frontal assault while the enemy was chasing him around their backyard would break the back of the Crutchtan resistance. Effectively, the war would be over. And on Terran terms.

Of course, once he saw what was there...and if things appeared more or less as he expected—

"*Commodore!*"

Cook looked up, startled back to awareness.

"Sir?"

"I said that I won't send you off unless you agree to the changes," Clay said crossly. "It's already too dangerous as you conceived it. That's what made CentCom balk in the first place, and I can't really argue with them. But I trust you enough—at least, as long as you're actually paying attention to whatever it is you're doing—to give you the chance to put your plan into operation. You've never failed me yet, and Miriam assures me that suicide missions are not your style. So if you're still willing to give it a go, even with Weatherlee's meddling, I'll cut whatever orders you need to get this thing out of the docks."

Cook sighed; he knew the gamble he was taking. Every Crutchtan from here to the enemy capital would be gunning for him. But every instinct he had told him it would work. His only worry was that he had killed so often that death had lost its meaning to him. In that state of mind, he feared he was a menace to everyone around him.

"I'd need some time to get my ship ready. And I'll only accept volunteers for the mission."

"Agreed."

Cook paused for what seemed an eternity.

"Give me the rest of the day to mull over the changes," he said at last. "And I'll need time to pour over whatever list you give me for the rest of my mission team."

"We'll talk again tomorrow, then," said Clay. "Looking Glass out."

"Over and out."

As the images from the viewers faded into blackness, Cook leaned back in his chair. Wearily, he looked across the room toward Janet, who shrugged lamely in return. He wondered if he'd finally succeeded in taking on more than he could handle. And if he really was condemning them all to a pointless death, he wondered whether, in those final few seconds before eternity closed around them, Janet would find it in her heart to forgive all the grief he had caused her.

* * *

A LIBERTY base was hardly plush by civilian standards. Hastily built from bits of metal and tempered plastics, the interior had the rough, unfinished look of a half-constructed building on the ground. Girders and beams crossed through hallway walls. Disposable doors and paper-thin paneling gave it an aura of haste, providing little or no privacy to the people inside. The entire project gave the workmen who built it little cause for pride, even if the design greatly simplified the task of tearing it apart.

But to those whose days and nights were the inside of a ship and the death that was war, anything else was a luxury beyond measure. And wherever existence was defined by the threshold emotions of panic and boredom, the greatest luxury of all was the chance to complain, far from the sting of battle.

THE CAFETERIA trays were stacked neatly on the next table. Scattered throughout the dining area, empty beer pitchers littered the room. Closer to the door, members of the *d'Artagnan*'s crew had come to relax, and laugh, and enjoy their precious liberty time. But off in the far corner, talk had turned to one group's favorite topic of discussion for the past few weeks. As a result, the mood at Table Seventeen was decidedly gloomy.

"An'I'll say't again," Gerlach shook his dizzied head as he emptied the remains of another pitcher into his glass. "I don'believe the gall of that guy. I guezzwhat he lacks in balls, he makes up in gall."

Ensign Cicotte, one of the new gunnery officers, nodded sympathetically. He knew all about superiors who abused their authority. He'd seen enough of that at officer's school to fill a book. The others at their table all mumbled their approval, though not too loudly; Chief Connors was sitting a few tables away and took a dim view of the lot of them.

"An' tha' goezf'r'the Skipper as well, putting'a pipsqueak like that'n charg'o'the rest of us," Gerlach slurred. "'S'enough t'make me sick."

"That's well and good to talk about," said Cicotte, "But now it's out of our hands."

His own eyes glazed with drink, Connors turned in his chair to face the chorus of blueshirts.

"T's only out'f our hands'f we leddit," Gerlach continued. "That four-eyed idiot can't do ev'ything by himself. There's a damn good bit we can do to make it clear that we don' appreciate the Skipper's lack of sense in the matter."

"What you're suggesting— "

Gerlach waved his hand, and laughed drunkenly. "Jus'a good bit'o'fun, Ricky, that's all. Nothing mutinous in that, now, is'ere?"

"Tha's all I need to hear," thundered Connors from his table. Struggling to his feet, and waving off his own companions, he staggered toward the blueshirts, spitting Demetrian epithets under his breath. Too tipsy to know better, Gerlach rose to meet him.

"Y'bladderbrained jackass," Connors muttered ominously. "Y'ain'hardly fit to polish'e Skipper's boots, an'y'have the bloody temerity—"

"I'm warning you, Connors," Gerlach slurred, waving an angry finger at the enraged greenshirt staggering towards him. Undeterred, Connors advanced on the young weapons officer until the two were swaying nose to nose, each barely keeping the other from falling into a drunken heap on the floor.

"Tha's'it, Yeoman! You're on report!"

"Ahh, repor'this, ye pea-peckered buffoon," Connors slurred, pushing Gerlach backwards. The blueshirt slid across his own table, disrupting pitchers and glasses before falling onto his head on the floor. The others at the table rose, indignant—until they looked to see Connors, collapsed from the exertion. They exchanged a long look with the greenshirts at Connors' table. Without a word, the entire complement from the *d'Artagnan* rose and stepped toward the exit as quietly as they could, dragging their fallen comrades with them.

* * *

JANET SAID nothing. When he was in this kind of mood she knew that keeping quiet was likelier to draw him out of his shell. She followed his gaze outward, toward the northwestern quadrant of the observation deck. She knew exactly where his mind was, and allowed herself the luxury of mild annoyance that his thoughts, as always, seemed to be elsewhere.

"Fools," Cook said at last, his voice carrying more amusement than Janet had expected. "In the last analysis, Mendelson, we're all fools."

"How's that?"

His eyes still light years away, Cook looked at her and smiled a wistful smile that always made Janet want to cry.

"How long has this madness gone on now? Is it a whole cosmic year, yet?"

"I think so. That, or nearly so."

"So we're all three solar years older. Millions have died in the process. We've probably killed a million Crutchtans all by ourselves, you and I."

A shiver ran down Janet's back. She hated when he started talking about numbers. It seemed so much more bearable, she thought, to keep the numbers out of her head.

Cook turned to face eastward. Toward Crutchta.

Towards the lines of battle.

"And all for what? For a cloud. A thin, wispy trail of gases barely visible unless you're right in the middle of it. All but indistinguishable from the void around it, except for its effects on a plane of existence that didn't even exist for Mankind, five hundred years ago."

"I suppose life was simpler, back then."

Cook laughed distantly. "I really wonder, sometimes. Life was probably just as plagued with dilemmas. The riddles seemed just as insoluble back in the old days. In the end, I doubt things have changed all that much. At least, Man hasn't changed. Our toys have, though. That just makes us more dangerous when we're naughty."

Janet nodded her head and forced a smile. She used to love it when he let his mind wander like this. Now she'd almost come to hate it.

"And I suppose we each have our own limited piece of creation that we can change, for better or worse. Looks like I've made a pretty good hash of mine."

He looked her squarely in the eyes; Janet's limbs started to feel numb.

"And there's a good bit that I'd change, if it were still within my power."

Janet felt her eyes begin to water.

Looking uncomfortable, Cook suddenly stood and held out his hand to help Janet to her feet. "Admiral Clay will be expecting my call any time, now."

Janet nodded quietly; gently, Cook lifted her chin, wiped a tear from her eye, and let his hand linger along her moistened cheek.

"It's time to go," he said softly, after the longest pause he could remember.

* * *

A SHORT time later Cook sat alone in front of a secured viewscreen in his quarters. Images of home adorned the walls, and scraps of paper and an unfinished model ship cluttered his desk. On the screen, Cook saw the crisp image of Admiral Clay shaking his head from an office on Looking Glass.

"I'm sorry, Cook. You know I'd help if I could, but my hands are tied in this thing. If you think it won't work with these restrictions...."

"It's not that it won't work, Admiral," Cook interjected. "But it's such a muddleheaded thing to do. The project's risky enough as it is. But you don't cut precisely those corners needed to provide some measure of safety."

"I can only relay the decision, Commodore. I won't try to defend it."

Cook paused a moment longer. He'd made his decision as soon as Clay relayed the news. Besides, with half the Terran fleet converging on Girshoona, the enemy would be pinned down. They couldn't afford to send many of their ships after him. Any Crutchtan ships he did manage to draw away from the battle would make the siege easier. In the end, it would work. It had to work.

"I've gone over the list of volunteers," he said at last. On hearing Cook's confident tone of voice, the Admiral's grin beamed broadly across the subspace channel.

"I'll take Fitzgerald."

"Good," Clay nodded.

"And Ashton."

"Ashton?"

Cook's second choice took the admiral by surprise. He knew that the two were friends, and Ashton was, by all accounts, able and industrious. But he was hardly what the Old Guard would have called "top drawer." He was competent, but no more, and would have done a fine job skippering a frigate in peacetime. To top it off, he was a rookie starship commander, and far from the best of the new crop. Under fire, Ashton was not the sort Clay would want covering his wing. The Admiral wondered whether Cook was letting friendship get in the way of his judgment.

"Far be it from me to tell you how to select a staff, Commodore."

Cook laughed. "You'll be the only one to spare me the lecture, then."

"Dammit, Cook, I'd have taken Fitz myself. But Jeremy Ashton? For the life of me..."

Cook held up his hand. He hoped that the reasons he'd given to himself were the right ones—that is, the real ones. "I know how his mind works, Admiral. And I know I can trust him. We've been through quite a bit together. What he lacks in experience, he gains in motivation. Besides, none of us has any experience in what we're about to do. Maybe his lack of seasoning will keep him from wearing the same bureaucratic blinders that seem all the rage in Covington."

Clay winced and shook his head. He was skeptical, but skepticism often drew the very best out of Terra's most ingenious tactician.

"When can you sail?"

"Soon. *Magellan* and *Morning Star* are only a few days away. But it'll be quite a while before we see port again, so I'd like to give my crew a few more days of liberty while we wait for Athos and Porthos. And it'll take some time for us to arrange a battle for the Three Musketeers to use as a springboard."

"I beg your pardon?"

Cook laughed. "Never mind, Admiral. Mixed allusions are confusing enough, by themselves. But we're lacking an Aramis, anyway, so I guess it doesn't really matter."

Admiral Clay frowned dourly, and shook his head. Cook was up to his old tricks, he thought. Babbling rubbish again, not caring who heard him or whose toes he stepped on. And never explaining anything he said.

Of course, he had no idea what the Isitian was talking about. But then, it was hardly the first time.

* * *

THE COMMAND office on the starship *Morning Star* was sparsely furnished. The stark white walls lacked even a finishing coat for the primer. The room all but swallowed the small desk and three cafeteria chairs huddling in the southeast corner, near the console unit that housed the command computer. Similar shortfalls plagued the sick bay, and crew lounges on each deck had taken to using packing crates for chairs. *Morning Star's* captain had placed an order for furniture each time the ship came into port. And each time, the Quartermaster's computer showed his ship fully furnished, so fleet headquarters routinely returned his requisition as already filled. It drove Jeremy Ashton to distraction, and made him think that Cook had been right in the early days aboard the *d'Artagnan*, when he'd told Jeremy that a freshly minted ship wasn't worth the trouble.

Jeremy was furious, but the ship's problems weren't what troubled him today. Today's target was the blue packet sitting open on the middle of his desk, bearing the code name "Mongoose."

Much as he liked and admired the Skipper, Cook cast a wide, suffocating shadow. Janet's life might be her own concern, but the way Cook treated her was unforgivable. Jeremy took it as a warning that, whatever his other gifts, Cook had an ugly capacity for using those closest to him.

Though Janet was to blame for dragging him into her private little mess, Jeremy realized that the whole episode may have sped him along the path to his own command. He still blessed the day when orders finally came through. Now he found himself right back where he started from: Cook's glorified errand boy.

Jeremy shook his head. Served him right, he admitted to himself. It would teach him not to go volunteering without a clearer idea what he was he was being asked to do. Or, at least who he'd be sailing with. The last thing he needed was to be under the Skipper's thumb again, Jeremy raged silently to himself. And no matter where he turned, whether on his own ship or anywhere else in the Universe, it seemed he couldn't get away.

Unable to contain his frustration, Jeremy seized the stack of reports from the "In" basket on his desk, and hurled it through the opening door, narrowly missing Frank Flanagan, his chief yeoman, who was just entering to discuss the latest glitch in the keel batteries. The old spacer jerked his head to look at the mess in the corridor. Slowly, he turned to look at his commanding officer, his eyes wide with amazement.

"Sorry, Chief," said Jeremy, his voice edged with embarrassment. He snorted angrily and raced to retrieve the various packets before anyone else noticed that the hallway was littered with statistics on fuel consumption and manpower efficiency. In an instant, Flanagan was stooping over to help his captain pick up the mess.

"I hate to ask, Captain."

"Then don't."

"But— "

"I apologize, and I would appreciate it if you'd just forget the whole incident. But I don't want to discuss it—I'm not going to discuss it—and if you say another word, I'll order you to drop the whole matter. And enter it in the log as a command directive!"

Flanagan shook his head as he gathered sheet after sheet, randomly cramming them together in no particular order, until it dawned on him that unless he was careful he might get stuck recollating the whole mess.

"Is the scuttlebutt true?" he said, trying to change the subject in a more promising direction.

"What scuttlebutt?"

"I heard that we're being tapped for some kind of secret mission, with no less than Commodore Cook!" Flanagan gushed. "Your old commander—imagine that! Boy, what a coup for us!"

Jeremy glowered at the greenshirt, and rose to his feet. "When you've finished here," he said acidly, "sort this mess and place it back on my desk. I'll be in the Cafeteria, having lunch."

"But— "

"That is all," snapped Jeremy, ignoring the baffled looks of all who were passing by them in the hallway. He strode smartly down the hall, leaving the baffled old yeoman to sort out his captain's ill humor for himself.

Flanagan watched Jeremy disappear around the bend in the corridors. "Officers," he muttered, slowly shaking his head as he gathered up the debris.

"You use people, Skipper."

"That's enough, Jeremy."

"You use people up, and spit them out when they no longer suit you."

"That is quite enough, Commander."

"That isn't the start of it, Commodore...."

"COMMANDER?"

Alone in the Executive Officer's quarters on the Conning Deck of the *d'Artagnan*, Janet sat on the bed, her knees drawn close to her breast. She tried to let her anger dissipate. He wasn't that blind, she thought. He couldn't be so inconceivably obtuse that he didn't know how this last little bombshell would affect her. She was staring out the small porthole, into the blackness around them, trying to understand what was happening to her life, when that familiar voice called through her closed cabin door—followed, when she made no answer, by a gentle knocking. Soon, she could stand it no longer.

"Go away," she snapped.

"Commander...."

"Go away."

"Would you at least give me a hint..."

"I want to be alone, Commodore. Nothing you do can make me open that door."

"But— "

"Go away."

For the next few minutes, Janet could feel Cook's presence outside her door. Anger burned at her insides. She was tempted to open the hatch, just to tell him what she really thought of this latest bit of news, this latest "wrinkle" in his pet mission.

Then, without warning, the feeling vanished. She knew he'd gone, and with him went much of her bitterness. She wondered why things like this upset her so much. But they always did, no matter how much she tried not to let it bother her. Seeing Jeremy again had opened many old wounds, many that she hoped she'd put behind her. As much as she liked him, Jeremy was a constant reminder of how little control she had over her own life. This latest development threatened to consume her like a burning cancer, wrenching her emotions and eating away what little self-respect she'd managed to retain over the last cosmic year.

She flopped onto her back and stared at the ceiling. For the longest time, she wondered how things had gotten so out of control, and why the one man in her life with the power to make her miserable could be so thoughtless.

Chapter 10

LIEUTENANT?"

Mason McGee turned his seat toward the radio-systems desk. His first officer was staring at his screens, shaking his head.

"What is it, Mark?"

"This makes no sense. It makes no sense at all."

"What is it?"

The young ensign beckoned Mason to come and look. Mumbling vague warnings about the risks of making the ship's commander troop across the bridge, Mason stomped from the command seat toward the main sensor screen. When he arrived, he understood why his first officer was reluctant to voice his concerns aloud. A thousand klicks ahead, arching around the Glincian freighter where they would deliver their load of cargo, were a dozen or so Glincian ships of unfamiliar design.

"Did ye scan...?"

"They have battle capability," Mark nodded, "but their guns aren't charged. Readings say they're no more dangerous than our own escorts. What they're doing here is anybody's guess."

The first officer raised his eyebrows and breathed deeply. "First time they've pulled something like this," he sighed. "Can't say as I like it, Macey."

"Neither do I, Ensign. Neither do I."

Mason stretched his back and rubbed his eyes as he walked back to his ship's hot seat. Transport skippers weren't supposed to have these problems. That was left for the regular Cozzie hotshots, not for conscript officers like himself, who weren't considered trustworthy enough to deal with the aliens except under the most highly controlled circumstances.

At last he plopped himself into his chair, the weight of unexpected responsibility making him feel suddenly older, and not one day wiser.

"Helm, hold this position until further notice."

"Aye, sir."

"Mark— ?

"Sir?"

"Get Dispatch on the line. Then, make as many readins as ye can take in the next few minutes. I'll not take us out on a limb by myself, and someone needs to know what we're facin, if they're to be figurin out what's happenin here."

"Aye, sir."

"Loony birds…never did trust'em, ye know."

"Well, Macey, looks like you might be right after all."

* * *

THE STARS glowed brightly through the atmospheric bubble shielding the main base from the eternal elements. On the horizon, the mother sun flamed like a million festival lanterns. Tomorrow it would set, leaving the base in darkness.

Seated on the metal flooring, leaning against the wall of the storage shed, Shl'Lanasha and his work crew rested from the day's exertion, reveling in the simple pleasure of breathing in the open, without a helmet. Their dusty pressure suits hung heavily from their bodies, though in the diminished gravity the weight bore less upon them than the heaviness of exhaustion.

Enjoying the silence, Lanash opened an outer pocket to retrieve a packet of letters from his parents and his son. Opening the last one he had received, he read it again, silently to himself. They were looking forward to his next visit, they wrote, and were proud of what they were hearing about efforts to ready *Gr'Shuna* for defense.

Lanash breathed with sorrow. The truth was too painful to laugh, yet each of them had too much at stake to accept the grimness of reality. They had accomplished much in the last full cycle. Yet everywhere was evidence that their own leaders doubted the planet could long stand against the onslaught of the Terrans, now less than two dozen astronomical units away. Already—though the civilians below could not see it, and he was forbidden to discuss it with them on pain of death—it was obvious that plans to evacuate the entire planet were being put into place. Ships were being assembled; docks and quays were being built in the skies; navigation lanes were being cleared, all to prepare the people below against the unthinkable, and to ensure the means to whisk to safety as many of them as possible.

At the same time, the bulk of their work was on fortification. Great fixed guns were being carved into moons throughout the star system, to blast away the invaders as they approached. Through telescopes, when his assignment carried him to the proper parts of the moon, he could see the giant guns and battlements being laid in the soil of the planet below, to give their armies the means to fight the barbarians on the ground, if it should come to that.

"Lanash?"

Shl'Lanasha looked up as ls'Shen approached and sat next to him.

"Our next turn is not until tomorrow," said Shen. "And you have not rested well these past few days. Why not take the chance to rest? I will have Lanaka summon you when the groupmaster calls us to Retreat.

Lanash clasped his friend's arm in gratitude, but shook his head.

"No, Shen, I cannot. An hour's sleep will only exhaust me further. It is better to take my rest all at once, rather than confronting the ordeal of rising twice in one day."

"Word from home?"

Lanash smiled. "All are doing well. But that has not changed since last I checked, twenty minutes ago."

Ls'Shen retrieved his own packet, and removed a likeness.

"This arrived today," he said, handing it to Lanash. The likeness showed a female, ls'Shen's mate Shenenda, and a small one, asleep in his mother's arms.

"You have not yet seen your son?"

Shen shook his head. "He is three weeks old today. My mate says that he eats like his father, and suffers from his father's lack of patience as well." He retrieved the likeness and placed it in the packet.

Lanash felt loneliness crest in the heart of his friend. "Perhaps a leave order will come next week," he offered. "Under the circumstances...."

"Perhaps," Shen smiled disbelievingly. "In the meantime, I should rejoice that my family will know an heir . And that my Shenenda will have a strong young man to care for her in her old age."

Shen breathed deeply. "If they survive," he added bitterly.

"We all survive one way or another," Lanash said sharply. "You cannot permit thoughts of tragedy to destroy your faith in the future. Without that faith we drive ourselves to madness."

"Perhaps, my friend. But I often wonder whether we are not there already."

Lanash laughed without humor.

"You are starting to sound like me," he said at last, in a self-mocking voice that masked the pain of his words. "And if that fails to alarm you, my friend, then you are indeed lost."

Soon, the Retreat call came, and the Second Shift assembled to share one last moment together before the end of the day. As the groupmaster droned on under the black, airless sky, reminding them about the importance of their work and the need to keep their spirits high, Lanash found his thoughts drifting to what remained of his own family on the planet below. He could not help wondering if all their suffering was in vain—whether barbarism would be too strong for the forces of His Worthiness, whether their own ways and the life they had known were both doomed to extinction.

Yet in the end he fought off such thoughts of darkness, as he did at the end of most days. Surrendering to despair was easy enough. Some days, it seemed to offer the only relief from the misery his life had become, a release as peaceful as death itself. But despair could never beat back the Terrans.

* * *

COMMAND MEMORANDUM

CC: 144-3284.6

FROM: CSO Captain A.J.Whiting
            Camp Greloosh #1

TO: Ft. Adm. Anthony Moeller
            CosGuard Deputy Chief of Staff,
            Security Division

Subject: Planet Greloosh, Preliminary Work on Primary Labor
            Facility

In the week after our arrival, we have completed excavations on primary location set forth in Command Memorandum 144-3189. Perimeter fortifications are completed, along with temporary barracks. Detention facilities for residents are proceeding on schedule, and should be finished in another two or three weeks. While final completion will likely take months, base engineers estimate that the Facility should be operational within the next five weeks.

Given the number of unneutralized enemy partisans still conducting raids on continents of Mainland, New Africa, and Amazonia, I have informed local military commanders that we will not accept transfers from those continents. Pacified continents are providing more manpower than we can process, and our Sanitation Facilities cannot accommodate any increase without a corresponding decrease in the security of our temporary holding facilities. I have therefore requested our local security officer to initiate neutralization procedures in all unsecured areas, to limit the disruptions that would accompany a noticeable increase in such activities on the grounds here. Once our Facility is fully operational we will, of course, transfer such operations to the Primary Facility.

Geologists report rich deposits on the Camp grounds, and are eager to begin work. Initial assay shows rich deposits of precious metals, iron, and nickel, and a lesser presence of copper and uranium. Petroleum fields appear largely unused throughout the Planet, but richest deposits are located in unsecured territories. Skill levels among surviving resident population appear quite high, but Training Officer reports greater than normal resistance to standard motivational techniques. Given tradeoffs involved, some staff members have suggested decreasing workday by four hours, in light of the number of enemy scientists currently in residence, as a way of encouraging a positive response. We would, however, use a second group as a control, to see if this approach will lessen unplanned attrition and increase production. If this meets with your approval, I suggest adding a trained psychologist to the Staff, to monitor progress and assess the results. I am dubious about the outcome, but am willing to try anything that could lead to greater output.

CSO Capt. A.J.Whitting
Commander, Greloosh I

* * *

"THEY'RE CLEAR of the goonie ring, Lieutenant. They're through."

"Ahh, Christ," sighed Mason. He wiped his sweaty brow with his hand, then turned to the communications station.

"Signal the hangar deck to prepare for docking. And radio the lorry. Tell them the skipper gives'em a 'well done' and hopes he never has to send them through anything like that again."

"Aye, Macey."

While it was all going on, Mason thought, he'd wanted to do nothing but get out of there. Now that the crisis was over, he felt angered and betrayed. And he wanted some answers.

He wanted to know what the goonies were up to. And he wanted to know whether Central Command was going to start taking their conscripts seriously—as spacers and as loyal Terrans, entitled to as much respect as any of the hotshots off fighting the lizards.

Most of all, he wanted to know why CentCom was putting them through all this, and whether it was about to become a part of life along the center-southeastern frontier.

"Hold her steady, Helm," said Mason, his accent creeping back into his voice. "We don't want them a-crashin into us. Not after all they've been through."

"Aye, sir."

"H-Deck reports lorry in position for docking."

"Activate the tractor, and tell them to hurry up about it. I want to get the hell out of here before those goonie birds start actin up again."

"Aye aye, sir."

Anxiously, Mason watched the monitor until the green light flashed on the screen, signaling that the last lorry was safely docked. Without a second's delay, the *McLintock* came smartly about and scampered toward the safety of Terran skies.

Chapter 11

I'M SORRY, SUZIE."
"Listen to me, Ben— "
"No, I'm sorry."
Suzie Yang glared into the vidscreen, her temper at the boiling point. Files and binders cluttered the undersized blue desk that CosGuard issued to all reporters with press credentials. Angrily, she rapped the desktop with her index finger. Her soft brown eyes were filled with rage, her pert mouth twisted in aggravation.

"It's not my fault— "

"Nobody said it was."

"This is the biggest story of our time, Benjamin Brewster. I'm not about to let you or anybody else tear me away from it."

Looking tired and quite abused, Ben Brewster looked back from his comfortable office in Covington and tried once more to get his best reporter to see reason. "You are one of the best political writers of this generation," he began wearily. It was the twentieth time he'd begun this speech, and its effect seemed to vary as little as the words he used. "But politics is writing about people, and that is your strongest talent. That and your ability to see through rhetorical cant."

"I'm warning you, Ben— "

"Listen to me," Brewster continued, vainly trying a different approach. "CosGuard has its people wrapped so tightly that you'll never get close to them. I mean, how long have you been trying to get a conversation with Jones, or Clay—let alone someone like Cook."

"If anyone can do it...."

"Look—what I'm saying is that there are a lot of strange things going on in the capital. A lot of strange things. I think you'd be more use to us here, writing about Covington, than you can ever be out there. On Looking Glass, all you can do is waste your time and talents trying to catch a glimpse of somebody famous. Either that, or serving up CosGuard hype to the public on a platter."

Suzie said nothing. Her burning eyes told Brewster that she hadn't changed her mind.

"This is getting us nowhere," he said at last. "I want you on the next press shuttle back to Demeter— "

"No!"

"You can catch a commercial liner back to New Babylon from there."

"I'm sorry, Ben."

"I'm afraid that's the final word."

"Then you'll have my resignation by trans-telex."

"Suzie— !"

"So long, Ben."

"Su— "

As the screen went black, Suzie rested her elbows on the table, her face in her hands. Though she couldn't see them, she could feel the unblemished, tan walls closing around her. Even the few pictures she'd brought from home seemed choked by the unbroken barrenness of life on a star base. She'd come to hate her quarters and the closed sterility of Looking Glass; now, she couldn't bear the thought of leaving.

She knew she was being stubborn. And stupid. And everything else Ben Brewster was probably calling her right now back in Covington. But she couldn't help it. She was fascinated by the drama of the war—the stark, human drama of life and death, the bitter, pointless struggle between rival races and civilizations. It grated on her pride to think that the real story—the waste, as well as the heroics—was being kept from her by the same brutally efficient machine that was grinding out victory after victory on the front. All she could ever do was write about the outlines: the biggest battles, the statistics, the most prominent personalities. Clay...Wright...Weatherlee. Jones...Grissom...Drexler. And, of course, Roscoe Cook.

Cook, she smiled, glancing at the thick folder on the corner of her desk. She picked it up and opened it. Like every other journalist covering the war, she'd kill for the chance to interview him.

Alone.

Without the prying ears of the CSO to whisk him away whenever the talk started getting interesting.

She was enough of a realist to know that it was a pipe dream. But it was a shame, she thought, for this one was a real puzzle.

Absently, she looked at the official, black-and-white photograph of the man all Terra hailed as a hero. The great Commodore Cook, a study in contradictions. Scholar, scientist—a prodigy in mathematics, music and philosophy from the one Terran planet that had rejected the war and turned its back on the rest of humanity. Yet he was also Terra's most ruthlessly effective commander, her grandest strategist and most daring tactician. He'd yet to lose in battle, and his victories were so stunning that his image was plastered on banners and placards all over Terra. Some CosGuard staffers she'd talked to insisted that if the brass ever turned him loose, enemy resistance would crumble like an Egyptian mummy exposed to the air of Old Earth. But the Fleet used him sparingly, as if afraid to tempt fate by exposing him to too much danger. In the beginning his advance had been relentless, held back only by the sluggish pace of the rest of the fleet. Now he was more like a wing commander without portfolio, called into action whenever an offensive stalled or the Crutchtans threatened to penetrate a weak point in the Terran lines.

Perhaps Ben was right, she thought. Perhaps the real answers were elsewhere. They certainly seemed in short supply in the press rooms on Looking Glass.

At last, she activated the screen again and dialed the number of the press relations officer. She booked passage on the next ship bound for Demeter. Feeling bitter and rejected, and numbed by her complicity in her own professional debasement, she called Burt Hollander, the new reporter from the *Times*—the same unmarried young hunk who'd tried to score with every woman on the press list—and accepted his standing invitation to dinner.

She knew she'd feel cheap and degraded by the next day. But she felt that way already. Besides, she was leaving tomorrow. Whatever the cost to her self-respect, she didn't want to spend her last night on Looking Glass alone.

* * *

THE ENTRANCE to the Command Center opened, revealing a great central chamber and a host of anterooms around the periphery. Shyly, fa'Shenali stepped through the doorway into the arching, cavernous nerve center of the Forces of His Worthiness. The Great Room was nearly deserted, its dimmed lights making him pause to let his eyes adjust. Yet the screens brightly displayed the Universe around them, as the Flagship's automated sensors continued their work undeterred by the lack of an audience, searching the heavens for the faintest trace of the enemy. The subaltern could hear muted and random voices as technicians went about their work, but could see nobody. Slowly, he walked toward the center of the room.

Beneath the arching canopy and endless bands of monitors, fa'Shenali felt the humbling lack of his own worth. Within these walls, he mused, the future of his people would be decided, by the dedication and energy of those who served the Lord Commander. He felt lost and bewildered, like a small child who had wandered into a Chamber of Solitude and had no notion of what Meditation really meant for the soul. If he had come to the Great Room for solace or inspiration, it was not working.

Continuing down the walkway, toward the far bank of computers, he stepped onto the grating that separated the command floor from the service area below. He stopped in front of the main tactical display screen. It was silent now, showing the stars beyond to the west. Somewhere, he thought—somewhere out there lurked the Beast, the One Most Hated. He knew that one day he would see the Beast's ship in battle. He hoped he would be ready.

As he mused to himself, he slowly became conscious of a bitter, acrid aroma filling the air, wafting up from below, carried on currents of circulating air.

"By your leave," called a voice. Fa'Shenali looked about, but saw none about him.

"By your leave, Subaltern."

Looking down, Shenali saw movement in the darkness below, underneath the grating. Curious about its source, he peered intently until he discerned its shape. It was a menial, a technician, assigned to attend the machinery. The menial sighed sharply, making no effort to hide his temper.

"By your leave, your Subalternness!"

"Yes, Menial…what do you require?"

"*Pffff!*" sniffed the menial.

Taken aback by the breach of manners, fa'Shenali undertook to repeat himself.

"I said— "

"If it is not too much trouble, Your Grand Lordship might try moving himself so that I am not trapped down here with the fumes."

Looking about to find himself standing on the hatch opening, fa'Shenali stepped aside. The grating opened and a technician climbed up to the main floor. The menial's face was darkened with soot, and his body reeked of smoke. He coughed to clear his throat, and took a deep breath.

"If you wished me to move..."

"Many thanks, Subaltern."

"If you will pardon the question..."

"My name is Iash'Hanna," the menial replied with a bow of politeness.

"If you pardon the question, One Called Hanna," repeated fa'Shenali, returning the bow formally, "but what were you— "

"The machines and augmentors need constant monitoring and adjustment," Hanna interrupted. Fa'Shenali stiffened at the interruption by one of his inferiors, but his show of rank went outwardly unnoticed. "My task is to keep them operating efficiently." Wryness danced across his lips, and he permitted fa'Shenali to sense his amusement.

"Or perhaps, Your Exaltedness thought that all this equipment maintained itself."

For a moment, fa'Shenali hesitated, unsure how to react to such a showing of familiarity. In the end, mindful of his own roots, he permitted himself an uncertain smile.

"Perhaps we are all too well insulated from the lives of others," he replied.

"You are the commoner," said the menial, wiping his hands on a rag hanging from his utility belt. "The One Called fa'Shenali?"

The young subaltern nodded.

"Your arrival has not gone unnoticed, fa'Shenali," smiled Hanna. "Many here rejoice at your good fortune."

"I am gratified. If only my work gave others similar cause— "

"*Pfff*— " scoffed Hanna. "Snooties are snooties, and it matters not how well you perform. To some, you will always be of the rabble. It has ever been, and will ever be."

Fa'Shenali lowered his eyes and bowed, acknowledging the truth in what the menial said.

"But what of it?" the menial smiled warmly. "Royalty is mostly pomp and little substance, a thinness of sugar on the excrement of worms. You are better off without most of them. As for Ga'Glish and his reformist breed—well, we shall see what happens once the Terrans are no longer baying outside their bedchambers."

"I see our mothers breed cynics like purebreds breed leeches."

Lash'Hanna laughed heartily. "Well said, fa'Shenali. I see our betters have not snuffed out your wit."

Shenali shook his head. "I wish it were so, though often I wonder. I make little progress on my work, and fear it will reflect poorly on the Lord Commander. But the task itself is impossible."

"And what task is that?"

Fa'Shenali looked toward the large viewer on the west facing of the arching canopy overhead. "It is the One Called *Khu'ukh*. He is my field of study, his mind and all its workings. I try to understand him, to help us find a better way to fight him, but my work is of no use. He remains a mystery to me, as to all others."

"Oh, the Beast is a clever one," Hanna nodded, his words carrying a conviction that fa'Shenali found surprising. "He soars far above our own simpletons—like an eagle soars above the vermin in the field. I fear your task may well be impossible, my friend. His art is like music from a troubadour's lute, but his bite is deadly as a viper's."

"How come you to talk so glowingly about an enemy you have never seen?" Fa'Shenali was astonished that a menial would dare talk of such things. He was even more astonished that his rebuke was met by the laughter of derision.

"Oh we have seen more than you might imagine," the menial replied good-naturedly. He stepped toward the control panel on the nearby wall. Pressing a few buttons, he turned to face his new acquaintance, a wry smile upon his lips. Soon, the remaining lights dimmed, and all around them was darkness, lit only by the dancing lights on the viewscreen above them.

"Attend."

At first he saw nothing but dots of light, darting about the screen like evening bugs on a warm summer night. To his amazement, he soon found himself recognizing the patterns, and realized that he was watching a replay of the Battle of Geroulanash. To the left were the doomed ships of Lord Grena, moving against a badly outnumbered Terran attack wing. To the right, the longnose ships moved along a broad front, slipping closer and closer to the *g'Khruushtani* until the Terran flank suddenly turned to strike at the heart of the oncoming forces of His Worthiness, the center pivoting sharply to shatter the *g'Khruushtani* battle lines, and splintering the fleet beyond recognition. Then, the Terrans turned upon and destroyed the helpless squadrons as they struggled to regroup. As fa'Shenali watched, he saw the dots forming together like the brushstrokes of an artist, arching and flowing their ballet of death into a beauty as cold as space. For an instant, he was floating among the stars, wondering at the regal grace and artistry that was filling his mind as stars filled the heavens.

Soon, the screen went dark, and light returned to the Command Center.

"How came you to make such a thing?"

"Such things are far beyond my capacity, Subaltern," Hanna smiled; fa'Shenali could sense the bitter irony in the menial's words. " I only work the machines. The computers do the rest."

"But why has no one told me? Why have we not...?"

Hanna's irony ripened into anguished laughter.

"Why? You may as well ask why our betters see only themselves when they look into a crowd, One Called fa'Shenali. Few bother to see a battle replayed in this matter, and no one uses it for study. Our leaders are mated to graphs and maps and wishful reports. They cannot see their own noses, much less remember that they have other senses with which to enjoy the Universe. And of course, none would condescend to listen to the rabble. Such a fall would admit that knowledge is not a prerogative limited to Royalty. But I am hardly the first menial to notice their limitations. Nor am I the only one who has seen the mastery of the Beast with his own eyes."

Fa'Shenali breathed deeply, and raised his eyes toward the giant screen looming above him. Lash'Hanna was right of course. They were incredibly stupid—all of them, himself included. After millennia of pursuing knowledge, it seemed that civilization had bred all the sense out of them. They could reach the highest pinnacles of attainment known to the Galaxy, only to be beaten bloody by a race of savages, too proud or too ignorant to know their own limitations. And if the Terrans knew no such constraints, who could truly call them savages?

Fa'Shenali harbored no doubt that the Terrans would use anything that would help them destroy an enemy. He also hoped that Fate would smile upon the g'Khruushtani at least once during this ordeal—that the Terran's primitive science would make machines such as the one he had just discovered beyond their capacity, and that they would be permitted at least this one small advantage in their struggle for survival.

* * *

"N<small>EARING</small> C-S<small>ECTOR</small> Supply, Commander. They want to know if any of us need anything before we head toward the lines."

"Mathison, radio the *Magellan* and *Morning Star.* Tell them this is the last rest station before the front lines. If they need to resupply, this is their chance."

"Yes, ma'am."

"And tell the Skipper that we're into C-Wing space traffic. He may want to take us the rest of the way himself."

"Aye aye."

"He does have this thing about grand entrances, you know."

"Oh, Janet. Really now."

"Don't tell him I said that."

"Janet?"

"Yes, Dexter?"

"Do you have any idea what's going on here? I mean, this is Grissom's attack wing, isn't it?"

"Yes it is, Dexter."

"Well, doesn't it seem kind of odd that— ?"

"Just mind your instruments, Lieutenant. We'll all find out soon enough."

"Couldn't you..."

"In due time, Lieutenant."

"But— "

"In due time."

Chapter 12

O N THE SIXTEENTH OF AUGUST, in the Earth Year 2555, during an interlude of clarity in the eternal storms and upheavals in and along the Great Cloud, Crutchtan subspace radar noted a massive movement of ships toward the reddish star they called *"Tza'shali-gra-Gen'zh"* – the "Guardian of the Bend." On the centerside edge of the great Shunian prominence, the star held the last Crutchtan stronghold protecting the provincial capital of *Gr'Shuna.*

With sensors stretched to their limits and straining to discern form out of the static, the monitors saw three Terran divisions advancing on the Crutchtan positions. Summoning all available ships to defend *Gr'Shuna* against the opening thrust of the long-expected Terran attack, the Crutchtans sent six of their own divisions into battle, hoping to buy time with their lives as they had done since the earliest days of the war.

Six light-years from *Tza'shali*, the Terran center broke forward, racing headlong toward the middle of the Crutchtan defenses. It was a common enough Terran offensive opening, but its execution struck fear among the Crutchtan strategists. It showed none of the Terrans' customary confusion on the commencement of battle, and nothing of their usual willingness to trade death for death to advance their lines another few light-years. Most ominously, the Terran starships were leading the attack, and risking his most terrible weapons of destruction at the onset of battle meant that the Terran commander hungered for victory more than he feared defeat. It also meant that he would rely upon his wits, and look to his own tactics and strategy, rather than the brute strength of his forces, to vanquish his enemies. It was the Crutchtans' first confirmation that the Terran called *Khu'ukh* was at hand, returning to claim skies that had once welcomed him in friendship.

After a moment's hesitation, the Crutchtans countered with thrusts of their own. Two divisions raced forward to meet the charging attackers from either side, seeking to cut through their ranks. At the same time, twin divisions each moved to attack the Terran flanks, to engage the remaining enemy forces and keep the Terrans from moving to reinforce the center of their line. Before long the heavens filled with panic and desperation, and the sky burned with death.

Converted from half the Conning Deck cafeteria, the Situation Room on the Terran flagship was a tense caldron. The tan walls were covered with maps and viewers. Monitor lights and shouts filled the air. Giant screens on all sides filled the room with the fluid, changing sights of the battle, turning the walls into a kaleidoscope of violence. Around the hub, officers and yeomen hurried about their business, knowing that wasted time meant life and death for others. It was little different than the same room on any of dozens of command ships in the fleet, except for the one at the center of it all.

Their eyes glued to their monitors, a half-dozen tactical officers reported endless changes that passed without notice by the man to whom their words were directed. Amid the noise and chaos swirling around him, he paced about a large, illuminated sphere, alone in a crowd of others, his eyes looking coldly at the holographic map in the middle of the command center. The color-coded dots of light told him all he needed to know, more quickly and intelligibly than his aides could relay the imprecise and belated information they received.

"Hodding reports minor realspace turbulence...."

"Gregg reports stiff enemy fire in Sector-A—he suggests...."

"Schultz requests permission...."

Oblivious to his surroundings and secluded with his thoughts, Cook's mind raced in a thousand directions, spinning attacks and counterattacks with each beat of his heart, every breath leaving behind a hundred discarded thoughts. All the while, he forced himself to consider each dot of light as a piece in a game of skill, rather than a host of breathing human beings whose lives depended upon the whims of his imagination.

"Tell Group C to advance another step, and move behind to support Weitzman," he said, his voice firm but quiet. A half-dozen aides sprang toward the radios, to relay his orders to the rest of the wing. "They'll stay there until I say differently.

"Move a squad from Company 6-J fifty klicks due west," he continued after a pause, speaking to no one in particular, but knowing that one aide or another would get word to the right people. "Tell Ramirez that once he gets his reinforcements, he's to attack—hard—and push straight toward the clearing."

"Yes, sir."

"Lt. Bellanger?"

"Commodore?"

"Go to the bridge and tell Commander Mendelson that we'll be holding this position for the time being. She can stand down, if she likes, in which case you will stand in at the systems desk, and Mr. Dexter will take the chair. But she's to have herself paged the second that the center line pivots, one way or the other. And the bridge is to stay in close touch with Commodore Grissom. When the time comes, I want command transferred to the *Constellation* without a hitch."

"Yes, sir." As the pretty young officer raced to carry out her orders, Cook's brow furrowed as the map before him showed another Terran position starting to sag.

"Tell Denning to retreat two hundred klicks, and regroup," he said, mildly annoyed that another CentCom hotshot was proving incapable of holding his forces together on the battle line. "And tell Matthews in 3-G to ready half his squadron to pivot to port and counterattack, on my command." A young ensign ran to a yeoman at the radio desk, to relay the latest order.

The space toward the east flamed with battle, and ships hurled toward each other, hatred burning inside each crewman on every vessel. Through it all, Cook's eyes remained coldly fixed on the situation map in front of him. As he battled the profound regret he felt at repaying the hospitality he had known under these same stars by returning as a conqueror, his mind was free to contemplate the transitory problems of victory.

* * *

PRESSING THE FIGHT for the battle's center, the main body of the Crutchtan fleet surged forward into the Terran midsection, bowing the Terran lines precariously and pressing the Terrans into a momentary frenzy of disarray. Within minutes, the Terran lines had firmed, locking the Crutchtans into a fiercely pitched battle, as the main body of the Terran battle group swung sharply to the right, toward the galactic center. While a stubborn rear guard struggled to slow the advance of the Crutchtans' main combat force in the center of the battle, the Terrans raced to come upon the Crutchtan left flank, catching the two enemy divisions in a sharp and sudden pincer.

The Crutchtans scrambled to reinforce their positions, shoring up their left flank and pressing upon the newly abandoned Terran center with all their available strength. But it was clear that their earliest fears were correct: the enemy commander was the Hated One. And while they buoyed each other with the thought that the future lay within their grasp, they all knew the grim truth. Altering tactics in the face of the rapidly changing strategy of the One Called *Khu'ukh* would be unavailing, like painting the rocks to catch a chameleon.

THE HATCH to the bridge opened with a rush of air. Janet looked to see the Skipper, his eyes preoccupied, striding straight for the command chair. Rising, she stepped down to the helmsman's station to relieve Simmons, her current apprentice.

"We're five hundred klicks from the front," she said over her shoulder, as she took her place on the bridge. Cook nodded quietly in reply.

"*Magellan* and *Morning Star* should be along shortly."

"Well done, Commander. As always."

"*Constellation* on security Channel E, Commodore."

"Thank you, Lieutenant. Put it on the viewer."

The communications screen came to life, showing the handsome, black-haired face of Commodore Grissom, who was standing by to resume command of the C-Sector battle wing. Janet thought that Grissom's normally glib smile seemed forced. Though he was never one of Cook's admirers, it seemed that the thought of taking over for the Skipper in the middle of a battle was enough to give any commander a moment's pause.

"I think we can take if from here, Cook."

"You have the battle draft I left you?"

"Looks golden to me, Commodore. But it won't be the same without its author."

"Well, it won't go like it does on paper. It never does, you know. But I'm sure you'll do fine, Matt."

"I hope you know what you're doing, Cook."

Cook smiled. "That's never stopped me before, you know. But if I do succeed in getting myself killed, I'll never have to live it down, so I guess it doesn't really matter."

Soon the screen went dark, and the *Constellation* departed to take charge of the Terran forces. Before long, two ships joined the *d'Artagnan* in the darkness; together, they waited in silence for the battle to take another turn.

* * *

SUDDENLY, THE Terran left flank withdrew and swung toward the center of battle, seeking to break through the middle of the Crutchtan forces and slice the enemy fleet in two. The Crutchtans countered by pivoting their right flank into a massive thrust toward the Terran midsection, pushing harder and harder toward the center of battle. Gradually, under the fiercest fighting of the engagement, the Terrans started falling back, drifting away from the lifeless system of the ancient star which dominated the local skies, drawing the fleet of defenders along with them, nipping at their heels in growing anticipation of their first victory over a hated enemy.

Then, alone and unmolested, three Terran starships suddenly came to life on the Crutchtan right flank, firing their engines and slipping into the darkness beyond the battle lines of their enemy. At the same instant, the main body of the Terran forces came alive once more, pressing the fight with the fury of the possessed and striking fiercely at the mystified Crutchtans.

As the battle continued, the Terrans becoming more bloodthirsty and less controlled with each passing moment, it was obvious that the Terrans would soon overrun the Crutchtan defenses, and that the better course for the defenders was to withdraw and regroup, preparing for the main battle for the planet *Gr'Shuna* that was certain to follow. Yet the growing Crutchtan confusion soon gave way to concern, and then horror, as their analysts poured over the sensor data from the episode.

The course of battle confirmed the vague sense of the local commander: there had been a change in the Terran command midway through the encounter. But the data also showed without question that one of the three Terran ships that had passed into Crutchtan skies had been that of the One Called *Khu'ukh*.

Among the people of His Worthiness, a single question now cried for an answer: Why?

Until they knew exactly what the Terran demon intended, none among the *g'Khruushtani* would rest peacefully.

Chapter 13

I T'S A BLOODY disgrace."
"Aye to that. A bitter pill, it is. But life's a daft, cruel bastard, don't ye know."

"A bloody disgrace."

"Watch the leg there, bucko. Hate to see the cleaning drone shave it off, now. We've a dozen holds to grease before mess and it'd put us bloody behind schedule, dashin' ye off to sick bay. And they're like to sew it on backwards, at that."

"To think of all the rotten— "

"Rotten it is, Laddie, for one such as he."

" — filthy things going on around us. And then for us to sit like a flock of pigeons...."

"Well, we can hardly do more than stew about it. 'Tis the Skipper's ship, after all. Though when a Cozzie's off to be drinkin'—after hours, so to speak...."

"Simply waiting around til God knows when. It's shameful, just— "

"Shameful it is. But as I hear tell, he did bring a lot of it on his own head."

"Well of course he did. He's the Skipper."

"Who??"

"Cook, you Ishtari moron!"

"When did we stop talking about the Chief?"

"When did we start?"

"What?"

"And ye little pantywaist, at least the last Man Jack to go insultin' me didn't wear a dress under his standard reds."

"You loudmouthed cretin— "

"Ye twerp-faced little poof— "

"*Fight—! Fight—!*"

"Security to Deck 5; Security to Deck 5...."

```
CC:            144-3496.1
FILE:          Log
ACCESS:        Command.
SECURITY:      Standard
OPERATIONAL STATUS: Normal
LOCATION:      circa 75/135/33/0-15e
```

We have settled into orbit around the sixth planet of a newly formed O-class star, just inside the Cloud. Though our precise position is largely a matter of conjecture, I estimate that we are about twelve parsecs inside the Crutchtan zone of control. We have detected no evidence of Crutchtan exploration of this star system, or this portion of the Cloud's interior.

The system is littered with high levels of post-formation asteroids. Space normal readings detectable through the fog suggest minimal debris outside the system, including significantly lower-than-normal presence of comets, rocks, and post-solar dust. Nearby subspace anomalies are also minimal. Magellan and Morning Star have taken positions just beyond the planet's outermost moon. D'Artagnan is venturing close to the third moon, to let Lt. Hatfield take readings of the liquid ocean on its surface. Several tertiary spirals are clearly visible in the surrounding skies to anticenter, and preliminary scans suggest a significant presence of heavy elements. Should Hatfield confirm the presence of liquid water on the moon, this system could provide a base for commercial exploitation of the area.

I have dispatched several scouting parties into the clear space outside the star system. They report wide-scale enemy sweeps still underway, apparently searching for us. With such dislocations of the enemy in progress, it is unclear why Command has not launched a major offensive, but all things considered I suppose it is not surprising. My intentions remain unchanged since the last entry: as soon as the enemy search abates, we will move deeper into enemy space, and proceed with the second phase of Operation Mongoose.

[PERS:CODE=<<Scooter>>:First Officer continues to observe a strict "radio silence." Radio Officer has added nothing beyond the cryptic comment that my choice of companions leaves much to be desired. So long as Helmsman declines to discuss the matter, I remain mystified as ever. Connors is also being stubborn./PERS]

Comm R Cook

* * *

STATELY PANELING and ancient artworks adorned the walls of Ga'Glish's command center. The soft lights, dimmed to highlight the projections on the Briefing Screen, cast long shadows that faded into the grayness that surrounded the meeting table. At times like this, few dared to speak inside the Lord Commander's inner sanctum.

"That is unacceptable!"

"But— "

"We cannot tolerate it, do you hear me?" Ga'Glish pounded the table with his fist.. "He must be found and destroyed!"

"Lord Commander," Dra'Lengish said sternly. His colleagues winced with trepidation. When it suited him, the Old One could be quite stubborn. In his present mood, the Chief of Tactics might say anything, and even the ancient gods could not foretell the reaction of Ga'Glish.

"Raging against facts will not find the intruders."

"We must mobilize. All available resources must— "

"You would divert forces away from *Gr'Shuna* to go chasing *Khu'ukh?*" The voice of Dra'Lengish reeked of uncharacteristic sarcasm. "With the Terran Fleet no more than ten units to the West, surely the Beast cannot hope to see us sending our fleet in pursuit of a phantom, can he? Or knowing that he threatens your homeland, Ga'Glish, perhaps he is simply waiting for you to render us all helpless with panic, so that he may— "

"Silence!" Ga'Glish hissed ominously. All present knew that the Old One had overstepped his place. In their present straits, and in his present state of agitation, all feared the reaction of their commander. When it came all were astonished, Dra'Lengish not least of all.

"You are right, Lord Lengish," Ga'Glish whispered, bowing regally to his obstreperous aide. "And you must forgive my ill humor. The weight of responsibility is often difficult to bear gracefully.

"But our problem remains."

Now fully in command of his emotions, the Tall One sat stiffly in his place around the table, placing together the tips of his fingers, and staring ahead at the projection screen.

"We cannot permit *Khu'ukh* to wander our skies unmolested. Yet now that the Terrans command the local bend in the Cloud, we cannot afford to divert resources from the defense of *Gr'Shuna*."

"But if his aim is the planet, need we bother worrying?" asked La'Gralokh, from *Glaroshana*. "We need only continue our fortifications."

Ga'Glish raged in silence. Gralokh was his newest comer, and possessed a keen sense of organization. Were it not for the Son of the Laglaroshani, the defenses of *Gr'Shuna* would still be largely theoretical, on someone's desk instead of in the skies and soil of the planet. But

Gralokh lacked a sense of strategic imagination, and could not comprehend the mind of a longnose murderer.

"He intends the destruction of *Gr'Shuna*," Ga'Glish responded. "But were that his sole aim, there would be no need for such theatrics. He could seek the same end merely by leading a direct attack.

"No," he continued, "I believe that Dra'Lengish is right. This *Khu'ukh* is seeking to provoke our rashness and to draw our forces away from the planet. But three starships— ?"

"*Gr'Shuna* can stand against three starships, Lord Commander." Gralokh announced proudly. Ga'Glish paled at the irony. With the Terran fleet massing, Gralokh remained blissfully insensitive to the looming disaster, but his words had just focused reality in the mind of Ga'Glish. With a single stroke, *Khu'ukh* just revealed the hopelessness of their position.

A fearful young aide entered and approached Ga'Glish to hand him a handwritten message.

Ga'Glish opened the note. It was from his mate, begging him to attend her. Angrily, Ga'Glish crumpled the paper in his hands. This was not the time for personal indulgences, he thought. And as he had explained to Glishana just the other day, his responsibilities were consuming. So long as the Terran menace threatened their home, he could think of nothing but duty.

"Dismissed."

"But Lady Glish— " began the aide.

"You are dismissed, Menial," Ga'Glish hissed hatefully. Fearfully, and with moistening eyes, the boy bowed and departed.

Immediately, Ga'Glish sensed the disapproval of his aides and regretted his impatience with the poor servant. The boy was, after all, simply a messenger. His mind soon turned to more important matters. In the crush of readying his forces to defend his homeland, he thought, a lack of tactfulness in dealing with inferiors was, after all, a small thing.

* * *

HE WAS DRIFTING in a Universe of his own, the gentleness of his dreams floating on a fragile cloud of music. Just as the flute was beginning a sublime journey through the most intimate reaches of his imagination, the intercom sounded, intruding upon a soft passage in his refuge from madness.

"Yes, Cathy?" Cook sighed.

"Crewman Connors is here, Commodore. You said..."

"Show him in," said Cook. He sighed and removed his feet from his desk. His feet plopped on the floor just as a sullen Gregory Connors, dressed in crewman red, strode through the door and walked up to the desk.

"Have a seat, Mr. Connors."

"No thank ye, sir. I prefer to stand."

Cook started drumming with his fingers. Without warning he rose to his feet and slammed his fist on the desktop.

"This is getting us nowhere, Chief. Frankly, I don't know what to do with you, and I'm running out of patience."

"Crewman," Connors corrected, in a stiffly formal tone of voice. "I might remind the Skipper that ye— "

"Can it, Chief! I busted the both of you because I will not have my officers and yeomen brawling in public like common spacers. Until I get answers, you'll both stay busted."

"Thank ye, sir, but I'll not be— "

"I don't want to hear it," the captain snapped. "Gerlach is no great loss to the bridge crew. I have a half-dozen gunnery officers who are just as good as he is, who'll give me less grief because their egos actually match their abilities, and who are perfectly capable of functioning with Lt. Dexter watching over them. He can stay a greenshirt until the end of the war, for all I care.

"But you, Mr. Connors, are disrupting the proper functioning of my ship. With enemy search squadrons starting to slack off—well, we'll be moving along any time now. I need you back at your post before we do."

"It's always the Skipper's prerogative— "

"Don't pull that crap with me, Chief. I have too much on my mind to wade through it all, and I'm not going to let it disturb our routine any longer. If we can't get back to normal, I'll just change what 'normal' means around here."

Cook rose to his feet, and fixed Connors with a stern, unforgiving stare. "Stand at attention, Mister."

By reflex, Connors snapped his heels together. Cook circled around him once, then returned to his desk and resumed his paperwork. After a few minutes, it became apparent that the Skipper had lost all interest in talking to him.

"Beggin the Commodore's pardon," Connors began.

"Crewmen at attention speak when spoken to," Cook replied absently, continuing with his work. As the minutes passed, Connors began to forget how hurt and angry he was for being busted, and started wondering exactly why the Skipper had him standing at attention.

"Excuse me, sir— "

"You're at attention, Crewman."

As Cook tended to his routine paperwork, the minutes passed in silence. Before long, Connors felt his feet turning numb, and his beard began to itch.

"Skipper— " he began again.

"I expect my crewmen to hold their tongues when standing at attention," Cook said sharply, not looking up from his desk. He initialed one report and took up another one from his in-basket. "I do, however, permit my yeomen a few more liberties," he added quietly.

Connors drew a deep breath. Finally, he understood what this exercise was about. He swallowed to clear the dryness in his throat.

"I guess I have been a bit of a jackass, haven't I?"

"I'd put it less diplomatically than that, Chief," Cook smiled, finally looking up from his work.

"You know, you make it a lot harder for me to run things when you're not there to help. With this particular mission, you're putting us all in danger. You don't have the right—none of us has the right—to put your personal problems ahead of this ship. And I know, Chief, because that's a struggle I have with myself every single day."

Connors lowered his eyes. Still dazed by his own blindness, he was amazed that self-pity hadn't landed him in the brig. Feeling very foolish, he was having trouble enough just maintaining his dignity. He hoped that the Skipper wouldn't ask him what had happened, for the truth was he didn't really remember.

"All right, Chief, get out of here. I still have rounds to do, and I have a mountain of sensor data to check, to see if we can venture out into the open yet."

"Aye, sir."

"I'll post orders tomorrow restoring both of you to full rank, and I'll delete the incident from the files. You can send your greens down to the laundry today, if you like."

"Thanks, Skipper," Connors smiled weakly, and did his best to hold his head high. Turning smartly, he snapped his heels and walked toward the door.

As Connors strode from his office, Cook sighed deeply and rocked in his chair. In the midst of all this death and destruction, Cook thought, it was easy to overlook the little acts of kindness that made the small tragedies of life less painful. In the end, it wouldn't matter to history. History would record the grand sweeps of battle and the tides of change. The human faces would fade into the gray past. It would only matter to those involved.

And to me, thought Cook.

Smiling inwardly, he chided himself for being such a sentimentalist. In the space of a single heartbeat, he returned to studying his charts, and to wondering what to do with his three starships, now that they were finally behind enemy lines.

* * *

"Captain?"

Jeremy swivelled to face the entrance to the bridge. The main viewer showed the giant mother planet rising over the horizon of the moon they were orbiting. McDermott, the ship's Security Officer, was standing at the entranceway, beckoning him.

"Carry on. Miss VanderBrook, take over."

"Aye, sir."

As his bridge crew went about the routine business of maintaining orbit, Jeremy followed McDermott from the bridge, into the small security hall that separated the bridge from the rest of the Conning Deck.

"What is it, Mac?"

The sound of the air pumps pouring through a small gash in the paneling made them shout to be heard. The engineers were working on it. In fact, they seemed to be working on everything, even if nothing ever seemed to get done. The sheer number of things going wrong made Jeremy realize just how big a starship was, something he'd never appreciated on board the *d'Artagnan*.

"Captain Fitzgerald still has two of our best technicians, sir. And he won't give them back."

"What do you mean 'won't give them back?'"

McDermott shifted uncomfortably on his feet.

"Well, he says that he's still making repairs on his mainframe, and can't spare them."

"Just who the hell does he think he is?" stormed Jeremy. "I need them here. And after he begged me to— "

"Well, sir...."

"Dammit, Mac! I mean—crap! They're our people."

"But Fitz has them, sir. And the *Magellan* is still out of range for the Molecular Transmitter."

"I'm sure he's seeing to that."

"Actually, he does seem to be keeping the moon between our ship and his."

Jeremy leaned back against the corridor wall, bumping his head against the bend in the hexagon. This was the last time, he promised himself. This was the last time he'd let himself get snookered like this.

"Get him on the security line—in my office."

"Yes, sir."

McDermott started dashing toward the A Ring hatch.

"And don't breathe a word of this."

"I won't, Captain."

The young Security Officer snapped to attention, and turned on his heels. Soon, McDermott was dashing toward the security office, to arrange a scrambled channel for his captain's call to the *Magellan*. The noise from the ventilation system was still ringing in Jeremy's ears, making it hard to hear himself think.

McDermott was a fine officer, mused Jeremy: diligent, capable, and entirely trustworthy. He enjoyed the tasks Jeremy delegated to him, and even asked to be given the kind of paperwork that used to drive Jeremy to distraction aboard the *d'Artagnan*. He was also the most annoying officer in his command, and quite paranoid about everything that moved. Jeremy scoffed each time he suggested changing their plans for reasons of security. It irked Jeremy to no end that Mac had cautioned against loaning Yanik and Biaselli to the *Magellan*—and was worried precisely about getting them back when they were needed. And it galled him to think that Fitzgerald would be so selfish as to steal trained people when the paint was barely dry on *Morning Star's* registry numbers, and her captain was still wet behind the ears.

But the most galling thing about it all was that there was only one superior officer within range. The last thing Jeremy wanted to do was to start running to Cook with his petty squabbles.

Slowly, he started toward the hatch, wondering what to say to Fitz, if and when McDermott could raise him. Life was simpler as a first officer, he thought. Simpler and less stressful.

Even if it meant enduring a hundred petty slights, and a thousand pointless stories.

And even if it meant slashing through an endless jungle of paperwork.

* * *

My dearest Mother--

Today is the saddest day of my life, for I must confess my failures to someone, and I find reality as difficult to face as another's countenance. Perhaps this is why I can admit weakness only to you, for I need not fear that you will cast me off, and distance will spare me the disappointment in your eyes. Through all our past storms, your love has never faltered. Perhaps mothers see through temporal mists with clearer eyes than their sons can ever appreciate, until the call of Death sounds in the darkness. But if reality makes these my last words to you, I pray that you will recall me with fondness, and that my failings as a son do not make you forget the Small One you once clasped to your breast, who will call you "Mother" through eternity.

By now, you will have heard that the Terrans are readying their forces to attack. I have ordered the evacuation of our homeland, and pray that my hopes have not blinded me to your danger and delayed my actions until we are past hope. The Beast is now loose within our skies, and I fear the worst is at hand. How Uncle retains his confidence in his bungling nephew, and in our cause during our years of darkness, is a source of amazement to me. But I am powerless to stop the barbarians from destroying all that ever brought meaning to my life. Should my impotence cost the lives of those I love, and leave me to face the monsters of our nightmares alone, I will gladly forfeit my own miserable existence to avenge myself upon them. However monstrous or barbaric such thoughts may echo in the soul of one bred to civilization, such are the demons that the longnoses arouse within us. Such is our hatred and desperation that we would gladly destroy ourselves, if we could only restore sanity to the Universe we once knew.

I have heard that Father intends to remain behind, to lead the planet's defenses from the ground. Please change his mind for him. If we cannot repel them in the skies, he will be condemning himself to death. And please tell him that his Son would gladly undo the past, were it within his power.

Glish, your Dutiful One.

* * *

"I DON'T KNOW how you stand it, Janet."

Taking a sip of tea, Mary Mathison placed her cup back onto the coaster on the end table. She felt a soothing warmth enter her body as she relaxed from the tensions of the day. Staring at monitors all day long had made her sensitive to bright lights, so she kept the lights dim in her living quarters.

Seated on the large floor chair next to the table, Janet had removed Mary's boots and stockings, and was massaging her friend's feet. It had been a hard day for both of them. With chaos surrounding them, and half the enemy fleet combing the skies for them, the days were hard on everyone. But when they came back to their empty quarters, where they couldn't really hide from their own peculiar loneliness, it was especially hard on the two of them. They could keep each other company, of course. And on their rare liberties, they could even see what else was available, elsewhere in the fleet. But it was hardly what either of them wanted—though Mary often felt, all things considered, that she was by far the luckier of the two. At least she didn't have a constant reminder of the past, pulling each scab off her heart as it formed.

"It's not so bad. Really."

"I mean, the way he treats you sometimes? Making you run and fetch, like that. Ordering you to take the chair or stand down, as if you didn't have sense enough to know when it was safe to turn things over to Dexter. I wouldn't put up with it."

Janet shook her head and smiled. Mary was a good friend, but there were just some things she could never make her understand. Some things were more important than the petty insults she had to endure. No matter how she hurt inside, imagining her life elsewhere always left her feeling empty.

"He is the Skipper," she laughed. "He can do things like that."

"But between what he makes you do around here—and everything else...I mean, I'd be gone at the first opportunity. I don't see why you choose to stay."

Janet sighed deeply and leaned forward, resting her elbow on the armrest of the chair. Mary thought Janet had the dreamiest, most hopeless look in her eyes.

"It's killing him, Mary. It's killing everything he ever dreamed about, or hoped to be."

Mary nodded sadly. "And that just keeps all the old wounds open, doesn't it?"

"Oh, he doesn't help matters any. He's either playing the perfect gentleman and driving me quite crazy, or else he's making some veiled, smirking reference to something he knows very well that only I will understand."

"Don't you wish he'd just let go?"

"Then he brings along Jeremy, of all people. After their little falling out, you'd think Jeremy would be the last person he'd think to take on a mission like this. It's as if he's just daring me to leave, but won't come right out and say so."

"But if that's true, wouldn't you really be better off someplace else?"

Janet shrugged. "I can't. Not like this, anyway. Not when he's like—"

"Well, if you ask me, I think Jeremy would...."

"I've told you a dozen times, I don't want to hear about it," Janet snapped. "I'm very fond of Jeremy, I really am. But sometimes, you're as bad as anyone. I don't like it any better when it comes from you."

Mary's eyes widened. Such a display of temper from Janet was unusual, but she was rather touchy these days. With all that was going on around them, it was only natural.

"Sorry," Janet said.

Mary smiled. "Want some teacakes? Fresh from supply? Salinger's trying to win my heart with food, now."

"No. After all I had at Liberty? I'll be watching what I eat for the next year."

"Nonsense. And you don't want to be rude."

"No, thank you."

"Well, just one won't hurt, will it?"

"No, really."

Ignoring Janet's protests, Mary went to the pantry and returned with a plate filled with dried fruits and crackers, and a half-dozen small cakes, marbled with jam.

"And what about Josephson? Now that Dexter is more than the ship's buffoon, she's sure trying to sink her claws into him. Do you think that she'll really get Dexter to notice her just by changing her simulator schedule to follow him around all day?"

"Really, now, Janet— "

"Aren't we just terrible?"

"Terrible but true. Just like the new power unit on the Centrax."

"You know, it just hasn't been the same since we left port."

"It's sluggish as anything. Not that Skipper would ever notice."

"Dexter says it's as slow as he can remember."

"You think I should bring it up?"

"With— "

"Well— "

"You are the executive officer, Janet. You have to start talking to him again, sometime."

"Not in a million years, Mary."

"Now, Janet..."

"Not in a million years."

* * *

SAD MUSIC FROM from a melancholy flute filled the air. Darkened to enhance the images on the screen, the room was a picture of desolation. Darkness had swallowed all traces of life, save one. Lit only by the eerie glow of the computer screen, points danced across the face of the lone occupant.

In the solitude of his room, seated on the floor by his study table and alone with his thoughts, fa'Shenali pressed a button and ordered the screen to display the Battle of *bhra'Bendi* for his viewing. He watched as the two adversaries crept toward each other—the *g'Khruushtani* in the green of life, the longnoses in the orange of sunset, clinging to the edge of the cloud and edging forward as shyly as a female at her first dance of maidenhood. The two fleets moved together slowly, fitfully, each reacting to the other like colliding glaciers on a planet of ice, until at last the green slowly withdrew toward the east, while the orange of the longnoses grew to fill the screen.

Pressing another button, Shenali sought to replay another battle, one that he had watched twice in the silence of awe. The *g'Khruushtani* commander was the same—but the Terrans had been led by their greatest commander, the One Called *Khu'ukh*. This time, the flowing lines of the orange advance grew into sweeping pincers and counterattacks that sprang from nowhere. They arched across the screen in a ballet of death, each movement showing such cunning grace and deadly precision that fa'Shenali found himself torn between the joy of discovery and the numbness of despair. In battle after battle, *Khu'ukh's* unerring instinct for surprise let him control the battle through the force of his imagination. Despite himself, fa'Shenali was transfixed, fascinated to see the alien's mind at work, thrilled by the texture of the Terran's thinking, the grandeur of his design, and awed by the Terran's ability to reshape his tactics within the beat of a heart. The Beast would strike wherever he was not expected, using his enemies' thoughts as toys. And they dared call such a one a savage, Shanali mused: they were leaves fighting against the wind, and dared to call the wind uncivilized.

It was hopeless, he thought. The *g'Khruushtani* were a proud people, a race of the highest accomplishments. But their memory of war had been lost over long millennia of peace. They could hardly hope to stand against the Terrans, a race with the blood of their warrior ancestors still burning in their veins.

Stiffening in his seat, the young subaltern purged his mind of such treasonous doubts. Opening his eyes once more, he pressed another button, and blackness filled the room. Soon, the screen filled with new patterns of light, and fa'Shenali returned to his studies with single-minded intensity.

* * *

The scent of blood stained the air, and screams of the damned rose like thirsty flames. Higher and higher they climbed, exploding at last in a devouring cataclysm of death and damnation.

Scrambling desperately up the side of the pit, the embers seared his flesh until he wanted to scream. But he knew that the slightest sound would rise into the chorus of lost souls and drag him screaming into the depths. Seconds passed like eons....

BOLTING UPRIGHT IN his sleeping chamber, Cook found himself spinning in the zero-gravity, his pulse racing wildly. Closing his eyes, he fought to concentrate on Christmas at home, on the bright-eyed wonder of a young boy racing down the stairs to greet a day filled with love and dreams. As thoughts of laughter calmed him, Cook steadied himself against the padded top wall. Working his way down to the control panel near the bed, he reactivated the gravity zone, bringing it into alignment with the ship. Settling into bed, he stared into the blackness of the artificial night until he had steadied his nerves, and dared to fall asleep once more.

Chapter 14

DAYS PASSED UNEVENTFULLY as the three Terran starships circled the dominant planet of a star system hidden from enemy sensors. On each ship, the crew went about its business, keeping the engines primed, manning the controls, and otherwise keeping their ships in proper trim. On the *Magellan*, crewmen took to betting on the number of days left until they left orbit; on the *d'Artagnan*, a few of the blueshirts started a new betting pool, wagering on the number of days their Skipper and his first officer would be speaking to each other until the next flare-up. Since whatever dangers their mission held for them belonged to the future, and as the routine tasks took little more than a skeleton crew to perform adequately, the captains authorized their crews to make liberal use of the small shuttles to exchange visits and pleasantries with friends on their sister ships.

But the interstellar fog that shielded them also kept them from following the Crutchtan ship movements. Each day sent a new wave of scouts picking its way through the Cloud, to sneak a hurried look at the clear skies beyond and return to the mother ships with whatever readings they could make.

* * *

THE NEEDLE ON the receiver danced at the low end of the band. As delicately as she could, Mary adjusted the controls, trying to focus the incoming signal. But it was little use: interference still flared over every channel, rendering each message from outside the star system unintelligible. As it had for the past week, the scout's transmission was scattered beyond recognition. The greater power available to the starship made their own broadcasts a bit clearer, but still hopelessly muddied.

"Do you copy, *d'Artagnan*-6?" Come in, Lt. Sheldon?"

"***s is ****. C** *_* ***r **? **m* ** ***_*."

"Shelly?" Mary pressed the earphone toward her ear. Like any radio officer worth her commission, she knew it would do no good, but reflexes were hard to ignore. With her free hand, she steadied the slender microspeaker.

" Sheldon? There's too much static on the channel."

"*****c? I** _**_** * ***'*_*_* ***."

"Switch to Channel Forty. Shelly?"

"****? "

"Try—Channel Forty—Four Zero. Channel—Forty."

As Mathison struggled to make herself understood through the subspace disturbances, the portside hatch opened and Cook stepped onto the bridge. His face all but shouted frustration.

"Any luck, Lieutenant?"

"Afraid not, Skipper. Sheldon is still out there, but we can't even make contact, let alone take a report."

Cook frowned sourly. He hated having to recall his scouts just to learn what they'd seen. It was a waste of resources and a waste of time.

"Dexter, any luck on the enhancer?"

"No, sir. We fixed the glitch on the computer, though."

"Great...as usual, our timing is impeccable. We always fix exactly the wrong thing.

"Sorry, sir."

"Don't do that, Dexter. Don't start looking hurt. I put up with enough of that already, and I'm sick of it. I am thrilled to death that you fixed the computer."

"Oh—thank you, sir."

"Sssh—Mathison?"

"Sir?"

"Transmit a low beam signal. That should cut through the fog, if nothing else will. Tell Sheldon to come home. We'll take his report in person."

"Aye, sir."

"And has anyone seen Commander Mendelson?"

"Ummm... "

"Mathison?"

"Well, sir... "

"Mathison!"

"I think she's in the lounge, Skipper."

"Thank you, Lieutenant. Carry on, people. Mr. Dexter, you may stand down. Mr. Gerlach, you have the chair. And Mathison, why don't you page Newcomb, to take over the systems station."

"Aye, sir."

"Gee, thanks, Skipper."

"Ssssh...."

Cook strode out the door, slowly shaking his head. As soon as the hatch closed, the navigator and radio officer turned to face one another. Each bore a look of giddy anticipation. At the helm, Ensign Lassiter, gently pounded the control panel with her fists, nearly sending the ship spinning toward the surface of the moon they were circling before catching the problem and bringing the ship back into a stable orbit.

"I hope no one noticed."

"Is he— ?"

"Yes, he's gone. I doubt he'll be back, at least not for a while."

"Well, Mary , what is it this time?"

"I think he's finally going to do it."

Lassiter smiled condesendingly. She didn't want to be seen as approving, but now that things were coming to a head she felt a rush of excitement in spite of herself.

As always, there was someone there to break the mood.

"What's he going to do?" puzzled Gerlach, rising on his way to take the command chair. He looked at Dexter, who shrugged dumbly. "And what are you girls getting so giggly about, anyway?"

"I think he's finally going to apologize," said Mary, here eyes beaming with satisfaction.

"Apologize? To who? And for what?"

"Oh, Gerlach, you have no sense, sometimes."

"Dexter—you know what's going on, don't you?"

"Well...no. Not really. Not that it's all that surprising, I suppose, but...."

"Really, now. You two are so dense, sometimes."

MINOR STATIC FLARED across the viewers, but it was static from the storms and disturbances from the great planet below, rather than from the vast cloud that surrounded the star system. However much it disrupted the proper functioning of the molecular transmitters, the proximity of their two ships made the interference too trivial to disturb routine, short-range communications.

"So you agree with me?"

Before Jeremy could steer the conversation back to his two missing engineers, Fitz pressed his point, growing more animated by the minute.

"How long have we been here now, Ashton? Two weeks, is it?"

"Actually, more like— "

"All we do is circle round and round. As if these bloody moons were creation itself, and we were limp-wristed, harp-strumming angels with nothing better to do than pluck away, waiting for the dead to rise. I'm sick of it, Ashton. Sick of waiting for some action. And damn sick of sitting on our butts doing little beyond playing floating bawdy house for some of the younger buckos who've a way with the birdies."

Jeremy nodded, and opened his mouth to reply.

"You know another thing?" Fitz went on. "I'm coming to wonder whether Cookie even has a plan for us. For all we know, he's just winging this whole episode. We've both seen him do that before, haven't we, Laddie?"

"Well you know— "

"You know what I think we should do? We should lay it on the line. Both of us—shoulder to shoulder and all. Tell him we're tired of all this extended liberty. All this time spent to no real purpose, circling these worthless hunks of rock. Tell him we want to see a little movement. A little action. What do you say to that, Ashton? Are ye with me?"

"You know, of course, that— "

"Great! Glad to hear it!" Fitz pounded his fist on his desk, disrupting the picture on Jeremy's viewer for a second or two.

"Ye know, with the two of us a-coming at him, flanking him on both ends, as it were, he'll have to see reason."

"Well, Fitz, I don't know if— "

"Glad we had this talk, Ashton. It helps to know whose guarding your wing. And mark me— we'll get Cookie to move this mission ahead, the two of us will. Ye can bloody well bank on it."

As Fitz signed off, Jeremy cleared his throat. Fitz was right, he thought. They'd waited long enough before moving ahead with the mission. And secretly, he was looking forward to having an ally in an argument with his former commander, an ally with half a chance of winning his point.

Still, he fumed at himself for being so slow to demand his own people back. At the same time, Jeremy felt vaguely uncomfortable about pressing Cook into something before the Skipper was ready. For all Cook's faults, Jeremy felt a great deal of loyalty toward his old commander, much like a student feels toward an old, eccentric professor. And when lives were at stake, the Skipper's instincts were almost never wrong.

Besides, he thought, his discussions with his wingmate were becoming rather one-sided. It was almost as bad as talking to Cook, except that he could usually follow what Fitz was trying to say.

"*Morning Star* out," he said at last, speaking into the empty screen.

"I HOPE I'M not interrupting anything."

Janet started in her chair. She looked up to see Cook standing beside her. They were alone in the officer's lounge. All was quiet, except for some soft music Janet had programmed into the speaker system. Janet felt herself blush; the tune playing was from a past she was trying to put behind her. Cook smiled mysteriously, as if sensing her thoughts. He pointed at the chair next to her; Janet nodded silently, and he took the seat. Desperately, she wanted Cook to ease the tension between them. She also felt foolish and vulnerable, painfully aware of her Skipper's ability to see through any of her defenses.

"Looks like you were right again," he said pleasantly. "The sluggishness you felt in the helm was a cross-wiring in the central relay system, probably a hold-over from our last spot of troubleshooting en route from Liberty-Twelve. It probably wouldn't have made itself felt—seriously, I mean—until the moment we needed it. Then— "

Cook widened his eyes and whistled like a flagging kettle.

"Well," he forced a laugh, "I guess we're just lucky you caught it."

Trying not to play the captain's fool, Janet struggled to keep her voice as subdued as she could. Cook sensed turmoil welling within her but saw only coldness in her eyes, and heard only the hautiness in her voice.

"Glad to help," she said at last, her voice as unforgiving as her gaze. "And it was nice of you to notice."

Cook sighed bitterly. "You know, this isn't any easier on me. It really isn't. And now, with Jeremy gone— "

"You sure brought him back in a hurry, though," Janet snapped reflexively, as all the old wounds flooded her senses. "Seems as if you can control everything as easily as you can manage my career for me."

Cook squinted, and slowly shook his head.

"I only meant," he began, trying to keep his own temper under control, "that without some sort of buffer— "

"Buffer!? You honestly think that Jeremy is nothing more than—and for both of us? I mean, my God, Skipper. How do you dare— "

"And what do mean, 'manage your career,'" Cook continued, raising his voice to drown out Janet's attempts at protests. "I've already explained that I had nothing to do with your assignment here. And you are perfectly free— "

"Right. In other words, you think I'm too stupid to see through— "

"Look here, Commander," Cook snarled. He'd told himself before entering the lounge that the last thing he would do would be to pull rank, but talking with Janet often made him forget his best intentions. "I will not have my first officer sniping at me, no matter how many claims she thinks she has on my conscience. I will tell you exactly one more time: it was Admiral Clay's idea to assign you to this ship, not mine. I have already apologized for not vetoing the notion. And I am sorry in more ways than I care to admit."

"If you say so...*sir*," Janet said icily. Cook winced inside, as she spit his rank back in his face.

"I mean, can you honestly say I've ever lied to you?"

Janet arched her back. "Once is quite enough, Commodore."

"I will apologize again," Cook said stiffly, his eyes narrowing angrily, "if it will do any good. Otherwise...."

Janet glared at Cook, her eyes narrowed angrily. "Don't worry," she said coldly, rising to her feet. "If I'm not here, you won't have anything to listen to."

Cook said nothing as Janet stormed toward the door. When she had finally gone, he leaned back in his chair, and took a deep breath to calm himself. With everything along the front falling into place, he wondered how his own life could be such a mess.

Perhaps Jeremy had been right after all, he thought. Maybe he was thoughtless and cruel to those around him. But life had been cruel to him, in many ways. He seemed to provoke anger wherever he went, just by being honest. And by seeing things nobody else could see. Maybe he was blind to things that others simply knew, and could sense the grander designs in the Universe only by missing the smaller pleasures that gave life its meaning. Or perhaps it was all an illusion, and he deluded himself with his own pretensions.

For several minutes, he sat by himself in the Conning Deck lounge, motionless and silent. But a starship couldn't run on self-pity, and soon Cook was angry with himself for being so vain as to suppose that his lot was any worse than any other man's. In the end, he allowed himself only a few minutes for his hurt feelings to fade before rising to finish making his rounds on the ship.

"HANGAR DECK REPORTS bay doors closing, and Number 6 aboard."

Gerlach swivelled in the command chair and scowled at the radio officer. Giddy as a drunken spacer, he'd been imagining himself on the bridge of his own ship, giving precise commands to the rest of his crew as they scurried about. The intrusion of mundane reality into his life put him slightly out of sorts.

"Do they have any word for us, Miss Mathison?" he said, his voice weighty with self-importance. "Anything that we need to pass along?"

Mary shot Gerlach a sour glance, wondering if it was just Gerlach, or whether it had something to do with the chair. "First report is that the enemy's still out there," she scowled, "but their numbers are decreasing. Sheldon thinks that they're getting ready to call off the search, but he can't— "

"Let's leave this one for the Skipper, shall we?" Gerlach said ponderously, rising to his feet. "Mathison, tell Lt. Sheldon to bring a full report to Cook's office on the double. Then page the Skipper, and tell him Sheldon is on his way."

"Okay."

"The proper response, Lieutenant— "

"Oh, stuff a sock up your nose."

* * *

THE CRISIS ROOM was flooded with exultation. Cheers rose from the throats of the command staff without restraint. The viewers showed the reddish dots withdrawing from the arena of battle, and raw emotion was pouring from every heart, save one.

"That is the last of them, Lord Commander. We have beaten them back again."

"We have known such success before, Gralokh," said Ga'Glish, "most recently just before the debacle at *Gr'Lusshe*. Another wave will come, as inevitably as the tides of home. And have you forgotten the Terran ships that are still lurking about the area? I rather doubt that the Beast hides in enemy skies because he is a coward."

Grolokh felt suddenly foolish, his elation turned to ashes.

"Lord Commander," he bowed in submission.

"But, enough of such talk," Ga'Glish said, rising to his feet and raising his voice. "The time has come. Without *Khu'ukh*, the Terrans are too disorganized to pose an immediate threat. We have dealt with this new commander before, and his tactics are like the rest. In the end, their numbers will prevail— "

Shouts of protest rose through the Room, only to be silenced by the Lord Commander's look of regal disdain.

"Their numbers will prevail," Ga'Glish thundered, "though their losses will be severe, almost as severe as our own. But our first concern must be the safety of our people, whose lives depend upon our valor."

Ga'Glish strode to the giant holograph that dominated the center of the room. From there, he spoke the painful words that each had hoped would never come. All knew that Lord Glishek's son spoke nothing but the truth. Out of respect for their leader, each kept a silent tongue.

"Our bravery, and the lives of our comrades, has bought us time. But we delude ourselves if we pretend that *Gr'Shuna* will long stand against Terran numbers and weapons. With the Beast now lurking in our skies, I fear that our time grows short as the winter sun. Our preparations are complete, and we have a short time before the Terrans' next attack. For the salvation of those we love, I am ordering the evacuation of the Planet."

Ga'Glish felt grief filling everyone around him. A consuming rage seized his heart, flooding it with a bitter hatred for all things alien and evil.

"But—Comrades All—this I promise you. Our day of vengence will come, when the Aggressor shall taste defeat. The blood of innocents shall rise from the grave to claim their Justice, and the Barbarians shall be put to rout!"

An animal cheer rose from the throats of his aides. Yet as his subordinates found the strength to prepare for death to protect the retreating population of *Gr'Shuna*, Ga'Glish found himself seized by despair.

Instantly, he purged himself of all such weaknesses. A leader could know no doubt, no lessening of resolve. But in a moment of sickening insight, the Lord Commander knew that their cause was all but lost. In the end, the Terrans had destroyed anything the *g'Khruushtani* threw at them. In the face of such barbarism, Science itself was but a eunuch.

He knew that such thoughts were unworthy of a leader. No matter how much he wished it, no matter how much peace surrendering to Fate might bring him, he also knew that he could not permit it. However hopeless their cause, he also knew that if they permitted this darkness to descend around them, his People might never know another sunrise.

* * *

THE GIANT PLANET loomed around them, dominating the sky like an alien god. The three Terran ships, circling a lesser moon and linked by subspace radio, were no more than insignificant specks in the newborn star system shielding them from the whims of the Great Cloud. Beyond the system's outermost planet, a small ionic squall had severed even low-frequency contact with the scouts scanning the space beyond. Waiting for the storm to subside, the three commanders held a council of war, each reduced to playing a talking head on another's video display.

It was their fourth such council since mooring in the system, and it was proving to be the least cordial of all.

"...and I'm sorry, Commodore, but I just can't understand it."

"Acch, Fitz— !"

"No, I'm sorry. There is no reason for us to be here. None at all, as far as I'm concerned. And begging the Commodore's pardon," Fitz arched his eyebrows and leaned forward toward the screen, his voice hushed and conspiratorial, "but it almost seems as if we're just trying to stay out of harm's way. Isn't that right, Ashton?"

Cook cut off Jeremy's answer.

"Your opinion is noted," Cook replied, in tones at once amused and patronizing, "but I'm afraid it's my opinion that will carry the day. And I regard any movement by us—now, with the enemy still combing the skies looking for us—to be rash and risky."

"Well then, what in Hell's name— "

"Certainly, we're under no great pressure to move. At least, none that I feel."

"But...."

"And the fact that we're so far behind enemy lines means that we need to be that much more careful when making any movement exposing us to enemy sensors."

"I can't argue with that, but— "

"I have been in this situation before, Captain. Well, not exactly this situation. Actually we didn't even know for sure that there was a war going on at the time, come to think of it, but that's beside the point. Even then, it was care and caution that brought us back to port."

Jeremy was about to mention something about the large rift in the Cloud that they'd found on the way back from Girshoona in the war's early days, but the conversation moved on before he could say anything.

"You think Command would have authorized the mission if they'd known about your timetable?"

Cook chuckled roguishly. "Operational tactics are the prerogative on the commander on the line, Fitz. And you know me. I never let details stand in the way of grander strategic concerns."

"Whatever the hell that's supposed to mean," Fitz snapped, "it damn well seems that we're just playing hide and seek with the enemy. And I bloody well know what Command would say to that, if you tried to sell it as one of your 'grander strategic imperatives.' "

"Fitz," Cook said, his head shaking beneficently, his voice dripping with tolerant smugness, "if we're supposed to be pirates, of a sort, then we have to act like pirates."

"Damn right, Cook! That means we attack!"

"No," Cook replied, pounding his desk for emphasis, his eyes as inflexible as his tones were reassuring. "That means patience—above all, patience."

Fitz opened his mouth to say something, but was cut short.

"And no foolish chances," Cook smiled. "An impatient pirate is a dead pirate. Remember," he raised his index finger." Patience."

"But...."

"Patience. *D'Artagnan* out."

As Cook's smirking image faded on the screens of his subordinates, Jeremy cleared his throat. He found it hard to inject his opinions into conversations between prima donas, but the exchange had crystallized some things in his own mind.

"You know, Fitz—, " he began.

"Thanks a bloody lot, Ashton," Fitz. "You were a big help."

"Well, you heard— "

"I sure hope ye fight a good bit better with your ship than ye do with your mouth."

Angrily, Fitz blanked his screen, without even the courtesy of a sign-off.

Jeremy cleared his throat again.

"*Morning Star* out," he said, wondering whether anyone else in the Cosmic Guard was so cowed by regulations as to sign off to a dark screen.

* * *

ONLY THE LIGHT from a single candle broke the dimness of the room. It was a ceremonial candle, lightly scented with the smell of Spring. In gentler days, it helped focus the senses at times of meditation. Today, Ga'Glish needed to be reminded of better times. As on many other recent days, his mind cried against the tragedy of life in an age of turmoil.

Today he would order the evacuation of his homeland. Whatever he might tell his comrades, or his mate, he doubted that he would ever walk the shores of home again.

The curtain parted, and Sra'Chengla entered into his sanctuary. His personal aide since before the war, the Young One had long ago found himself stripped of illusions, and now bore the heart of an old man.

"I am sorry to intrude, my Lord."

"Save your apologies," Ga'Glish intervened, a smile of politeness covering the wistfulness of his heart. "A commander has no Sanctuary from the present, Chengla."

The younger one bowed and took a seat on one of the ceremonial cushions across the table from his commander. The light, flickering from the unsettled air currents, cast dancing shadows over the face of the Tall One. Sra'Chengla felt his leader's anguish, even though the face of Ga'Glish was stoic and calm.

"Plan One is now in place," the aide said quietly. "We have redrawn the evacuation route to take the Convoy well out of the zone of danger, and shall keep ourselves between the enemy and our mates and children. Tracking the Cloud will add a week to their journey, but with the Beast loose in our skies, the added precautions are not unwise, Lordship. The new route toward Cloud's End should provide the added margin of safety you desired. It awaits only your order."

"How long...?"

"We will be ready in two dozen days. Perhaps sooner, if all goes as planned. And if the Terrans continue to regroup, rather than pressing their attack."

Ga'Glish closed his eyes in contemplation. Plan One required tens of thousands of Imperial vessels for its operation, yet was the least ambitious of the contingencies under Directive Twelve. It would take the children of *Gr'Shuna* to safety, along with the elderly and all females of child-bearing years. Close to a billion souls would be wrested from the world they knew and whisked into the interior of the Empire. They would be leaving behind mates and fathers, whose rescue would be left to an uncertain future and whose end would probably come fighting the Invaders on the soil of their homeland. To have ships enough to secure the evacuation against sorties from the Terran fleet until the Convoy was beyond danger would require recalling all the search ships, leaving a vast expanse at the mercy of the Beast. It would also mean placing everyone at risk, for they could never be certain where the One Called *Khu'ukh* might strike next. For the present, they were simply forced to compromise with reality.

"Order this date, from the Lord Commander," Ga'Glish said, with a firm voice and impenetrable heart; his aide took a transcriber from his waist pocket to record the directive from the Lord Commander.

" 'Evacuation Plan One is operational,' " Ga'Glish continued. " 'First priority is assigned to the evacuation of the Planet *Gr'Shuna*. All Imperial forces are directed to give fullest attention to their assigned tasks under Command Directive Twelve. All Hail our Grand Imperator—all unite for victory over the Aggressor.' Sign it 'Ga'Glish, a Son of *Gr'Shuna*.' "

Sra'Chengla bowed in acknowledgement. When he raised his head, he saw tears flooding the eyes of his commander.

* * *

SLOWLY, THE SKIES cleared around the bluish star that would one day bear the Crutchtan name *gla'Shenzhi-Khu'ukhtari*—"Hiding-Star of the One Called Cook." It quickly became apparent that the Crutchtan forces had withdrawn from the vicinity. Even the Terrans' most adventuresome scouts could not detect the faint soundings of active enemy subspace radar, or any other signs of an enemy presence lurking beyond the range of detection. A few days later, the *d'Artagnan* and her two companions began moving slowly through the fog of the Great Cloud, inching forward toward clearing skies.

Coming about just outside the Shunite Prominence, the Terran ships moved steadily east, tracking the edge of the Great Cloud and hugging its outermost wisps for concealment and protection. For days, they sailed, seeing no signs of life, until at last the Cloud swung sharply to anticenter and they faced the crystal skies at the western rim of the vast Crutchtan Basin, opening toward the very center of the Crutchtan Empire. Eighty parsecs east of Girshoona, they were the first Terrans to see the end of the Great Cloud, and the first to see just how close Terra was to final victory. However awkward the Terran battle lines moved when navigating the currents and eddies along the Cloud, the Terrans were the masters of clear skies. And once past the Grand Bend, nothing but clear skies would stand between their starships and the Crutchtan homelands.

Venturing tentatively into the clearing, the Terrans had a matchless vantage to detect the movements of enemy ships moving west, toward the battle, or east, toward the rest of the Empire. Finding a modest star some twelve parsecs center-south of the Cloud, the three Terran ships swung into orbit around a planet with oceans filled with frigid salt water and floating continents made of ice. From there, the most feared and hated Terran of the age would launch his final effort to bring the war to an end.

His own mind raged against the blindness of his superiors for altering plans that, he realized now more surely than ever, would have forced the enemy to sue for peace. Now, he was hatching ideas that were different still than those he had brought with him.

* * *

IT WAS LOVELY, in a heartbreaking way, thousands of lights moving in the darkness. Through eternity's silence, the fragile hulls began their long journey, filled with countless souls who were leaving the only home they had ever known.

"Lord Commander?"

Ga'Glish turned from the observation window toward the sound of his aide's voice. The lights from the hallway poured through the open door, casting a carpet of light onto the plush flooring of the viewing room. Ga'Glish blinked his eyes to bring them back into focus.

"What is it, Chengla?"

"I am sorry to intrude."

Ga'Glish smiled sadly. He clapped his hands to summon the room lights. "It is unimportant, Young One. Today is a day none of us shall forget."

Sra'Chengla nodded, but kept a respectful silence. At last, the Tall One's thoughts returned to more pressing concerns, and the aide felt his leader's resolve return.

"You have news from the Front?"

"Our scouts report that the Terrans are still regrouping, with more reinforcements arriving with each day that passes. Estimates vary widely on the time before they are ready to attack again. When they do it will be with increased strength."

"Our reinforcements should be ready as well," Ga'Glish remarked. "With luck, we shall have the convoy escorts back with us as well. Yet it is not like *Khu'ukh* to decline the chance to press an advantage. I suppose that we can do little until the longnoses are ready to strike. But I do not like it."

"Our own forces increase in strength daily, said Sra'Chengla. And the evacuees should be well beyond the zone of battle by then. Luck is with us, Lord Commander."

"Luck is an unmated lady," Ga'Glish smiled sadly. "She bestows her favors as she pleases."

"Then it is only a matter of time until her fancy changes," Sra'Chengla bowed in reply. "We need only wait for her to drop in our lap."

"I hope we do not all die waiting, my young friend—as well we may, if we do not court her more actively. Even a courtesan needs prodding, from time to time, in order to find the proper lap."

Walking toward the command center, the two men passed the Concourse of the Ages and the Fountain of Victory. As their footsteps echoed over the floor and across the hallways, Ga'Glish was at ease with himself for the first time he could remember. It was almost liberating, he thought, though he doubted that the feeling would last. The cruel realities of what his life had become would, he feared, be deferred only for a short time. But for now the women and children of *Gr'Shuna* were on their way to safety, his own family among them. And he had resigned himself to dying in defense of his home.

Chapter 15

G EYAAAAAA—!!!"
        Her mate's scream of terror ringing in her ears, Segusha raced
        to the controls. She arrived in time to see portly ts'Segu rise
        from the floor, the color drained from his neck and eyes.

"Segu— !" she began.

"Terrans!!—*Terrans!!*" screamed Segu, suddenly reanimated. His jowls fluttering wildly in terror, he pointed at the central monitor. Segusha ran to the viewer, where her own heart nearly failed her.

There she saw three ships, closing at speeds beyond their own instruments' capacity to discern. A quarter-unit distant, the power readings surged past all scales known to the merchant vessels of the Empire.

Segusha turned to her mate, who paled and fainted once again. She willed herself to signal their companion vessel and learned that they had also seen the demons lurking in the skies of home. And they were fighting the effects of panic, as well.

"Mother— "

Segusha turned to see Seguila and Sargai, her small ones, peering into the control room.

"Is something wrong? What is the matter, Mother?"

"Silence. Back to your cabins, both of you." Segusha started toward them, clapping her hands loudly as she walked.

"But— "

"No arguments. Return to your cabins! At once, do you hear?"

As the small ones scurried back toward the living compartments of their vessel, Segusha turned the radio to the emergency setting. Small and slender as she was, she suddenly felt the strength of a bull saurus rising within her. Behind her, ts'Segu rose to his elbows, then to his feet once more, then staggered toward the forward control panel.

"Distress—distress," Segusha called into the speaker, on the emergency channel. "Three Terran vessels, reading Twelve-zero-twelve-nine-seven. Please acknowledge."

As Segusha repeated her message, over and over, she began to feel quite ill. Life on a merchant vessel had never been easy for her. The cramped quarters made her long for the blue skies and warm shores of her native land, and she constantly regretted mating herself to the simple fool who shared her bed and enjoyed her favors. She never tired of reminding him of the pleasant life she abandoned the summer she lost her senses to love, and succumbed to her own fancifully romantic notions of life among the stars.

Of course, that was when ts'Segu was a handsome, dashing star pilot, long before his growing girth made her forget her fanciful notions of being carried off like a heroine in a children's myth. Now her mate's livelihood threatened to kill them all. Now the Terrans were upon them!

"What shall we— "

"We are changing course," hissed Segusha, her eyes fixed upon the three images growing ever stronger on the monitor screens. "We must lose them somehow, and hide until they are gone."

"But we cannot...it is impossible...."

"Tell me nothing of impossibilities, Fool. It is impossible for the ships of the longnoses to be where they are. They are a hundred units to the East, you told me. We shall easily have a safe passage, you told me. To bring delicacies and knickknacks to the Forces and return with pockets filled with riches, you told me. But our instruments do not lie. The Terrans are all but upon us. If we do not act quickly, we are lost."

"Give me the wheel."

"I shall keep the wheel. You can barely navigate through the center of a door well, let alone bring us safely to harbor. Confer with your friends in our brother vessel. Perhaps you imbeciles can devise the means to save us. I am too busy trying to change our course setting."

"Permit me to— "

"You have locked the controls! How are we to— ?"

"My Pet—a minor adjustment—permit me— "

"Fool! How are we to escape if you have disabled the controls?"

As Segusha flailed at his hands, Segu reached over his mate's shoulders and unblocked the computer. Soon, the vessel returned to manual controls. Placing his hands on the wheel, he began a steeply banked turn, narrowly missing their companion ship, whose pilot had similar notions.

"They are upon us!" screamed Segusha, pointing to the observing panel behind and to her right.

Clearly visible in the darkness through the viewing window, three bright balls loomed in the darkness like glowing apparitions. To her left, a small flicker from their companion's weapons briefly glimmered in the heavens, followed by a brilliant flash of light from one of the Terran pursuers. In a heartbeat, the fiery remains of a dying ship lighted the sky, as the Terrans destroyed the other ship in the small merchant convoy.

"Aiyee—we are lost!" Segusha screamed, her voice crackling with animal terror.

From behind her came a dull thump, where her mate had fallen into a heap on the floor.

"*MORNING STAR* REPORTS that they have moved to seal off the lane of retreat," reported Mathison. "Captain Ashton says that the enemy vessel is holding course. And Captain Fitzgerald wants to know why— "

"I don't care what he wants to know," Cook fumed. "The order is to hold fire. That goes for everyone—including the *Magellan.*"

"Incoming message...it's the *Magellan.*"

Cook sighed harshly. He didn't notice the small smile of pride dancing across his helmsman's lips. He only knew that things were not going at all as he'd planned. In fact, this first operation was turning into an altogether Isitian hash. Perhaps it was better to have it out now.

Actually, he thought, there was no real alternative to having it out now. Besides, his best ideas often rose from the flames of some disaster or other.

"Put it on the screen, Lieutenant, and hail the *Morning Star* as well. We may as well get everyone's perspective on this.

"Aye, sir."

Soon, a glaring Captain Fitzgerald filled half of the main communications screen. The other half showed a fidgeting Jeremy Ashton, who looked very uncomfortable.

"Opinions, gentlemen?"

Jeremy opened his mouth, but it was Fitz's voice that filled the *d'Artagnan's* bridge.

"Have you lost your bloody mind, Cook?"

"Settle down, Fitz," Cook snapped. Too late, he realized that putting this discussion on the main screens had been a blunder of the first magnitude. He should have adjourned the conference to his office, where they could have it out in private. His bridge crew, eyes wide in amazement, looked embarrassed and worried as the commanders tore into each other. Cook figured that the effect was the same on the other ships. This was probably exactly how they'd do it on Isis, he mused, but it was too late to do anything about it now.

"Settle down?" Fitz hollered. "Settle down? The devil to settling down. Do you have any idea of the risks we're taking, this far inside Lizardland? You brought us all this way—through bloody clouds—circling dead hunks of rock until we're dizzy as a Demetrian gold-digger. Now you want us to hold fire while you consult your bloody Isitian navel? I mean—my God! What are we doing here, if not trying to cut their bloody supply lines?"

"That's enough, Captain," Cook said angrily.

"No that's not enough."

"That's enough—unless you want to be relieved of your command here and now."

After a few more seconds of grumbling, Fitz had calmed himself enough for Cook to have his say.

"I think it only fair to tell you," said the commodore, his eyes narrowed, anticipating the eruption he was sure would follow, "that I have serious reservations about firing on civilian vessels."

"Oh, for the love of tripe!" Fitz groaned.

"Commodore." Jeremy's face was weary, almost resigned. He'd seen Cook in this mood before, and knew just how little good arguing would do. "With all due respect...."

"Good God, Cook!" Fitz shouted, his face starting to redden. "What the Hell are we doing out here?"

"We are disrupting enemy shipping." Cook said through his teeth.

"Then we damn well better kill something! I mean, my God—how disruptive can we be if all we do is jump out from behind an asteroid and yell 'Boo!' every now and then?"

"Just let them man their lifeboats before we fire," said a voice of reason from the d'Artagnan's helm station. The ship commanders were all too busy discussing the matter to pay any attention.

"We already have a rather embarrassing advantage in forces," Cook said, coldly, "I do not intend to sink to the level of a cutthroat like Chadborne Wilkes. Besides, we don't need three starships to overpower unarmed civilian freight haulers."

"Unarmed??!" Fitz protested. "I took a bloody shot right to my Number Two shield!"

Cook glowered menacingly at the screen.

"Not much of one, granted. But it was still a shot."

"I will not let us degenerate into a band of pirates— "

"Then let them take to their lifeboats," Janet grumbled. Her impatience was growing by the minute. She found that whatever vicarious thrill she felt at her commander's civility was being crushed by the weight of his thoughtlessness.

"And as long as we're still half-way through our first raid," Cook continued, his eyes narrowing fiercely, "it's as good a time as any for us to set some rules of engagement."

"Rules of—? This is a bloody war, Cook! Or have you quite forgotten?"

"Lifeboats— , " Janet snarled.

"Nevertheless, there's no need to kill civilians." Seeing Fitz's eyes bulge in fury, Cook was quick to add: "Not unless we have to—not unless they fire on us first. We can make that clear right here and now, to this ship and to any that follow. If they fire on us, we destroy them—quickly, and without reservation. But if they surrender immediately, we will...."

"We'll what?"

"We'll...well...we'll let them escape in their lifeboats. Or whatever damn emergency facilities they have in Crutchtan ships...and let them go on their way. After destroying their cargo, of course. Then we can fade into space to await another day, striking terror into the hearts of the enemy and landing another blow for the good guys."

Fitz and Jeremy winced in tandem. Obviously, further arguments would be useless, but both had deep misgivings about what they were about to do.

Janet was livid.

"Well, gentlemen, any last comments?"

Seeing Fitz open his mouth, Cook was quick to close the discussion.

"Good! Glad it's settled. That's why I wanted all this talk out in the open. Air out our differences and all that. Work out our goals with a feeling of camaraderie. Team spirit and all. Good for morale."

Ignoring the exasperated looks on the faces of those around him, Cook ordered Mathison to clear a hailing channel to the Crutchtan ship now surrounded by the three starships.

"Hailing frequencies open, Skipper."

"All right," Cook said, pounding his armrest for emphasis. "Helm, hold her steady."

"Gee, sir," came the reply from the helm station. "Wherever do you get all these clever ideas? Or is that where they come from on Isis, as well?"

"Miss Mathison, let's see who we've got on the other line."

"Aye, sir."

"And Mendelson, let's not be quite so snippy, shall we?"

HER MOUTH DRY as desert sand, Segusha helped her mate to his feet and fought the urge to panic. The paleness of her mate's eyes told her that she could expect little help from him. Until he steadied, it would be all he could do to keep his balance.

"Mother...."

Segusha spun around, her voice trumpeting urgency.

"Back to the cabins."

"But— "

"Back to the cabins."

"Mother!!" screamed Sargai, her eldest. "Look! The screen!!"

Segusha turned to face the main viewer and nearly fainted herself.

The screen bore the hideous image of a long-nosed simian. Its face was the scowling countenance of a nightmare, its eyes the glowing embers of a demon. Her own eyes widened in fear. She felt the color drain from her face, and her last meal started rumbling ominously in her belly.

Behind her, she heard the dull thud of her mate, falling to the floor once again.

"Help your father to his feet," she whispered softly. "And then return to your cabins."

"Mother— !" Sargai called, his voice trembling with fright.

"At once!" she hissed, hoping that the firmness in her voice would give her courage enough to face the longnose.

"MATHISON?"

"The translator is engaged, Commodore. They should be receiving."

Cook cleared his throat, preparing to have a go at establishing contact. The two Crutchtan images on the screen stared back dumbly, like stone statues. He smiled and nodded his head. Pushing the translator button, he spoke slowly and deliberately into the translator, as he had once done in the Governor's Palace on Girshoona.

"Hello."

The console lights glared from all sides like spotlights on a stage. The Crutchtans simply stared silently from the screen. Undaunted, Cook pressed ahead. He knew that the other ships were monitoring his transmission. He hoped he wouldn't sound as foolish as he felt.

"This is Commodore Roscoe Cook of the Terran Cosmic Guard, commanding the Starship *d'Artagnan*." The Crutchtans made no reply, but Cook noticed that the green slits on either side of their necks had paled considerably.

"As you know," Cook went on, "our people are at war—which, I'm sure you agree, is a tragedy of cosmic proportions, but...."

Janet coughed loudly, and shot him a look that would have soured a ton of sweetener. Outwardly undaunted, Cook changed the thrust of his remarks.

"In any event, our mission is to interdict enemy shipping. I am afraid this means that we will have to destroy your vessel."

With a dull thump, one of the Crutchtans fell out of sight, toward the bottom of Cook's screen.

"We regret this inconvenience— "

"Oh, for crying out loud," Janet muttered; Cook frowned at his first officer and pressed on.

"But we do not wish to cause unnecessary civilian casualties. As we have the time needed to avoid needless killing, we will permit you to evacuate your ship before we open fire. We would have afforded the same opportunity to your companion ship," he continued, struggling to find the coherence in what was still a rather shaky affair, "but they chose to fight, rather than surrender."

The impenetrable stare from the lone remaining Crutchtan made Cook uncomfortable. He swallowed, wondering whether it had been a mistake to undertake visual contact, but quickly dismissed the thought. He hated the thought of scuttling the vessel like a common pirate. And it was too late for second-guessing, anyway.

"Even so," he continued, staring directly into the eyes of the remaining enemy civilian, "we cannot permit you to delay leaving your ship. We expect your people to come with reinforcements soon, and we must not dawdle ourselves, in getting on with our mission. We can give you only five of our minutes to gather your belongings and abandon your ship. I suggest that you hurry."

Suddenly the screen went dark; the Crutchtans had broken contact. Cook had no idea whether they had understood him, or what they meant to do. All in all, he thought, this was turning into rather a sloppy operation. Disjointed. Out of focus. And altogether too Isitian.

But Cook couldn't indulge his own doubts for long, for the communications monitor didn't remain dark. The electronic ghost of the Crutchtan's image had barely faded from the screen when Fitz flashed onto the viewer.

"All right, Commodore—!"

Cook cut him off.

"We have five minutes," the commodore said coldly, the steel returning to his voice. "If you want to discuss the matter, we'll do it in private."

Before Fitz could utter a word in protest, Cook rose from his seat and bounded toward the door.

"Mendelson—with me. Dexter—take the chair."

ONE OF THE lighting panels flickered on the ceiling. It was a common defect in starships, caused by a wiring robot somewhere in Eastern Terra that had been running short of conducting fiber at the time of manufacture. Janet had seen it the last two times she'd been in Cook's office; she wondered how long it would take him to notice.

She settled into the plush visitor's chair, beyond the line of sight of the communications viewers, and listened to the three commanders haranguing one another. She was coming to regret her impatience with the Skipper. Not that he didn't deserve it. If he ever bothered asking her opinion, there were a thousand things he should be doing differently. But for all his other faults, and however painful it might be for himself or those around him, he really did try to do the right thing. After seeing the fire in his eyes when he took a stand for something he believed in, she found herself fighting against a flood of old feelings.

"So what do you think, Jeremy? Is he completely crazy, or has he just misplaced his mind again?"

"Well...."

"Look," sighed Cook. "This is our first interdiction. I want us to do it right."

"Then don't go getting squeamish on us. Right, Jeremy?"

"Well...."

"And I want us to settle on a policy for handling civilian vessels. Eventually, I'll want us to separate. We can disrupt a larger area if we're not clumped together. But I won't have us losing the discipline or cohesion that comes with fighting as a unit."

"You know what I think?" Fitz squinted. "I mean, no disrespect intended—but you know what I think, Cook?"

Cook leaned back in his chair. Janet caught his eye, and he smiled as he winked at her. "Not that I could really stop you from telling me," he said, turning his attention back to the screen.

"You've just got too much to worry about in that head of yours to think straight. There's so much bouncing around up there that your brain fritzes out on us, every so often. Like an overloaded computer."

"I suppose that's more flattering than many other explanations I've heard, Fitz."

Janet heard the sound of Captain Fitzgerald's rough laughter coming over the monitor.

"Really, I'm serious Cook. You've too much on your mind, and your head is already filled with all that trivia. You just have trouble pulling it together, sometimes. You can't keep it all from crashing. That's why you go daft on us, every now and again."

Cook chuckled amiably. For now, he would play the diplomat, he decided. It was not the time to pull rank. "Well, Fitz, practicalities do throw me, sometimes, I suppose."

"And now that you've seen the error of your ways...."

"Well, not quite," Cook said, looking Fitz straight in the eye. "For the time being, we'll just muddle along without killing any more civilians than we need to, and see whether that slows down the war effort."

"You're a stubborn man, Cook. I wish you'd listen to reason."

"Reason's singing us the same tune, Fitz," Cook said, his eyes twinkling mischievously. "But as long as I'm in command, we'll use the Isitian version of the lyrics."

"Come again?"

"We'll do it my way."

"I want the record clear— "

"I'll note our difference of opinion in my log, Fitz. If you like, I'll even draft a formal order outlining our engagement policies on civilian merchant vessels."

"I'd appreciate it, Maestro."

"*D'Artagnan* out."

As the teleconference ended, Cook sighed and rose to his feet, stretching his arms and yawning. Janet thought he looked tired. But since the war started, he rarely looked well-rested. He walked to the large star map in the anteroom; Janet stood and followed.

The anteroom was dark, except for the illuminated, spherical map, now set for the local skies. Cook stared intently at the points of light, each denoting a nearby star. Around the edge of the sphere, dominating the western edge, the Cloud glowed like burning embers. Janet approached until she was beside him, but said nothing. After a few minutes of silence, she turned to leave.

"Don't go."

Janet stopped and turned to face him. "I wasn't sure you wanted company."

"I wasn't sure you cared what I wanted."

The frosty look on her face told Cook he'd said the wrong thing.

"Sorry. That was a thoughtless thing to say."

He returned his gaze to the star map, his brow furrowed deeply. Janet came to stand beside him.

"It's been a long time since I've had anyone to talk to. Not since Jeremy left. And not for a few weeks before then."

She stared straight ahead, afraid that he was about to open all the old wounds again. But his next words were in a soft tone of voice that she'd almost forgotten.

"What do you make of this, Janet?"

She noticed that he used her first name; he hadn't done that very often. Since their last days aboard the *Constantine*, she could count the times on the fingers of both hands. And she remembered all of them.

"What do you mean?"

He stared straight ahead, his thoughts buried under a facade of intense concentration. She could tell that something was deeply troubling him. He might be an enigma, and a particularly mulish one at that, but she still knew him better than anyone else. Perhaps, at times, even better than he knew himself.

"We have them at our mercy, you know," he said at last. "We can blast the poor devils to kingdom come. And Lord knows, whether they live or die makes no real difference to us, or to the war."

"But we were once in the same spot, weren't we? And the Crutchtans were civilized enough to let us return home."

Cook turned to face her. She saw the troubled eyes of a gentle philosopher who once captured her soul and captivated her mind.

"You agree with Fitz and Jeremy?" he asked softly. "You think we should just blast away, then vanish into the blackness? It makes more sense tactically, I suppose. Exposes us to less danger. And it would probably cause a good deal of panic among the natives, at that."

Janet took a deep breath, and felt the years melt away like dew before the sun. "A friend once told me never to be ashamed of my own sense of humanity," she said.

Cook turned to face the glowing lights of the star map. Janet felt the full weight of the past crushing down on her shoulders, and wanted to cry. She looked at Cook's face—the brow furrowed in thought, the distant eyes that could see through everything—and wondered what new mysteries she would find, if times were different, and she were given the chance again.

It was several moments before he spoke. "That friend was very young," he said at last. "And the times were very, very different."

Suddenly, the page signal sounded. In an instant, Cook was at his desk, pressing the intercom.

"Cook here."

"We have movement from the target, Commodore." It was Mathison, from the bridge. "They've separated from the cargo bins, moving away at flank speed. Captain Fitzgerald wants to know if he can do the honors."

"That vulture," laughed Cook. "Tell him that it's my mission, and he's already had the first kill."

"Aye sir."

"Tell Dexter to stand by; Mendelson and I will join you right away. Out."

"Before we go," Janet said, stopping Cook as he began his dash to the bridge, "answer me one question."

"Sure."

"I can't believe that you would have given no thought to the prospect of blasting civilian ships to kingdom come."

Cook started laughing, a lusty laugh of the sort she'd missed for longer than she cared to remember. It was good to see, she smiled—though after a second or two she thought it would be nicer to have him take her question seriously.

"And I don't think for an instant that you could have sold this mission to the brass if you told them you were going to let any Crutchtan spacers go, whether they fired first or not."

"Now that you mention it," Cook smiled mysteriously, "I suppose it does seem a bit odd, doesn't it?"

"Well?"

"Well, what?"

"Don't get cute with me, Skipper."

"The truth?"

Janet nodded.

"Well, cutting the enemy's supply lines was always an objective. It was—and it is—a worthy mission. Well worth the risk, even by itself."

"But?"

"I suppose I did lose a few details to hazy thinking while concentrating on my other plan. This is Plan B, after all."

"And?"

"And the original plan called for ten starships."

"Skipper!"

Janet's flaming eyes told him that she was in no mood for further teasing. Cook squinted and scratched his ear, but decided he was having too much fun to stop.

"So?" she demanded at last.

"So?" Cook stiffened his back proudly, as if the explanation were self-explanatory. "I was hoping to find the Cloud pretty much as we found it, tailing off just past Girshoona, providing a clear shot into the heart of Crutchta. And I thought that, once past the front, we'd find that the Crutchtans are without reserves to speak of. I guess we'll never really know for sure. At least, not for a while. Though, of course you know that— "

Janet's eyes narrowed angrily. "*Skipper—*!"

"Well, sailing ten starships into the middle of Crutchta would have carried the war right into the enemy's homeland. It would have forced them to choose between calling their fleet back from the front to meet us, or letting us roam freely in their home skies. Or so it seemed to me, anyway. Unmolested, we could lay siege to five or ten of their planets, until they sued for peace. If attacked, we'd destroy whatever forces they sent to meet us—at least, within reason; ten massed starships would let us deal with quite a lot of bother before we ran into serious trouble, you know. And it would open up the front to attack by our main fleet. But whatever we found, we'd have forced them into a strategic crisis. And it would have ended the war within a matter of weeks."

Cook pounded his fist into his open hand for emphasis.

"At least I think it would have. I guess we'll never know for sure."

Janet paled, her eyes wide with amazement.

"You mean..."

Cook laughed roguishly. "Well, it was just a thought."

"But— "

"And you know, regulations do give the line commander the discretion to take the initiative, so I really wouldn't have been disobeying any orders. Not technically, anyway—though I suppose making a hash of things might have gotten me into a spot of trouble, even with Admiral Clay. But when we finally got here it seemed that three ships gave us too small a margin for error, so I just trashed the whole thing and moved on. Except, of course, there were still a few details to sort out. Things should go more smoothly next time."

Her wits still reeling, Janet shook her head in disbelief. She was about to say something when the page signaled once again.

"On our way," Cook said into the speaker. Hurrying off at once, he paused just outside the door to the bridge.

"Coming?"

The door caught Janet on her way out of the office. Startled, she waited for it to open again before racing after Cook onto the bridge.

* * *

IT WAS QUIET in the Room of Discussion. The lights of the tactical holograph were many-colored dots on the face of fa'Shenali. Beyond, in the dim underlighting, he sensed befuddlement, tinged with traces of fascination. Soon, all would be darkness and silence, all except for the lights of the holograph, and the sound of his voice. He smiled to think that if he was not about to make them understand at last, then at least he had gotten their attention.

"What is it that you will be telling us, fa'Shenali?"

Shenali turned to face his interrogator; for once, he heard no derision in the voice of Dra'Lengish, the Chief of Tactics. For the first time, he sensed genuine interest, laced though it was with a healthy dose of confusion.

"I will be saying little that is new, Subcommander. I am asking only that we approach the problem in a different way."

"Is that not using different words to say the same thing, Subaltern?"

"I will leave you to judge such matters, Subcommander," fa'Shenali replied, smiling at the humor he sensed welling in the crowd. He paid little notice to the page who came running down the aisle to whisper something into the Lord Commander's ear. But he felt a deep disquiet to see Ga'Glish visibly pale before rising from his seat to race up the aisleway toward the door.

Too disciplined to let such passing matters deter him, he began his presentation. The page, meanwhile, remained to pass his message to selected others in the assembly.

"We all know that the One Called *Khu'ukh* has earned his reputation for daring at the cost of much *g'Khruushtani* blood," said fa'Shenali, sensing the distress rising within his listeners. "Yet, if we watch his forces in motion, we can see the contours of his thoughts and watch his plans as they emerge. Pay heed...."

Shenali pressed a button, and the holograph sprang into motion again, the lights of Terran and *g'Khruushtani* forces swirling about the enclosed spheroid projection like the trailings of rival fireflies.

"I am sorry, Subaltern." It was Dra'Lengish, who had risen from his seat to interrupt.

"A question, Subcommander?"

"I am afraid this meeting is cancelled," said Dra'Lengish. He raised a hand to silence the murmurs of perplexity.

"This ship is now under a Class-1 Emergency. Everyone is directed to return to his station and await instructions."

"What is the matter, Lord Lengish?" called a voice from the middle of the assembly.

"The details are still uncertain," replied Dra'Lengish. "But it appears that the One Called *Khu'ukh* has surfaced again."

The murmurs began again, this time with undercurrents of distress. Dra'Lengish breathed deeply and continued, his voice calm and firm.

"We have an unconfirmed report that three Terran starships have attacked and destroyed a convoy of civilian merchantmen in the skies off Cloud's End."

Fa'Shenali did not hear the rest of what Dra'Lengish had to say. The subcommander's words were drowned in the chaos that gripped the room like a sea of madness.

Chapter 16

WE HAVE REPORTS of rioting in the streets, Lord Commander."

"Enough."

"And the Convoy groupleader is still pressing for details. All he hears over the radio— "

"Enough, I said!" hissed Ga'Glish. Fury in his eyes, he turned to face Dra'Lengish.

"Surely some word of encouragement or comfort— "

"Silence!"

"I am sorry, my Lord, but— "

"Sorry?" Ga'Glish thundered imperially. "With less regret and more outrage at Terran banditry, perhaps the Empire would not be teetering on the brink of ruin. Go—!"

Ga'Glish stretched his arm toward the Monitorium.

"Go and do something useful, Dra'Lengish. Find us something to erase this latest Terran trick."

"My Lord— "

"Go discover some bit of magic to send the longnoses scurrying for home. And if such alchemy eludes you, my fine Chief of Tactics, then return to your models and your simulators and stay there until you find me a way to explain to the People exactly how the Imperator is going to make the Terrans disappear."

"But, my Lord— "

"*Begone!* – or I'll send you home in chains."

Leaving his anguished Chief of Tactics on the verge of tears, Ga'Glish stormed down the broad Common Corridor, heading toward his morning briefing in the Analysis Section. The Flagship was buzzing with rumors and on the verge of panic. Ga'Glish stepped quickly down the corridor, keenly aware that all eyes followed him as he passed. As miserable as his life had become, the past few days had been the worst. Each day brought new word of another attack by the Terran bandits;

each day pushed his homeland further toward the madness of animals. He had no doubt that inflicting such horrors had been the Beast's purpose: terror was an effective means of disarming one's enemies. Yet Ga'Glish could not comprehend a creature like the Terran monster—one who could inflict such torment upon those who had once offered him friendship.

In the back of his mind lurked the same dark fear that haunted everyone: the Convoy. Alone in skies infested by the Terrans, the Convoy was now at the mercy of one who had shown himself merciless. Whether the One Called *Khu'ukh* would destroy it outright or hold it hostage was barely a thought to those below. The panic gripping the planet came from the same horror that had seized the High Command. From the moment *Khu'ukh* had made civilians his targets, *Gr'Shuna* became expendable.

Ga'Glish took refuge from the prying eyes of outsiders behind a large, brass door that shielded the Analysis Section from the rest of the Flagship. He leaned against the wall, his forehead resting upon a blinking direction indicator, his soul aching with each flash of light.

It was his own incompetence at work, he told himself. Whether through negligence or wishful thinking, it had been his incompetence that forced the choice upon them. Now his own ruthless objectivity made him feel just how painful a choice they confronted.

They could try to defend *Gr'Shuna*, or they could move to protect the Convoy. They could stand fast, fighting to deny *Gr'Shuna* to the enemy; or they could move to insulate their children and females from the Terran Beast who lurked like death in the unprotected skies of the Empire.

Ga'Glish harbored no illusions that they could do both. Though it would mean sacrificing his homeland, there was no doubt about the course they would pursue. Yet it grieved him to give such an order. His mind filled with visions of the millions he would be condemning to slaughter at the hands of barbarians. As he had many times in the past few days, he found himself weeping like a doddering old grandmother.

It would never do for his subordinates to see their leader in such a state, he kept telling himself, until at last anger at his own weakness was enough to overcome his shame and despair. Composing himself, he rose to his full height and headed down the hallway toward the Room of Information, hate and fury flooding every fiber of his being.

* * *

COMMAND DIRECTIVE

TO: All Command Officers
FROM: CosGuard Chief of Staff
Date: cc:144-3597.6
Re: Command Reorganization

Following final implementation of the Central Command Reorganization Plan outlined in Command Directive cc:144-3580, it is my intention to examine the feasibility of realigning the entire command structure. All staff officers at the Theater, Regional, Division, and Wing Command levels shall prepare a written report, outlining their major duties and responsibilities, together with an evaluation of all personnel under their direct command. All command officers of the line are instructed to begin keeping and forwarding weekly summaries of their activities to their Regional Command officers. These reports, together with any evaluations received, will assist the Command Staff in determining future assignments, and shall be kept as a distinct and separate entry from the official Ship's Log.

All command officers are hereby notified of the formation of an Executive Liaison Committee, consisting of the CosGuard Chief of Staff, the President's Chief of Staff, and the Chairman of the Senate Governmental Affairs Committee. This Committee is now responsible for collating information, formulating policy recommendations for the President, and expediting any matters deemed necessary or prudent for the War Effort. All command officers are ordered to cooperate in all respects with any and all Committee inquiries, and to provide whatever assistance the Committee requires. In addition, anything in the Manual of Administration or Protocols of Command notwithstanding, all Theater Commanders, Security Agencies, and Prison Administration Command officers shall, until further notice, report directly to the Committee, through the Chief of Staff.

Ft Adm W.W. Weatherlee
CosGuard Chief of Staff

* * *

"NEXT GROUP, stand at the ready."

The words sounded harshly in the earphones of Shl'Lanasha. Stepping up to the loading platform, he looked up, through the airless sky. The stars glowed like bright embers, filling the heavens with a dusting of light. He looked eastward, along the rocky horizon of the moon he was about to leave forever, and thought of the son he might never see again. Shl'Glisen, now the sole pride of his heart, was still living in nightmares, thought Lanash. For all he knew, the poor boy would never outlive the terror of his dreams, or the horror of seeing his mother butchered before his eyes by the Terrans. He still remembered the spot among the stars where the Convoy had faded into nothingness, and it drew his eyes now. He grew sick with the knowledge that he would not be there to ease his troubled son toward manhood and that, if something dreadful happened along the way to safety, he would not be there to ease his passage into eternity.

The shuttle door opened, and Lanash stepped inside, moving quickly to take a seat by the window. The vessel was crowded, and soon every seat was taken. He looked in vain for the rest of his company, but the hold was wide and his view of the interior was limited. Though it would have been nice to have a friendly shoulder beside him, there would be time to rejoin his friends when they reached the planet.

The warning signal sounded, and the shuttle shuddered under the weight of its thrusters. Shl'Lanasha gazed silently outside as they rose from the ground, heading for the transmission station that would send them down to *Gr'Shuna*. As his vantage of the moon increased, he saw the fortifications and massive blasters radiating in all directions from the launch station. He saw for the last time the gleam from the tiny, fragile pressure suits of those who would be left behind, assembled in formation to salute those like Lanash who were leaving to join Lord Glishek in defense of their homeland.

Lanash felt his eyes growing weak as he watched them wave at the last shuttle. Those remaining on the moon would man the large guns and massive fortifications built as the planet's first line of defense. Though it passed unspoken, everyone knew that these outer fortifications would be the first line of defense shattered by the Terrans when they finally attacked.

Like everyone around him, Shl'Lanash tried to avoid the thought that those staying behind were doomed. But as the shuttle rose higher and higher in the airless sky, the fortifications began to look smaller and smaller. And Lanash knew what they all knew. The defenders on *Gr'Shuna's* moon would only be the first to die in defense of the planet; it was beyond hope that they would be the last. Like Lord Glishek, all viewed surrender as unthinkable. They had each heard the stories of the Terran death camps. And they were resolved to die, rather than see *Gr'Shuna* suffer the shame of Terran atrocities.

* * *

THE ATMOSPHERE was tense in the Fleet Command briefing room. With the new theater commander finally named and installed, many of the old timers had been given their walking papers. New arrivals would be taking over their posts any day. But even as the new staff aides were busy scurrying to and fro, it fell to the old veterans to set out the day's incoming data, and to explain to the new Briefing Officer what it all meant. Having to watch the greentail desk jockey present it all for their new commanding Admiral galled the old timers ever more.

"What is your summary, Commander?"

Lt. Commander Rex Wolfe cast a cold smile at Commander Jennings, Admiral Wright's old staff aide. Carefully concealing any gesture that might reveal the slightest hint of emotion, Jennings turned his head and focused his gaze at Miriam Wright's replacement. It never ceased to amaze the old spacer how cruel life could be, but he'd be damned if he'd give the brash newcomer the satisfaction of lording it over him. It had taken Wolfe nearly an hour to collate the most routine set of reports that Jennings had seen in more than a month. And Jennings had to explain it all to him anyway, once the idiot refused to listen to anything his senior yeoman had to say. All things considered, Jennings reflected, he'd prefer supply duty back home to watching his replacement mangle some of the more sensitive readings, helpless to stop the young fool from making life miserable for the most talented and dedicated staff he'd ever worked with.

"Commodore Jones' final analysis is that the Lizards are still pressing their counterattack, pushing our initial thrusts back," said Wolfe. "The Intelligence report is different: CSO indicates a massing of ships on the eastern rim of the star system. If we didn't know better, I'd swear they were about to launch an attack in the opposite direction."

"Your evaluation?"

"I don't know what to think, Admiral. But I can't believe they're abandoning the planet. Not without a fight."

Admiral Medwick rose from his chair, and moved to stretch his legs. It was a knotty puzzle he thought. The lizards were tricky, but not tricky enough. Maybe for his boneheaded predecessor, but not for him. They wouldn't draw him out. Not before he was ready.

"Continue preparations, Commander," Medwick said at last, resuming his seat. "We'll launch our attack on Girshoona on schedule. In five weeks, not one second sooner. Inform Jones to keep up the pressure, as best he can."

"Aye, Admiral."

Wolfe saluted, then turned sharply and left the room.

Medwick watched the young aide disappear, then cast his eyes about the silent, sullen faces that surrounded him. It would be a relief when his own people arrived, and he no longer had to rely on aides whose loyalty might be less than absolute. If it took a few more weeks, then so be it; certainly, the lizards weren't going anywhere. Besides, it had been a long time coming. A long time before he'd finally gotten a battle command of his own. He was determined to let nothing stand in the way of a victory. And if it meant waiting until Third Fleet Command was staffed by people he could trust, then they'd simply wait.

* * *

COOK PACED about the bridge, impatient as a clockwatcher in a sweatshop. It was enough to put his whole bridge crew on edge. The crew was used to many of his idiosyncrasies, but this was something new. For the past three days, it had fallen into an unsettling routine: every hour on the hour, he paced the bridge, waiting for the scouts to report their observations. Each time the next report arrived, he grunted and left in a minor huff, disappointed by the results.

This batch promised more of the same. Nine of the first ten squadron leaders showed clear screens; even Squadron Eight showed the Crutchtans leaving the zone at flank speed. Before long the hour's last reports were logged into the *d'Artagnan's* records.

Two indicator lights flashed on the control screen at the communications desk. Mathison sighed, her ordeal nearly done. She had little doubt that the incoming messages would be disappointing. These days, the Skipper dripped disappointment wherever he went. But it didn't really matter; soon he'd leave, muttering something unintelligible under his breath. And then she'd be free to summon her apprentice, and catch some needed sleep in her quarters.

"Reports from Sectors Six and Twelve, Commodore," she said, struggling to keep the weariness out of her voice.

"Yes, Lieutenant?"

"Ensign Targas reports that enemy shipping has disappeared from her sector," Mary read from her screen. "No contacts in the past ten hours.

Even her squad's active sensors report no activity within range. Apparently, the three ships they'd spotted all turned tail and headed back East."

"And Twelve?"

"Shaw reports some strange readings coming from the West. He wants to take half his squadron a few parsecs past his zone limit to investigate."

"Radio approval," said Cook, his brow furrowing intently. "And order *Morning Star* into Sector Twelve for support, just in case."

Turning in her seat at the helm station, Janet looked at Cook and winced. From the systems desk, Dexter looked up curiously.

"You think they're going to detach a force from the Girshoona?" asked Janet. "Is that what all this fretting has been about?"

"The thought had crossed my mind," said Cook.

"But with a major battle looming to the West— " Janet interjected.

"And no reinforcements coming from the East— " Dexter continued.

Cook held up his hands, palms outward. "Indulge me."

"But—?"

"Dexter, run a new cross-check on the duty rosters of all three starships. I want some fresh blood in the scouts. It's been a week since we sent the current batch out, and I don't want them getting stale."

"Yes, sir."

"I'll be in my quarters, Commander," he said to Janet, rising to his feet.

"Yes, sir."

"Call if anything develops. Otherwise, I'll be back in a couple of hours."

"Aye, aye."

Striding from the bridge to his cabin, Cook knew that he was making everyone nervous. He couldn't help it; he was getting nervous himself. He knew he wasn't being completely honest with his senior staff, or with the rest of his crew. But he wasn't sure he was right. Until he was certain, he wasn't about to share his real concern.

His cabin door whooshed open. Cook walked to his desk and plopped in his chair, listening to the sounds filtering through the walls: Mendelson chattering away on the bridge; a yeoman bellowing down the Conning Deck corridor at some malfeasant; the whirring of the cleaning drones as they scrubbed the tiles on the floor below.

There were infinite variations on how the Crutchtans could respond to what he'd done, Cook thought. In the end, they distilled down to two:

they could run the blockade, or they could try to break it. It astonished him to think that they'd already chosen the latter. Withdrawing all civilian craft from the sector suggested they'd be coming after him in force, even if it meant losing Girshoona without a fight. And it implied that destroying him was more important to the enemy than a planet full of their own people. That was something he hadn't expected.

It was a compliment, in its own way, he smiled to himself, though he'd had similar compliments before and could have skipped this one without feeling slighted in the least. He only hoped that Fleet Headquarters had the wit to make the most of it.

Chapter 17

THEY RAN IN lockstep down the paved streets, their feet sounding as one, their minds locked into place by the hypnotic rhythm of their pace. Surrounding them was little of the world they had left a brief cycle earlier. As Regiment Blue plodded along, toward a still-unknown destination, it was like running through a graveyard of shadows from the past.

The manicured gardens along the wide boulevards had grown wild and unkempt. No longer did the city echo with the laughter of children, nor ring with the gentleness of females. To the left a building burned out of control and untended, for none had the time to squelch the fire. Garbage littered the streets along the ancient houses of the aristocracy, and vermin from the forests were finding homes amid the refuse. Wherever the soldiers looked they saw chaos.

Shl'Lanasha kept his eyes focused ahead. So long as he concentrated on his duties, his heart beat as one with his comrades. But whenever he permitted himself a sideways glace he saw an unspeakable horror in the eyes of his countrymen, and could feel their consuming terror.

His helmet and body armor were light, nearly as comfortable as bathing in the warm summer sea. They had taken the design from some garments found on a dead Terran in the early days of the war. Though the clothes were as alien as the longnoses, it had been a simple task to adapt them to the needs of the *g'Khruushtani*. The visor on his helmet adjusted to the light, permitting him to see the warmth of those around him in the darkness. Coveralls the lightness of air swathed his body; yet woven into the fabric of his armor were threads of an alloyed metal that gave his clothes strength and resilience, shielding his vital organs from all manner of projectiles. Like the others, Lanasha did no know where they were headed; they knew only that they had been ordered to the edge of town. And so they ran in unison, as they had been trained to do, giving as little thought to what they saw as to the air they breathed.

Down the boulevard they ran, oblivious to the distant scuffles and screams that followed their passage. Up the Hill of Remembrance, they continued past the perimeter of the Old City and out the ancient Gate of Judila, away from the sea, toward the hills and forests to the west.

As the sun reddened and set, the onset of darkness found them running still. As the creatures of the night stirred from their rest, and began their daily labors of survival, Regiment Blue found no rest. There was only the dull rhythm of two thousand soldiers, plodding onward, twelve abreast, to the call of night beetles and the lonely screech of the raptor.

* * *

Fo'Rendish struggled to keep a stoic calm. He knew the importance of his task, and strove to do it well. But having One of Importance watching his every movement made him uneasy. When such a One was also the Lord Commander, uneasiness could not help but affect his performance.

"Well?"

The monitor watched his instruments, waiting until the motion sensor made another sweep of the screen before venturing an answer.

"All remains clear, my Lord."

"You can see nothing?"

"Not from this distance, Lordship."

"Not even the Convoy?"

"No, Lordship."

"Have you used all of your instruments, Monitor? Can we not raise them on our screens by using more sophisticated methods of detection?"

The young Monitor sighed deeply, and repeated the answer he had given a dozen times before, to officers whose rank and importance had increased with each duty cycle over the past two days.

"We are in low frequency radio contact with the Convoy, Lordship. They are still beyond the range of our most sensitive instruments. And they still have not encountered the Terrans. Until they do there is no reason to disclose our presence, or theirs, by using our active sensors. Passive observation will do just as well."

"I would prefer additional readings, Monitor."

"Please allow me my professional judgment, Lordship."

"But the difference in sensor range— "

"The Convoy is alerted, Lordship," fo'Rendish said, more sharply than he had intended. "Their scouts are combing the skies for any trace of the longnose bandits. It is unlikely that the Terrans will be able to come upon them undetected. And you surely must remember that the Terrans possess sensing devices of their own. If we probe the skies too aggressively for them, they will detect the probes long before we detect the Terrans."

"You are certain of this?"

"Yes, Lordship."

Ga'Glish bowed and turned to go, the sensor soundings echoing in his ears. He knew that the monitor was right, and felt foolish for having troubled the young man. Yet he ached to think that they were helpless in the face of Terran atrocities, that as they sought to cut across the Gulf of Shuna he could do no more than pray that the Terrans did not find the Convoy before help arrived.

He strode down the corridor toward the Intelligence Section. Such a crisis called for action, he thought; he would not accept their own impotence in the face of impending disaster. Whatever it took, he would find a way to intercept the longnoses before they could murder any more Small Ones. Before they destroyed the last shreds of the heritage and traditions of his home.

* * *

"ALPHA LEADER, acknowledged. This is the *Corona*--go ahead *Dauntless*."

"Chandler? Is the channel secure?"

"Yes, it's secure."

"Anyone else— "

"No one is within earshot and I'm alone in my quarters. What is it this time, Detwiler?"

"You hear the latest order?"

"Same as the last one, isn't it? Hold position and await instructions? What's the problem?"

"Are you serious? Just what the fuck is headquarters thinking? We get the lizards on the ropes, and what do they do? Leave us farting around till we're too fat and lazy to do anything. For all his other faults, at least the Old Man wasn't such a snort. But I guess the Waddler wants us as dull and dim-witted as he is. Reminds you of DemCom, doesn't it? What the hell you think we should do about it?"

"Watch your mouth, Detwiler. The Brass doesn't take kindly to ridicule these days."

"That's why..."

"Why the secure channel? Sheesh...paranoia becomes you, Detwiler. It blends in with the rest of your personality."

"And so we sit here like saps. And all because— "

"We sit here because we're ordered to sit here."

"You're no fun anymore, Chandler."

"I'm sick of it, David. Sick of watching friends die. Sick of having nothing to look forward to, except trying to keep from getting killed."

Soon the channel went clear, and another security message took its place. For the longest time, Chandler sat alone in his quarters. His mind was numbed by all he had seen in the last cosmic year—the narrow escapes, the blinding flash of death in the heavens, the war that went on as endlessly as the Clouds and skies around him. Even his hatred for the lizards had all but left him, replaced by a mindless routine that deadened his senses and killed his capacity for outrage.

Soon he rose from his seat and left to tend to his rounds. The door opened, and he stepped into a world of familiar faces and sounds. The corridor teemed with crewmen going about their duties. A cleaning drone nearly bumped into him, coming to a halt and sounding its warning horn less than an inch away from his leg. A ship was a way of life, he mused. Its rituals and diversions dulled the awareness that in other realities, existence could be as different as shadows were from sunshine.

In its own way, he smiled bitterly, war was the same.

* * *

"NEXT!"

Lanash stepped through the circle of fellow soldiers into the center of the ring. Numbness coursed through his body. The blood-green sand felt soft beneath his feet, and he shifted uncomfortably from one foot to the other. He stared silently at the small wooden post that faced him, a few paces away. Soon the circle parted, and he heard the throaty protests of the woodland animal that two soldiers were dragging by the neck into the makeshift arena. As the drillmaster fastened its leash to the post, Lanash took several deep, reassuring breaths and looked at the animal now bleating at him, loudly and pitiably.

"Shl'Lanasha!" commanded the drillmaster. "Take the ready!"

Lanash drew his dagger from its sheath and crouched low, looking into the animal's frightened eyes. Forcing himself to be strong, Lanash fought the urge to empty his stomach on the ground beside the terrified beast.

"Your home is in ashes and your mate's entrails are filling a barbarian's stomach!" hissed the drillmaster. Lanash felt hate gnawing at his belly, and his mind was on fire.

"Listen to my voice," the drillmaster continued. "Death is a phantom and the longnoses are but shadows of evil."

Lanash felt the fire of passion and lost all sense of time and self. He never heard the command to halt, stopping only when two of his comrade's physically grabbed his arms and held him fast against their bodies.

Looking down, he saw his chest covered with his victim's lifeblood. The creature's shredded remains were scattered across the circle. Led away from the exercise ring, behind the mutilated carcass of the dead animal, Lanash felt his heart reawaken, and could feel it pounding thunderously in his breast even as his belly weakened. Falling to his knees, he bent over and emptied his morning meal onto the sandy ground. As his companions helped him rise to his feet, he felt his legs give way. His head floated lightly over his body as he struggled to remain conscious in the face of a growing faintness. He did not hear the drillmaster's harsh voice sounding behind him.

"Next!"

* * *

THE SMALL audience in the Briefing Room stirred visibly. Fa'Shenali could sense their growing excitement, a single thought growing stronger, much like a snowflake starting its fall from the mountaintop.

"So it is your belief— "

"It is not a belief, Lordship," fa'Shenali interrupted, "so much as a theory. Whether it proves correct, of course— "

"I understand, Subaltern," said Ga'Glish. "But your idea brims with wit as well as promise."

"Thank you, my Lord."

"Do you know the range of their sensors?"

"Lordship?"

"From what distance will they be able to detect our active probes?"

"No one knows with any certainty, my Lord. My guess would be that their range is approximately the same as ours—twelve units, more or less.

That is how long it takes for the signal to fade into the background noise of the galaxy."

Ga'Glish thought a moment. They would have to be careful. Too many probes might make it easier for the longnoses to sense a trap; too few might make the bait so hard to perceive that the Terrans might never notice. But the idea itself....

Ga'Glish rose from his seat and began to pace. The logic of fa'Shenali's plan was flawless. Searching for new merchantmen to attack, the Terrans would be looking for any signs of activity in the sector. Active sensor probes from the fleet—not many; just enough to make the Terrans aware that ships were headed toward them—should draw the Terrans away from the Convoy and toward the relief force.

Then they could set their ambush for the Beast. A few ships in the middle, to serve as bait, surrounded by the bulk of the *g'Khruushtani* fleet, concealed by distance or shoals, or wisps of interstellar gas. When the Terrans attacked, the *g'Khruushtani* would surround and destroy them. The Beast and all he symbolized would die in flames, and *Gr'Shuna's* future would reach haven, beyond the reach of the murdering Terrans.

And if the witless longnoses surrounding the planet delayed their attack long enough, the Fleet might even return soon enough to repel the attack on *Gr'Shuna* itself.

"The plan is brilliant," Ga'Glish said.

"Thank you, my Lord."

"Your commander salutes you, One Called fa'Shenali. And your people owe you a Grand Debt that is beyond measurement.

"Come!" Ga'Glish gestured grandly, his arm sweeping full circle and coming to point toward the archway leading to the tactical computers. "Let us see just how cleverly we can plot to reclaim our debt of blood from the longnoses."

Cheers ringing in his ears, fa'Shenali bowed proudly, and watched as the assembled High Commanders converged on their leader, their voices brimming with excitement. Yet as others thrilled at thoughts of victory, secret and treasonous doubts clouded the subaltern's mind. The One Called *Khu'ukh* was slippery and unpredictable, and Legends told of the brave one who died, eaten by a seashark while trying to catch a fish with his own bare hands. He could assign it no reason—and if reason governed their lives, then his doubts were little more than madness. But as others felt the thrill of budding triumph, fa'Shenali felt the coldness of disaster lurking unseen in the darkness.

Chapter 18

T HERE IT IS again."

"Where?"

"Look at the screen—two o'clock. Right there."

"Where?"

The panel lights flashed an alert on the command console. The young ensign, seated in the pilot's chair, glanced about. A look of confusion filled his clean-shaven face.

The grizzled old yeoman, assigned as the small ship's co-pilot and navigator, had all he could bear. Wearily, he rubbed his eyes and tried to control his temper. Flanagan's beard was as scraggly as the summer fur of a wild tree cat from his native Ceres. He'd spent his whole adult life as a Cozzie greenshirt, rising to the rank of Yeoman Chief by hard work and toeing the line. But for the third time in the last two days he was on the verge of strangling an officer. It was one thing to endure a tyro's foundering in the comparative safety of home. At least on a mother ship, there were others to keep the greentail in his place, and plenty of help within the sound of a voice. Now they were a half-dozen parsecs from the nearest friendly face. He couldn't afford to let this rookie test his wings by trial and error.

"You're hopeless, Finley," he snarled, leaning over the young blueshirt's shoulder to activate the scout's command computer.

"Two o'clock?" Finley squinted at the subspace radar, his eyes searching for a small dot that would reveal an enemy position. He was embarrassed at missing the diffuse, cloudy readings that had caught the yeoman's eye.

"Computer on," barked Flanagan.

"Computer working..."

"Log entry, cc:144-3796.9: 'Subspace radar reading, heading 557, south 020; origin unknown. Will request permission to investigate.' End entry."

"—acknowledged."

"Flanagan— ?"

"Quiet !"

"Log entry confirmed."

"Flanagan!"

The yeoman turned toward his nominal commander, exasperation burning in the pit of his stomach. "All right, Ensign—you do know how to work the low wave transmitter, don't you?"

"There's no need to get sarcastic, Yeoman. I am fully certified on Class-E scouts. I just wanted to tell you that I saw it, too."

"Right…well, we're going to check it out, anyway. That is, Mr. Ensign Tyro, unless you have some objection. You blip the message to *Morning Star*, while I start setting the controls."

"Uhm…"

"What is it?"

"I can't find the codebook."

"Aaach! Finley, you're hopeless."

* * *

AS THE young blueshirt and his yeoman navigator began searching for signs of movement, a lonely sentry gazed upward, at the clear night skies of *Gr'Shuna*.

It was a bad dream, thought ls'Shen, gazing at the stars that had seen him grown to manhood. A raptor-of-night passed overhead, her prey shrieking as she held it in her cruel talons. The rustling wind brought a chill to the air. Shen covered his shoulders with a blanket, and drew closer to the warmth of his watchfire.

Fate—the Fate of the ancient myths and the Sacred Teachings—could not be so unkind, he mused. The light from his fire danced across his face, like spirits of the damned. Civilization was precious, and as fragile as a whisper of love. Surely, the ascent of the *g'Khruushtani* from barbarism could not be as dust in the wind, to be blown and tossed like sand along the shore. One day, rather than shivering in the night, he would wake to the warmth of sunshine, and all would be as it was. Fate would be revealed as the creature of myth, puckish and fickle, but mistress to the needs of all.

He glanced at his timepiece: it was nearly midnight. Another would soon take his post, and he could return to his cot to sleep. Yet the moments hung like timeless stars. After endless musings in the darkness, and an eternity spent shivering in the cold, another glance at his timepiece showed it to be nearly midnight, once more.

* * *

COOK LEANED back in his chair, staring at the ceiling. Seated across from him, Janet and Van Horn were listening intently to the voice from the communications speaker. The crackling of interstellar static blurred the voice, but not enough to disrupt the message. The scouts they were using as signal relays might not be as sophisticated as the standard relay buoys, but they were functional enough.

"It appears to be a small convoy," said Jeremy from the bridge of the *Morning Star*, nearly five parsecs east and toward galactic center. "Its current heading would bring it around the horn in another week, if we let it get that far."

"Ye said your point man is a rookie?" teased Van Horn. "The pilot on our forward scout is a bloody tyro? That's how serious ye're taking our mission, Jeremy?"

"I made sure he had a good crew," came the reply.

"A Demetrian, then?"

"Well, he's half-Ceresian," Jeremy laughed. "Though I did take a lead from the Skipper and bend the rules a bit. I gave him a yeoman for a navigator."

"We'll make a skipper out of you yet, Ashton."

"Not to belabor the point," Cook said, suddenly sitting upright in his chair, "But you said your scout detected them—how?"

"Sensor echoes," said Jeremy. "The Crutchtans were using probes to make sure there weren't any shadows lurking in the dark. The scout just honed in on the signal."

"Dumb lizards," scoffed Van Horn. "Excuse me, Skipper—but that's just about the dumbest thing I ever heard tell of."

"Actually, Mr. Van Horn," Jeremy interjected over the radio, "I've heard stories about a certain chief engineer's last leave on Looking Glass— "

"Hush, Ashton," bellowed Van Horn. "There's a lady present. Besides, ye were there yourself."

"I'm surprised you remember that," Jeremy laughed. "In fact...."

As Jeremy and Van Horn exchanged quips and insults, Janet watched Cook carefully. He seemed distant and withdrawn. It was obvious that the commodore had long since stopped paying attention to anything being said. The furrowed brow and intense eyes told her that his mind was spinning with activity. She had no idea what he might be thinking; he just sat in his chair, rocking back and forth, back and forth. Soon, Janet was queasy with motion sickness.

Quite abruptly, the commodore signaled the end of the transmission, and ushered Janet and Van Horn out of his office. As they walked down the corridor, passing crewmen rushing about as they saw to their duties, Van Horn was puzzled and slightly offended by Cook's sudden aloofness.

"And at the end of it all," he said to Janet, as they walked toward the on-duty officers mess, "I don't even see what the bloody problem is. I mean, we've been waiting for the lizards to show themselves. Now that they have, the obvious choice for us is to investigate—and then attack the buggers."

Janet laughed softly. For all his gruffness, Van Horn was a kind man. But without Jeremy on the staff, and with her own particular problems with the Skipper, Van Horn was now getting stuck dealing with Cook's moodiness and eccentricities. It was apparent that Van Horn had neither the time nor the patience for it.

"I don't know, Van," she sighed. "Skipper rarely sees things so simply. Sometimes I think he spends all day dreaming up solutions where nobody else can spot a problem, just to be difficult."

She didn't want to tell him that she'd seen that look in Cook's eyes before: distant, self-absorbed, lacking its normal mixture of mirth and condescending humor. It usually meant that he was getting ready to do something goofy.

Something really goofy.

* * *

"THERE'S SOMETHING coming over the channel."

At the sound of his commander's voice, Yeoman Sergeant Kevin Ward briskly turned his chair to face the viewing screen. Activating the advance station's monitor, he leaned back to view the incoming report:

INCIDENT REPORT

CC:	144-3801.2
FROM:	CommJMJones
TO:	FleetCom, Third FleetHQ
Code:	<<Omicron>>
Flags:	Yellow1;Yellow2;Red3
RE:	Arena Status, Girshoona

Girshoona sector reports continuing Enemy resistance on all fronts. Terran casualties remain significant: one Starship, one Cruiser, six Frigates lost to date, along with scores of smaller vessels. (See prior reports, filed under code <<Omicron>>). This date, major casualty was Frigate F D Roosevelt, lost with all hands during skirmish near Silverman's Star; enemy losses included two Class-B warships, and a dozen smaller support vessels....

"You know, Commander," said the crewman, pressing the button to pass the information along to Fleet Command, through the established channels. "I can't help wondering why they don't just attack and be done with it. Seems like the lizards are doing all right, picking off our ships one by one. Why not just rush the bloody planet and take the fight to them?"

"Can't say I disagree, Mr. Ward," replied Jim Jefferson, the commander of the monitor station at Liberty Base 223, who was filling in for the regular Quarter Watch radio officer. "But that's a decision for the Brass. And with the state of things back at CentCom, I doubt they'll be issuing any orders for a while longer."

"Aye on that, Commander."

"Carry on, Mr. Ward. I'll be in the Office, sorting through the mess the last crew left us."

"Yes, sir."

* * *

BEYOND THE outer hulls of their ships, the stars hung in the distance like burning gems. A series of makeshift relays linked the starships across the twenty parsecs of open space that marked the Terran blockade line; Fitz glared across the void, his anger filling the communications screen. In the awkward silence, the tension was growing more poisonous by the second. Janet shifted uncomfortably in her chair in *d'Artagnan's* conference room. Alone with her commander, the security scrambler made sure that only the captains and their first officers would be discussing the decision Cook was announcing. She had a good view of both screens, and neither junior commander was taking the news well at all.

Actually, she reflected, she didn't like it much herself. But arguing with Cook was like trying to reason with an avalanche.

Finally, the *Magellan's* commander broke the ice.

"This is the stupidest thing I ever heard."

"Your opinion is noted, Captain Fitzgerald."

"*No!*" Fitz thundered; the thud of his fist on his desk was felt even aboard the *d'Artagnan.* "You don't get off that easily, Cook."

"Captain Fitzgerald— "

"We've been out here risking our necks behind enemy lines for what? Eight weeks, now? Maybe three weeks since we split up to patrol different quadrants. And what've we got to show for it? Eight merchant vessels. One bloody kill per week for the whole lot of us. And not their crews, mind you, just the ships themselves. We let the lizard crews waltz away to come after us another day."

Cook glared at the screen, cold fury on his face, his jaw locked hatefully as he listened.

"This mission is a failure, Cook. A complete failure. A bloody disaster of the first magnitude. If and when we do get home, my report won't spare you a single detail, do you hear me? Not a single one."

"Are you finished?"

"Finished? I'm just getting started!"

"Captain, when we get home you can make whatever report you wish. But as the ranking officer on this mission, it is my judgment that carries the day. And I've heard just about all the caterwauling I care to endure."

"So with the first contact we've had in days, we're going to turn tail and run? And why? Because you're getting skittish. Have you forgotten what the hell we're doing out here in the first place? Or have you just lost your stomach for a fight—like the rest of your prickless breed on that flower-garden you call home."

"You forget yourself, Captain," Cook said, glaring at the screen. "And your inability to reason under pressure does not commend your opinion as something worth my attention."

"So that's it, then? We're just— "

"You have two hours to recall your scouts, or arrange a rendezvous," Cook interrupted, his voice cold and unforgiving. "You will then plot a course to Hatfield's Star, where we will rendezvous ourselves. If you're not there in three days—either of you— "

For the first time since the transmission began, Cook glared at Jeremy, who visibly started.

"I will relieve you of command, and you'll spend the trip home in your own brig. Understood?"

"Yes, sir," replied Jeremy.

"Do you read me, Captain Fitzgerald?"

"Yes, Commodore."

"*D'Artagnan* out."

As the faces on the screen began fading into black, Janet saw Fitz's face redden with rage. She hated listening to the commanders squabble. She felt awkward, almost resenting Cook for the challenge to his own authority. She couldn't see the logic in his decision, either, and winced at the thought that he might ask for her own opinion. It wouldn't do the slightest good, of course; when he was like this, nothing anybody said would change his mind. But it would force her to choose sides, and she didn't want to get caught in the middle. Not again. And certainly not with him in this cantankerous mood. It was almost a relief when the question finally came.

"You agree with Fitz, don't you?" He leaned back in his chair, hands locked behind his head, a mischievous, taunting smile on his lips. Janet turned a deep crimson.

"You think," he sat upright, a hint of resignation in his voice, "that we should intercept and attack."

Janet took a deep breath, then looked him straight in the eye. Not for the first time, and despite all the pain he had caused her, she was grateful for his ability to see into her soul.

"Yes, I do."

"Well," he sighed, "all of you may be right, and I may well be running away from phantoms."

"Then why?"

Cook smirked, hoping that his bittersweet laughter would not be misunderstood. As good a first officer as she was, Janet could never fully outlive the past. Actually, he thought, neither would he—but then, where Jeremy would be content to state his opinion, Janet felt the need to convert him to her point of view. Despite himself, Cook smiled, he often felt the same way. As far as Janet was concerned, it was probably for the very same reasons.

"Where is all the civilian traffic?" he asked.

"What does that have to do with— "

"Why would the Crutchtans go to the trouble of clearing space for twenty parsecs in all directions of all traffic, radio transmissions, even sensor echoes...and then suddenly, out of the blue, start broadcasting active sensor probes? Calling to us like a beacon. Doesn't that strike you as the least bit odd?"

Janet shrugged blankly. Cook smiled to himself, aware that nothing he said was making sense to her.

"Well, I don't know either. But I do know that if I were about to clear a zone of enemy vessels, I'd make damn sure that all of my own people were out of the way. And I'd want a whole quadrant to myself, a place where anything moving that wasn't mine would be the enemy."

"So you think— "

Cook turned his chair to look at the observation screen, and watched the passing stars.

"I don't know what to think, Commander. I don't know if we're being invited to an ambush, or whether the Crutchtans are just getting careless. Or whether Fitz is right after all, and I'm just losing my nerve. But I won't retreat east, because I can't know what might be coming up from the Crutchtan heartland. And I won't take us center-west, because it seems that's exactly where they want us to go.

"So," he spun about to face her again, his voice resuming its peremptory tone of command, "we are coming about, heading anitcenter-west. We'll use the Cloud for background cover until I can figure out what's happening. If that means inching our way back to our own lines, so be it. But something is happening. I can feel it in the shadows. Until I can explain it to myself, I won't even try explaining it to anyone else."

Janet looked to see a great sadness flash across his face, appearing just for an instant before fading into the self-confident smugness that he projected to the rest of the universe. For just a moment, through all the bluster and posturing, she saw the little boy inside him—a boy who was quite alone, and frightened by the realization that he was very different than everyone around him.

"Except for you," he added, his voice reaching for a cockiness that Janet no longer found convincing. "But I'd rather you didn't tell anybody else about this conversation."

Janet nodded quietly. She didn't know whether he was right or wrong; she knew only that, despite herself, she wanted to cry. And that no matter what happened, as long as they could be together, she would never be the one to let go.

The thunder rumbled distantly overhead, and the wind fluttered against the side of the tent. Janet felt her heart beating wildly, as if she were one with the storm outside and soaring with the wind. Her pulse slowing, she moved to turn over, only to find her arms, still reaching past her head, being held gently against the tent floor. Arching her back, she stretched lazily, smiling at the light, playful touch that greeted her belly.

What was she doing? she asked herself. Her head was still swimming, and she wasn't sure she wanted an answer. They'd waited too long on the beach to head for cover before the storm hit, but didn't care. Her leave was over in two days, and she knew she'd never see him again. But something about the stranger with the odd accent was eerily familiar. Something about his manner made her think she'd known him forever.

"You're sure we've never met?" she whispered, wriggling her tummy beneath his free hand.

"I'd remember," he answered.

"Does everybody really call you 'Skipper?'"

"Only my friends. My enemies have other names they like to use."

Janet laughed languidly, her attention elsewhere.

"My parents called me 'Scooter' as a boy. That's one of the reasons I joined the service. Well...not really."

"I didn't think so."

"You're quite a mind reader."

"So are you, Skipper," Janet purred lowly. "Oh—I do wish you didn't have to leave so soon."

"I've already changed my plans."

"But you're due back tomorrow."

"I'm the Skipper, remember? I change my plans whenever it suits me."

"And it suits you?"

"It suits me quite nicely, Missy."

Pinned firmly to the ground, Janet arched her back, her head soaring above the thunderclouds and reaching toward the stars.

Chapter 19

*B*LIP.

The lights from the corridor cast shadows into the dimness of the Monitorium.

Blip.

A breathless silence filled the great room. Only the radar sounded, transfixing all with the dull rhythm of yet another circuit.

Blip.

For twelve days they had watched their instruments scour the heavens, searching for the slightest trace of the enemy. For twelve days, the green lights of the screen had danced across the faces of monitor after monitor.

Blip.

"Still nothing?"

The technician started as the voice behind him broke the spell. He relaxed to see a familiar face, peering over his shoulder.

"Nothing, Subaltern."

"Have you checked the augmenter?"

"Only moments ago. We remain linked to our forward surveyors, and all instruments show optimum efficiency. If they are out there, they are as shadows in the night."

Rising to his full height, fa'Shenali breathed wearily. They were living on the edge of knives, he thought. Things were not going as planned, and the past dozen days had brought no news and little rest. The Terrans could not have missed their signals, yet if the Beast were going to appear he would have already attacked.

Fa'Shenali knew that something had gone wrong. He longed to know what was happening. Yet each passing hour brought only pain, and his ears still rang with the angry words of his Lord Commander at their last briefing, moments earlier.

"Anything," Ga'Glish had cried, as he slammed the meeting table with his fist. "Anything would be better than this endless waiting."

All at the table agreed with him.

They were soon to find out just how wrong they could be.

* * *

"FLANAGAN?"

The old yeoman stirred in his seat. "Sorry, Finley. I must have dozed off." The lights in the control room were dimmed. As his wits returned, Flanagan glanced out at the stars and noticed that they had come to a dead stop.

"Look."

Finley pointed to the sensor screen. Rubbing the sleep from his eyes, Flanagan looked—then looked again, his mind jolted awake. Their subspace motion sensors were showing movement. It was slow and steady, but it was definite movement. Even at this distance, the mass readings were off the scale, yet the screen seemed to show a single object. It couldn't be a star: stars didn't move through the sky at speeds faster than light. Yet no ship could be that massive.

"What do you make of it, Chief?"

"Damnedest thing I ever saw," whispered the yeoman.

"That's why I stopped," Finley said, staring at the screen with a fascinated gleam in his eye. The lights from the console swept his face as the receiver swept the heavens.

"I was sure it was a misread, but it holds steady, even at 'all halt.' And I've double-checked all the circuits."

He turned up the volume on the speaker; Flanagan winced under the noise, until Finley adjusted the instruments to filter out most of the interstellar static. Then the old yeoman heard it: the rhythmic beeping of the radar—faint, masked by static, but unmistakable, sounding in tandem with the image on the screen. It confirmed the sighting; at least, it confirmed that the instruments were receiving something. What it meant was still a mystery.

"Looks to be anti-center west," said Finley. "Just past our zone of responsibility and heading right for us, as I've got us positioned now."

"Have you radioed for instructions?"

The ensign turned to look at Flanagan, his eyebrows arching mischievously. "In twenty minutes, it'll edge into our sector," he said.

"Then we can take a look for ourselves, without having to clear it with Captain Ashton."

Flanagan chuckled deeply. He had to admit it: young Finley was right. The captain was a decent sort, but had an annoying tendency to think problems to death. Give him a riddler, like this subspace anomaly, and he'd spend the next two days conferring with his command staff. In the end, nothing would be decided until ten seconds after they finally passed the buck to Commodore Cook.

No, the need now was for action. Waiting twenty minutes was a small price to pay for the right to investigate the matter themselves.

"What do you think, Chief?"

Flanagan scratched his beard and smiled to himself, then looked the blueshirt straight in the eye and winked.

"We can cut the time down to ten minutes if we fire our engines for a few seconds, Mr. Finley. At this distance from the anomaly it shouldn't give away our position. But she's your ship."

Finley beamed; it was the first time Flanagan had addressed him politely, the first time any greenshirt had shown him anything but contempt.

"Plot us a course, Yeoman, and stand by to engage the engines."

"Aye aye, sir."

* * *

"....AND SO, Lord Ambassador Drub'd and other distinguished members of the panel, it remains our steadfast and unalterable hope, on behalf of the Terran People...."

As the Terran prime minister droned on, prattling about planned improvements along the shipping lanes to the Glincian outposts, a signal sounded in Drubid's earpiece. He looked to the wings, and saw Fralama, the Official Confidante, motioning intensely and holding a yellow piece of paper. Drubid closed his eyes, wondering whether service in the diplomatic corps had ever been as lofty a calling as the histories described. Rising from his seat, he lightly stepped from the dais, heading toward the corridor.

Once outside, he found Fralama in a state of agitation.

"You won't believe it," the old man trilled, his mind in a state of perplexity. "It is an outrage, Drubid. An outrage of the highest order."

"Calm yourself," Drubid said sharply. He had come to appreciate many of Fralama's charms; the passing of years often brought a passing of faculties in its wake, but Fralama retained the remnants of a vigorous and active mind—at least, on his good days—and was an indispensable store of knowledge from days long past. Unfortunately, his many gifts did not include steadiness of nerves among them. The fact that the Embassy had sent one such as he to fetch him sent shivers of foreboding through his bowels.

"It is the Terrans again," he spat indignantly. "They have increased their demands once more. It is simply beyond belief, Drubid. Beyond all capacity for tolerance."

Drubid whisked him to the side, mindful that in the Terran capital the walls often heard tales that found pathways to unfriendly ears. "What do they want now?" he asked in hushed tones. The severity of his tone reminded the old man of the dangers that lurked in the hallways of diplomats.

"They demand the right of moorage," Fralama whispered intensely, his hands shaking under the weight of Terran insolence. "These barbarians insist that we permit their ships to dock at our outposts, and that we permit these—these—*savages*—to walk about on Glincian soil. Have you ever heard of such unmitigated gall? From a bunch of—of—simians?"

"Has the Government yet made a formal reply?"

"Formal reply? You mean...?"

"Have we made a formal reply to the Terrans?"

"— to the Terrans?"

Drubid breathed deeply to calm himself. He bore much affection for the old diplomat. But whenever the Official Confidante confided something, he tended to plunge the Glinci delegation into chaos.

"Has the Government replied to the Terran demands?"

Fralama spat vigorously. "Of course not—no! Never!"

"Let me see the Communiqué." Drubid motioned for the yellow paper, and was annoyed when it was not forthcoming. Snatching it from the trembling hand of Fralama, he read the message from the Capital for himself:

*to Fralama, High Confidante of the Synod of the Ages, Glincian House
of Munificence, in the Mode of Discretion and Highness of Purpose:*

GREETINGS:

Granting Terran requests for refueling rights along the Fiduni Perimeter
has led to new requests for the right to moor at Glinci bases, and for full
grounding rights on the settlements there for Terran nationals. Garola has
demurred, awaiting a convening of the full Synod for consideration of this
and related concerns.

Counselor Garola has noted that the refueling concession was made at
behest of Envoy Drubid, and requests his opinion on likelihood of Terran
satisfaction with the next round of concessions. Specifically, you are directed
to determine whether Drubid truly believes that Terran accommodation
is in our best interests, and determine for yourself whether further
concessions by the Government will dull or sharpen the simian appetite
for more. Also, you should discreetly inquire whether our Allies remain
willing to bear the attendant risks of continuing our clandestine dalliance
with Terra.

Independent confirmation of the latter point is requested, but not
required at present.

MINISTRY OF STATE SECURITY
Lenorsa, First Deputy Director

"Fools," whispered Drubid. He turned with rage in his eyes toward
Fralama.

The whiteness of age blended into the paleness of fright in the old man,
whose tongue was silenced by the worry that Drubid might take the
messenger to task for the message. But he need not have worried. Drubid
found Fralama too valuable a source of information to vent his anger on
the doddering old fool. Besides, his quarrel was with the Security Office,
whose meddling once again threatened to cripple the assertion of
Glincian interests.

The mongrels in State Security could barely see past the horizons of
the capital, thought Drubid. They were certainly incapable of thought
on the grand scale of the Elite. And things were more ticklish now than
at any point since the Outward Expansion had begun nearly a dozen
generations ago. The smallest misstep could bring the whole enterprise
crashing down upon their heads before their mission was fully
accomplished and the riches of the Cloud were under Glincian sway. If
that meant replacing the staff of the Security Ministry with more
malleable souls, then his superiors should be apprised at once. And if

Counselor Garola was being manipulated by those with their own selfish interests to advance, then it was time for the Ruling Body to intervene again in the Synod.

In the meantime, the Terrans were pushing things along far too quickly. If the Synod did not respond in kind, events would overtake them and the savages would seize the initiative. As long as Glincian science lagged Terra's in matters of destruction they would be at risk, for they could never bring the savages to heel. Not until they could make the barbarians understand that resistance meant terror, and submission alone brought peace.

"Come," Drubid said at last. "We have much to do."

"What? Much? What?"

"Come along, Fralama. We must reply to your superiors."

"You mean...?"

"Yes, I will help you draft your answer, Elder Fralama." Reassuringly, Drubid patted the old man's arm. "We must make them understand that we have matters well in hand, and that our initiatives are about to bear fruit. But first, I must tend to my duties here, and you must return to your own."

As Fralama trundled down the corridor, a chill of foreboding came over Drubid. He turned toward the meeting hall. He could hear the droning voice of the Terran, muffled by the thick, wooden door. The Terrans were giving them an opportunity, their best in generations. He hoped that the savages would not prove to be their undoing, instead.

* * *

"My God."

"The channel. Dammit, Finley—reopen the channel!"

"My God, look at them all."

"Mr. Finley!"

"Sorry, chief." The young ensign lowered his eyes toward the radio; in a few seconds, the speaker was alive with the random noise of subspace static.

"*Echo Bay*-One, this is *Morning Star*-7," said Finley, adjusting the fine tuner on his transmitter. "Do you copy? *Echo Bay*-One...."

The scout shuddered under the gentle whining of the engines. At one-quarter sublight power, they were engaged just enough to keep themselves going, while minimizing interference with the scout's finicky instruments. As his pilot tried to raise the relay ship positioned between themselves and the nearest starship, Flanagan gaped at the sensor screen. Each turn of the sweep hand sounded through the deck of the small ship, as the dull, metallic ping confirmed the contact.

But the contact wasn't what had taken the wind out of them, thought the yeoman. Not until they'd gotten close enough for a better look.

"*Morning Star*-7, we copy," came the reply. The voice was scratchy, though plainly discernible over the background noise.

"Do you have an update for us? Over."

"Roger, *Echo Bay*," said Finley. He cast a worried look at Flanagan. Neither wanted to imagine the worst, but a convoy this size could mean either of two things. One of them could spell disaster for all of them.

"We have a strong sighting of enemy vessels, bearing 730, heading right at us."

"How many and what kind? Over."

"We have no idea, *Echo Bay*, but the readings are off the scale. Repeat, off the scale. The computer cannot resolve separate images—repeat, at this distance, our computer cannot resolve separate images. But we show a massive movement of ships. So massive that we get only an aggregate reading that exceeds our measurement capabilities at this distance. Over."

"Hold the line, *Morning Star*."

The channel dissolved into static. Finley smiled sheepishly at his greenshirt navigator, who winked to buck up his pilot's courage and shook his head. A burst of turbulence whipped against the ship, nudging them slightly off course. They were nearing a small star cloud, still in the primary stage of formation, and their ship was small enough to feel the buffeting of the heavens outside. The static on the speaker billowed loudly. The young ensign found his courage sinking into his boots, afraid that space would claim their channel, leaving them without contact or instructions. For days they'd been alone, with only themselves and the stars for company. He'd never felt their isolation quite so keenly.

Soon, the disturbance passed, and over the channel came a voice that both men recognized instantly.

" --...--peat, *Morning Star*-7, this is Command Central, do you copy?"

Flanagan's eyes went white, as if about to pop from their sockets.

"This is *Morning Star*-7," Finley said into the transmitter, summoning all the poise at his command.

"This is Commodore Cook, *Morning Star*. Who's this?"

"Ensign Finley, sir." He strained to hear the voice on the speaker, over the intermittent static on the line.

"How well are you reading me, Ensign? Things are a little staticky on this end."

"The channel could be clearer, Commodore. But I read you just fine."

"Well, Mr. Finley, we seem to have a bit of a puzzler on your end, don't we?"

"Yes, sir. We sure do."

"They tell me you're moving ahead at sublight, not quite two parsecs from the contact, and that the source exceeds the mass and size of a Grade-C moon."

"Roger, sir. That's affirmative."

"Ensign, now listen carefully. It is very important that you get me accurate information on the composition and numerical size of the contact."

"Aye, sir."

"There are many things this could mean and a number of different ways to handle it. But it is absolutely vital to know what's coming before we commit ourselves. Do you read me, Mr. Finley?"

"Roger, Commodore. I understand."

"I want you to ease in, close as you can, and get me some numbers. If you can manage it, get some configuration readings from a few individual ships. Better than anything else, that will tell me if this is a convoy, trying to run our blockade—or an enemy fleet, sent to intercept us."

"Understood, Commodore."

"Now don't do anything foolish, Ensign. You're exposed and alone out there, and the nearest help is four parsecs away. Try to stay undetected. At the first sign of trouble, withdraw and reestablish contact with your mother ship. I'm redeploying the rest of our scouts to back you up in case things get rugged. And the starships are two days behind you, so there's no need for heroics. But you're on our foremost point, *Morning Star*-7. If we lose you, we'll be advancing blind—so we're all counting on you."

"I'll do my best, Commodore."

"I know you will, Mr. Finley. You and your crew have already proven yourselves capable and alert. I'm sure you won't let me down."

"No, sir."

"*D'Artagnan*, over and out."

"Over and out."

Static returned to the speaker, and Finley switched off the transmitter. His heart was soaring, and he needed a moment to savor the feeling. He looked toward the navigator's chair to see Flanagan grinning from ear to ear.

"Now that's one to tell to your grandchildren, Finley," the old yeoman laughed. "A 'well done' from Commodore Cook himself. We sure drew the brass ring on this one. Now all we have to do is keep from getting ourselves killed."

Finley beamed. "Heading 730, ahead one-half," he said. "Prepare to engage subspace engines."

"Aye, Finley, course marked and on the screen."

The young ensign felt himself swelling with pride. They were all counting on him, he thought. Commodore Cook was counting on him.

Whatever it took, Finley thought, he wouldn't let the Commodore down.

* * *

From the Trans-Terran Dispatch, 30 September 2555:

To the Editor, *Trans-Terran Dispatch*:

I have noted with some concern the continuing references in your fine publication to my Planet by certain "senior officials in the Terran Government" in terms carrying no small measure of disparagement.

It seems to me that if these "senior officials" do not wish to make their pronouncements in public, it might be kinder of you to spare these poor souls the distress of making them in private. Given the intemperate nature of their remarks, I am sure it would cause them no end of embarrassment if their identity were revealed. They seem to have quite enough trouble on their hands these days, after all, and eliminating this source of worry might permit them to concentrate their attention on ending the War a bit sooner.

IRENE N. McINNIS
Chancellor, Isitian Senate

* * *

THE TROUBLES of home passed unnoticed among the fleets and forces in the East. And events were soon overtaking the players in the skies east of *Gr'Shuna*.

"This is incredible."

A large aquarium filled the west wall of the makeshift conference room. Normally the officer's lounge, Cook often commandeered it for briefings and staff meetings when his smaller office simply wouldn't do. The large, curving tank was filled with tropical fish from several planets in eastern Terra. In simpler times, Janet would find herself drawn to it, to watch the tranquil movements of the fish and lose herself in thought. Now, she looked to see Cook rocking in his chair in front of the tank, shaking his head as he read and reread the report from the *Morning Star's* advance scouts. Around the oblong conference table, the *d'Artagnan's* senior staff watched quietly, as the mission commanders considered the new intelligence. Fitz and Jeremy stared in silence from the viewscreen on his desk; the static from the screen lent an air of random eeriness to the room.

"This is incredible," Cook repeated. "Absolutely incredible."

"Not that I'm telling you what to do, " Fitz began, only to be cut off by Cook's rapid fire questions.

"How sure are they of their numbers?"

"Even accounting for the background noise from the Cloud, the computer puts the probability in excess of 99%." answered Jeremy.

"I didn't ask about the computers."

"They're positive."

"How close did they get?"

"They made visual contact with the enemy point ship. It was one of their convoy cruisers. We've seen them before, at— "

"How close to the main body did they come?"

"Half a light year, maybe less."

"And their heading?"

Jeremy nodded. "Straight for us, as if they were guided by a navigation buoy."

Janet arched her eyebrows. "Christ," she whispered. Other voices rose from around the table; everyone present took her cue. The time had come to voice opinions.

"If you ask me...," interjected Fitz, only to have his voice drowned out by the growing chorus on board the *d'Artagnan.*

Cook slumped in his chair. The voices quickly faded from his consciousness; soon they were little more than a blur of indistinct sounds and emotions. Summoning the star map of the surrounding skies that he'd etched into his memory, his mind skipped past the known clouds and shoals, running along the most promising lanes of travel and commerce, those that he might choose himself if plotting a course. But it all made no sense: the Crutchtans had trapped themselves. Any way he looked at it, they had cut off every avenue of retreat.

Trying to make sense out of senseless circumstances, his mind circled the same questions, over and again. Why would the Crutchtans send such a major movement of ships so far from the best routes of passage, and so far away from reinforcements? What could they possibly have in mind?

Finally, he gave it up. There were too many missing pieces to the puzzle. But one thing seemed clear. He'd been right to avoid the bait the enemy had set out for him. He was more convinced than ever that the active sensor probes they'd detected had been set for the express purpose of drawing him away from the convoy. That was the only conclusion that fit the facts. It also meant that they were running headlong into a major enemy ship movement, heading eastward, for some purpose as yet unknown.

"Well, Cook?" demanded a voice from his screen. It was Fitz; quickly, Cook turned his attention to the discussion at hand.

"Well, what?"

Fitz scowled menacingly. "Everyone else thinks that we should attack, but we've yet to hear from you."

"Oh, I agree," he said softly. "At this stage, I don't see that we have much choice."

Fitz looked surprised, almost disappointed.

"Jeremy," he continued. "I'm ordering medals for the crew of that advance scout. Finnegan and— ?"

"Finley and Flanagan."

"Well, whatever. You supply the names, I'll draft the letter of commendation myself."

"They'll both be very proud, Commodore."

"All right, people…we'll have company in a few days, so I suggest we start getting ready. Prepare to increase speed to C-12; I'll plot the intercept course myself."

"Aye, aye," chorused the group.

"It's about time," Fitz grumbled.

Cook laughed softly. "You may well be right, Captain Fitzgerald," he said, leaning back in his chair, his weary eyes still managing a twinkle. "But a Sage once said that anticipation is the meat of life… "

"Oh, Christ."

"Well, Fitz, you asked for it, you know." Janet laughed brightly.

" — and action itself is but the anticlimax."

"What the hell does that mean?"

"That's a dumb question, Fitz," said Jeremy, from the captain's quarters on the *Morning Star*. "What does he ever mean? I mean, 'meaning' itself being such a subjective concept?"

As the raiding party's command staff enjoyed a laugh at his expense, Cook found his mind drawn to the enemy convoy. He exchanged a glance with Janet, who could tell that he was worried but could not understand the source. She smiled and shrugged her shoulders, wondering why something that seemed so obvious should bother him.

In the end, he tried to dismiss his concerns as groundless. He knew it was silly, and he was usually so careful about wasting his time and energy on things beyond his control. He turned his chair to face the aquarium, listening to the bubbling of the air filter and watching the gentle motions of the fish as they floated through their element.

Something was waiting for them in the blackness, Cook thought. Something whose outlines he could barely sense, and whose existence might be no more than a shadow. He couldn't help wondering whether the Crutchtans had finally caught on to him—whether this all wasn't just part of some grand trap for him and those under his command—or whether he was just losing his grip on his own mind.

* * *

"THE SCREEN is clear."

"Acknowledged."

Bra'Lendt relaxed in the monitor's seat. It had become routine: every ten minutes, he would glance at the monitor, to see whether their instruments had detected anything. He had come to view his responsibilities as mindless and uninteresting, even though he knew how critical they were. The Convoy depended upon his industry and alertness; his ship was the forewardmost reconnaissance vessel, responsible for guarding the safety of the precious cargo filling the holds of the thousands of transport craft plodding behind them in the blackness of space. But as with all things, repetition deadened the senses. By the end of his turn of duty, he often found his mind dulled by the monotony of his tasks.

On the other side of the station console, Gar'Shedra, his commander, smiled at him. Lendt felt considerable affection for the old pilot. They had served together since the early days of the war, and soon found that they had much in common. Each had served as a planetary scientist in the Colonial Expedition of His Worthiness, and had come to regret the long hours and tedious work that exploring the stars entailed. Yet neither would have chosen a different profession for all the riches on Balarium. They shared love of the stars, a common bond that each had nurtured through solitary walks on moonless nights on the world of their youth. And they, along with half the adult population of *Gr'Shuna*, shared an unspoken fear—that the longnoses were about to despoil their home forever, and that they would never again know the peace and serenity of another summer on their mother world.

"You have Landana on your mind again, Young One."

Lendt smiled and nodded. She rode on Ship Number Twelve, on the other side of the Convoy. It had been weeks since he had seen her, and even then, it was like meeting her for the first time. Their time together had been short. Between engineering assignments in the Life Support Unit of the Command Ship, and his duties as a convoy scout, their mating would barely blossom before duty forced another separation. Perhaps it would be different this time, he thought, though he feared that nothing had changed. Once the Convoy reached a safe haven, he would again be summoned to duty. So long as the Terrans were clanging at the gates, he would always be summoned to duty.

"Is it not always the way with us?" Lendt laughed softly. "No matter what we are doing, they are never far from our minds."

"Perhaps it would help our cause if we were not so obvious," returned Shedra. "Coy indifference works so well for females. Perhaps we should give them a taste of it in return."

"But love does not drive them mad," smiled Lendt. "And once we are caught—well, it is just their way of keeping us in line."

Shedra laughed. The old pilot had seen many changes in his day; but when they talked of their mates, it seemed as if nothing ever changed. He noted the clock: once again, it was time to check his instruments.

He glanced at the control panel, and the blood frooze in his veins. For the second time in his life, he knew such a feeling—a paralyzing fear, gripping his entire being with a steel fist of terror and hate.

The readings showed on his screen, strong and steady as a star. Though it was the first time he had seen anything like it, he knew at once what they were: first one, then another; and finally a third showed on the screen. They were enemy ships—Invader-class death ships—ships the Terrans called *sht'argh-she'eps*. The third vessel had a configuration known to all *g'Khruushtani* sworn to defend the homeland with their lives. Each had burned its marks of distinction into his consciousness. Even at this distance, where the others were indistinguishable, the *g'Khruushtani* could sense the ship that carried the mortal enemy of all they held dear. The realization of what lay ahead filled Shedra with terror. His mind could think of little beside the shadow of Death slicing through the skies, toward the fragile ships that he was helping to guard.

The three alien ships loomed in the darkness, moving toward them like demons in the night. Gar'Shedra stared at the screen, unable to move or speak, afraid to utter a sound lest his existence shatter like a brittle glass frozen in the deepest days of winter.

Chapter 20

INCENSE BURNED IN the lamp overhead, filling the room with the fragrance of meditation. It was the Festival of Meditation on the planet *Gr'Shuna*, a time of thought and contemplation halfway between the winter solstice and the dawning of Spring. Like the grayness that filled the skies of home at this time of year, the room of Ga'Glish was stripped of its finery. The tapestries were being cleaned; the portraits were in storage; everything that might distract the mind was hidden away, to be reclaimed at the proper time.

Seated on the floor, Ga'Glish sat stiffly on a pillow of plainest brown. A look of confusion filled his eyes. Across the table, his brightest junior aide was sipping from a cup of freshly brewed tea. The report from the Convoy lay open, its contents reflecting the horror in everyone serving in the rescue fleet.

"What you are saying...," began Ga'Glish.

Fa'Shenali closed his eyes and nodded with the solemnness of a tribal elder passing judgment.

"That is correct, Lord Commander. The earlier reports are confirmed."

"I thought it little more than gossip. The hopeful prattlings of village grandmothers."

"I was never so sure," fa'Shenali continued, "though I would not have taken the matter on faith."

"And the proof?"

"Our people have spoken to the survivors themselves. There is no mistake."

"Why would the Terrans permit them to live? Why would *Khu'ukh* not simply kill them, like an insect under his boot?"

"Their reasoning is alien to us, my Lord, but it appears that...."

"By your leave, my Lord."

Ga'Glish turned to see his own Chief of Tactics, standing at the entrance to his living area, his eyes pale as the moons of *Gr'Shuna*.

Panting and out of breath, Dra'Lengish leaned against the archway, his body aching for rest. He had long since left youth behind him, and the run from the Monitorium was a long one.

"Enter," said Ga'Glish; at once, he could sense anguish in the heart of his old friend.

"It is—the longnoses," panted Dra'Lengish. "They are— "

"The Convoy?"

The Old One nodded, his eyes cast down in despair.

Ga'Glish jumped to his feet and raced down the corridor, battling to contain his emotions. As his mind raced with plans and alternatives, he struggled with his own anguish, horrified to think what the barbarians would do to the helpless Convoy.

Every fiber of his being told Ga'Glish that it was hopeless. In the privacy of contemplation he knew that he was to blame for sending the children of *Gr'Shuna* to a certain death, and for the evil awaiting them in the blackness.

He would spend the next hours in agony, wondering how the One Called *Khu'ukh* had known. How had the monster sensed what the vastness of space itself hid from view? How the Evil One set himself against the *Gr'Shuna's* last hope for the future with such unerring accuracy?

Most of all, a thought thundered through the brain of Ga'Glish, a single thought that had long dominated his being and gave him the last remaining thread of solace that Fate had left for him.

If *Khu'ukh* destroyed the Convoy, Ga'Glish promised himself—if the Beast killed what little remained of his homeland's future—then he would kill the Beast himself.

Come what may, and though it would take his own life and those of all around him, the Beast would die.

* * *

to the Lord Commander, in the name of Ja'Rend XCVI,
Imperator of all g'Khruushtani:

Greetings:

As you commanded, we have completed our pivot and increased speed to narrow the distance between ourselves and the advance body of your forces. Our scouting parties report sighting Terran vessels less than two days away. Several of them no longer respond to our signals, and I fear they have fallen to the longnoses.

At risk of insult, I am constrained to remind you that our defenses will not last long against the Terran warships. Our situation will soon be desperate. Please hurry.

AD'DRANAKA, CENTURION
Commander, Convoy of Hope

"Enemy defensive perimeter showing on our screens."

Finley looked at the monitor. Everywhere he looked, enemy ships filled the skies. Adrenalin surged into his veins, and he could feel a relentless hammering in his chest. In less than a minute, his squadron would make contact with the enemy. He looked at his tactical screen and checked his alignment with the others. They'd been sent ahead to scout the enemy's defenses. The Commodore wanted to know exactly what they'd be fighting, and that meant sending someone to make as close a pass as possible. Since he'd been the one who'd found the lizards, the brass sent him ahead with reinforcements.

Actually, he thought, it was a kind of compliment, though if he got out of this alive he'd try to avoid such compliments in the future. In the meantime, it was all he could do to avoid ruining his flight pants.

"Bandits at three o'clock," Flanagan said. "Scrambling into attack formation. From this distance, they look like Vipers."

The news sent shivers through Finley's body. To his amazement, he felt his head clear and and his hands stop shaking. Calmly, he checked his tactical screen. He'd expected his stomach to be twisting into knots. Instead, hate coursed through his body; the green dots on his screen became no more than an approaching menace, to be destroyed without pity.

"Blue-Leader, this is Blue-Seven," Finley said into the transmitter, his voice clear and firm. "Hostiles closing at 740, north two degrees; range, one-hundred astrokilometers."

"Roger, Seven," came the reply over the speakers. "Hostiles confirmed. Blue Squadron, prepare for engagement; stand by Attack Plan Bravo— repeat, Bravo. All acknowledge."

Finley pressed the confirmation button. With a wink toward the old yeoman seated at the navigator's station, his hands settled in at the controls, easing his craft into its place in their battle wedge as they neared the Crutchtans. With the first flash of enemy fire, he found himself one with his vessel, twisting and turning in space with no thought except survival—and the destruction of the enemy.

* * *

"...IN THE meantime," said Van Horn, standing beside the holographic projection of the *d'Artagnan* in Cook's darkened office, "the weakness we detected in our Number Six shield appears to extend from the seam south of port— "

He pointed with the cursors; a reddish light danced along the left side of the ship's image. Seated on opposite sides of the conference table, Cook and Janet gazed intently at the image of the ship hanging suspended in mid air.

"...half-way across our port side, just aft of the auxiliary hatch. The slit's barely detectable, but could cause a peck of trouble if we don't fix it before we run into the enemy."

Cook rubbed his eyes. Weary of the bickering among his subordinates, he didn't want to hear any more problems. He was coming to the conclusion that this mission was snake-bitten: nothing was going as planned. And just when they could use a spot of luck, everything was starting to unravel.

"Before we left," he sighed, "I thought...."

"Aye, sir," Van Horn said. "We gave them the once-over ourselves. They were even checked at dry dock. Everything came back clean."

"Then what— "

"I haven't a clue, Skipper." Van Horn shook his head, staring harshly at the image of the ship. "Until we start making repairs, I couldn't even venture an intelligent guess."

Cook was about to ask for an unintelligent guess when the pager sounded at the door. Before the commodore could lean across to his desk to press the admittance button, the door whooshed open and Dexter bounded into the room.

"Skipper!" Dexter panted.

Wearily, the commodore turned to face his young aide, expecting the worst. He knew that Dexter wouldn't barge into his office unless it was an emergency. Or at least something that the young lieutenant perceived as an emergency. But Cook found that little excited him anymore. He'd seen too much death to fear it, and too much killing to harbor any fond illusions about the depths of the human heart. The intrusion of yet another crisis was hardly enough to alter his mood.

"They've made contact, Skipper! The scouts have made contact!"

His voice racing with excitement, Dexter relayed the news: the lead squadron had encountered stiff enemy resistance, and was trying to regroup. But Cook paid little attention to the report: he knew at once what was needed; his instincts sensed what to do without thinking. He'd seen it all, and all too often. Wherever he looked, he saw nothing but death and dying.

As Dexter prattled on, bringing the senior staff up to date, Cook's mind was already redeploying his forces, advancing his scouts and their reconnaissance drones on the enemy positions from all angles. His instincts told him that the Crutchtans couldn't be everywhere at once—that somehow, some of his scouts would get through. Soon, he'd have enough intelligence to plan a proper assault on the enemy position. After that, they could obliterate whatever the enemy was sending toward the east. Intercepting and destroying the big convoy might salvage something from this mission.

At the same time, he felt sickened by the endless killing. As he had for nearly a cosmic year, he longed for nothing so much as rest.

"Mr. Van Horn," he said at last, interrupting the spirited discussion that was going on around him. "Looks to me like you better get cracking on those shields. We need them ready for the Crutchtans."

"Aye, sir."

"Miss Mendelson, Mr. Dexter—summon the entire bridge crew. I'll meet them on the bridge in twenty minutes. It's time to bring everyone up to date and rig our shifts so that the first team is rested by the time we reach the enemy convoy."

Soon, alone in his office, Cook leaned back in his chair, staring at the ceiling and wondering when it would end.

THE SHIP veered wildly to port, barely avoiding the blast from the enemy's forward guns. Pressed against the padding of his station, Finley gripped the armrests of his chair. Shock waves shuddered throughout the ship; his knuckles were white as a ghost. He'd seen half his squadron die before his eyes, their ships lighting the skies like funeral fires. The sight sent terror coursing through his veins. Now, he was numb to everything but his own survival. Other thoughts would wait until later.

"Starboard shield back on line!" Flanagan hollered from the navigator's seat. "That was close, Mr. Finley. That was damn close."

Finley had no time to respond. Afraid that the lizards in the Viper would come about and try again, he pressed the throttle ahead to full. Pushed into his chair by the force of acceleration, he counted to twenty, as his endless drilling had trained him to do. Just before his ship was drained of her last reserves of power, he cut his engines and drifted, slowing below sublight until if felt as if he had come to a halt. While the battle raged aft, as fiercely as ever, all around him, the skies had cleared. Nothing but emptiness lay ahead; and his attacker, perhaps tiring of the chase, had moved on to another quarry.

"Reading a friendly on the screen," said Flanagan, "Twenty points off the port beam, closing at a crawl."

"Probably doesn't want to attract attention," laughed Finley. "Lord knows, the last thing we need is a reason for the lizards to turn their noses this way."

As the friendly neared, Finley let himself relax for a moment. He noticed his heart racing and felt himself getting lightheaded. The stress of battle was catching up with him, and he realized just how close he'd come to dying with the others. Whoever was coming toward them couldn't have any less experience than he did. Whatever might lie ahead, it would be nice to have a wingmate.

Soon, a voice crackled over their high-frequency receiver. Unscrambling the signal, Finley recognized the speaker—it was McKeever, one of his hazers from the *Morning Star*.

" . . .— -ing unidentified Starhawk; this is *Morning Star*-12. Come in please. Over."

"This is Finley, on Number 7; is that you, McKeever?"

"Finley?" came the reply. "You're the last one I'd expect to see back here. How the hell did ye manage it? Over."

"Can't really say, Mack," smiled Finley. "Just sort of happened. But I'll tell you, I haven't the foggiest notion of what to do next. Over."

"All ye ensigns are a worthless lot," laughed McKeever. "But I'll give ye this much, Finley: you're a scrappy damn bastard. And I've a confession of my own to make, Laddie-buck: I've lost my own bearings on the communications relay—and I haven't the foggiest notion of how to call home to Mother. Over."

Anxiously, Finley cast a glance at Flanagan, who laughed and gave him a thumbs-up sign.

"Maybe we can help each other, Mack," said Finley. "We've still got a fix on Com-One. If you have any ideas.... "

"I've always got ideas, Laddie," interrupted McKeever. "I'll be right beside you in about five minutes. Just stay on my wing. Maybe we'll win us a couple of commendations. But keep an eye on your screens. I wouldn't doubt that the lizards might send some reinforcements along, to finish our lads off."

"Shouldn't we go back...."

"Tut, Finley. A real Cozzie looks ahead, not past his own stern. We've penetrated their lines, Ensign. Our mission is to find out what's ahead. We can't do that by going back."

"I don't like it, Mack."

"Neither do I, Finley. But we've a job to do, and so do they. They'll keep the lizards busy. It's up to us to make use of the chance they're giving us."

The young ensign looked at Flanagan, who could only shrug and grunt his agreement. Finley knew they were right. But being right was no comfort when people you knew were being killed.

"Bring your heading due west, Finley, and prepare to ease up ahead. We'll be hard enough to detect, but we don't want to take chances. Not till we leave the lizards sensors far astern."

Soon, the two scouts were streaking toward the strong sensor readings to the west. Darting this way and that, to confuse enemy sensors and avoid enemy patrols, they closed on the enemy convoy.

Before long, they were staring at their screens, wondering how both sets of instruments could be wrong, yet reluctant to call home.

Not until they confirmed what their scanners showed.

Not until they saw it with their own eyes.

* * *

"We are waiting for your answer, Brother Cook."

The boy looked up at the instructor, who was smiling kindly at the front of the classroom. Slowly, the lad rose to his feet and took a deep breath.

"What is your conclusion?"

"I conclude that Socrates was a fool."

His eyes twinkling with mischief, the old man leaned back against his desk and folded his arms. "Explain your conclusion, if you would."

"The citizens of Athens did not really want his death. They just wanted him to leave them alone. If he simply left, they would not have followed and, given what we know about the fickleness of

mobs, they may well have changed their minds within a very short period of time. Mere stubbornness being no excuse for suicide, his death served no purpose and was therefore needless. Thus, I conclude that Socrates was a fool."

The instructor stood and strode to the board, writing the name "Socrates" with his electronic marker.

"Were there any other teachers of philosophy in Ancient Greece, Brother Cook?"

"There were many."

"Do we study all of them?"

"No. We study a rather small number of them."

"So, Socrates lives today through his philosophy, does he not?" The boy paused a moment. "Yes, he does."

"And if he had saved himself by abandoning his philosophy, and thus lost the respect of his pupils, might not his philosophy have died with him?"

"Plato wrote—"

"Plato wrote about a teacher willing to die for his principles. He might not have chosen to write about a coward and, if he had, we might not find the tale instructive. And so, we remember Socrates in large measure by the manner of his death. And since death eventually comes to all, will you grant that perhaps his perception of life was not so foolish as it seems to you?"

As the boy furrowed his brow to consider the point, the old instructor took his marker once again, to write "What is 'Duty?'" on the board.

"COMMODORE?"

Cook looked up, his reverie broken. Ahead to starboard, the *Magellan* loomed like a giant in the darkness. Far ahead and to port, the *Morning Star* kept a steady pace in the lead, her advance position making her the logical choice for monitoring communications from the hundred or so scouts that Cook had ordered into the surrounding skies. He shifted in his seat, clearing his throat before he spoke.

"Yes, Miss Mathison?" He looked to see his communications officer beaming.

"*Morning Star* reports that two scouts have penetrated enemy defenses. Captain Ashton is ready with a full report."

"Put it on the viewer, Lieutenant."

Mary pressed the buttons to get the *d'Artagnan*'s former first officer on the communications screen. Cook took a deep breath and looked about him. Everywhere, he saw nothing but eager anticipation as the crew prepared for the coming fight. Soon, Jeremy's face was on the viewer, grinning from ear to ear.

"I take it, Jeremy, that you've got good news," Cook smiled absently, his voice distant and detached.

"Skipper," Jeremy laughed, "this time, I think we've struck the mother lode."

"It's about time," chimed a voice on the ancillary communications screen. It was Fitz, using the security code to beam his transmission directly to his companion ships. His face was animated, and he was grinning almost as broadly as Jeremy. But Cook noticed an ugly harshness in Fitzgerald's eyes.

"Our scouts report a massive movement of enemy shipping," said Jeremy. "And massive is an understatement.

"Two scouts have penetrated enemy defenses, and made visual contact with the alien convoy," he continued. "They report observing a line—an endless line—of enemy ships heading centerside-north along a broad front. They say an accurate estimate of numbers is impossible. But their computer reading places the figure in excess of ten thousand ships."

There were whistles and gasps across the *d'Artagnan's* bridge. Jeremy chuckled and held up his hand, palm outward, to prevent interruptions.

"And the odd thing is," he went on, "that the Crutchtans line is distended. It goes on forever, setting up a killing row for us. Almost like...."

"Like they don't want us to know just how large a group it is," Fitz spurted, slapping his thigh. "Christ, but I like the sound of this, Jeremy. Looks like we finally got us something worth going after."

"I hope the scouts make it out," interjected Cook. "Sounds to me like both of them deserve medals."

"I'm sure they'll be glad to hear it," laughed Jeremy. "They're both mine, you know."

"Damn hard to believe that," Fitz chuckled. "Ship full of rookies. Can't even crap by themselves without making a mess of things."

"Well, this squadron took a lot of casualties, getting the reconnaissance for us. And one of them actually was a rookie. That tyro Finley, if you remember."

"Finley!" roared Fitz. "That lucky klutz. I didn't think he could turn in his chair without getting lost!"

Cook smiled, but didn't find the news surprising. He remembered the young ensign's voice, tense and wavering but full of spark and determination. A lot like Dexter in his early days, he smiled. And except for a noticeable lack of arrogance, not unlike himself.

"All right," said Cook, leaning forward in his chair, his eyes just short of twinkling. "We'll continue this discussion later. We have too much to do now to waste any more time cutting down our junior officers."

His jaw twitching, Fitz stared sullenly from the screen; Jeremy chuckled and nodded.

"Prepare for engagement," Cook continued, a measured firmness in his voice. "Come to Attack Formation A and stand by for all ahead at C-17, on my command. *D'Artagnan* out."

As the images from the viewscreens faded, Cook's bridge crew eagerly turned to their duties. Gerlach adjusted his controls to let him trigger all main batteries with a single command. Dexter reset the radar settings, calibrating the sensors to probe the enemy defenses; Mary activated the radio jammers, coordinating the IFF codes with the other ships and clearing the channels they would use during the engagement. Only Janet noticed that their commander's eyes lacked any fire, and his face registered a disturbing lack of enthusiasm.

"All right, people," said Cook. "Let's hope that our readiness check on the port shields weren't a misread. Helm, slow to C-4. Wait for the *Magellan* to come athwart our bow and into formation."

"Aye, aye."

"Mr. Danley, set a course for the convoy, and feed it into the communications computer. Optimum approach should give us about four degrees of arc to port, I'd say, given our present distance from the enemy."

"Aye, sir."

"You know what I don't understand?" asked Dexter, scratching his head.

Groans filled the bridge. Patiently, Cook swivelled his chair to face his systems officer.

"We are all dying to know, Mr. Dexter," smiled the commodore.

"Why would the Crutchtans be going in such an odd formation?" puzzled the lieutenant. "I mean—they'll be lined up like—like— "

"The term is 'enfilade,'" said Cook. "We'll be approaching along their axis, quite simply turning their flank, minimizing our exposure and maximizing our own firepower."

"But why?"

Cook shrugged. "Probably heading for help in the quickest way possible," he said, after a brief pause. "If they're panicked, and they haven't had time to redraw their formation, it may be the only way they could come about, en masse. If that's true, that means that there's trouble coming toward us, aportside." The commodore turned to face the forward viewer.

"Either that," he continued, "or we're being suckered into a trap."

Janet turned in her chair, facing aft. Underneath her furrowed brow, her eyes flashed with impatience. "You worry too much," she scolded.

"Eyes front, Missy," Cook said softly. "Prepare to increase speed to C-17."

* * *

SUDDENLY, WHERE there had been only blackness, there it was, glowing as brightly as the hottest star. Yet their computer still gave them hope, for the configuration did not quite match. And there was always hope in the *g'Khruushtani* heart. Through this entire nightmare, they had little else for sustenance.

At the command station on his Protector-class fighter, Al'Drenga closed his eyes, then slowly opened them again. He did not really expect the image on the screen to change. But such were the thoughts of a rationality long since fallen..

In the seat beside him, la'Shalan cleared his throat, then pressed his slender fingers against the activation switch of their radio transmitter.

"The channel is open, Altern," Shalan said, his voice thin and lifeless.

The screen before them registered its second enemy ship approaching; this one glowed as brightly as the first. His own fingers trembling nervously, Drenga pressed the analysis button. The computer gave its answer: it was as they had feared; yet it was still not the One for whom they waited.

Al'Drenga looked at his navigator and smiled sadly. In the short time since Fate had thrown them together, they had grown to be friends. Now he knew the truth of the old proverb, "to die among friends"—for their deaths were now as inevitable as the Terrans approaching on their monitor screens. And it was truly a source of comfort to face the end with a trusted companion by his side.

Then it appeared, glowing as brightly as the others, yet seeming to dance through the blackness like an evil god from an ancient myth. In a saner time, Drenga would have reflected that it only seemed so—that foreknowledge colored the perception of truth, and that legends often fed upon legends. But the times were hardly sane. And he had no more time for reflection.

"Advance Force 1 reporting," Al'Drenga spoke into his transmitter. "The Terrans are approaching. Summon all ships to battle positions."

"I hope Life has been kind to you," the young commander whispered to his companion.

"And to you as well, my Final Friend."

Drenga fought against thoughts that would distract him, thoughts of the love he would never again touch, the soft sands he would never walk, the young ones he would never father. As coldly as he could, he willed the tears back into his heart. He knew that death would soon claim him, and Shalan, and countless others like them. He prayed only that the time that their deaths bought for the fleet would be enough.

Silently, his fingers worked at the controls, bringing his small, fragile ship into its place amid their defensive perimeter. Behind him, sensors showed all of the military ships in the Convoy, massing to make their one, desperate effort to fend off the Terrans for a day—a single day—until help could arrive.

Silently, his mind counted off each moment as it passed.

Chapter 21

"MORNING STAR'S SCOUTS report main body of enemy convoy consisting of Class-C transports," said Mathison.

"Thank you, Lieutenant. Mr. Gerlach?"

"Aye, sir?"

"All guns, fire at will."

"Firing."

The interior lights of the *d'Artagnan* dimmed, and the ship shuddered under the force of its own guns. Cook saw the exploding enemy ships on the forward monitor. Another barrage had reduced yet another wave of Crutchtan defenders to interstellar dust and ash. But he found his mind drifting—not to the next enemy wave, already forming just beyond the range of his guns, but to what might be lurking in the darkness, in the black skies of the East.

And to the furious but hopeless assault being mounted by the overmatched enemy ships now hurling themselves at the three Terran starships.

"Commodore?" Mathison swiveled her chair to face the command seat.

"Hold steady, helm. I expect we'll have more company before too long."

"Sir," Mary tried again. "The *Magellan*...."

"Enemy wave obliterated."

"Thank you, Mr. Gerlach. Dexter?"

"Sir?"

"Data on enemy forces?"

"Commodore, the *Magellan*...."

"Chaser class, mostly, " reported Dexter. "I thought I detected one or two communications relay ships."

Cook leaned back into his chair to think. Nothing was making sense.

The fierceness of the enemy assault was out of all proportion to their strength and numbers. It was suicide. Nothing less than suicide.

"Commodore!"

Fury in his eyes, Cook glared at his radio officer. "What is it, Mathison?"

"Incoming message from the *Magellan*."

"Accch!" Cook waved his hand in aggravation. He didn't want to talk to anyone—and Fitz least of all. Not when his brain was screaming at him, trying to tell him something that he wasn't seeing. Something important. Something he was missing.

"Put him on the screen."

Soon the glowering image of the *Magellan's* captain was staring from the communications screen; Cook stared back angrily

"What is it, Captain?"

"How long, Cook?"

"How long what, Captain?"

"How long are we going to sit here, letting this charade continue? In five minutes, I could slice past the enemy small fry, and... ."

"You will remain in formation until I say differently, Captain."

"Begging the Commodore's pardon," Fitz said. "But I see no reason—"

"I am in command, Captain. That is reason enough."

"My opinion— "

"Is noted and overruled."

"Dammit, Cook! This is the biggest lizard convoy we could ever hope to—"

"That is quite enough, Captain," Cook said acidly. "The next thing you say or do containing the barest hint of insubordination will find you relieved, your Executive Officer in command of the *Magellan*, and you riding home in your own brig. Am I understood?"

"Perfectly."

"Return to your duties, Captain."

"Yes, *sir*." Fitz smiled tightly. "*Magellan* out."

As the image faded from the screen, Cook struggled with his own feelings of anger and betrayal. The enemy's actions were making no sense. Rather than circling the convoy to make it easier to defend, they were wasting their ships and personnel, throwing everything they had into a hopeless fight. The last thing he needed was another distraction. Until he figured out this puzzle, everything else could wait.

"Mathison?

"Sir?"

"Send out the word for the reconnaissance scouts to make another pass at the convoy. This time, for a sensor probe."

"We've already had one," piped Dexter.

"Then they'll do it again," snapped Cook.

"Yes, sir."

Class-C transports, mused Cook. The Terran equivalent was bulky and awkward, fine for short-range shuttles but poorly suited for longer-range convoy duty. The transport trains were much more efficient.

"What in creation is going on here?" he muttered.

"I beg your pardon?"

Cook raised his eyes to see his helmsman frowning at him, a worried look in her eyes.

"Talking to myself again, Missy," he smiled sheepishly. "Nothing to be concerned about. We do that all the time on Isis."

Janet sighed and shook her head. Cook fell back sullenly into his chair, wondering if Fitz wasn't right after all. Maybe everyone else was right. Perhaps he was so busy running from phantoms that he was letting his imagination run wild.

"*Morning Star*, acknowledging."

"Thank you, Miss Mathison."

"Bandits closing, dead to port."

"Thank you, Mr. Dexter. Weapons, fire at will."

"Aye aye, Skipper."

As the ship shuddered gently under the outgoing fire, her captain breathed deeply. Not for the first time, he wondered whether he was losing his touch.

Or his nerve.

Or maybe just his mind.

"Not that it would be much of a loss," he mused aloud.

"I beg your pardon, Skipper?" Janet asked.

"Just steer the ship, Commander."

"Yes, sir."

AD'DRANAKA TURNED away, sickened by the sight.

Behind him, the screen flashed brightly, as it registered the deaths of another squadron of ships. Horror filled the room like a ghost, haunting the thoughts of all. But the ghosts on the screens were real, and the phantoms that floated through the blackness filled more than a Small One's imagination. They littered the heavens with death and destruction, filling the sky with a nightmare of fire.

Finding an isolated nook, out of the sight of his underlings, the centurion rested his head against the wall and let tears fill his eyes. He looked about him: his ship was manned by young ones barely past childhood themselves. He saw the fear in their eyes, and felt the same terror that seized them all. Yet each remained steadfastly at his post, mindful that the fate of all depended upon the courage of each of them. Ad'Dranaka had spent half his life slicing through the heavens, piloting spacecraft in the service of His Worthiness—whichever Worthiness happened to occupy the Seat of Honor. The Lord Commander had chosen him specially for this assignment for the clarity of his judgment. Now the honor seemed a cruel joke. Even with a lifetime of experience, he could barely control himself, much less command the respect of his underlings.

Struggling to master his weakness, Ad'Dranaka, Lord of the House of Adoshi, slowly recovered his composure. Hoping that the others were too occupied to notice his own flagging courage, he returned to the control room, his head proudly erect, his eyes passionless and brave.

"Report," he commanded.

"All lost," came the reply, from a Young One whose voice until recently cracked from the dawning of manhood, and now cracked from fear.

"Ready the next attack," the centurion said. He sensed the failing spirits around him. They needed his leadership now, more than at any time since this horror began. He filled his lungs with air, and rose up to his full height.

"And prepare to radio the Lord Commander," he continued. "We cannot hold back the Terrans much longer. Tell him that we will defend the Convoy to the last breath of the last defender."

"Yes, my Lord."

Ad'Dranaka turned his eyes to the viewing screen overhead, just in time to see another squadron disappear under a barrage of fire from one of the longnose death ships. He ached with the knowledge that he was leading his command to its death. He closed his eyes and inhaled deeply, savoring the sensation of air flowing into his aging lungs. He refused to believe that all was lost; somehow, he kept telling himself, help would arrive in time. But he felt tired, very tired. And he permitted himself the bitter comfort of wondering if death would prove more restful than the life he had been leading since the war began.

* * *

EXPECTED THOUGH it was, the news fell like a mountain upon Ga'Glish, and upon all around him.

"There is no mistake?" he asked.

Dra'Lenish closed his eyes and bowed deeply. "Their final message was of resistance, my Lord. They were committing their last ships—their reconnaissance and communications vessels, along with the last remnants of their armed escort. Now, all is silence. And we are still a day away."

From his place behind the Lord Commander, fa'Shenali felt revulsion and hate rising to consume everyone present. The slaughter of innocents stained the heavens, and cried for vengeance.

"One day," whispered Ga'Glish, his heart screaming in anguish, his face a stone statue of g'Khruushtani pride. "One day from salvation, only to die like caged animals."

Ga'Glish rose to his feet. Hunger for retribution filled him, and his soul thirsted for Terran blood.

"Order to all ships," he hissed, his bitterness a lash whetting his passions and stirring a primal lust for atonement.

"Change course for the Shuninari Channel. There we will intercept the Beast, and destroy him."

An animal roar erupted from the throats of all. Fa'Shenali felt himself rising amid the clamor, buffeted by the emotions around him as a feather upon the wind. Soon he woke as if from a dream, to find himself screaming as loudly as the rest.

FLANAGAN STAMMERED, his face white as a sheet.

"I-i-incoming fire!"

Finley pulled desperately on the pilot's wheel. The small scout banked sharply to port, then dove dead south, as straight as the laws of physics allowed. His insides fluttered wildly as he struggled to stay calm. That was what they taught at the Academy; that was the only way to stay alive in battle. As soon as their course stabilized he pulled back, determined not to make the same mistake again.

"Damn lizards," he muttered. "Can't trust anything that looks like its mother breathes fire."

Flanagan shook his head. With the danger passed, laughter was the best medicine to ward off a post-crisis collapse.

"Don't go in so close this time, Laddie," he said gruffly, his face ash-white. "We're here to take some readings. We can do our job without coming close enough to shake their slimy hands."

Nodding his head, Finley tried it slow this time. Easing his way closer, ever closer, he crept into place, just beyond the ranger of the enemy's guns, then signaled to Flanagan to begin his half of the job. With Finley holding steady, matching the enemy's speed and course, Flanagan stepped from the navigator's chair to the large black panel at the back of the cramped bridge. Hunching down to read the controls, he activated the small scout's sensor probes, holding them steady as he could. After a minute that seemed to stretch into eternity, he ended the probe and pressed the Analysis button.

The reading from the instruments astonished him.

"It can't be."

"What's that, Flanagan?"

"It must be a mistake."

"Let's have it."

"They're jamming the probes—cluttering the sky with noise to confuse the sensor gear. But it seems there's a lot of junk here. Mostly equipment, I'd guess. All I can get for most of it is a density reading."

"Not chapter and verse, Yeoman, just the bottom line."

"Water."

Finley spun about in his chair, gaping awkwardly at his navigator.

"What?"

"The lizard ships are loaded with water."

"Water?"

"That, or something with the exact same density."

"If that don't beat all."

Finley turned in his chair, facing forward, and stared at the enemy ship slicing through the skies dead to starboard. Flanagan eased his way back from the sensor controls, and resumed his post as navigator.

"What do we do now?"

Finley shrugged, his hands reaching for the radio controls.

"Report it, I guess. Let someone else figure it out. But then, I don't understand what all the fuss is about, anyway. Not when we could just blast them out of the sky."

He turned to face his companion.

"How do you figure it?"

"Well, Mr. Finley, with officers involved...."

"Belay that, Mister!"

"It's no wonder nothing makes sense."

Laughing, Finley pressed the transmit button on his radio and steadied the microphone with his other hand.

* * *

"MATHISON?"

Turning toward the Skipper, Mary shook her head.

"Still no response."

"How about the space normal bands? Have you tried...."

"Begging the Commodore's pardon," she interrupted, "but I've tried all available channels. The enemy isn't responding."

As his bridge crew exchanged puzzled looks, Cook rose to his feet and started pacing about the bridge. It made no sense, he thought. None at all.

"Commodore?"

There was still a piece of the puzzle missing. Or was it something he was overlooking? Though more than willing to die for their homeland, he'd never seen Crutchtans behave like lemmings, and this engagement had been more like a frenzied mass suicide than a battle. They always had a purpose for their sacrifice, whether to cover a retreat, or simply to kill as many Terrans as possible against hopeless odds. Here, they'd been sadly outmatched. They would have known it from the outset. Yet knowing that three starships could reduce the whole convoy to interstellar ash in minutes they refused even to return a hail. And for what? Ten thousand shipfulls of water?

He was missing something, he told himself.

Something important. And probably obvious.

"*Dammit!*" he muttered.

"Commodore, it's the *Magellan*."

"I don't want to talk to him."

"It's not a hail, sir," Mary said, swiveling her chair to face him. "It's a communiqué—logged and entered."

Cook sighed harshly. With everything spinning around him in a muddle, the last thing he needed was somebody trying to force his hand. He sensed tension infecting his bridge. Whatever façade he tried to maintain, he wasn't immune.

"What's it say?"

"Inter-ship Memorandum, from...."

"*Mathison*! Get to it, for crying out loud!"

"Sorry." Mary cleared her throat. "'Note enemy warships neutralized; awaiting order to attack.' Signed— "

"Thank you, Lieutenant."

"Sir?"

Cook's eyes narrowed. He tried to ignore the nervous faces of his crew. Struggling to hold his own temper in check, he needed to pull everything together.

"Sir, it's the *Magellan* again, this time on a standard channel."

"Ignore the hail."

Janet's ears perked. She glanced up from the helm. Cook's voice suddenly had its familiar ring of steel, and the distant glaze had left his eyes. He must have figured out whatever was troubling him, she thought. Or maybe he'd just decided what to do about it. But this show of resolve, too subtle to be noticed by anyone else, had no effect on the stress gripping the bridge crew. Cook strode to the command chair and resumed his seat.

"Mr. Gerlach?"

"Sir?"

"Commodore— ?" Mary spun around in her chair.

"Charge a single forward gun."

"Aye sir; charging."

"Captain Fitzgerald wants to know...."

"Not now, Mathison."

"Guns amain. Forward Battery 1-A charged and ready."

"Commodore— "

"Prepare to fire a single shot across the enemy's bow—close enough to singe the paint on their outer hull, if you can manage it."

"Aye, aye. Target locked."

"Commodore—the *Magellan*."

Fuck the *Magellan*, Cook thought.

"Fire!"

The shot flashed through the sky, appearing on the viewing screen as a luminescent blue streak. It pierced the blackness just past the bow of the convoy's lead ship.

"I'm glad you targeted the right ship," smiled the commodore. "Fitz can't always take a joke. I guess I should have been more specific."

A wave of nervous laughter crept across the bridge, breaking the tension. Cook sensed them starting to relax.

"Mr. Gerlach, charge all forward guns and stand by for further orders."

"Aye aye, sir."

"Mathison, try another hail. Tell them if they don't respond, our next shot will destroy their ship and we will commence an immediate attack on the rest of the convoy."

"Yes, sir."

THE SHOCK waves from the near miss echoed through the ship. Ad'Dranaka himself was still reeling from their brush with death when the monitor's voice sounded through the noise.

"The Terrans, my Lord. They order us to respond on pain of death."

Angrily straightening his back in a display of dignity and pride, Lord Dranaka strode to the Monitor's station, half-inclined to return the Terran fire. It was bad enough to die by banditry, he thought. He would not permit the Terrans to think them cowards as well. Groveling for bare existence was beneath the dignity of all but the meanest commoner. He would not let the Terrans gloat over their meaningless victory. If they meant to taunt their victims before the slaughter, he would show them the face of true *g'Khruushtani* courage. They would see no fear, even if he had to stare into the eyes of the Beast himself. Hardening his resolve, he nodded to the Monitor.

"Put it on the viewer, my young friend," he said, summoning all his strength, hoping to avoid melting into a puddle on the floor.

Soon, he was staring into the ugly countenance of the Most Hated One, for the Elder had no doubts that the hideous image on his viewer was that of the Beast, himself. The orbs of the Terran's eyes floated in pools of white; his pointed snout protruded menacingly from the middle of an otherwise featureless face. Several moments passed before the monster opened his mouth to speak and flashed his sharp white teeth. He uttered the sharp staccato yelps and barks that Terrans used for language.

"I am called *Khu'ukh, kh'am'dar,*" spoke the Beast. The translating computer captured a rough, grating voice as it reduced his primitive speech into words Lord Dranaka could understand. "A Son of *Shtarsh'iep-da'Rkhtahy'n.*"

"I am Ad'Dranaka," the Groupleader said, foregoing the customary bow of greeting. "And I know of the One Called *Khu'ukh.*" He sensed the mindless terror of his underlings, but managed to crush the urge to surrender himself to similar feelings.

The Terran bowed in acknowledgment, momentarily distracting the centurion by the display of manners.

"Your actions have been puzzling to us," the Terran barked suddenly; his predatory scowl sending chills into the feet of Dranaka.

"But then, I make no pretense of Cosmic Understanding, most particularly the labors of foreign brains. Although, with such aside a tipped sharpness, our custom has been toward granting the inhabitants of every vessel we have encountered, in the recency of Time, the election of retaining themselves through renouncing one's ships and surrendering one's cargo. Presently I tender to you the identically random opportunity for personal salvation."

The Terran tongue was so odd, so inscrutable, that it took a moment for what the Beast was saying to register in the mind of the centurion. Even then, he was not certain that he understood.

"You mean," he asked, "if we abandon our charges, you will permit us to escape with our lives?"

"Yes," said the Beast.

Hatred boiled inside Ad'Dranaka, and rage took charge of his mind. He spoke as if already burning in the firestorm he knew would follow. Tears filling his eyes, his universe reduced to raw emotion, he would remember nothing of what he said. Those hearing him speak would tell him that he spoke with the heart of an imperator.

"I have heard enough of Terran lies and barbarism," he hissed angrily, his face flushed, his eyes aflame. "We will die defending them, rather than surrender a single one to you and your atrocities."

* * *

THE CROWDED corridors were alive with movement, but it was not the normal bustling that attended each day's feeding hour. Tearful females of all classes raced down the frenzied hallways, screaming for their children. The anguished cries of small ones, searching for a comforting pair of arms, filled the air.

Lonely and unnoticed, a young one named Shl'Glishen stared out the viewing window, fascinated by the longnose ship hovering in the blackness outside. Long shunned by his peers as "Glishen the Strange," few had ever taken notice of the sad, empty eyes that lurked on the edge of the children's play. Without a mother, and with his father in the service of His Worthiness, his relatives had slowly given him up as a Wounded One—one dispossessed of feelings or tenderness, caused by the trauma of watching his mother die at the hands of the barbarians. There were no comforting arms beckoning for him, none who could ease the terror of what all knew would be their last moments of their existence. Alone in the midst of the panic swirling around him, he felt strangely unmoved by the chaos. Numbness had long insulated him from the feelings of those around him, and his long isolation from any real companionship had calloused his soul. With a sadness that no others could comprehend, he watched horror enveloping those near him.

"They are here— they are here! *Terrans*!!"

The hysterical voice of a young female caught his attention. He watched her run down the hall, nearly getting trampled in the stampede that raced past him. Turning his eyes in the opposite direction, he saw them.

Ghosts from his past, coming for him again.

"Run! They are going to kill us all!!"

"Run—everyone—*run*!"

They were dressed differently, this time. Not in tattered rags, but in neatly pressed cloth, the color of sand. Each held a weapon of some kind, either a long stick, glowing brightly on the end or a small black box, of the kind that haunted his dreams.

"*Run*—!!"

A woman called to him as she raced past, tugging his shoulder until the press of the crowd pushed her past.

"Run, Young One! They are coming!! Save yourself! Hide! *Hide*!!"

He turned to face the approaching longnoses. He knew better than the others. He had been through it before. He knew there was no escape, just as he had known that they would someday come for him. One could not fight ghosts, for they simply vanished into shadows. If they had come for him, there was no use fighting; there was no use for any of them to fight. Not any more. There were fates worse than dying, the Young One knew. Living with nightmares and phantoms was one such fate. This time, there would be no running away. This time, he would die with the others.

He closed his eyes, awaiting the inevitable, his heart coming alive for the first time in his young memory. His feelings returned to him in a flood, crying out at the suffering the monsters had caused, anger and hurt and hatred filling his awakening soul until he thought it would burst.

After what seemed an eternity, he opened his eyes again. To his amazement, he saw that the longnoses were gone.

And they had taken his ghosts with them.

* * *

D'ARTAGNAN'S BRIDGE was silent as a graveyard.

Janet looked at her instruments, and adjusted the controls to keep them hovering just within the range of their molecular transmitters. Aching inside, she turned her head to starboard.

Cook stood in front of the starboard viewer, looking at the broad line of enemy ships, stretching into the void as far as he could see.

"Number Twenty is reporting, Skipper. That's the last of them."

"And?"

"Same as the others. Aside from the piloting crews, and two ships half-filled with the old and sick, all twenty teams show nothing but shipfuls of young Crutchtans on board. Young Crutchtans and their mothers."

Cook closed his eyes and took a deep breath. What kind of monsters did the Crutchtans take them for, he wondered. He smiled weakly, half-amused by the thought that a little knowledge of human history might not ease the aliens' minds, after all. And if anyone else had been in command....

Without a word, he strode back to the command seat, and resumed his post.

"Mathison, radio their lead ship," he said, his bearing firm, his peremptory tone reassuring his crew. "Tell their commander that Terrans do not make war on children. We wish them a safe journey, and they are free go on their way."

"Yes, sir."

"Then radio the *Magellan*, and tell Captain Fitzgerald to keep anything he has to say to his own damn self."

"Aye aye."

"Helm, come about and take us away from here. Head us west, bearing 750, five points north."

"Aye, Skipper."

Soon, the ship whined and shuddered as the engines pulled her into a tightly banked turn. Cook felt his arm press into the soft cushions of his chair. He closed his eyes and longed to do nothing but fade into oblivion, and sleep for a hundred years.

Chapter 22

STANDING AT THE head of the darkened amphitheater, fa'Shenali raised his hand to shield his eyes from the bright light, and shifted uncomfortably on his feet. Behind him loomed a giant projection of the local skies, the multi-colored stars hanging like jewels in the air. Blue points of light, suspended just west of a protruding cloud of interstellar gas, marked the three Terran starships; to the east, a sea of green specks showed the Imperial fleet moving to cut off the longnose retreat around the bend in the Cloud. Fa'Shenali raised his eyes to see the spectacle of space, reduced to allow its perception. He wondered how sentient creatures could chose to kill each other in the midst of such timeless beauty.

"As we all can see," boomed the Lord Commander, his thunderous voice filling the room with the confidence of royalty, "we have contained the longnoses in a recess from which there is no escape. At our present course and speed, we will reach the Point of Shuninar Cloud in less than a day, well in advance of the Beast. We will be able to settle into our positions, and await his approach."

"Are the reports true, Lord Commander?" called a voice from the darkness.

"Which reports?" asked Ga'Glish.

"The rumor about the Convoy. Is it true? Did the Beast spare the Convoy?"

A low hiss signaled the Lord Commander's displeasure at the interruption. "Perhaps our young expert can enlighten us," he said at last.

A long silence followed.

"*Fa'Shenali!* "

The young subaltern was startled back into awareness.

"My Lord?"

"The Convoy, Subaltern," snapped Ga'Glish. "Tell us about the Convoy."

Fa'Shenali stepped forward, out of the darkness and into the merciless glow of the projection lights. He sensed the anxiety among those present, but knew there was little of substance he could tell them.

"Nothing has changed," he began. "At least, nothing of which we have confirmation. We have had long-range contact from a source claiming to be the Convoy leader, reporting that the Terrans have destroyed their escort ships, but that they are presently unharmed. It could be genuine, or it could be a Terran trick, designed to mislead us. Until we dispatch a patrol, we have no way of knowing to a certainty."

"And we will dispatch no patrol," interjected Ga'Glish. "Not until we have reduced the Beast to ashes."

Fa'Shenali bowed in acknowledgment, for he could have no quarrel with the decision. Whether the Convoy lived or died could have no bearing upon their quest for the Beast. Yet deep within himself, the Young One hungered to know.

"What possible reason would he have to spare them?" asked a voice, one that fa'Shenali had come to recognize. It was Dra'Lengish, the Chief of Tactics.

"I cannot say for certain," the young subaltern replied. "Our information is too incomplete to do more than speculate."

"This from our Beast expert?" scoffed Va'Nazze. "Any of us could profess our ignorance, my Lord. Perhaps the Young One has learned the lesson of humility too well."

As the room filled with laughter at his expense, fa'Shenali closed his eyes and forced himself to relax. A loss of temper at such a time would not be wise. He reminded himself that derision was a prerogative of rank. As a mere commoner, he was lucky to be standing amid the Chosen Ones. Showing outrage rather than submission at their exercise of privilege would be a breach of protocol.

"Assuming the communication to be genuine," fa'Shenali continued over the fading wave of amusement, "it may reveal that the Terrans have broken yet another set of our codes, and were dictating the contents of the transmission. Or it may simply reflect the Beast's own primitive sense of honor."

"Honor!"

Va'Nazze's voice rang out over the clamor. Fa'Shenali looked across the auditorium to see the scowling face of the Lord Commander, and realized that his opinions were being carefully noted. Cursing his own impulsiveness, he realized that it was too late to recall his opinions. Now he would have to defend his innermost thoughts in public.

"You dare speak of Terran honor before such an assemblage? The very word insults the memory of all who have perished under the lash of such Terran '*honor.*'"

"Terran atrocities are too well documented to deny, and I speak of no more than speculation," Shenali replied, bowing to acknowledge the point. "But the fact is that in the early days of the Conflict, the One Called *Khu'ukh* did respect his promise not to attack any *g'Khruushtani* until he had returned to Terran skies. To my own mind, this suggests a heart that respects more than mere expediency. And I am sorry to offend, but I use the word 'honor' only for lack of a better one."

"Is it 'honor' that causes him to slaughter our people by the thousands?" hissed the Lord Commander.

"With all respect, my Lord, we are trying to kill him at the same time. Perhaps he perceives no difference. But we should recognize his strengths even as we search for signs of weakness. As we confront the effects of his abilities every day, we do ourselves no dishonor by studying him objectively—most particularly as I think his own kind does not fully appreciate his skills."

"Appreciate?!"

Too late, fa'Shenali sensed the implications of what he had said. He wished to crawl into a crack in the floor to hide. Murmurs of outrage among the assembly made him feel small enough to achieve such a goal.

"Perhaps you can *appreciate* one who murders your countrymen, Subaltern. But such kind thoughts toward our enemy will hardly bring back the dead."

Fighting the impulse toward further argument, fa'Shenali bowed stiffly. "I mean no disrespect, Lord Commander," he said mildly. "And I apologize for my common choice of words."

During the awkward silence that followed, fa'Shenali relaxed every muscle in his body, struggling to show obedience and determined to offer no further tendencies toward nonconformity. As Ga'Glish held a fierce scowl of displeasure for heartbeat after heartbeat, the Young One wished mightily to let deference rule his own tongue. Soon, he saw the Lord Commander relax his gaze, and a cleansing sense of relief washed over the young man.

The discussion soon turned to matters of tactics, and fa'Shenali found himself excluded from the debate. As he stood silently, listening to the voices of his superiors, his mind cried at the realization that he had offended his sponsor and only defender. If Ga'Glish chose to dismiss him, fa'Shenali knew that his future would be as bleak as the gray clouds of winter. Yet as he lifted his eyes to the star map, and saw the *g'Khruushtani* fleet moving into position to crush the Beast, he felt a profound sense of loss. Though its source was a mystery even to himself, he was shocked to make the treasonous discovery that he, alone among his countrymen, would mourn the passing of the longnose called *Khu'ukh*.

* * *

JANET LOOKED up from the helmsman's station to see the commodore's lonely figure, standing before the sensor screen that scanned the eastern skies. He had been there forever, it seemed. He'd barely moved a muscle for the last cosmic hour. But their course was unchanged. Unless they changed course, their present heading would take them into a promontory of the Cloud in less than a day.

"Commodore?"

Janet looked to the communications station. Mary looked at her, confusion filling her face. Almost a minute passed, without a response.

"Commodore?" Mary repeated.

"What is it, Lieutenant?" Janet asked at last.

"The *Magellan* wants to know exactly where we're going. Captain Fitzgerald says— "

"Tell Captain Fitzgerald that we're going exactly where I say we're going," said Cook. He turned and glared sternly at his radio officer. He would later regret venting his anger at such a helpless target, but for now he cared for little but lashing out at anything or anyone that crossed him.

"But..."

"We are holding course, Lieutenant. And the *Magellan* is ordered to remain in formation until further notice. Is that clear?"

"Yes, sir."

Motioning for the navigator to watch her station, Janet rose and walked to the monitor. She could see nothing but stars and empty space. Yet Cook kept staring at it, his eyes intense and troubled.

"What is it?" she whispered.

"Nothing," he replied. "Go back to your seat."

"You're making the whole crew nervous, including me. At the very least, I think you owe me an explanation."

Cook smiled tightly, laughing at some private joke that she knew only he would understand.

"Everyone thinks I'm running from phantoms," he said, a wistful softness to his voice. "And I can't be sure they're not right. That's all the explanation I can give you. And more than I'll give anyone else."

"What are you afraid of? You think we're being followed, is that it?"

Cook turned to look her straight in the eye. His voice was deadly serious, but she could see sadness written on his face.

"I can feel it, Janet. I can't explain it, but I know they're out there, and I know they're after us. Until we get home...."

Stopping in mid-sentence, Cook turned toward the screen again, his face a stone facade once more. Janet felt hurt and defeated; it was like he was casting her aside all over again.

"Well, that's all quite beside the point. And that's all the explanation I care to give. Return to your post, Commander. I have a lot on my mind. And you have a ship to steer."

"But— "

"Missy—return to your post."

"Yes, sir."

"THE BLOODY fool! The bloody damn idiot!"

Fitz slammed his fist so hard on his desk that he drained it of feeling for a minute or two. He was too angry to worry about the possibility that he had broken his hand. His mind was already racing with thoughts of revenge. Soon, but not soon enough, the bell sounded at the entry door.

"Enter," Fitz barked.

A young greenshirt entered, his eyes wide with apprehension, uneasiness etched across his face.

"Ye sure took your sweet time a-gettin here, Hartman," Fitz snapped.

"Sorry, Cap'n, but with the maintenance check in full swing, and all...."

"Hold your bloody motormouth," barked Fitz. "Stow the chatter and take a seat."

Hartman, his face flushing a deep red, quietly sat down in one of the chairs across from his commander.

"Computer on," barked Fitz.

"Working."

"Security clearance, 'Eyes Only.'"

"Please enter access code," droned the machine.

As Fitz prepared his log entry, the young yeoman felt a wave of guilt. It was the same every time the captain had called him to serve as a witness. The young man had no idea what the skippers were up to. He hadn't a clue about whether Cap'n Fitz was even being fair about it. But he did know that Commodore Cook was a hero, who never did anything without a reason. He felt like a traitor for sitting silently and becoming a party to what Cap'n Fitz was doing. Even if it was all being done by the book.

"Witness required," said the computer. "Please enter identity code."

"Go to it, Laddie," smiled Fitz, turning the console to face the young yeoman. Without a word, Hartman entered his serial number into the computer and turned the keyboard back to his commander.

As Fitz switched the machine to an audio feed, dictating his observations so that Hartman could hear them, the young yeoman felt as worthless as a dust speck on Ishtar. The yeoman leaned back in his chair and tried to close his ears. But his conscience wouldn't let him rest, and echoes of his complicity rumbled through his head.

"DISTANCE TO outer limits of Cloud—two thousand astrokilometers," said Dexter. "At present speed, estimated time of contact.... "

Cook leaned back in the captain's chair; he barely heard his system's officer's report. He had computed and recomputed the distance in his head a hundred times already. He didn't need to hear it again. He stared into the looming interstellar fog, now growing until it filled all their sensor screens, his doubts growing by the second.

Taking them through the Cloud was dangerous. Their instruments would be useless, and at these speeds a collision with anything larger than a large rock would blow them apart more surely than a hundred enemy gunners.

Taking a deep breath, Cook looked at the back of Janet's head. Her long, flowing hair, falling across her back, brought memories of better times. He had taken her half-way across the galaxy, and caused her more grief than she ever deserved. If he actually was leading them to their death, he hoped she could forgive him in those final milliseconds before the Universe closed around them.

"Steady as she goes, Helm. Miss Mathison, radio the others. Tell them to remain in single-file until we emerge on the other side. That is, unless they detect an explosion ahead. If we go down, they're on their own."

"Aye, sir."

Before long the first wisps of the Cloud whipped the sides of the ship. The readings from the sensors dissolved into an impenetrable static. Only the motion sensors showed signs of life, displaying faint signs of subspace motion dead astern. As the three ships dove deeper into the fog, a profound silence gripped the *d'Artagnan's* bridge.

"THERE THEY go."

"No! They can't. Dammit—they can't do that."

"I tell you, Mr. Finley, they just did."

"*Morning Star*-7 calling Mother—come in."

Flanagan looked at his young commander and shook his head. The lad had spunk, that much he had to give him. But there came a time when spunk reached its limits, and a man had to believe the truth of what his own senses had to tell him.

"Finley— "

"Come in, *Morning Star,* come in."

"Ensign—it's no use, Laddie. Bad luck, that's what it is. But there's nothing to be done about it now. Try to relax."

"Relax! And just what in the name of Molly McGee are we supposed to do now?"

Flanagan squinted in contemplation, and scratched his head thoughtfully. Truth to tell, he didn't really know. He supposed they could try going around the Cloud, but they'd have a devil of a time finding the starships on the other side.

At last, the old yeoman shrugged his shoulders. "I guess we follow them."

"What?"

"Do you want to set the course, Mr. Finely? Or shall I do it?"

"But—but— "

As the young ensign sputtered incoherently, Flanagan adjusted the instruments to take them into the teeth of the Cloud, following the trail of their mother ship. He just hoped that they could keep close enough. Aside from going into the Cloud in the first place, the last thing they wanted was to lose the trail and have to find their way out by themselves.

At least with Cookie leading the way, Flanagan thought, they stood half a chance of getting out with their hides intact.

"Entry in ten seconds."

"But—but— "

"Five seconds."

"But—but— "

"Here we go, Laddie. And here's hoping that the way out's as easy as the way in."

"But—but— "

"Mr. Finley, you're taking the words right out of my mouth."


```
                    COMMAND MEMORANDUM
        CC:         144-3902.7
        FILE:       Special Log
        ACCESS:     Command
        SECURITY:   Voiceprint
        OPERATIONAL STATUS: Normal
        LOCATION:   Indeterminable: vicinity of eastern approach to
                    Girshoona
```

This duly witnessed entry updates and supplements Command Memorandum 144-3897.2, outlining and detailing the continuing derelictions of mission commander, Commodore R. A. Cook.

We have entered the interior of the Cloud, ostensibly traversing a promontory en route to rendezvous with Terran forces at Girshoona. Despite continuing contrary advice from Captain Ashton and myself, Commodore Cook has taken it upon himself to abandon our mission and head toward friendlier skies.

Since sparing the sole major convoy we have encountered since this Operation began, Commodore Cook has shown increasing signs of stress, and his decision-making continues to be erratic and ill-conceived. Our current heading—single file, through an Interstellar Cloud of undetermined depth and density—is solely due to his insistence that we are being pursued. Yet sensors show no signs of any approaching enemy force, nor signs of any enemy ships.

As Captain Ashton continues to demur, I can offer no formal challenge to the Commodore's authority. However, it is my firm belief that Commodore Cook is, by cowardice or increasingly pronounced paranoia, losing his capacity for making command decisions. And it is my regretful intent, should we safely traverse the Cloud and reach friendly skies, to recommend that he be relieved of command.

Capt. B. Fitzgerald
BNF 45711D810-1

* * *

THE LORD COMMANDER spoke the words, but he merely echoed the feelings of all present.

"It is a disaster."

Ga'Glish looked at the giant monitor screen. He ached with disbelief, yet he could do nothing to summon back the longnoses, nor see them emerge as from a dream. Instantly, he sensed the awful truth: the Beast had known. Somehow, he had known. Unless luck smiled upon the g'Khruushtani, the Hated One would escape.

"How much of a residual force did we leave?"

"A reconnaissance outpost, my Lord. Two, perhaps three dozen ships."

Ga'Glish closed his eyes and struggled to keep from surrendering to despair. Three dozen small reconnaissance vessels to stand against three Terran starships; it would be another massacre. More g'Khruushtani sacrificed to the ravages of barbarism. All to an end for which success was nowhere in sight.

"Order all ships to reverse course," hissed the Lord Commander. "We will make our way back toward the Lesser Bend without delay. Relay this order to the outpost at *Fruseniti*: they are to delay the Terrans at all costs. Whatever casualties they must endure, they are to use every means to slow the longnose retreat so that we may intercept and destroy them."

"Yes, my Lord."

As the others all nodded their approval, fa'Shenali squirmed with discomfort. Try as he might to conceal it, his uneasiness did not escape attention.

"You disapprove, Subaltern?"

Fa'Shenali turned to see Ga'Glish glowering unforgivingly. The rest stared at him, contempt filling their eyes. By instinct and years of training, he found himself suddenly standing stiffly in place, showing his readiness to answer the questions of his elders and accept whatever correction or other judgment they had to offer.

"I do not agree that this is the wisest course, my Lord."

"And why not?" asked Dra'Lengish. "How come you to wisdom in such matters? Or would you dare to keep secrets from your Lord Commander?"

Casting his glance downward, Shenali knew that his only chance for salvation lie in humility. But arrogance filled his heart, such arrogance as he had never known. It surprised him fully as much as it amazed the others, and was as mysterious to him as the paradox of Life itself. Lifting his eyes defiantly, his body quivering with fear, the young Subaltern spoke quietly, but firmly. His gaze never left the dour face of Dra'Lengish, whose countenance softened as he heard the Young One speak.

"No, Lord Lengish," he said with a bow of respect. "And I would never think to mention it, were my opinion not sought. But it seems to me that the Beast has either destroyed himself by entering the Cloud or that, having cut his escape route by half, he will emerge unscathed from the Cloud and move directly to *Gr'Shuna* to lead an attack against the planet. In either case, we should move with all speed toward *Gr'Shuna*. For if the Beast dies in the Cloud we lose nothing, even as we gain by reinforcing the planet while the Terran Fleet sits idle. But if the Beast emerges safely, he will surely beat us to the planet. And we would benefit by pressing our fleet upon the Terrans before he has the chance to organize his forces. Thus, simple logic dictates that— "

"*Silence!*" thundered Va'Nazze, who turned at once toward the scowling face of the Ga'Glish. "Lordship, such impudence cannot be tolerated. Surely, you can entertain no further doubts about this commoner's unfitness for continued service."

His eyes filling with the prideful gaze of royalty, Ga'Glish stared silently at the young officer. Shenali felt an eternity of humiliation pass before Ga'Glish deigned to speak. Even then, the Lord Commander spoke with the precision of one not unused to putting a rabbler in his proper place.

"Of what are you speaking, Lord Nazze? For I have heard nothing. When he is ready, I am sure that the Young One will make his answer."

As the attention of the assembly returned to the task at hand, fa'Shenali wished for nothing so much as a painless death. But as he was not dismissed, he had no choice but to stand rigidly in place, watching those around him go about their duties. Worst of all, he had to endure the ignominy of their inattention, even as he felt the haughtiness of their disdain. Struggling to contain his emotions, his mind and body soon became numb as he sought to lose himself in thoughts of happier times—of boyhood outings with his mother, or the joy of discovering the fleeting worlds that formed in the seaside pools left by the changing tides.

Moment after moment passed into oblivion, as orders were received and executed, and all around him joined as one in the firmness of their resolve to strike at the Beast. It left the young man isolated and alone in his public abasement. And he remained, standing rigidly in place, until the last of them had gone, and he was free to collapse into the anguish of self-despair.

* * *

A WHOLE DAY passed.

By the second day, La'Shendra had started feeling hopeful once more. Checking his instruments to ensure that they remained in position, he let his eyes wander over the vast expanse of hydrogen that stretched in all directions around them. The *Frusenite* Eminence or Lesser Bend, stood between them and *Gr'Shuna*, screening their operations from the intrusive eyes of Terran sensors; *Shunita*, the major promontory between *Gr'Shuna* and the Grand Basin, lay before them, its whirling eddies and flashes of interstellar lightening casting an eerie glow over the blackness. The intervening cosmic *cul-de-sac*, the *Fruseniti* Clearing, at once gave the small reconnaissance squadron a shield for protection and a dagger pressed against their throat. Though it gave them room to hide from the enemy while they kept track of the curiously inert Terran movements to the west, it also trapped them inside. None could leave its safety without revealing their position to the longnoses. And with their newest orders, if the Beast were to emerge from the Promontory....

La'Shendra shuddered, as if from the cold. He would not allow dark thoughts to burden his mind today. Such imaginings belonged to the past, for today was a Day of Hopefulness. It was nearly two days since the Beast disappeared into the swirls and storms of the Promontory; each passing hour strengthened the probability that the monster would never emerge. As Shendra kept a vigilant eye, carefully watching his zone for signs of approaching Death, he amused himself by listening to his subordinates talk about the past. Or their hopes for the future. Or the females they had enjoyed.

For himself, he thought, it was enough to watch the Universe around him, to marvel at the unending size and complexity of creation. He thought of the mate he had left behind on his home planet, far to the East, of the endless torment she must endure with news of each new disaster. And he thought of his parents—of the child they still fussed over, and the grandchildren he might never be able to give them.

So involved in his ruminations was he that he missed the first changing readings on the monitor board. Several moments passed before he noticed his screen showing levels of energy on a scale occurring nowhere in nature outside an interstellar storm. It was several moments more before his could admit to himself the truth of what his senses were telling him.

"All ears," he called into his voicephone and into the transmitter, broadcasting his message to subordinates throughout the nearby skies. His voice was unwavering and firm, as expected of a Centurion in the service of His Worthiness. His underlings deserved no less, and the strictness of his training made anything else unthinkable.

"Unidentified readings show on the monitor screens, emerging from the Promontory. All ships, converge toward the source of the readings; all hearts, converge toward death for the Beast."

Steering toward the spot where the longnoses were beginning to make their way clear of the Penultimata, the last wisps before interstellar condensation cleared the skies of sensor-fogging gasses, Shendra felt his soul shatter like brittle glass falling against a stone. He soon burned with hatred for the barbarians who were destroying everything he knew, and he tried to force himself not to think of all he would be leaving behind.

The end would come soon enough without getting morbidly sentimental, he told himself. Dwelling on what he was about to lose would only reduce him to a quivering mass of emotions, and leave him unable to turn his final heartbeats into moments of eternal pride.

Chapter 23

LOOK—HERE HE COMES."

The three young yeomen each turned from a monitor screen, standing as the blueshirt stepped through the door and slowly walked toward Monitor Bank Two. Stooping slightly at the shoulders, the oldtimer walked with the patience of age, knowing that life was too short to hurry.

Jim Jefferson had seen this day coming for a long time. The Monitor Stations were CosGuard's advance warning system, able to discern enemy movements days in advance of the tracking systems available on the line. Since the early days of the war they'd worked well, giving the Terran fleet warning of every major enemy counteroffensive since the terrible days of the first Lagrush campaign. Yet the changing of the guard meant changes throughout the lines of command. Having swept through the front lines like a cleaning drone, was only a matter of time before they took the broom to the support staff as well.

Bright lights danced across the equipment, as the computers collated and compared each second's readings with the one just passed. Jefferson stepped slowly toward his favorite monitor team. The three young greenshirts waiting for him at the other end of the ramp brought with them an infectious irreverence and enthusiasm for their jobs. It was enough to make him feel good about the future again, he thought. Almost enough to make him sad about getting sacked.

"Commander Jefferson...," began Gentry, the tall one on the left. He was tall and gangly, just like his sister's oldest boy.

"As you were, Lads," the commander barked, as gruffly as he could through a wistful smile. "Don't mean to interrupt; you boys just carry on. I'm just passing through to say my goodbyes."

The soft blips of the subspace radar faded into the background as the three young greenshirts shuffled about, embarrassed to give voice to their thoughts. Goodbyes were a common thing in this day and age, and friendships of a lifetime were often made and broken weekly. But a good commander was as rare as ever. It was hard to bid farewell to someone who'd been a bedrock for such a big part of their lives.

"We think it's a damn shame, Mr. J," Gentry said at last.

"A damn rotten shame," interjected Ramsey, a short, stocky Demetrian.

Jefferson laughed softly. War might make men out of boys overnight, he thought, but the lads were still green as the shirts on their backs. They might never know just how lucky he'd been in his life. And he hoped to God they'd never come to know just how little a man could come to care about losing a post he'd spent a lifetime working to get. Not after what he'd seen happen to those who'd tried fighting back. And not after learning just what kinds of boots he'd be licking if he wanted to keep his position.

"At ease, Lads. I'll have none of that rank sentimentality, if you don't mind. A change in command often brings changes across the boards. And at my age—well, I doubt I'd be here much longer here, anyway."

He laughed at their protests, afraid to let show just how much their loyalty in the face of his disclaimers meant to him. Finally, he held up his hand.

"Anyway, it's all official. I'm shipping back to Looking Glass tomorrow for reassignment. Your new commander will be shipping in any day now. I expect you to show this newcomer the same respect you've always given me."

"He'll have to earn it, Mr. J, same as you," said Gentry.

"Or she," the commander laughed. "I hear it might well be a birdie, and something of a greentail, at that. Fresh from behind a desk."

"Well, so long as the tail's a lively one, Mr. J. That's all that concerns the rakes on this hunk of tin."

As the four men shared a final laugh, Jefferson thought back to some of the strange readings they'd seen the past few days. Signals as strong as a dozen ion storms, raging for an hour, then fading away into nothing. It was as if the Cloud were about to break loose with the full fury of the heavens, and Lord knows they'd seen their share of storms along the way. The Cloud was a natural incubator, hatching ill winds like a flatulent spacer. But there was something odd about this one; it was like nothing he'd seen before.

"Any new readings?" he asked, regretting the need to let business intrude upon the moment.

"Not a peep," answered McCauley. "The whole field's as clear as the night sky on Ishtar. Or a class-one whore on the *Flying Duchess.*"

Shaking his head at the follies of youth, the old commander bid his charges a last farewell. As he left, he found himself wondering about the changes he'd seen as the Old Guard found itself brushed aside by the New. He'd heard about some of the top-level reassignments, and wondered if the general exodus to New Babylon would include the middle level brass. Wars were not undertakings for the old or faint-hearted, he smiled to himself. He was coming to wonder if the same saw applied to office politics. But he was surprised to find himself actually looking forward to assignment to a less demanding post.

As his footsteps sounded down the metal floorings, he never once thought about the unusual sensor readings they'd uncovered. Duly reported along the new chain of command, now that it had faded he dismissed it as the echoes of a brewing storm, or an anomaly of the sort that cropped up from time to time, swirling madly for a frightening instant, then disappearing into the nothingness of space.

He came to the lift, which would take him down to the next level for another round of goodbyes. Though too modest to acknowledge it, the polished trim and spotless tiles were silent tributes to the man who'd run the station with pride and the patient eyes of experience. For good or ill, the New Guard was coming east with a vengeance. Now that his own battle was over, he wished them well in the fight against the lizards.

* * *

FROM THE elation of emerging alive from a hazardous and seemingly endless fog, the *d'Artagnan's* bridge was struck dumb by the news. Cook stood up, his eyes fixed on the screen. The last thing he expected to find on this side of the Cloud was the enemy, closing as if they were expecting him.

"Range?"

At the systems desk, Dexter hurried with the calculations.

"Twenty klicks and closing at flank speed."

"Readings on their size and strength?"

"Not yet, but they're near enough for close-range sensors. I'll have the data analyzed as soon as I can."

As the seconds crept by, Cook forced himself to concentrate on the outlying skies. The advancing enemy was coming from anticenternorthwest; to center, the skies opened westward. And he recalled the promontories just east of Girshoona. It was possible—in fact, he was nearly certain—that this was a small *cul-de-sac*, a clearing around a newly condensed star. Commandeering a small auxiliary sensor screen on the starboard wall, he scanned the surrounding skies intently. Soon, he found what he was looking for, a small, blue star, right in the center of the clearing, still trailing a spiral of gas and debris in its wake.

Immediately, he relaxed. The oncoming enemy was there by accident, and would be outgunned and overmatched. But now, he was certain that he was right: they were being chased. Otherwise, without someone else to radio ahead with a warning, the Crutchtan outpost would never have been expecting the enemy to emerge from inside the Cloud. The only question in his mind was how much time they had to get out of the *cul-de-sac* before the main force appeared.

"Three dozen enemy ships, Chaser-class," reported Dexter. "All armed and...."

"Anything approaching from the East?"

"Pardon me?"

"Do the screens show any enemy ships approaching from the East?"

Confused, Dexter looked at his instruments, then shook his head.

"No, sir."

"You sure?"

"Yes, sir. But the Chasers will be here in about...."

"Mr. Gerlach, charge all shields; stand by to charge the forward guns."

"Aye, sir."

"The Chasers will be— "

"Helm, stand by to increase speed to C-15—heading 125, twenty points south."

"Yes sir."

"The Chasers— "

"Mathison, radio the others and tell them to match our speed and heading. Single file, same as in the Cloud. They're to avoid engaging the approaching enemy except as needed to defend against attack. Transmit the order in written form. I want there to be no mistake about the command."

"Aye, aye."

"Mr. Dexter— "

"The Chasers— "

"Never mind the Chasers, Lieutenant. Keep your sensors focused due east and let me know the second you see anything unusual."

"But sir— "

"Yes, I know. The Chasers are armed and on their way. And you have your orders."

Dexter exchanged a nervous glance with Mathison and Danley. Concern in their eyes, the three junior officers worried that Cook was digging himself into a hole. Eyes forward, her attention to the screens in front of her, Janet was too busy with her own worries to communicate with the others; she just hoped that Skipper knew what he was doing. Only Gerlach seemed unconcerned about the events unfolding. But he was busy with the ship's weapons systems, and knew that he'd soon have to deal with a few dozen enemy chasers scrambling around the sky.

"Helm—engage."

Soon, the ship shuddered under the increased stress, and Cook felt himself pressed against the side of his chair. As the ship swerved sharply to port, he turned his chair to face the eastward screens. Brow narrowed in concentration, his eyes scoured the skies, intently searching for the first hint of the enemy fleet as his crew went nervously about their duties.

"TRACTOR BEAM'S engaged, Mr. Finley."

Collapsing into his seat, Finley smiled weakly at the old yeoman. He peered out the forward viewer, to see the *Morning Star* looming as she drew them toward her. It had been a harrowing ride, trying to keep right on the starships' trail without ramming the Mother Ship from astern. And it was unnerving, Finley thought, keeping their eyes peeled for the odd chunk of debris that could send their small ship to kingdom come. Focusing that much attention for such a long time was exhausting. It was a relief to have it all behind them.

"Plans, Mr. Flanagan?"

"Sleep, Mr. Finley. Nothing more than sleep."

"I think I owe you a beer, Yeoman."

"Only if you take your change in whiskey."

Finley laughed. The two of them had been through a lot together, he smiled. It would be nice to leave someone else in charge. And Flanagan was right about another thing. Once safe and sound aboard the *Morning Star*, he doubted that he'd find the energy to stir for days. Let the war tend to itself for a while, he thought. For now, it was somebody else's turn to take the chances, and worry the worries.

"WHAT!?"

Wincing visibly, Cindy Stockman swallowed hard and took a deep breath. "We are ordered," she repeated, "to disengage the enemy and to follow *d'Artagnan* and *Morning Star*, heading 125 under 20, around the last bend in the Cloud, en route to Girshoona."

Fitz slammed his fist onto his armrest, then leaped to his feet. His jaw locked in anger, his brown eyes dark with hate, he paced about the bridge, his nervous energy impelling him toward motion. There was much about the Isitian he could never understand, Fitz told himself. But running away from a fight, especially against an enemy that seemed so interested in self-immolation, was positively criminal. He could overlook a lot. Talent often came with eccentricities, after all. And for all his shortcomings, Cookie was a force of nature in battle—a regular whirlwind. But this sort of rank cowardice was unforgivable.

"Anything else?" he snapped.

Cindy nodded, almost afraid to give her commander the other half of the message. "We're ordered not to open fire, not to engage the enemy in any way except in defense. And we're to signal confirmation of the message."

"Confirma—," he began, stopping in mid-thought. Storming back to the command seat, Fitz activated the small viewer on his armrest and glared at the message for several minutes. Gradually, his eyes softened, and he managed a small smile of self-satisfaction. When he spoke, the anger was gone from his voice. But his cold, humorless eyes sent shivers of foreboding through the spine of his radio officer.

"All right, Miss Stockman. And relax, for crying out loud. There's no cause for concern, here. Radio your confirmation. And tell the *d'Artagnan* to lead on, and that we'll fall into line, right behind the *Morning Star*."

"Aye, Captain," Cindy nodded warily. The forced calmness in the captain's voice did little to help her relax. She heard just enough overtones of defiance to make her wonder what the captain had in mind.

As he listened to Lt. Stockman relay the message, Fitz leaned back in his chair. Rocking back and forth, he turned his eyes westward, to the regrouping enemy formation that was lurking just beyond the range of his blasters. The corners of his lips turned up in a tight, determined smile. Cookie was learning, he thought, documenting his orders like that. But nobody ever accused the Isitian of being slow. It was almost like he knew they'd be fighting each other, once they got back to the safety of their own lines. If their next battle would be fought with paper, then so be it. There wouldn't be anything Cookie could do about it, he laughed mirthlessly. Not this time. Not the way Cook had worded his order. And certainly not the way any board of review would see it. If Cookie's career was about to go down in flames, it was his own damn fault: the Guard had no room for cowards. Not in this day and age.

Fitz gazed sternly into the starboard screens, staring contemptuously at the two-dozen small enemy ships left alive after their initial pass. He vowed that if it was the last thing he did, he'd see those lizards burning. Heaven itself was littered with the remains of men—women, too— friends he'd known in better times, lads who'd given him more than he realized at the time, whose fate was now to float the frozen cosmos as the charred remnants of happier days. The lizards could light the darkness, and he'd scatter their ashes before the winds of Hell. For the sake of all who'd gone before him, he'd fry as many of the slimy buggers as he could.

* * *

A SINGLE CANDLE lit the entranceway. The incense of mourning filled the air, and a lone presence sat on a ceremonial pillow, beside a silken tapestry in a darkened corner of the room. Ga'Glish sat by himself, meditating on the cruelties and imperfections of life. Tears filled his eyes, and he rocked gently, back and forth, gently chanting the songs of his youth, made all the more painful by his own lack of innocence. It was hard enough to mourn the passing of a mate, he thought amid the dimness. To live through the passing of one's home was more than anyone should have to bear.

Sensing a change in his surroundings, Ga'Glish looked up to see that a second presence had intruded upon his solitude. The beads of the entranceway were still swaying gently, their disruption casting shadows of movement in the stillness.

"Forgive me, my Lord," said the interloper. It was Dra'Lengish, his Chief of Tactics. Ga'Glish could sense the pain his old friend felt, and knew at once that the news Dra'Lengish brought would be quite unpleasant.

"What is it, Lengish?"

"I regret— "

"Courage, Old Friend."

Lord Lengish fell to his knees beside his Commander, his voice heavy with emotion.

"I regret to inform Your Lordship that our stratagem has failed. The Terrans are departing. They are even now sailing toward the Lesser Bend at greater speeds than our ships can muster. They will surely pass beyond the bend before we can arrive to intercept them. I am sorry, my Lord. I have failed you."

Ga'Glish bowed his head; when he spoke, his words came directly from his heart.

"You have not failed, Lengish. None of us has failed, my Trusted One. We cannot command the enemy to do our bidding. Perhaps the task has been hopeless from the start."

"Lordship—"

"Leave me, Old Friend," whispered Ga'Glish. "I wish to mourn our Homeland in silence."

As his friend departed, tears flowed down the cheeks of Ga'Glish. How had he known? Ga'Glish asked himself over and over again. It was as if the Beast could sense danger in the barren winds of the Cosmos, like a bird fleeing a storm just beyond the horizon.

The Tall One knew the star maps well enough to recall them from memory: hastening toward the Bend, the Terran ships could easily outrace the fastest ship in the Imperial Fleet. Once past the Bend, nothing would stand between the Beast and *Gr'Shuna*. Their Home would fall to the barbarians, who could even now claim it without shedding any but the green blood of the *g'Khruushtani*. The longnoses would attack at long last, their mindless, primitive evil destroying all he had known and loved, laying waste to the dreams of countless generations. A jewel of the Empire would fall to barbarism, and he could do nothing to stop it.

Worse, it seemed as if he trailed doom in his shadow: all he had done merely hastened the coming disaster. Every decision he made, every step he took, seemed only to lead further in the wrong direction, bringing catastrophe all the nearer.

Crying aloud in anguish, Ga'Glish lifted his face to the ceiling and wailed, the pain of failure flowing through his veins. He had no illusions about what was to come, and little hope. Nothing short of a miracle could stop the Beast now.

* * *

AN OPPRESSIVE STILLNESS gripped the *d'Artagnan's* bridge. Only the clicks and whirs of the ship's computers broke the silence. His jaw twitching angrily, Cook glowered at the aft viewer. In the six minutes since Mathison reported the message from the *Magellan* and Dexter noticed that she was breaking formation, only Cook and Mathison had exchanged words. In the minutes since the radio officer reported no response from their Red Priority hail, nobody had dared to speak. They just tended to their duties and tried to avoid thinking about what the Skipper might do next.

Suddenly, Cook whirled around and glared at the radio desk.

"Well?" he demanded.

Mary shrugged her shoulders and shook her head.

"Damn fool," Cook muttered. He plopped sullenly into his chair.

"Mathison," he continued, his voice angry and cold, "log the following communication to the *Magellan*: 'Captain Fitzgerald—you are ordered to return to formation at once, and to acknowledge this order immediately.' Let me know when a full minute has passed."

"Aye, sir."

Cook rocked sullenly in his chair, replaying the message from Fitz over and over in his mind. "Moving to cover retreat against enemy attack," it had read. "Will follow when threat is over." A blind idiot could have seen this coming, Cook told himself. And any dolt would have made sure that the *Magellan* wasn't bringing up the rear.

"Sensors show *Magellan* moving to intercept enemy attack squadrons," reported Dexter. "Range, ten klicks; heading...."

"Thank you, Mr. Dexter, but that will be all. Keep your sensors trained to the East."

"But— "

"Mathison?"

Mary shook her head. "No reply."

"Is the minute up?"

"Half-way there, sir."

Cook rose and paced slowly about the bridge, marking off the seconds until the deadline passed. It would be less infuriating, he decided, if he could be certain he was right.

"Mathison?"

"Time coming... *mark*."

"Inform Captain Fitzgerald that he is relieved of command," Cook said, staring at his aft viewer. "Instruct his executive officer to assume command, and return the *Magellan* immediately to formation. Log the order, same as the others."

"Aye, aye."

Cook strode to his seat and resumed the chair. His eyes were angry. His voice was cold as the void surrounding his ship.

"Helm, maintain course; Mathison, tell *Morning Star* to set course for the point dead ahead."

"Aye aye."

"Yes, sir."

"*Morning Star* acknowledges."

"Helm—stand by for full speed ahead, C-15."

"Ahead at fifteen, yes sir; standing by."

"Mathison— "

"Sir?"

"At this speed, we'll pass out of audio range in about ten minutes. Dexter—in five minutes let me know if the *Magellan* is returning to formation.

"Aye, sir."

"Helm?"

"Ready, Skipper."

"Engage."

"Engaging."

* * *

CINDY STOCKMAN felt her courage sink into her boots. Like the first two, this third message was unmistakable. But this time it was her neck on the chopping block. Third in command on *Magellan's* bridge, she could do little but stand by while the Captain and his executive officer defied the Commodore. Now Cook had dropped everything onto her lap.

"Weapons?" barked Fitz.

"Last pass wiped out all but a half-dozen of the slimy bastards," crowed Landrum, the *Magellan's* weapons officer. "Next pass should see us finish off the lot o' them."

"Cap–Captain?" stammered Cindy.

"Not now, Missy," snapped Fitz.

"It's another message from the *d'Artagnan*. This time...."

"I said, not now!" roared Fitz. He turned in his seat to face the forward screens. His chest was pounding like a kettle drum. He watched the last straggling lizard ships regroup, and move slowly into formation for their last charge. His eyes narrowed bitterly, and a consuming hatred for the enemy flooded his brain. He could think of nothing beyond crushing the life out of the few lizards he saw coming into formation, beginning what would be their final attack. He knew exactly what Cookie was trying to do. But Fitz was determined not to let anyone keep him from ridding the Universe of a few more slimy bastards.

With all attention focused on the looming battle, the systems officer never noticed the faint readings just starting to appear on the aft sensors.

THE BRIGHT FLASH of light to his left caused La'Shendra to wince. He did not need to look to discern its cause. He knew, as well as he knew the face of his mate, what the flash meant. There remained but two ships left of their attack force; two small ships making their hopeless charge against the death ship of the longnoses.

Quickly, Shendra purged his mind of such notions. They could lead only to despair and cowardice, he thought. He would not have his last moments alive sullied by cowardice. Around him, he sensed the growing fear among his underlings. All aboard knew the fatal truth, and none harbored illusions about their fate. But he was their leader. And he had vowed to make his final heartbeats moments of pride.

"Steady at the wheel," he spoke, in a reassuring tone of voice. "Keep on course." Around him, apprehension hung in the air like a mist, yet none uttered a word except in duty. He felt the hardening crystal of courage inside them. Sensing their terror at the prospect of the Grand Journey, he felt a surge of royal pride in his subordinates. But this surge carried with it the aching of loss, for he knew the truth even if the thought was forbidden. He longed for the freedom to weep for the loved ones he would never touch again.

A flash lighted the skies to his right, and Shendra knew that they were continuing their lost charge against the barbarians alone.

"Weapons at the ready?" he asked, his voice ringing with the courage of a thousand generations.

"Ready," whispered the wide-eyed young man to his left, his finger poised over the release button. He was the son of a shopkeeper, and had left home shortly before the birth of a son he would never see.

La'Shendra sensed the young one's numbing fear, and flushed with the pride of blood. They were all of one blood now, he reflected sadly. And their ashes would mingle through eternity.

"Fire!" he cried.

At the same instant, a fearful flame burst from the Terran ship. His own craft shook violently under the impact of some unseen force. Horror erupted everywhere, and he heard animal screams, and the shouts of souls consumed by their own mortality. A wrenching fear rose in his chest, forcing open his mouth to join the chorus of terror, unleashing the innermost reaches of his being amid the earsplitting roar building beneath him. Then a gentle warmth washed over him, and everything dissolved into peace.

* * *

OBLIVION MARKS neither time nor space: time is but a marking-post of life, just as space merely defines its corporeal limits. Without consciousness to note its passing, time is without meaning, and space is only emptiness.

But in the silence of eternity, darkness blends into shadows, and shadows pass into light. As life dawns in the Universe, light ripens into awareness.

Slowly, Fitz stirred in his chair.

It took several moments for Fitz to orient himself, and another minute or two for the magnitude of what had happened to register through the fog. The scene felt like a bad dream. The acrid smoke, the half-light, and the sensation of weightlessness, left Fitz fighting the urge to escape back into unconsciousness.

When he was fully awake, reality struck him like a bolt of lightening. He looked about him, and recoiled in horror. Half his bridge crew lay unconscious, floating in the air like ghosts. The rest remained fastened into their seats, held in place by their lap restraints. He tried to call their names, but words froze in his throat. Terror seized him, and to his horror he discovered that he couldn't utter a sound to save his life.

He pressed down on the control panel on his armrest, and nothing happened. Again and again, harder and harder, he slammed his hand down onto the buttons.

Nothing.

He pressed the emergency button to signal the engineering deck.

No response.

He signaled the hangar deck.

Silence.

He tried to power up the self-destruct controls.

Nothing.

Suddenly it registered: he was weightless.

None of the systems lights showed on the consoles.

And he couldn't get a single control working; not a single one.

The ship was without power.

He had no idea what had happened, and no clue about what had left his ship powerless and adrift. His head swimming, he tried to activate the emergency override, to seize control from the bridge, to get the engines going again, if only to garner enough power to set the self-destruct sequence. He pressed the override button, again and again, but it was no use: his ship was a lifeless hulk. And he was floating helplessly through the void.

Fighting panic, he rose from his seat and sent himself floating toward the auxiliary controls rimming the topside of the bridge. Circuit after circuit was dead. At last he pressed the lever for the emergency distress beacon, and the panel sprang to life. He would never know that he'd stumbled across a fluke of engineering, put in place by a long-forgotten technician who somehow managed to convince his superiors that the distress beacon should be on its own self-generating circuit. His mind nearly paralyzed with fear, Fitz initiated the long-wave signal for "Ship in Trouble"—three short blasts, three long, three short. He programmed the small computer to send his "SOS" out into space, and said a small prayer, hoping that he hadn't been out of commission for too long.

And he prayed that his sister ships still hadn't rounded the Point. That there would be someone out there—someone other than the lizards—to hear his distress call.

His beacon set, Fitz moved to check the rest of his ship to see what was happening belowdecks. He hurled himself through the air toward the handhold beside the entrance ramp leading to the interior of the ship, only to collide with the barren metal. The door sensors, like the rest of the ship, were drained of all power, all life.

Cranking open the emergency compartment beside the entry door, Fitz took out a handblaster, aimed it at the midpoint of the hatch, and burned a hole through the metal.

His head reeled with horror and terrified wonderment. He thanked whichever malevolent gods had brought him to this state for leaving behind something that still worked. Fitz stepped through the open hole and into the blackness that lay beyond.

Chapter 24

I DON'T WANT AN ARGUMENT, Jeremy."

"I'm sorry, Skipper—"

"And I won't have you risking—"

"You hold it right there!" Jeremy snapped, his dark eyes flashing with anger.

Staring directly into his viewer, Cook would later reflect that he'd never seen such determination in his friend's eyes, or such concern for the selfish, foolish neck of another. At the time, all Cook felt was an angry frustration.

"Just look at the damn sensors!" Jeremy shouted. "Hundreds of enemy ships are pouring into view. With more popping onto the screen every minute. All of them heading right for us. They'll cut you off so fast—"

"I've seen them, Jeremy. I've seen all of them."

"Then they still haven't registered through that thick Isitian hide of yours."

"That will be all, Captain."

"Like hell it will, Skipper. We've been through too much together—"

"Don't get maudlin, Jeremy. You know I hate that."

"Skipper—"

"I've always been able to wriggle out of danger, and I can do it a damn sight better all by myself."

"No, sir."

"I beg your pardon, Mister?"

"I won't stand idly by while you go risking everyone on board your ship. Not like this. Not when we're so close to home. And not when you're about to go off, flying by the seat of your pants again on some half-baked rescue mission. You need someone to cover your wing, Skipper. Someone to absorb a bit of the heat, if it comes to a fight. Like it or not, mine is the only starship around, so I guess you're just plain stuck."

Cook glowered at the image on the screen. Friendship would excuse a lot, he'd recall in less stressful times, and a less fallible human being would have simply thanked his best friend for the help, and for the instinctive selflessness in a moment of crisis. Even at the time, Cook had the passing thought that Jeremy was one of the most thoroughly decent men he'd ever met. But the commodore's ego made it hard to admit the need for help. It made him want to strike out at the first available target. The fact that Jeremy seemed to be right just made him angrier.

"All right, Jeremy," Cook snarled. "You want to risk your foolish neck, you come right along. But you watch your step, Mister. I won't have another subordinate stepping out of line. Not by so much as an inch. And so help me, Jeremy, I've had all the crap I can stand for one mission. If Fitz is going to insist on drawing a court-martial, don't tempt me to make it a twosome."

Jeremy drew a deep breath.

"Understood," he nodded.

"I intend to accomplish two things," Cook said coldly. "I want to find out what disabled the *Magellan,* and I want to save as many of her crew as possible. Those are the objectives, in that exact order. You will provide cover, nothing more. And if I tell you to take off, I will accept nothing less than an 'aye-aye,' followed by an immediate departure. Clear?"

"Absolutely," Jeremy replied, hurt showing through his narrowed eyes.

"We leave at once. Match my speed and heading. At top speed, we'll arrive in five minutes."

"Fine."

"That should give us another thirty minutes before the approaching enemy fleet starts nipping at our heels."

Jeremy closed his eyes, took a deep breath, and nodded.

"Anything else?" he asked after a long pause.

"*D'Artagnan* out."

As the image on his screen began to fade, Cook saw Jeremy shaking his head. A wan smile crossed Jeremy's lips as Cook heard him say, "Over and out."

"You use people, Skipper."

"That's enough, Jeremy."

"You use people up, and spit them out when they no longer suit you."

"That is quite enough, Commander."

"That isn't the start of it, Commodore. You had no right to treat her like that. And no right to keep her dangling like – "

Cook backed Jeremy into the wall and stood, inches away, glaring hatefully....

* * *

STANDING BEFORE the giant screen in the Monitorium, Ga'Glish closed his eyes and lifted his head. Cheers rose from the throats of all around him, filling his ears with shouts of triumph and jubilation. Feeling the clasp of a hand on his shoulder, he looked to see Dra'Lengish smiling more broadly than he had in weeks.

"Are we delivered?" his friend shouted, struggling to make himself heard above the tumult.

"Nothing in life is guaranteed," Ga'Glish shouted in return. "But it looks like the gods have taken to smiling upon us at last."

And indeed it had. As Ga'Glish looked at the screen again, it showed the Terran ships streaking faster than ever toward their disabled comrade, making their way back into peril from the safety of the Bend.

The distress call from the comrade, thought the Lord Commander: they must have heard the distress call as well. How anxiously the longnoses guarded the secrets of their ships, he mused, for he had seen similar behavior before. The *g'Khruushtani* had yet to capture a Terran starship intact; the Terrans, it seemed, preferred destruction to surrendering their most powerful weapon of destruction. On past occasions, the only reply a trapped Terran starship would make to a demand to cease hostilities was an explosion, and the self-immolation of all aboard. Even the One Called *Khu'ukh* was bound by the Terrans' barbaric Code of Honor—though it pained Ga'Glish to recall that on the eve of the War it was only his own civility that had spared the Beast from this grim duty of self-destruction. Ga'Glish found it astonishing that this Code could still bind one such as the Beast, the one Terran commander whose name meant terror to all *g'Khruushtani*.

Ga'Glish let out a bellow of such laughter that heads turned from all across the Monitorium. Why the derelict ship had strayed in the first place remained a mystery, but its very presence was nothing short of miraculous. He found the irony in such a turn of events to be delicious, for it had never occurred to him that a reminder of his darkest moment would prove to be the very instrument of *Khu'ukh's* destruction.

"The Terrans are nearing the source of the distress signal, my Lord," reported an underling from a monitor station. "They will arrive in the next few moments."

"All ships arm themselves," thundered the voice of Ga'Glish, silencing the crowd with the force of his exultation.

"Victory is at hand—death to the Beast! All hearts resolve to destroy the Invader. Death to the Beast!"

"Death—Death," began the chant. Soon, the frenzy of their resolve brought them together as with a single thought, a single focus. They were as one, lost in devotion to the task at hand.

"Death to the Beast!"

* * *

//LOG-ON SWITCH ENGAGED; cc:144-3918.491939.

From its vantage, on a massive metallic ball in a lazy orbit around the bright yellow star of a warm blue planet, a strange sequence of readings tripped a switch in Automonitor 6-East. Earlier, an invisible surge of subspace power had penetrated a thin spot in the thick clouds of the East Girshoonan Promontory. Now, its sensors had detected the dull, indistinct rumble of low frequency signals.

The computer whirred and clicked, its primitive brain noting and collating the anomalies. But the rumble quickly faded, as shifting cloud patterns scrambled, then screened the signal. Searching its memory banks for an analogue, the computer found and logged the likeliest source:

/NOTE PROBABLE TERTIARY STAR CLOUD, IN SECOND STAGE OF CONDENSATION; quadrant: e 134 n 043, range: 12-25 parsecs(est)/

The information stored, the machine turned to its next assigned task. The rumble had lasted less than a second. Unless it recurred, the requisite for tripping the paging program was three.

/LOG-OFF SWITCH ENGAGED, recorded the computer; cc:144-3918.492017//.

Chapter 25

THE *MAGELLAN* HUNG IN THE blackness like a floating tomb, showing no signs of life. Listing to port, she drifted helplessly through space, her running lights as dark as death.

On the bridge of the *d'Artagnan*, Cook paced stiffly about, his eyes fixed on his forward screen, his jaw twitching angrily. Nobody dared to break the silence; they knew from experience that the first to do so would bear the brunt of their Skipper's temper. Yet each was reluctant to speak for another reason as well. The unspoken questions on everyone's mind were the same.

What had happened? How could mere chasers disable a starship?

Though his mind burned with curiosity, Cook had no answers. The ship showed no outward signs of damage, ruling out a wayward asteroid or other freak accident. Yet facts were facts. No matter how mad he might be at her captain, or how mysterious the source of her condition, the *Magellan* was now a derelict hulk. And he had less than thirty minutes to figure out why. Lost in thought, he returned to the command seat.

"Mr. Dexter," he said at last. "Molly over with a search team. I'll give you twenty minutes. Make each minute count."

"Aye aye!" Dexter was on his feet in an instant.

"Draw two squadrons of redshirts," Cook called out as Dexter raced up the ramp leading to the interior of the ship. "One to find answers, one to search for survivors. And make it quick. Don't forget, the enemy's right on our tail."

"On my w— "

As the closing hatch door cut off his system's officer reply, Cook swivelled his chair to his left. He watched the tactical display on the Number Two screen as it showed the Crutchtans approaching, their numbers increasing with each passing second.

Thirty cosmic minutes, he thought. Three thousand seconds. At top speed, the Crutchtans would be upon them in three thousand seconds.

He turned to the westward screen and stared at the image of swirling interstellar gases fading into the distance. He knew it to be a vast promontory, jutting out from the great Cloud, standing between them and Planet Girshoona.

They had already cheated death once, he told himself. They'd dashed blindly through one small cloud and lived to remember it. With the advancing enemy cutting off their only remaining lane of retreat, it seemed they'd have to do it again. Only this cloud was a lot thicker than the last one.

Smiling cryptically, Cook tried to keep from computing the odds on safely traversing another gas cloud. He knew it would only depress him, and was too variable a calculation in the first place. There was simply no way of knowing, and nothing he could do could reduce the risk. But wondering whether they'd be alive in a few hours was likely to prove a far more compelling topic of contemplation than figuring out what had sucked the life from the *Magellan*. He had no intention of letting his bridge crew dwell silently on such a morbid subject.

"All right, Mr. Gerlach, run another check of the weapons systems," he commanded. "We may need them before long. Mathison, stay in contact with the search team. We may have to yank them back at a moment's notice. Mendelson—Danley—I want our course plotted and set for departure, heading 750."

"Into the...."

"That's right, Commander. Smack into the Cloud. I don't like it either, but I will not hear another word about it."

With his bridge crew busily engaged in their duties, Cook sank glumly into the command chair and activated the controls for his console screen. Silently, and however much he tried to distract himself by trying to pinpoint the thinnest, wispiest segment of cloud he could find, he found his mind returning to the frailty of men, and the shortness of life.

Sensing the regal presence behind him, the monitor looked up from his screen and turned to see the Lord Commander, accompanied by his entire retinue, filling the Monitorium until it was about to burst.

"Report!" commanded the voice of Ga'Glish.

"The Beast and a second ship have rejoined their disabled companion. How long they will remain cannot be known."

"Why did the third ship stay behind?" asked Dra'Lenish.

"That is also unknown."

"Had we wished to know what we know not," smiled Va'Nazze, "we would have summoned fa'Shenali the Common."

All eyes turned to the slender youth at the edge of the crowd. As the royal retainers enjoyed some small merriment at the expense of the junior aide, Ga'Glish carefully pondered his next move. The Beast was cunning and dangerous, and one could never discern his next movement. But they had succeeded in cutting off his only path to safety. This time, surely, he would have no choice but to fight.

"Order to all ships," thundered the Lord Commander, who waited until his scribes were ready to record his command. "Fall into attack formation; all battle groupings to the fore. Support Groups Three and Four to the rear, to serve as reinforcements. All other Support Groups to the flanks. Let us fill this Rille with *g'Khruushtani!* Let us leave the Beast no room to escape!"

From all sides, voices rang in unison, cheering their good fortune and saluting the valor of those who would slay the Beast. Only a single throat kept still, unwilling to speak and barely daring to give thought to his misgivings, lest his thoughts betray his doubts.

Yet even fa'Shenali could not remain a skeptic for long. And as the *g'Khruushtani* fleet hurled swiftly toward their most hated enemy, he even began to feel relief at the prospect that such a glorious victory was at last within their grasp. And in the end he found his voice joining in the celebration as all called for the destruction of the One Called *Khu'ukh.*

THE ENTRY HATCH to the Molecular Transmitter opened with a soft rush of air. As he entered the transmission chamber, Dexter felt his mind racing like a motor, and fought against a growing sense of mental paralysis. The Skipper had shown him a lot of confidence, he thought, but this was his biggest responsibility yet. With great effort he calmed himself. Time was in short supply, and he couldn't waste it worrying about everything that needed doing.

Coming upon the pods that dotted the circular platform, Dexter looked in vain for a green jersey. Running to the control panel on the south wall, he pressed the intercom button. Soon, from a station on the control deck overlooking the transmission chamber, a disembodied voice answered, giving him the answer before Dexter could even ask the question.

"Chief Connors is on his way, Lieutenant."

"Connors? His name wasn't on the duty roster."

"He asked to replace Yeoman Agacinski. The Chief had friends on the *Magellan*. A lot of us did, Mr. D."

"Page him," ordered Dexter, surprised at the edge in his own voice. As he stormed back to the pods, he heard the shipwide speakers fill the ship.

"Yeoman Chief Connors, report at once to the Molecular Transmitter—Chief Connors to Miss Molly, on the double."

Dexter just stepped onto the transmission pods when the hatch opened again. In ran Connors, jersey askew, a sidearm strapped to his belt. He sprinted to the platform and jumped onto the pod next to Dexter.

"Sorry, Lieutenant."

"Stand by," Dexter shouted. He looked up to see Ensign Torraco at the viewing window. She leaned over the console and spoke into the microphone.

"Ready when you are, Dexter," she said, a wave of her hand turning into a small salute. "Good luck."

Dexter glanced about one last time, to make sure that everyone was in position.

"Transmit," he said.

Tightly shutting his eyes against the flash of a blinding white light, Dexter felt an enveloping warmth bathe his body, and drifted with the sensation of floating through space and time. Soon, lost and disoriented, his heading spinning wildly....

....Dexter opened his eyes to see a charred, gaping hole staring at him through the darkness. Raising his flashlight, he saw a blackened hole where the *Magellan's* control panel for the hangar deck should have been. Lifting his eyes, he saw the smashed windows of the control tower. Everywhere, the acrid smell of burned circuits mixed with the odor of smoldering flesh. He could sense dread rising inside him, tickling his spine as the odors of death sickened his stomach and made his skin itch.

Stepping carefully over the shards of shattered window panels, he made his way to what was once the intercom. He ran his fingers over the cold, jagged metal edge and looked inside. Melted into the fused hulk of metal and plastic, he saw the singed remains of a human head, half consumed by a fiery heat, a single eye staring back at him.

Feeling a ghostly hand grab at his neck, he dropped his flashlight and wailed a high-pitched scream, turning to do battle with the very devil only to find that this particular devil was the spitting image of Chief Connors.

"Lieutenant?"

Taking a deep breath, Dexter tried his best to stay calm.

"Something wrong, Mr. D?"

"Never mind, Chief. We've little time and a great deal to do."

"Aye on that, Lieutenant."

"Assemble the men into two teams," Dexter said, recovering enough composure to regain his wits. "You take half the party to Engineering. Scout the Engine Room for damage and molly any survivors back home. I'll take the rest to the Bridge to see if anything there will give us a clue about what killed the *Magellan*."

"What do you think happened, Mr. D?"

"I don't know, Chief. I just don't know."

"Whatever it was.... "

"Don't think about it, Chief. Not till we've done what we came to do. It'll only get in the way of doing our job, and we've little enough time as it is."

"Aye sir," said Connors. As Dexter returned to examining the ruins of the *Magellan's* molecular transmitter, Connors strode back to the center of the chamber.

"Ears open, ye bunch o'lame-brained laddiebucks," he bellowed. "All right—yaps shut. Squad One, front an' center. You'll be helpin the Lieutenant here—and mark me like a preacher, the first man steppin out o'line'll have hell to pay for it, so help me he will. Squad Two, you'll be a-followin me—an don't any o'ye come to squawkin an jabberin like a flock of birdies on leave. We've bloody lots to do, an the last thing we need is for some fartassed redshirt to be wandrin off for not payin attention."

Leading his men through the open hatch, into the darkened corridor, Connors turned left, heading towards the emergency crawlway that would lead them toward Engineering. Turning right, Dexter headed toward the Bridge, his squad of redshirts in tow. Silence lurked everywhere. In the shadows beyond the beams of their flashlights, they saw no signs of life.

Rounding the last bend in the corridor, the squadron came to the walkway leading to the Bridge. From the direction of the Bridge, a gentle glow fell across their path, casting jagged shadows onto the opposite wall.

Dexter rounded the corner and stood there with his mouth hanging open, his flashlight pointing down to the floor.

Illuminated dimly, and still as death, the captain's chair was clearly visible through a gaping hole in the entry hatch. Striding quickly down the ramp, Dexter stopped to examine the opening; running his fingers over its black, jagged edge, he felt moistness on his fingertips. Shining his light onto his hand, then quickly to the source on the hatch, the reddish liquid he saw was as unmistakable.

It was blood.

Fresh blood.

A cold chill tickled Dexter's spine.

Carefully stepping through the hole, willling himself to ignore the relentless pounding of his own chest, Dexter led his squad onto the rampwalk leading down into *Magellan's* bridge. He hoped he could find some answers. He knew they'd find more questions.

"Blood!" exclaimed a young crewman behind him, his voice flushed with panic.

Dexter didn't even hear him; his mind was already wondering about the next mystery, already asking himself whose blood it was. And how it came to be smeared across the hole in the bridge hatch.

"CHIEF!"

Connors stopped suddenly and turned on his heels, causing the procession of redshirts to clatter into a gnarl of confusion.

"Hold, ye bloody fools!" he snapped at the two young crewmen behind him, as they collided into his massive frame. Standing his ground, Connors pushed back hard against the press of bodies.

"Chief!"

This time Connors recognized the voice; it was Johannsen, whom he'd posted aft. He heard urgency in the crewman's voice, and Johannsen was the most level-headed of the present motley bunch.

"What is it, Johnny? Speak up, Lad—an the rest o'ye, stop whinin like a herd o'natt'rin nanniegoats."

"Chief Connors—quick! I found one. Still alive, he is. Out like a sot in the wastelands of Ishtar, but breathin' like a baby."

Making his way through the rest of the squad, Connors stepped down the corridor, toward the sound of the voice, his flashlight casting a ribbon of light through the dark. Soon, standing over the kneeling figure of Crewman Johannsen, he shined his light on the limp body of a young greenshirt. Half the lad's face was badly burned, as if caught by the flash of a great explosion, and blood trickled down from his ears. Around his eyes, like pockets of death, the seared flesh hung like tattered rags, looking to all creation like the poor boy had been struck by the devil himself.

"Hartman," Connors whispered. "It's Hartman."

"Ye know him, Chief?"

Connors didn't answer; he lifted his eyes toward the ceiling and drew a deep breath.

"Call home. Call home and have a medical team a-waitin on Miss Molly," he said at last. "I hope we'll be havin more than this one to be sendin back. An' join us when ye can, Johnny. We'll be up ahead, by Engineerin."

"Aye, Chief."

"The rest o'ye, follow me."

Suddenly fighting his way to the front through a rush of stomping feet, Connors' found his temper growing by the minute.

"I said follow me, ye deaf-eared pack o'mulebrained lemmings. Don't be tearin off blind like that. Let me through—let me through."

As the group started back down the hallway, groping their way through the darkness, Connors tried to push the image of the unconscious yeoman from his mind. He'd seen injuries like that before. Pirates mostly, survivors of their own efforts to flee the pursuit of the Law. The lucky ones didn't make it; those that did often awoke to find themselves blind. Most woke up screaming at the top of their lungs, never to stop. Whatever it was that melted their flesh was often enough to addle their brains, as well.

Maybe this time would be different, he thought. He pushed on toward Engineering, struggling mightily to fight the emotions building inside him. Maybe he was an ignorant fool, always living in the past. Wars always brought about great advances in Medicine. Maybe the doctors had learned enough to bring people back from the ranks of the living dead.

In the meantime, they had work to do. If there were any more survivors, they had bloody little time to find them.

STEPPING THROUGH the jagged opening in the hatch, Dexter walked down the ramp leading to the *Magellan's* bridge. Quiet as a catacomb, the narrow passageway opened into the small, arching dome that had been the great ship's nerve center. Across the room the emergency lights cast eerie shadows that moved and altered with each step he took.

Dexter looked up and nearly screamed: three of the *Magellan's* bridge crew were floating through the air, their limp bodies hanging like ghostly specters suspended in time and space. The rest sat slumped and lifeless at their posts, their faces burned beyond recognition. Soot-stained arms waved aimlessly in the weightlessness of death, as their chairs continued rocking under the impact of whatever had killed them.

Forcing himself to stay calm, Dexter counted the bodies: there were seven in all. Systems, navigation, helm, radio, weapons, command, plus two redshirts. Security most likely, he thought. But something wasn't quite right. Counting again, it became apparent: someone was missing. Aside from the two redshirts, only the radio desk and the captain's seat were empty. The others all died at their posts.

Rushing past him, the rest of his search team poured into the bridge, racing to check the bodies for signs of life.

"Captain Fitzgerald," Dexter whispered.

"What's that, Lieutenant?" asked the young redshirt nearest him.

"Nothing."

"Mr. D, quick! This one's still alive!"

Quickly stirring, Dexter ran to to portside, where one of his redshirts was bringing one of the floaters toward the floor. It was a female, a blueshirt. The radio officer, Dexter concluded.

"She's unconscious," panted the redshirt. "But she's still breathing."

"Get her back to the ship," said Dexter. His cold eyes hid his horror at the sight of the once-pretty young bluebird. The left side of her face was now little more than a bloodied, charred sore.

"*D'Artagnan*, this is Dexter. We've got a survivor, a member of the bridge crew. Have a medical team standing by the transmitter."

"Acknowledged," came the reply.

Soon, the young survivor disappeared in a dazzling flash of light, leaving Dexter to wonder about their next step. He'd always dreamed about his own command, about making all the right decisions and leading his crew through crisis after crisis with a the detached coolness of a Commodore Cook. Now that the crisis was upon him, and everyone was looking to him for answers, he was all but paralyzed. He hadn't the foggiest notion of what to do next, and they were running out of time. He looked at his watch; he had ten minutes left.

Fighting the urge to panic, he made himself think out his next step. Just the next step, he told himself. One step at a time.

"Allison," he said, fighting to get the words out. "Plug the recorder into the log outlet. Retrieve anything you can. We'll play it back when we get home.

"The rest of you, finish checking the others here, then go back into the corridor and start checking the Conning Deck for signs of life. I'll try to get the intercom working to call for survivors. But keep an open channel, all of you. And stand by to molly back home at a moment's notice."

* * *

AS LOUDSPEAKERS blared a message through the silent decks of the *Magellan*, summoning all with the strength to walk or crawl to come to the transmission points for passage back to the *d'Artagnan*, a ghostly echo rose across the ship. On every deck, the faint moanings of the helpless and crippled rose like the howls of desert wolves. Unable to walk, too weak to move, they pulled the rescue team in a dozen directions, as the rescue party from the *d'Artagnan* desperately tried to answer the lost sound of each voice they heard.

Ten, then twenty, then forty wounded beings were carried to safety. Their tear-stained faces were twisted by pain and gratitude; their bodies were torn and burned by forces beyond their comprehension.

Ten minutes later, it would all come to a halt.

The voices, now awakened from hopelessness, would continue their calls in the darkness; the halls would still echo with the sounds of pain.

Soon, the calls would go unanswered.

* * *

"CAP—CAP—*CAPTAIN!*"

Bellamy's hoarse whisper sent chills down Jeremy's spine. Of all the officers on his bridge, Jack Bellamy was the most experienced, the coolest in a crisis. He hadn't expected the scanners to show any good news, but the suppressed panic in his voice of his systems officer told him to expect the worst.

"Yes, Mr. Bellamy, what is the prob— "

"Christ, Jeremy—look! Screen Three—look!"

Jeremy swivelled his chair to the right. Lifting his eyes, he saw what had panicked his executive officer, and felt his whole body go numb.

The enemy now filled the screen. Where the skies were nearly dark only moments before a thousand ships now registered on their monitors, from one end of their sensors to the other. Each passing second brought more enemy ships into view.

"It's the whole damn fleet," Jeremy whispered. "They're all after us. Every last one of them."

Worse yet, the Crutchtans were streaming past the leeward side of the Cloud and were almost to the edge of the Grand Promontory. Before they could even start for home, Jeremy realized, their only lane of retreat had been blocked. They were caught in the middle of the cul-*de-sac* like sitting ducks.

"I hate to say this, Captain— "

"Then don't," snapped Jeremy, his sudden Cookean curtness startling even himself. "Miss VanderBrook, raise the *d'Artagnan*. Red flags all around, top emergency priority."

"Yes, sir."

"They've cut us off, Jeremy. There's no way out. Not a single fucking way!"

"VanderBrook?"

"Channel open, sir. Putting it on the screen right now."

"*D'Artagnan*, this is Captain Ashton of the *Morning Star*. Come in, please.

"This is Captain Ashton...."

LIFTING HIS eyes from the chart on his computer to the monitor screen overhead, the *d'Artagnan's* chief medical officer checked on his current wards. All but the single bluebird in Ward Number Six were resting peacefully. But each minute brought more survivors from the *Magellan,* and he was running out of room as quickly as he was running out of patience. Rubbing his eyes with his hands, he tried hard not to let his temper get the better of him. He was, he kept telling himself, an officer of the Cosmic Guard. Today, whatever his medical training told him was right would have to defer to the greater needs of the ship.

The lights of the sick bay were dimmed at his insistence. The loudspeaker hissed with background noise, trying to keep voices and disturbances away from the patients. At the medical officer's directions, all distractions were to be kept away. The survivors from the *Magellan* were too frail for anything more taxing than sleep. The disfiguring burns on their bodies and faces were too painful for many of them to bear without sedation, and too repulsive for anyone but the medical staff to deal with in a tactful manner.

But his authority ended at the entrance to Ward Six, and from his office desk across the hall the doctor looked sternly and disapprovingly at the goings-on. Despite his best efforts, the battered young blueshirt was being questioned. Softly, gently, perhaps—but it was still interrogation, as irresistible as the tide, and as about as useful to the patient's health as the rising sea was to a sand castle on the shore.

Breathing deeply, the doctor returned to his charts and readings. He avoided thinking of the horror that had maimed all the young, healthy bodies that now filled his sick bay. And he tried not to let the peremptory usurpation of his authority distract him from the task of trying to heal.

SITTING ON the edge of the bed, Cook spoke quietly, the soothing gentleness of his voice barely audible above the soft rumbling of the ship. Out of the young officer's vision, half the command staff listened and waited, hoping to hear something to help them understand just what went so terribly wrong.

"Cynthia, isn't it?" he smiled. "I had a neighbor back home whose name was Cynthia. We called her 'Cindy.'"

On the bed, her arms strapped to prevent her moving too quickly for her own good, her eyes wide with fright, Cindy Stockman struggled to force her mouth to respond.

"C—c—commodore...," she stammered.

"Shhh," whispered Cook, looking directly into the poor girl's eyes, trying to keep her from noticing the half-dozen other officers seated around her. Gently, he took her hand and squeezed it. "It's all right, you're safe now. You're all safe."

"B—but the *Magellan*. What happened to the *Ma—Ma*—"

"What do you remember, Cynthia?" Cook asked, his eyes kind and gentle, his voice soft and soothing. "Tell me, what do you remember? It will help you. It will help all of us."

Drawing a deep breath, the young lieutenant struggled to calm herself. A moment later, her attention locked by the strong gaze of the commanding presence sitting beside her, she spoke—haltingly, breathlessly. Her face was as pale as death, and her eyes bulged as if she was staring into the face of a ghost. Cook knew that each passing second would bring her closer to a relapse into a fog of incoherency, and time was quickly passing. They were already past the point of danger; any further delay might cost all of them their lives.

"We—we had them. We had them all," she whispered. "All but one or two. Then we got another—another one. I—I saw the flash on the weapons screen. And then Captain Fitz gave the order again."

"What order?"

"The order to—to fire."

"And then?"

The young woman's face crumpled into a wrinkle of agony, and she opened her mouth to scream. But nothing came out.

Not a single sound.

Narrowing his eyes, Cook's voice rang with the steely edge of command, hoping that the young bluebird's training would lead her to respond before they lost her again.

"What happened after he gave the second order to fire?"

"No—no. That's all—that's all—that's all."

It was too late; sobbing hysterically, shaking her head back and forth, they had reached the end. It was all she could manage.

"That's all—that's all."

Lifting his eyes as the medical team raced to her aid, Cook barely noticed the way they rudely pushed him out of the way. As in the past, Cook was somewhere on its own plateau, where no others ventured and time and space were a seamless fog. Detached from the chaos around him, he tried to sift some grains of sense out of the poor girl's torment. She obviously remembered nothing of the actual source of her ship's disablement. The cataclysm had erased whatever had happened from her memory. Yet it was obvious that all systems were functioning right up until the end. And there is nothing that Fitz—or anyone else—could have done to overload the ship's power systems to cause the circuits to fry themselves, and everyone around them.

No, the answer had to lie outside the ship.

Something from outside. Something that entered the ship just as it was preparing to fire.

Or maybe just as it was engaging its....

Suddenly, the blaring of the alert buzzer shattered Cook's reverie, and he heard Janet's voice ringing over the intercom.

"Red alert—all hands to battle stations; Commodore Cook to the bridge. Red alert—all hands to battle stations."

At once, everything was a blur of activity as the ship erupted with energy. Crewmen ran to their posts as they'd done a thousand times before, scurrying to retrieve damage control gear from the storage compartments, straining under the dint of endless drilling to reach their assigned stations in record time. Racing through the halls to take his place on the bridge, Cook found his brain still lingering over the mystery of the *Magellan*.

But then, what was happening in the eastern skies was no mystery at all.

Not to him.

* * *

"Next up—on the double!"

The next-to-last squad from the search team began to shimmer, starting the transmission that would take them back to the *d'Artagnan*. Dexter trotted down the corridor, shining his flashlight into the darkness and calling for any last stragglers that were within the sound of his voice. He could hear footsteps—at least, he thought they were footsteps. The *Magellan* echoed with eerie creaks and rattles, low moans and whimpers of helplessness. He knew that they were leaving people behind, but the order had been quite specific: they had to leave at once.

Everyone.

Without exception.

They were out of time. The enemy was breathing down their necks—and anyone not catching the last molly would be left forever.

"Last call—anyone down there? Last call!"

"Mr. Dexter— "

"Last call!! Anyone down there—last call!!"

"Message from the ship, Mr. D—they're ready to molly us home."

Racing to the transmission point, Dexter stepped into position. He took a last look around, then pressed the button on his radio.

"Dexter here," he said. "All accounted for on this end. Transmit."

Almost instantly, the enveloping whiteness of the transmission signal wrapped itself around his senses, and as the last image of the Magellan faded from his vision, he felt a dreamy warmth washing through him.

As he materialized on the landing pad of the *d'Artagnan*, a shiver of terror gripped his spine. The last impression he carried away from the doomed ship was the cry of a human voice screaming in agony.

"Well, Mathison?"

Trying to fend off her Skipper's impatience long enough to hear the report coming through her earphones, Mary held up a hand, then turned to face the Skipper.

"Molly reports the last squad from the search team is back. All hands accounted for, and we've brought back more than— "

"Dexter can give his report later," Cook silenced her with a wave of his hand. He turned his chair to face the forward screens. They showed the *Magellan* adrift, a helpless and listing hulk, dead to creation. Half her crew might still be alive. The early reports told of corridors strewn with bodies, some dead, some unconscious, some wailing in the dark, unable to move. He had to put all that from his mind; time had run out for the *Magellan*. It would take all his skill, and more luck than he could expect, to escape the massive enemy fleet racing toward them.

"*Morning Star* hailing us on the Emergency Channel," said Mathison. "They're a minute away—and the enemy's two minutes behind them."

"Mr. Gerlach, ready a single forward battery," Cook said firmly.

"Aye, sir."

"Jeremy suggests that we rendezvous— "

"Tell him to stay on channel and hold course," barked Cook. "We'll find him by his broadcast signal, if nothing else."

"Forward Number One amain, Commodore; standing by."

As Cook opened his mouth to give the command, Mary whirled her chair around, her eyes wide with amazement.

"Skipper—!! It's the *Magellan!* My God—it's Captain Fitzgerald!"

"Hold fire," shouted Cook. "Mathison, put it on the screen."

Cook forced himself not to wince as the *Magellan* faded from the forward viewer, replaced by the frayed image of the man who had commanded her. Sitting at the helm station Janet closed her eyes, unable to look at the pitiable remnant of a starship captain staring back at them. Soot-covered and dripping with sweat, Fitz had the look of death about him. His eyes were hollow and lifeless, and he looked haunted by shadows. In the background, a small auxiliary monitor showed the same approaching enemy fleet that filled *d'Artagnan's* full screens.

"Fitz—for God's sake!"

Fitz shook his head, managing no more than a weak smile. Cook felt part of himself dying along with his old wingmate's doomed ship.

"Sorry, Cookie. I'm sorry for everything."

"Mathison—flag Molly on the double. Fitz—we don't have any more time. You have to come over— "

"Sorry to disobey, Commodore. Not that I haven't done enough o'that already."

"Systems—tell Molly to scan the ship to pinpoint the source of the transmission."

Fitz laughed wistfully, his eyes filling with tears. "No, Cookie, can't be lettin' ye do that, now. I finally found a generator that works, and I've sealed off the auxiliary bridge. But I don't have the power to set things off myself. Guess you'll just have to do it for me."

"Fitz— !" Cook jumped to his feet, his voice cracked with pain.

"Ye were right, Cookie—ye were right about everything. I just had to tell ye that."

"Listen to me, Fitz— "

"I should have, Cookie. Should've done that all along. I killed my own ship, ye know. I killed them all. Every last one."

"Skipper!" Mary's voice was tinged with panic. "Jeremy says—"

"Fitz—!"

"*Skipper*!!" shrieked Mary, her face ashen.

"Enemy coming into sensor range," announced Gerlach. "Range...."

"Goodbye, Cook," Fitz smiled sadly, his eyes taking on the faintest glimmer of the spark that once lighted his soul. "My hat's off to ye, for all the good it does. Ye're a bloody magician, Roscoe Cook. I'd forgotten what a privilege it was, seein' ye work your magic."

"*Skipper*!!"

"Fitz—you son of a bitch! Don't do this!"

"*Magellan* out."

"*Fitz*— !"

Fitz faded from the screen, replaced by the image of crippled *Magellan*. Cook wanted nothing more than to sink into his chair and hide—hide from the prying eyes and the approaching enemy fleet. But he couldn't do that. Not now. Not with the full madness of war about to come crashing around them.

"Skipper—enemy's approaching at C-14. Range— "

"Helm, prepare to come about at full emergency speed; Weapons...."

"Standing by," said Gerlach, his eyes tightly closed.

God forgive me, Cook thought to himself.

"Fire," he said firmly. "Mendelson—take us out of here. Maximum acceleration, 500 points dead astern, heading 750; stand by the spin stabilizers."

A blinding flash of light from *d'Artagnan*'s guns forced his eyes shut, and Cook felt the ship shudder gently beneath him. Opening his eyes, he took a deep breath, and swivelled to follow the dying flash from screen to screen as the ship spun sharply toward the Cloud.

"Goodbye, Fitz," he whispered.

The ship sped away to join the *Morning Star*, accelerating with every passing second. Soon, with the *Magellan's* fireball fading into the blackness of space, he turned again to face forward. Putting all other thoughts behind him, every synapse in his brain was straining to find a way to escape the oncoming enemy fleet.

Chapter 26

T"HERE IT GOES again."

"Hmmm?"

"Same as before. Only clearer this time."

Yeoman Sergeant Kevin Ward leaned over the console to peek at Monitor Seven. The young redshirt technician was right: his lower screen clearly showed movement—subspace movement. This time the signal was strong enough to register through the remnants of last week's ion storm. But the motion sensors lost all readings at the edge of the promontory, as if the enemy fleet were diving behind the bend in the Cloud. It was a puzzler, thought Ward. With their own ships stalled and waiting for Headquarters to give the order to attack, the arrival of enemy reinforcements could spell trouble.

Real trouble—though with all the politicking going on these days, the Brass could hardly be bothered to see it.

"Convinced, Mr. Ward?"

"That I am, Laddie," said the old yeoman, thoughtfully stroking his newly-shaved chin. Under the New Regime, his beard was strictly forbidden, and their new commander was a by-the-book sort. Too green to know the mechanics of subspace radar, she was determined to keep her crew in Cozzie trim. Now, he smiled, they'd get to see what kind of head she had on her shoulders—considering that she'd failed to impress them with anything else she had to offer. He pressed the intercom button, and leaned over to talk into the speaker.

"Miss Wiggins, please report to Monitor Seven-East."

"Not the Iron Bitch, Mr. Ward."

"Mind your manners, Crewman," the greenshirt chuckled good-naturedly. "I hear she's just rusty. Needs a little oil, that's all. To keep her from squeaking all the time. Do I hear any volunteers?"

Young Jason Jeffries winced at the thought. "I'd rather chew on Demetrian carrion worms."

As the two monitors shared a laugh, the door to opened, and the shift commander entered. Pauline Wiggins was a short woman, who wore her uniform loosely around her waist and hips to hide the overabundance of her figure. Her hair was drawn back tightly into a bun resting just off the center of her crown. As she approached, the two men retracted their smiles and shifted uncomfortably at their posts, determined to show their commander the respect due her official rank. Their noses noted her other ranks as she drew nearer.

"What is it now, Yeoman?" she barked in a low, rumbling alto.

"Same as before, Commander," Ward replied. "Still no indication of numbers. But this time the readings are even clearer."

Wiggins peered at the monitor screen, looking it over from top to bottom. She nodded thoughtfully, her eyes almost disappearing into the crinkles on her brow.

"I'd say it was the enemy fleet," she said at last, "except for the fact that they're all heading off in the wrong direction, well beyond the other side of the promontory."

The old yeoman's eyes widened with surprise.

"Would that deployment make any sense to you, Mr. Ward?"

The greenshift cleared his throat. "No, ma'am. I think that if it's an enemy fleet approaching, they'd be heading straight for us."

"That's what I'd expect, too," she nodded. "If they're reinforcements for Girshoona, it makes no sense for them to go hiding behind the Cloud. But who can tell with lizards? Log it, and send it on up the line. Maybe they can make sense of it."

"Yes, ma'am."

As the portly lieutenant commander waddled out of the station, Ward chuckled quietly to himself. Entering the appropriate codes into the computer, he pressed the transmit button and officially made the entry someone else's problem. Some things never changed, he chuckled to himself. In many ways, maybe this New Regime wasn't so different after all.

"What'd you make of that, Mr. Ward?"

"I dunno, Jeffries. Maybe there's something inside her head after all."

"Sure ain't much on the outside, though."

Ward returned to his duties with a smile. "Aye on that, Mr. Jeffries," he laughed, adjusting his own instruments to hone in on the source of the motion readings.

"Aye on the lot of it. Now, train your sensors on the Bend—train all of them, Jeffries. Let's just see if we can't get a bit more information by triangulating."

"For all the good it'll do, Mr. Ward. I mean, it's not like anyone's in any kind of all-fired hurry to move out there, or anything."

"Well, Crewman—there are two ways to take an enemy planet, you know. The right way--"

" –and the Cozzie way. Yes I know, Mr. Ward."

"It's more than that, Laddie," the yeoman laughed, fiddling with the instruments as he squinted at his screen. "It's the way of the Universe. An eternal constant in an ass-bloody churn of chaos and catastrophe. The military mind ain't changed since the beginning of time. Grunts like us ain't about to change it one whit."

* * *

THE GLOW from the Cloud filled the observation platform of the Imperial Flagship, casting faint shadows across the width of the Room of Grand Visions. Alone with his thoughts, the Lord Commander faced west, hatred and rage growing inside him.

Two points of light. He could see them. The longnoses were streaking toward the thinnest stretch of the perilous *Dibishi* Transverse of the Great Cloud. They were so close he could almost smell the mustiness of their flesh, yet still they eluded his grasp. No matter how swiftly his fastest ships approached, the Terran ships were faster. So long as their path remained unobstructed, the longnoses could maintain their lead merely by willing it.

Screaming with rage, Ga'Glish slammed his fist against the wall. He was certain what the Beast would do. The Terran had plunged headlong into the fog before, when only the acuteness of his own senses gave him any warning of danger. Ga'Glish had no doubt that the Beast would do so now, when to turn back meant certain death.

He also knew what his course would be.

What it must be, if he was to rid the skies of the Terran menace.

Coldly, his emotions now under firm control, he stared past the Hated One, ahead to the swirling gases that dominated the heavens before them. His decision was already made. It was made the moment the Beast had taken flight, and would be changed only if the Terran turned to fight.

In a single unit of time, the Terrans would enter the Cloud, hoping to penetrate to the other side before being blown to bits by a random hunk of interstellar rock.

And the *g'Khruushtani* would be right behind them. His scientists told him that he would likely lose at least a third of his forces in the pursuit. But they would track the Beast to the ends of creation.

"AM I interrupting something?"

Cook turned his chair to face the door, blinking his eyes as the light from the hallway poured into the darkened room, and wordlessly shook his head. Janet entered the captain's office, and the door closed behind her. Only the light from Cook's monitor split the darkness. The screen cast their faces in a soft, greenish glow, throwing eerie shadows into the corners of the room. Janet stumbled her way to the nearest chair.

"You wanted to know when we were two minutes from the Cloud," she said.

Staring at her, Cook said nothing; he just nodded silently, and rocked back and forth in his chair.

"I know how hard it must be...," Janet began.

"They're still on our tail," Cook interjected, suddenly sitting upright. "They're following right behind us. And they're going to follow us into the Cloud."

"Losing a friend like that...."

"They're two minutes behind us," he continued, "and showing no signs of slowing." He pressed a button on the console to rotate the angle of projection.

Cook lifted his gaze from the screen, and looked Janet straight in the eyes. "I'd say they were mad," he smiled wryly, "but I know what *we're* going to do, and I won't admit to being insane myself. Perhaps a little dotty, from time to time, but— "

"Stop it!" Janet cried. "Just stop it! How can you just sit there, without a care in the world, and pretend that nothing's happened? You just watched someone you've worked with for years die right before your eyes. One of the few friends you had left—along with who knows how many others aboard that ship. And you don't have the decency to—you can't even pause long enough to.... "

Janet sprang to her feet and ran to the door. Sighing harshly, Cook closed his eyes and shook his head.

"Janet," he called after her. But it was too late; the door was closing by the time he opened his mouth. Leaning back in his chair, Cook stared at the darkened ceiling, the squeaking of his chair cutting the silence.

"Two minutes," he said aloud.

After what seemed an eternity, he rose from his chair and walked slowly toward the rear door. He felt the pounding of his own terrified heart. Traversing the Cloud once had already been the risk of a lifetime. Racing blindly at incomprehensible speeds, past hidden rocks and shoals with sensors blinded by the fog, was enough to cause nightmares in the most foolhardy of men. Doing it a second time bordered on suicide, and he wondered whether he was being needlessly self-destructive—whether the risks he was undertaking might not be his way of atoning for all the lives he'd destroyed.

In a way he almost envied Janet. He took a deep breath to steady himself for the command seat. He had too many responsibilities to spend time grieving over a lost friend. He doubted that time for reflection would improve his mood. The knowledge that he'd dispatched his old wingmate into the Great Beyond left little room for solace.

With a rush of air, the door opened. Out into Corridor A—taking a long, roundabout way to his Bridge, his stern gaze and stride bristling with limitless confidence and bracing the spirit of all who saw him—walked the great Commodore Cook.

* * *

"*D'ARTAGNAN'S* ON Channel 1," announced VanderBrook, the *Morning Star's* radio officer. "She says to maintain single file, try to keep radio contact, and match her speed and course—just like last time."

"Acknowledged," nodded Jeremy. "Helm, come to 750, fall in behind the leader."

"Aye, sir."

Jeremy turned to face forward, his eyes fixed on the reddish fog that dominated the main viewer. The anxious faces and nervous voices around him faded, and he pushed them from his consciousness as best he could. In the distance, well beyond the range of their sensors but clearly visible on the screen, bright flashes of light erupted from deep within the Cloud. The surrounding skies were dense and filled with storms, as dangerous as anything that lurked behind them and just as deadly. Cook had chosen the thinnest part of the Cloud to make the attempt; at least, it looked to be the thinnest from where they were,

Jeremy thought. There was no telling what might lie just beyond the reach of their sensors. They'd cheated death once already. He had little stomach for taking the risk a second time.

But he understood why they were doing it. No matter how chancy it was, the risks of a blind shot through the Cloud gave them better odds than sending two ships into battle against the whole enemy fleet.

"Coming into position," announced Braddock, the helmsman. His voice was thin and reedy; his face was beading with perspiration.

"Steady as she goes."

"How long this time, Captain?"

"As long as it takes," replied Jeremy. "As long as it takes."

As the two ships neared the first wisps of the Cloud, the fog began disrupting their equipment, fouling their link with the other ship. Jeremy found himself wondering how he'd ever let his fate come to rest upon the whims of the skipper of the ship ahead. And he swore that when they came out of the Cloud on the other side, he'd never—ever—let Cook's shadow swallow him again.

In a way, it was kind of ironic, he thought. Cook wandered the Universe in a fog of his own; now, the fog threatened to destroy the lot of them. One errant rock—one misplaced hunk of interstellar ice, and...

"*D'Artagnan* says to slow to C-4."

"Helm?"

"Aye sir—slowing to C-4."

"Static increasing on the channel, sir. It's getting hard to make anything out."

"Do the best you can, Lieutenant."

"Yes, sir."

"That's all any of us can do."

"Aye, sir."

"And don't worry about anything," he continued, sounding as resolute as he could for the sake of those around him. "It's out of our hands now, anyway. We're just playing follow the leader, troops. If anyone can get us through this infernal haze, it's good old Cookie."

* * *

THE MOOD in the Monitorium was black as the void of Eternity. At his station, Monitor fo'Rendish felt his manhood fade under the stress of attention. His voice shrank nearly to a cracking whisper.

"They have disappeared, my Lord. They are off the screen, and into the Cloud."

"Continue the advance," Ga'Glish replied harshly, glaring over the hapless monitor's shoulder at the screen. "Order all ships to disperse, attack crescent number six, three units abreast. All ships will maintain constant speed until I order otherwise."

The monitor hesitated for the briefest of instants, only to feel his seat turned violently in its moorings. His face came to rest before the angry stare of the Lord Commander.

"Take account of your situation," hissed Ga'Glish, hatred dripping from his voice like acid. "And question me not, Small One, or you shall suffer the consequences of your disobedience."

"Yes, my Lord."

"To your duty, Monitor—it is my command!" thundered the Tall One. He could sense terror in the Monitor's belly, and the underling's fear fanned Ga'Glish's own rage nearly to the point of madness.

"Yes, Lordship."

Quickly, fo'Rendish relayed the orders of the Lord Commander to the rest of the fleet. From their places behind him, the balance of the command staff kept a respectful silence, many seeking desperately to mask the treasonous feeling that perhaps, just perhaps, the Lord Commander was losing control of his emotions. And perhaps—just perhaps—it would benefit His Worthiness to effect a substitution of leadership.

Of course, each also fancied himself the Worthiest successor to His Lordship. But such thoughts were masked, along with the rest.

* * *

From the Trans-Terran Dispatch, 17 Nov 2555:
To the Editor, Trans-Terran Dispatch:

I hate to keep bothering you with trifles, but once again a remark attributed to a "senior Cabinet officer" seems a bit wide of the mark.

While I am aware that much of Terra regards my Planet as inhabited mostly by "daisy-sniffers," the fact of the matter is that very few "daisies" were ever imported onto Isis, owing to an abundance of native flora. The "daisies" which inhabit our Planet are native plants, more closely resembling the Old Earth daffodil than a true "daisy." And while many of us enjoy the wonderful sweetness of our lilacs in the Springtime, Isitian daisies are, by and large, without a strong fragrance at all.

I hope that this clears up the point. If the "Cabinet officer" has any further questions on the matter, he is always welcome to consult our Department of Horticulture.
IRENE N. McINNIS
Chancellor, Isitian Senate

* * *

ONLY THE soft sounds of whirring machines broke the silence on the bridge. Across the command center, and at any station with access to the central computer, frightened eyes were focused on the viewers around them. Glowing gases filled the screens on all sides, admitting nothing to view but swirls of interstellar hydrogen. Even so, the screens had captured eyes and minds throughout the ship. Everyone searched desperately for a patch of clear space, wincing in terror at the sight of each flash of lightening.

This wasn't like the last time, Janet thought. Harrowing as their first trip through the Clouds might have been, they didn't have the nascent storms and unstable gasses to contend with.

From the command seat, to which she had found herself banished, Janet watched what was happening with a helplessness that approached despair. As each painful second passed, her anxiety grew until she could not contain it any longer.

"Skipper...," she began.

"No talking," snapped a cold voice just in front and to starboard. Taking a deep breath, Janet struggled to hold her fear and tongue in check, like the rest of the bridge crew. She tried to force herself to watch the screens for signs of danger—signs that she was not certain she could recognize.

Seated at the helmsman's station, Cook's eyes were fixed on the forward screens, his fingers hovering just above the controls. His penetrating gaze searched the skies for clues of what might lie hidden from view—dappled clouds hinting at the presence of shoals, a small eddy suggesting a star aborning. Like a sculptor surveying a raw stone, or a mystic listening to the wind, his eyes saw life in the meaningless puffs and tumbles of the clouds. Though enough of a skeptic to question his own abilities, with each new perceived detail he altered his course ever so slightly, trying to steer between the forces of Nature, aware that his first mistake would mean destruction for all of them.

Sensing danger in the subtly shifting reddish shades just coming into sight, Cook edged the ship slightly to port, trusting the *Morning Star* to follow in his wake. Banking around the disturbance and back onto course, without taking his eyes off the forward screens, he called to the systems desk.

"Dexter?"

"Jeremy's still on our tail, Skipper—following the change in course exactly."

"Remember: Tell me if...."

"Right, sir. I'll let you know if we lose them."

"Mathison?"

"Unchanged, Skipper. Nothing but static."

He had just realigned their heading with the position he sensed for Girshoona when he saw something out of the corner of his eye. It was a small, unexpected disturbance on one of the aft screens, followed by another and another, and yet another. Waiting until he felt he could spare another moment of attention, he eased the ship into a thin stretch of clouds, unmarked by any signs of interstellar condensation.

"Readings aft?"

An awkward silence followed.

"Mr. Dexter?"

"Aye, sir."

"Well, what is it?"

"Just speculation, sir."

"Dexter— !"

"I read it as a series of non-natural explosions. Fairly massive, I'd say, to register at this distance. Actually, in my opinion..."

"In other words, probably the enemy," Cook concluded aloud. He continued to focus his gaze on the forward screens.

"Well—yes, sir. Although that fact is far from established. In fact, the readings seem to indicate.... "

"That will be all, Lieutenant," Janet quickly interjected. "Log it, and carry on with your duties."

"Sorry, ma'am. But the Skipper wanted to know— "

"Shut up, Dexter."

"Yes, sir."

* * *

Fa'Shenali peered out his viewing tile to look at the undulating vapors as the Flagship passed through them. Through the eons they had swirled and danced, he thought, unseen and untouched by any living thing. And they would continue long after Terrans or *g'Khruushtani* ever dared disturb their silent sanctuary.

In the distance, he saw the reddish glows of heated gases, and the bright flashes of static discharge. Here and there, he could see the dying brilliance of a *g'Khruushtani* vessel, lighting the fog for the briefest of moments as it collided with the rocks and debris that made traversing the Cloud so perilous. Safely to the rear, far from the front of the advancing Fleet, the Flagship was in little danger of quick destruction. But such a thought gave him little comfort, as he considered the folly of their course. He found himself wondering just how much courage it took to order others to risk death, while keeping it safely at bay for oneself.

As he sought to dismiss such treasonous doubts about their Lord Commander, the ringing of his summons bell broke his reverie. Rising to his feet, he walked to his access panel and activated the speaker.

"You have reached fa'Shenali," he said into the screen. Instantly, the image of Dra'Lengish, Chief of Tactics, appeared.

"You are summoned in the service of His Worthiness," the image spoke. "Come at once to the Tactical Alcove, near the Command Center."

"I hear and obey," said the young subaltern, trying to contain his elation at being lifted from his exile. Soon, racing from his quarters toward the heart of the Flagship, he had forgotten all thoughts of danger and despair, and felt a sense of purpose beating strongly inside him once more.

"*D'Artagnan's* banking gently to starboard," called the systems officer.

"Helm?"

"Yes, sir—making the change now."

Jeremy stared at the forward screens. Gray with static, Forward Screen One showed little more than shadows moving in the darkness. Below the main viewer, the tactical screen showed the faint contour of a starship, as it slipped through the fog.

Jeremy didn't like it; he didn't like it at all. Groping about like blind beggars was bad enough. What made it almost unbearable was watching his life trying its best to flash before his eyes, but being so keenly aware of their predicament that he couldn't pause for more than an instant of reflection.

"New course, Heading 760," volunteered the navigator.

"Cookie's easing back over now," the system's officer reported. "Coming back to the original heading."

"Helm?"

"Already underway, Captain. Sure wish he could make up his damn mind—eh, Captain?"

Jeremy smiled, but didn't reply. For the moment, all he could think about was the last image of fireball that was once the *Magellan*, fading into the Black..

* * *

THE TACTICAL Alcove's marble walls arched gracefully into the air, surrounding the visual screens and tactical viewers like a sea surrounding the islands of home. As the moments passed, fear and concern gripped the mind of the young commoner. He thought he was to serve at the side of the Lord Commander, as in past battles. He had not expected to find himself alone with Dra'Lengish. Sensing the darkness of the Tactician's mood filled the young commoner with a dread.

"I do not understand," said fa'Shenali. And truly he did not—for Dra'Lengish had never before spoken a civil word to him. Yet he could feel the Elder's intentions as if they were his own, and they bore not a trace of malice.

"I understand it not, myself," said the Chief of Tactics, his mood becoming black as the depths of eternity. "I have known him since his own boyhood, and have loved him like my own sister's son, for the sake of his father. But he is consumed, One Called fa'Shenali."

The subaltern took note of the tone of politeness, and his mood instantly improved.

"He is consumed as if by fire. I fear that he is leading us to ruin. All of us. All for the sake of the phantom that haunts his soul."

"But what have I— "

"You have studied the Beast, fa'Shenali," continued the Tactician. "Alone among us, you have examined the longnose *Khu'ukh* with the open eyes of youth. However slow your progress, your own ways, untutored in the dictates of protocol, have been as honest as the breezes of autumn. In my despair to acquire insight into our predicament, I confess that yesterday I read your last report....the first I have read from start to finish."

Dra'Lengish tapped the desk beside him.

"I am ashamed to admit it, but to my amazement I found it filled with insight beyond your years."

"I thought it was filled with rambling incoherence."

"You have not spent the last few cycles watching the Beast slaughter your countrymen," Dra'Lengish said, his mood darkening from melancholy to despair. "But there is more."

The old man leaned forward and spoke in the whispers of conspiracy.

"I have watched your suffering over the past months, Subaltern. At times I watched with eyes of self-righteousness, exulting in your abasement. In the past, I watched with the contempt I felt was simply your due. Yet events have always sustained your judgment. And I have come to respect your courage, Young One."

Fa'Shenali fought the urge to surrender to flattery. From one of such importance, kind words meant a great deal. But the young subaltern sensed a darker side to the Tactician's praise, and struggled to keep his sense of proportion.

Sensing fa'Shenali's conflicting moods, Dra'Lengish quickly pressed his point home.

"There are changes coming, Subaltern. Mere breezes now, they are growing with each passing gust. And as with the changes that brought you here, chaos is coming as well. But before the gales of change raise too much dust, it is well to know the loyalties of those around you."

Hopelessly confused, fa'Shenali stared dumbly, his tongue wagging incoherently."

"Certainly, Lord Lengish, you cannot suspect—I mean, I have never given reason for any suspicion. And my entire being belongs to His Worthiness—as does the very breath of my life. Surely— "

"Enough, Young One," Dra'Lengish smiled, his mood masked by a humor as black as his mood. "All of life is unending change, fa'Shenali. Even civilizations evolve, much like any other form of life."

"Most assuredly, Lord Lengish. But— "

"The best advice, for one so young in worldly ways, is to avoid scandal as best he can, and to steer clear of danger. For it comes, Young One. And it often comes shrouded by the piteous wails of a tortured mind."

"I am certain you are right, my Lord, but I confess that I have not the slightest idea of our topic of discourse."

"That is for the best, Young One. Perhaps the best will come about for all, if the Fates are kind. May such topics never come to haunt you."

"Yes, Lord Lengish."

"You are excused, One Called fa'Shenali," said Dra'Lengish. "You may resume your station in the Command Center."

The subaltern bowed and took his leave, his wonderment at the reason one such as the Chief Tactician might concern himself with a lowly subordinate overshadowed by his elation at the chance to redeem himself. And as Dra'Lengish sat alone in his alcove, the Old One rocked himself in gentle contemplation. He wondered what lay ahead for them when they emerged from the Cloud, and felt a great sadness at the changes he sensed in the wind.

* * *

THE FROZEN rock tumbled slowly through the void, pulled along its way by the mass of a greenish spiral that split the blackness at the edge of an endless field of hydrogen.

As on countless times through countless eons, the rock slowed as it passed its closest approach to the cloud, at the apogee of its circuit around the spiral. The large bulge near its southern pole gave it the lopsided contour of a misshaped fruit, twirling endlessly through time. An impact crater midway scarred its northern hemisphere, a relic from a massive asteroid that nearly shattered it into pebbles in the timeless past. Slowly turning as the rock wobbled on an ever-changing axis, the crater passed from the greenish darkness of the spiral to the reddish darkness of the cloud, and back again, under the watchful eyes of countless lights in the clear blackness that reached toward the center of the galaxy.

On its surface, reflecting the changing lights of an icy sky, were the shattered remnants of several small, metallic cones. Fallen silent under the impact of meteor strikes and eons of neglect, they littered the barren landscape where once they called warnings to the heavens, bearing the silent inscriptions of makers that once charted the skies for lost and wayfaring souls.

Chapter 27

"THE CLOUDS ARE getting thinner."

Janet started at the sound of Cook's voice; it had been hours since he'd spoken in anything but a harsh, guttural monotone. In fact, it seemed like ages since he'd spoken at all. Janet looked at the chronometer; it showed she'd been asleep for nearly two hours, and the crick in her neck confirmed it. Looking about, she saw that the rest of the bridge crew was sound asleep. A few were beginning to stir, but only she and Cook were awake.

"How long...,"she began.

"Actually, the peace and quiet were a refreshing change," smirked Cook. Janet could read a shortened temper in the tone of his voice. "And if there's nothing for you to do—well, I thought you'd all better get some rest. I have no idea what's waiting for us up ahead."

"How far...?"

"Check the systems log," he smiled. "When Dexter checked out, I programmed it to record our passage. You'll find the elapsed time and distance, cloud thickness and relative velocity. And anything else along the way that wasn't hydrogen."

"You must be exhausted."

Cook laughed humorlessly. Once again, Janet was right on target, but he was in no mood to give any compliments. "Panic does tend to concentrate the mind, Missy," he replied. "But I've allowed myself a few catnaps along the way, whenever the skies permitted."

"Jeremy's still with us?"

Cook nodded, and looked at the auxiliary scanner at the left of the helmsman's station. "Two seconds behind," he said, adjusting the dial to bring the *Morning Star* into sharper focus. "Where they've hung for the last eight hours."

"Eight cosmic hours?"

Cook laughed.

"That means this 'thin spot' is— "

"So far it's nearly three parsecs across. I think we're nearing the end, though."

"I don't see how you managed, Skipper."

"The last part hasn't been bad. The first two hours were the real killers. That's where all the storms were. But I'll tell you...."

He motioned behind them, to the main aft screen.

"The Crutchtans took a real pounding for the first parsec or so. But I haven't seen more than a half-dozen explosions in the last five hours. Either they've turned back, or they've followed us into the clearer skies. And I doubt that they've turned back."

Just as he finished, the aft screen showed a burst of bright yellow light, brightening the skies behind them for a full second before fading slowly into the dull red glow that surrounded them on all sides.

"I see what you mean," said Janet.

"Wake the others, Commander," said Cook, his face grim, the brusqueness of command filling his voice. Janet groaned; tired as she was, she'd hoped for a bit more rest. She longed for nothing so much as a return to oblivion.

"I think we're nearing the edge of the Cloud. I want everyone at battle stations when we emerge."

"All right, Skipper."

"You know," he continued, the edge in his voice suddenly gone, "it was nice to have the company, Janet. Even if just for a little while."

Stretching herself until she could feel all the kinks start vanishing from her body, Janet felt gentle waves of emotion warming her like the summer sun. As she started to open her mouth to say something, she felt her jaws begin swelling into a yawn that spread until she was feared her jaws would pop.

"Of course," Cook laughed, his eyes softening one last time before the battle he sensed was coming. "I'd hate to put everyone to sleep in the middle of combat. Maybe I'll just handle it myself."

"Don't be ridiculous."

"Sorry—force of habit."

"CAPTAIN?"

Startled, Jeremy shook his head to clear the fog from his mind. He didn't know how long he'd been asleep; he only knew that every cell in his body cried with exhaustion. With a monumental effort, he forced his eyes to stay open, and turned to face his radio officer.

"Yes, Miss VanderBrook. What is it?"

"*D'Artagnan's* on the line. Near as I can tell through the static, Cook thinks we're nearing the end of this mess and wants us standing at red alert. He thinks there may be trouble waiting for us when we emerge from the clouds. Wants us all to be ready."

"Sound alert, Missy," Jeremy said, his mind coming into focus once more. "All hands to battle stations."

"Aye, sir."

"And signal the third scouting team to the hangar decks to stand by. We may need to send them out again, once we get clear of this mess."

"Aye, aye."

"Let's keep alert, people. We've come this far. It would be a shame to blow it all now."

As the rest of the bridge sprung into action, Jeremy found exhaustion creeping back into his mind. Like everyone else, he found waiting oppressive—and all the more tiring, because there was nothing else they could do.

Staring ahead, he tried to focus on the task ahead, on keeping his ship in line and maintaining their formation behind the *d'Artagnan*. But as the seconds passed into minutes, he found himself hoping that they'd find clear skies when they emerged from the fog. The prospect of emerging into the midst of another battle was too brutal to face. Before long he found himself lost in thought, hypnotized by the endless clouds, the fragile wisps of interstellar gases that hid the heavens from their sight and sensors. Before he realized it, his head was nodding insensibly, as his mind drifted back into oblivion.

"YOU SUMMONED, Lordship?"

Glaring angrily, Ga'Glish turned toward his Tactical Advisor with hatred in his eyes. Anticipating the reaction, Dra'Lengish took it with calmness and grace, raising his eyelids in feigned surprise, struggling desperately to conceal the treachery welling inside him. He hated what he was doing. He loved Ga'Glish as he loved his own son, and had served him faithfully for dozens of cycles. Yet he knew the truth; and if events forced his hand, he would need all the help he could find to return the Fleet's commander to stability.

"What is he doing here?" Motioning violently with his hand at fa'Shenali, the Lord Commander's voice rang with accusatory tone.

"Forgive me, my Lord; I confess that I summoned him here myself."

"You did what?"

Struggling to remain calm, the Chief Tactician breathed deeply and resumed his explanation.

"We are nearing the end of our Transit," Dra'Lengish continued, apologetically. "Young fa'Shenali may be tactless and brash, but his studies might prove useful in the event that the Beast chooses to fight. He is under strict instructions to say nothing unless asked."

For several moments, Ga'Glish said nothing. Dra'Lengish sensed the Lord Commander's anger subsiding, and let himself relax.

"You should have asked permission."

"You would have refused, my Lord. And you may still send him away, if that is your pleasure."

Ga'Glish lifted his eyes to the forward screen, noting the changing speed and thickness of the blanket of fog. Soon they would emerge, and could survey the damage to their fleet. It had been quite some time since the last explosion, the last evidence of collision between one of their ships and the interstellar debris hidden from their sensing devices. The lack of debris augured well for their prospects, for such an open stretch of fog meant that most of their casualties from the transit were behind them. It also meant that there would be nothing but clear skies between themselves and the Hated One.

If the gods were smiling, the Beast would have no place to hide, no avenue of escape. And if they were fortunate enough to have overtaken him in the fog....

"He may remain," Ga'Glish announced, his voice cold and detached. "You are right, as usual, old friend. Let us hope he can prove himself useful."

Dra'Lengish bowed and withdrew, leaving the Lord Commander alone upon his watchtower.

Surveying the scene below him, Ga'Glish felt anger gnawing at his innards, as he thought of all who had perished at the hands of the Terrans.

"Grant me this," his said, his voice lower than a whisper, his mind churning with hatred. "Let all who have died be avenged—and all who are to die, die in glory."

Alone upon his watchtower, Ga'Glish stared ahead at the thinning clouds, flames of anger surging inside him, the depth of his emotions strengthening the resolve of all he commanded.

* * *

"FOCUS?"

"Sorry, Skipper," said Dexter, fiddling with the sensor controls. "That's the best we can do."

It was good enough, Cook smiled to himself. The bright green glow was a sight to warm a spacer's heart, he thought: the hot, young star was showing them the end of the Cloud, its brilliance shining through the fog like a beacon. They were nearly out of danger, about to pass into clear skies. The light would be from the first star system past the Cloud's outer fringe. From there, they could signal the rest of the Fleet, and at flank speed the trip back to friendly lines should be less than an hour.

Trying to recall the map of the area he'd studied before leaving, Cook scoured his memory for a greenish star near the Cloud, seeking a clue to their relative position. They had to be in the uncharted skies east of Girshoona, he concluded, but wasn't sure how far east they'd be.

Of course, there was the small bend in the Cloud, the promontory he'd noticed on his first trip to Girshoona, hosting six newborn stars in a cradle archipelago much like the Pleides in western Terra. As far as he knew, it was still uncharted when they'd left, and was probably unexplored still. That would explain the apparent thinness of the Clouds, and the large amount of debris near the fringe on the other side. Most of the debris on this side would be gathered up by the gravitational pull of the forming stars.

But if that were the case—

Cook bolted upright, adrenalin surging through his body, his eyes alert for the slightest break in the clouds, the smallest indication of a gravitational disturbance. As they neared the edge of the Cloud, the fog thickened ominously, blurring their instruments even further and making visual discrimination nearly impossible.

"Helm, prepare to slow to C-2; Mathison, signal the *Morning Star* to match our exact speed and heading."

"Aye, aye."

Suddenly, he saw it—right in their lane, obscured by the blinding light of the nearby star, but just discernible. The faint, sweeping ripples in the clouds made it unmistakable. In another instant, they'd be on top of it.

"*Panic climb!*" Cook cried. "Due north, engines amain!"

The bridge lights flickered and dimmed as the engines drained energy from other systems. Cook felt himself pressed against his seat, as the ship strained and creaked to carry over the rippling clouds. As the ship broke clear of the fog, into the clear skies beyond, the monitor showed how close they'd come to destruction: nearly skimming the surface of the rocky planetoid, the ship swerved under the sudden force of its gravity, before breaking clear and streaking clumsily toward the hot, young star that lit the local heavens.

As the shock of their narrow escape registered on the faces of his crew, Cook felt an instant wave of relief surging through his brain.

Then he remembered.

Spinning about, he opened his mouth to speak.

"*Jeremy*—!" he screamed.

Even as the words came, he knew it was too late.

THE SYSTEMS officer's shriek caught Jeremy's attention. Normally stoic and detached, Bellamy was not the sort to express himself so viscerally. Jeremy had just started smiling at the incongruity when his eyes caught sight of the forward viewer.

To his amazement, his last thoughts were not the mindless terror he expected. Rather, he found himself gripped by a consuming curiosity, an enveloping sense of wonder that grew until it consumed him.

THROUGH THE eerie silence of *d'Artagnan's* bridge, everyone could see that the force of the explosion would scar the planetoid forever. The silence of space carried images, not sounds; but as the seconds burned into their memories, their relief at their narrow escape faded into a sickening numbness, an emptiness as wide as the blackness through which they sailed.

Her throat aching, Janet blinked to clear her eyes as she brought the ship about. As she watched the dying embers of the fireball that was once the *Morning Star*, tears streaked her cheeks. Dexter stared dumbly at the aft viewer, his own screens unattended, his eyes watering. Mathison was sobbing audibly; Gerlach teetered on the edge of losing control.

A stern voice brought them back to reality.

"Mathison!" Cook bellowed, his eyes filled with hate. "Mathison, *dammit!*"

Her breathing hard and tortured, Mary struggled to respond.

"Stow the blubbering, Missy. Priority channel to Fleet Command."

"S—sorry, Skipper— "

"Priority channel to Fleet Command—*on the double!*"

"Aye—aye— "

"*Acch*— " Cook spat contemptuously. Slapping at the console beside him, he overrode the radio controls at the communications desk and opened the channel himself.

"Mathison—stand down. Return to your post when you're of use to me. Gerlach—charge the guns. Helm—prepare to attack."

"But— "

"Prepare to attack, dammit!"

A light flashed on the communications desk, signaling an acknowledgment of his hail from the Fleet. But the reply merely invited a response; it contained nothing to identify the sender, a minor breach of protocol. Discretion not being unknown to officers of the line, it was one that most radio officers would consider justified by the odd location of the hailing source, but the hailing officer was not in a forgiving mood.

"This is the *d'Artagnan*," Cook said angrily. "Just who the hell is this?"

Chapter 28

PEERING BACK OVER HIS SHOULDER, fo'Rendish looked at the intense eyes of the Small One behind him. He felt sadness in the young subaltern's soul. Given the readings on the screen it was a sadness that defied reason.

"Your heart frets, fa'Shenali," he whispered, "though its cause escapes me."

Fa'Shenali barely heard the monitor speak. His eyes transfixed, he stared intently at the screen before them. The explosion registered plainly, that much he could tell. The rough calculations he managed to do in his mind told him that it came from a few heartbeats ahead, in the space through which the longnoses would now be traveling. As to the source and magnitude, time alone would reveal such secrets to them.

Suddenly, the guards at the entry door snapped to attention. With his retinue of attendants close behind, the Lord Commander strode through the entranceway, triumph flashing across his face and gladness all over him. Fa'Shenali glanced at the young monitor seated before him. Like himself, fo'Rendish was a commoner, whose hard work and dedication had often earned him the praise of Ga'Glish himself. It was the young menial's good fortune that he had not yet risen sufficiently through the ranks to make him a threat to his betters.

"I mourn the ghosts of paths untraveled," the subaltern smiled wanly. "Just as I mourn the felling of any monarch of the forest. But please do not mock me, One Called fo'Rendish. It is woman's folly—the weakness of sentiment, and nothing more."

"Hail!" came the call from the ranking officer. At once, everyone sprang to his feet and returned the salute.

"Hail!" they cried.

Beaming like a triumphant king, Ga'Glish strode to the center of the command center.

"I hear we have news—news fit to set to song!" he thundered, and all thrilled in the forcefulness of his voice.

"We read a massive explosion ahead, Lord Commander," nodded Dra'Lengish. The Chief Tactician beckoned for Ga'Glish to follow, and led the way to the central monitor station. Perceiving that the time had come for him to fade from sight, fa'Shenali stepped away from the monitor and blended into the entourage.

"And its magnitude is that of a Terran death ship?" Ga'Glish came to the monitor and halted. He gazed greedily at the screen, his eyes anxious to learn everything that could be detected at this range. Dra'Lengish bowed as the Lord Commander smiled broadly, filled with a relief that knew no bounds.

"Our instruments estimate slightly more mass—as if the Terran ship collided with a small planet."

"Excellent," nodded Ga'Glish. "Excellent. This is a day of triumph! A day of History—a day of Supreme Victory!"

All around cheered loudly, all except the young subaltern at the far corner of the room. As their shouts of joy rang in his ears, echoing the undiluted elation of the Lord Commander, fa'Shenali wondered if he was the only one to remember that the Terran party had entered the cloud with two ships.

Or that the Beast, like so many creatures of their mythology, seemed to live a charmed life.

* * *

"YOU HAVEN'T done *what?!*"

The young ensign cringed under electronic image glowering at her from the communications screen. She felt her face redden, as she suffered embarrassment for the omissions of the brass. It didn't help knowing that their transmission was on an open channel, and that her inarticulation was being broadcast to the whole fleet. She was never so glad to see Captain Chandler, striding onto the *Corona's* bridge in response to her page.

"What's all the commo— ," began Chandler, until the image on the screen all but froze the blood in his veins.

"What's this crap about the Fleet sitting on its ass instead of taking Girshoona?" Cook demanded, not bothering to acknowledge his old nemesis.

Taken aback as much by Cook's unexplained rage as by his mysterious presence on the screen, Chandler took a moment to respond.

"When—where did you— " he began, only to have Cook cut him off.

"Just what the hell have you people been doing all this time?"

"We have orders—we haven't finalized all the details, and— "

"You fools have nearly squandered your chance to take the planet without opposition. You know that, don't you? Now we have the chance to break their back. We can gut their entire fleet if you fools can get off your collective butts long enough to do something. Only you're too busy scratching your candied little asses to be bothered. Don't want to let a war get in the way of needlepoint, and all that."

"No, Commodore—you see— "

"The whole damn enemy fleet's right behind me and I'm in no mood to argue. Send a small force to take the planet. A lone starship should do it; send three, if you want to play it safe. And any troop carriers you have standing by. The rest of you follow my signal to join me in battle. You take care of the details, Chandler—but they'll be here in less than five minutes, and I can't hold them off forever by myself."

"But— "

"That's a direct order, Captain."

"On whose— "

"On my authority as a Wing Commander of the Cosmic Guard."

"You're assuming command, then? Formally, I mean?"

"I don't recall being relieved. If I was, I'm afraid it just slipped my mind."

"Well then—we're on our way, Cookie. Just as long as we know whose neck..."

"I don't care, Captain. I don't give a shit, any more. Just get your ass over here. And bring as many ships with you as you can."

"We'll be there before you can say— "

"Cook out."

"Yes, sir."

Cook's image faded from the screen. Chandler had never seen the Isitian look so wild, so consumed with rage. His own stomach fluttered at the thought of what they were about to do. Of course, there could be hell to pay, but it had been ages since they'd seen any action. Besides, Cook had never steered them wrong.

Sinking into his own command seat, he relayed the order to attack the planet—and to follow CosGuard's best tactician into battle. Soon, for the first time in weeks, the skies filled with movement. As the dormant fleet slowly stirred into motion, events started edging toward what History would later conclude was the most eventful encounter of the war.

* * *

"GOR'FERADAN -- ARE you there?"

Dr'Zenzi adjusted the tuning dial on his radio; the long hours spent traversing the Great Cloud had not been kind to their instruments. It was obvious that many of their most sensitive equipment would need recalibration.

As his fingers sought out the proper frequency to communicate with his wingmates, Zenzi let his mind wander for a moment of precious contemplation. The Fog was passed, he kept telling himself; they had survived the ordeal—though not without the intervention of Fate, which had spared them from the forwardmost point until well after they had passed through the Zone of Shoals.

"This is Gor'Feradan. Are we in contact?"

"Ferad," smiled the young pilot. "It appears that we are in good health. I wish that we could say the same for our equipment."

"I shall stay on the station to signal the others. Do you wish to do the initial recalibration? Now that we are out of the infernal Fog...."

"Yes, I concur. I will orient my instruments; you monitor further contacts. I shall inform you when my adjustments are complete."

Looking out the front window, Zenzi saw the clear blackness of space before him, with stars festooning the skies on all sides as far as he could see. Straight ahead was the golden light of *Shunara*, home star of *Gr'Shuna*; to the right shined the bright, glowing disc of a newborn star. Quickly checking his chart, he discovered that the system was strewn with rocks and giant balls of ice; reaching to activate his radio, he was about to warn the others to watch for debris when he lifted his eyes.

"Merciful heavens," he whispered.

To his left, in the same space where the ship of Gor'Faradan had sailed two heartbeats earlier, the sky was immersed in a massive fireball. All around, he saw the ships of friends scattering like embers on the wind. Without radio contact, he could not know what was wrong. But wherever he looked, all was chaos.

Then he saw it.

Like a ghost from his thousand darkest nightmares, it emerged from the flames and shot past him like a demon. Turning like a bird of prey, it came about and began madly blasting the heavens in all directions, shooting fire like a creature possessed. A terrified glance at his instruments to check the enemy ship's configuration confirmed his worst fears.

It was the Beast.

"Advance Patrol to Number One!" he screamed into his speakerphone. The only reply was static; the Cloud had cut them off from the main fleet, and there was no time to establish contact with his comrades. He hit the control button, alerting the rest of his crew to the presence of danger, and unsealed the emergency power override on his control panel. Designed to keep the ship's engines from overheating during normal operations, the circuit breaker would prevent any excess surges of power from pushing the engines into the danger zone. It was now a dangerous extravagance; they could afford to keep nothing in reserve.

Not if they were to live.

A flash of light to his left caught his eye; it was the ship of Ba'Randa, He of the Wicked Grin, now dying in flames amid the eternal cold of space. In the next instant, the ship of Da'Grana was no more. Summoning all the power his engines could muster, Dr'Zenzi raced his ship toward some nearby shoals, hoping to discourage the Beast from pursuit. He could taste the aroma of death, even across the void.

Twenty heartbeats away! he thought to himself. Another twenty beats of his heart and—if they did not crash on the shoals—they would be safe. They could hide in the rocks until the rest of the fleet emerged from the Cloud.

The rest of the Fleet!

Another flash of light lit the skies—then another, as the Beast trained his powerful guns first on Al'Tran, then on Fa'Raddah. Zenzi could not pause to reflect upon their times together—the close encounters with death they had survived; the even closer encounters with the Fleet concubines they had shared. It was all he could do to keep from screaming in panic himself, at the realization that Death was stalking them all, and the knowledge that surrendering to panic would only seal his fate. Raddah and Tran were gone; his mind was too numb from panic to digest the thought.

Their death fires were not even starting to fade when two more light flashes wrote death across the heavens.

Two more flaming lights—seven of his squadron gone.

And now, only he was left.

He could see the shoals coming up quickly on his left; he estimated twelve heartbeats—now ten—now eight.

He saw cratering on the foremost asteroid; edging his ship to the right, he planned to skim just over the top of the highest crater, before cutting hard to the left, hoping to cross out of the Beast's sensors, and use the small hunk of rock as a shield. His mouth as dry as a desert, he felt his chest echoing each beat of his heart. Mercifully, he did not see the Terran ship gliding smoothly into position, passing just behind his ship and slightly overhead.

His last sensation was sensing the sound of his own voice screaming in his throat as his ears exploded under the force of a tremendous noise.

"PLAY IT AGAIN."

"It will not change, Lordship," said the young monitor. The Clouds—"

"Play it!"

The menacing scowl of Ga'Glish burned itself into the young monitor's memory, much as the hatred in His Lordship's belly seared itself into the minds of everyone nearby. Nodding respectfully, fo'Rendish replayed the transmission from the scouting party. Try as he might, the clouds scattered too much of the signal to render it intelligible. But enough had come through to cause the sweat of fear to bead upon his forehead.

"Please, Monitor."

The soothing voice of Dra'Lengish calmed the monitor's jagged nerves. Fo'Rendish could feel the Chief Tactician's concern, and the young man was grateful for the intercession.

"His Lordship is anxious. We all are anxious to know what lies beyond the fog."

"Yes, my Lord."

As the graininess of the signal filled the air once again, fo'Rendish closed his eyes and tried to calm himself. It was a distress call. They were a few dozen heartbeats away from the Great Cloud's terminus. The main body of the Fleet would be entering clear skies within moments—and they were getting a distress call.

There were too many gaps to be certain, but it sounded ominously like a signal of danger, like one of the scouting party was calling for help.

Or sounding a warning for those who would follow.

"Your thoughts betray weakness," sneered Ga'Glish. "You are frightened, Small One. Frightened by fragments of thoughts which the sky itself has blocked from our senses."

"It sounds to me like trouble, my Lord. And caution in the face of danger...."

"Caution suits a concubine, Monitor, not one who would be her master."

"I respectfully suggest— "

"Silence!" thundered Ga'Glish, just as the summons bell signaled another incoming transmission.

Clear as a winter sky, two short pulses registered on the speakers, followed by a pause—then a long pulse.

It was the signal warning of the Beast.

Two short pulses rang again—then nothing.

As an organism with a single mind, all eyes rose toward the main visual screen at the front of the command center. There, they saw the last of the clouds melt into clear blackness. As they passed into the clearing, they saw nothing but an endless array of stars, burning brightly in the eternal dark.

Suddenly, a terrified voice broke the deathly silence.

"Look!"

The sky to the left of them was alive with fire. Ships from Lord Reyna's division were darting about in panic, some crashing headlong into others; some vanishing into the fiery cauldron. Without order or discipline, every ship in sight was scattering desperately, wildly—as from a demon.

And at the center of the firestorm, a bright disc slipped with menacing grace across the blackness, trailing destruction in its wake, scattering the Fleet with its every movement.

A frenzy of madness gripped the command center. Running bodies collided and fell, then rose and collided again, as everyone hurried desperately to his assigned station. Dra'Lengish ran to the tactical display terminal, to begin tracking the progress of the Terran ship, trying to bring some semblance of order to the panicking forces of His Worthiness.

A heartbeat later, Ga'Glish appeared on the communications screen, broadcasting a message to the entire fleet.

"Sons of the *g'Khruushtani*," thundered Ga'Glish, his eyes dark and filled with the fire of hate. "Our destiny is within our grasp at last. Do not shrink from the task at hand—fearful though it may be.

"The gods of the Ancient Ones have brought us the means to destroy the enemy," he continued, his voice rising like a growing tide along the shore. "It is within our power to destroy the Beast, now and for all time. From his ashes shall come the ruination of all things Terran—barbarism, war machines, their demonic engines of destruction. Throughout the Empire, our sons and daughters will sing our praises through Eternity.

"Go forth—let us go forth to crush the enemy. Centurion Gal'Reyna— to arms. Come west, to take up the Outermost Flank. Al'Nadra, come eastward, to skim the surface of the Cloud. All other groups, follow the Flagship—for His Worthiness, and for the glory of the Empire!!"

The animal roar within the Flagship found echoes spanning the width and breadth of the Fleet. Soon the ships of His Worthiness stopped their reckless flight. As the *g'Khruushtani* ships formed their perimeters of battle, and began stretching a seemingly endless crescent across the sky, a lonely disc, the brightest object visible in the nearby heavens, slowly arched its way northward, then west toward a bright, yellowish star. Away from the stirring battalions it sailed at a leisurely pace, taking care to keep well within sight of the frenzied sons of *g'Khruushte*, yet just beyond their grasp, receding into the distance like a phantom lake amid the desert sands.

* * *

AS THE CONTOURS of battle unfolded on the screen before him, fa'Shenali watched from the far wall with a mixture of fascination and horror. The Beast was a formidable adversary, but his lone ship could never stand against the assembled might of the Imperial Fleet. As the *g'Khruushtani* battalions formed into a wide crescent of death, the subaltern willed his heart to rejoice that so dangerous an enemy was about to meet his death.

Yet doubt gnawed at fa'Shenali: though a barbarian, the Beast was not a fool. His daring and ingenuity was legendary, causing the ruin of many noble commanders and the destruction of countless brave *g'Khruushtani*. Now, as a Day of Retribution neared and the Fleet closed to destroy its most dangerous foe, it was he—the One Called *Khu'ukh*—and not the *g'Khruushtani*, who controlled events. The Beast could have been half-way to *Gr'Shuna* by the time the Fleet emerged from the Cloud.

If he had so chosen.

But he had stayed behind to strike at the advance positions, inflicting mass devastation among the reconnaissance vessels only to depart upon the arrival of the main body of the Imperial Fleet. And now, he was leading them all into the darkness.

Suddenly, fa'Shenali found himself gripped by a coldness he had never before known. A coldness of foreboding; and he was not alone.

"I share your anxiety, Subaltern."

Fa'Shenali started at the unexpected presence of Dra'Lengish. So intense had been his musings, so keen his feelings of isolation, that the young one had not noticed the approach of One of Such Import. Instantly, fa'Shenali's mind flooded with embarrassment, and his mouth babbled words of apology.

"Lord Lengish, I—I— "

"Stay your prattling, Subaltern," hissed Lord Lengish. "I need your judgment—not evidence that part of you remains a child."

Chastened, fa'Shenali nodded respectfully.

"After risking so much to escape, why would the Beast have remained to attack, rather than moving at once to safety?"

"I know not, my Lord. At least, not for certain. But— "

"Could the loss of his companion ships be having any effect on his behavior?"

"I know not, Dra'Lengish. I suppose— "

"Is he leading us into a trap?"

"I am sorry, Lordship. But I cannot— "

"*Aaaahh* !" Dra'Lengish waved both his arms in a gesture of impatience. "Is there nothing you can tell me, fa'Shenali? Or am I wasting my breath, asking questions of a rock?"

"You ask questions to which there are no answers," fa'Shenali snapped, his temper getting the better of his discretion. "I can speculate—anyone can speculate. But without facts, my guess is like a seed falling in the forest: luck and time will determine if it bears fruit. And I will not warrant the results—not to you or to His Worthiness. If you wish more precision, you may consult an Augurer, my Lord. But then, do not expect an omenmonger to tarry, once you have paid for her services."

Despite himself, Dra'Lengish smiled at the Lowly One's brashness. The Young One was right, of course; but more importantly, Dra'Lengish sensed the proud honor at the core of the subaltern's being. Of low birth or not, the young one was unashamed of his opinions. Yet he would not pretend that they were worth more than their true value.

"All right, fa'Shenali. Perhaps my questions demand too much prescience. What, then, can you tell me—and speak quickly, for we are closing on the Beast with every second."

"I sense danger."

"Why—from what source?"

"I do not know, Lord Lengish. But *Khu'ukh* chose to fight rather than flee. And he lets us draw nearer, rather than leaving us to track his energy trail. He is not prone to carelessness, and yet his boldness approaches the realm of Myth."

"And so you think he is luring us headlong into a trap—a trap of some sort, the shape of which is beyond your power of discernment."

The Tactician's words were spoken calmly, without passion or qualm. And though the precise formulation had not gelled within his mind, fa'Shenali found that they captured his fears exactly.

"Yes, my Lord. That is precisely what I believe."

The Old One's clear eyes showed sadness, a sadness that burned deeply into the mind of the young officer.

"I agree, Subaltern. Yet I fear that we are the only ones who see the danger."

"If we are heading into a trap— "

"It will most likely come from the West—from the Terran fleet at *Gr'Shuna*. And it will likely be most unpleasant."

"Yes, my Lord."

"Subaltern, I want you to watch the western screens like a bird of prey. Let me know the moment that anything unexpected appears in the darkness."

"Yes, my Lord."

"I will try to convince Ga'Glish to abandon this madness. Anger has conquered his judgment, and hatred blinds him to all signs of danger."

As Dra'Lengish strode into the center of the room, fa'Shenali felt a brief sensation of dizziness. The Universe was turning inside out, and it was all he could do to keep his mind focused on his assigned task. Riveting his eyes to the screens, alert for the first sign of the approaching Terran fleet, he forced out all thoughts but duty, training his senses and his every conscious thought on the task of keeping watch over their westernmost flank.

* * *

HIS BACK TO the giant screen, Ga'Glish looked over the Command Center like a prince surveying his manor. Everywhere he looked, his underlings scurried about, all resolved on the task at hand, no trace of doubt or other treason poisoning the air. His soul sang with triumph, knowing that he was nearing his Moment of Atonement, that he would finally make amends for all the evil done since he spared the Beast in a moment of misguided compassion.

Turning to look at the screen, the Lord Commander's eyes searched until they found him—the bright dash of light in the center of the screen. He raged with a fury that almost scared him. Thoughts of death and destruction pounded upon his conscience, as they had daily for nearly a full cycle of time—millions lost, drawn screaming into the hole of Eternity by the monster now lurking before him.

His mind screamed at the thought of his complicity, of the weakness in himself that had caused it all. He could have easily stopped this demon, he told himself once again. He could have spared countless lives simply by snuffing out the Evil One when he had the chance, when War was just a word lost to history and sanity still abided in the Universe . The thought had never left him, tormenting him whenever he was alone, through countless days and endless nights. But now he could see—touch—almost taste the end.

"Monitors show us within seven astronomical units of the Beast, and still drawing nearer," reported a voice from the throng below. It was the a young technician—a strapping youth, whose technical skills with the machinery of Space would have earned vast rewards in the Days Before the Darkness. Now, thanks to the enlightenment of the Lord Commander, those same gifts spared him from toiling as a common soldier on some forsaken battleground.

"Order all ships on the flanks to increase speed," thundered the voice of Ga'Glish. "Let us have at the Beast, now that he is within our grasp."

Redemption would be glorious, he thought, as those near him sprung into action to fulfill his command. He was ready to shed a crushing weight, at last be freed from the mindless guilt that sapped his strength and consumed his mind. With the Beast destroyed, the mighty Terran offensive would crumble—crumble like an arch deprived of its keystone. Of this much he was certain.

Soon the advancing flanks were visible on the giant monitor screen. Ga'Glish watched eagerly as they came nearer, nearer, until the Beast was almost within range of their long-range weaponry.

Suddenly and without warning, the wily Terran made his move—his last gamble at escaping. Swerving sharply eastward, snapping into one of his wrenching spirals, he fled to the east-southeast, surging just past the bellowing guns of the *g'Khruushtani* flank, and racing back in the direction of the Great Cloud.

At first raging at the Terran's apparent escape, a surge of triumph coursed through the body of Ga'Glish. The longnose had just sealed his fate, by choosing a path from which there would be no escape.

"Orders to the Fleet," thundered the Lord Commander. Instantly, he commanded his staff's attention; raising his arms to silence them, his voice bellowed with the sounds of triumph.

"The Fleet of Lord Ladrasha shall divert to the South, to take the position near the *Ling'tari* Crescent." At once, an Underling appeared with an indicator, and Ga'Glish beamed a point of light toward a faint, spiraling mass of gasses and rocks near a southern bend of the Great Cloud.

"The forces of Lord Reyna shall maintain their position here—the rest, shall follow the Flagship. All hearts—to the attack."

Cheers echoing in his ears, Ga'Glish glowered angrily at the images on the screen. The Beast had blundered at last: he had chosen a course taking him directly toward the small, intense storm that was brewing near the strands of *Ling'tari*. With his back to the storm, and surrounded on three sides, the Beast would meet death at last. There would be no escape this time. No reprieve from the Judgment of Souls.

The Forces of His Worthiness divided near the star they called *Shuno'la-shi*—the "Point of the Shunites." Ga'Glish watched as the Beast receded into the distance, only to slow and come about near a dull, reddish star a few units away from the simmering storm. Eyes burning with hate, Ga'Glish watched the progress of his fleet toward their most hated enemy, glowing with vengeance as the Imperial ships came closer, ever closer to the enemy receding into the distance.

He did not hear the first gasps of horror from the monitor stations below. Nor did he notice the first frantic signals from the rearmost positions, conveying their terrified warnings of a disaster approaching from the blackness to the West.

* * *

"GO AHEAD, DETWILER."

"Can you see it?"

"At four o'clock?"

"You think that's the storm Cookie mentioned?"

"It's the only storm I can see—the only ionic disturbance that shows on the screens."

"Well if that's the case then, where the devil...."

"My God!"

"Is that—?"

"That's the whole fucking fleet!"

"— Jesus Christ—!"

"Starship *Dauntless* calling Red Leader; *Dauntless* calling Red Leader. Over."

"Jack—?"

"Hang on Dewey—and what say we don't just hold position here? And wait until the rest of the gang joins us."

"Well—Cookie promised us action, Detwiler."

"Yeah, and it looks like he's about to deliver."

"This is Red Leader; over."

"Chandler, hold on to your seat. In about ten seconds, check your forward screens. You're going to experience the shock of a lifetime. Ready...."

"Captain Detwiler, this is no time for riddles. And remember the new command protocols. You're to use standard regulation exchanges on regulation channels. I didn't make them up, but rules are rules. And the new brass are a big fat lot of sticklers. Among other things. Over."

"Any time now...there you go."

"Holy shit."

"Didn't hear an 'over,' there, Captain."

"Shut up, Dewey."

Chapter 29

FOOTSTEPS SOUNDED DOWN THE lonely corridor of Liberty Base 223, through Emergency Hatch Twelve and over the metal grids that divided the commander's quarters from the rest of Third Fleet Headquarters. As with most temporary structures, the building engineers had redesigned the liberty base for ease of construction, not for the comfort or convenience of those consigned to duty there. And if that meant there was no quick route from the communications center to the Commandant's quarters—well, engineers never considered the problems of command, either. Like a security communications blackout. Or the possible need for a courier to relay a particularly sensitive message in person, without the risk of divulging the information to those without a real need to know.

The young lieutenant thought little of it as he hurried past the grid toward Hatch Twenty-six and onto the Officer's Deck. He knew nothing of the Old Days—the days before the war. To hear the oldtimers tell it, the bases back then were filled with shops and people, pleasure centers and libraries. Milling crowds lent an almost civilian aroma to the sterile confines of military life. And the smells of baked goods from real, honest-to-God bakeries filled the air around each concourse.

But that was before the War. Before he was drafted to play his small role in advancing the cause of Terran civilization. Or, more particularly, before his father-in-law—the Chairman of Mid-Terran Mining & Manufacturing and one of Senator Chen's biggest contributors and most valued advisors—secured him a position as adjutant to Fleet Administration, where he had no reason to fear the thunder of enemy blasters and was as safe from the enemy as any of the Top Brass.

All he knew was that so long as he did his job, he'd never have to face a lizard blaster or slog through the mud, trying to pick the buggers off one by one. Until now, that meant little more than fetching coffee and relaying staff requests for the next day's lunch menu. Today, with something important to deliver, he didn't want to be late. More than this, he didn't want to get lost along the way.

The young man ran past Hatch Twenty-six and out into the Residential Concourse, dodging the occasional cleaning drone or staff officer until he arrived at the outer door to the Commandant's Quarters. Panting heavily, he pressed the page button, then tried to smooth his ruffled hair. After a few seconds passed, he rang again, only to be greeted by the arrival of an ill-tempered young ensign, a pretty young girl barely out of her teens.

"Yes, what is it?" demanded the young adjutant. "And what could possibly bring you around at this time of day? The Admiral is just having breakfast. I'm sure you know how testy he gets, if his routine is interrupted."

"I was told," panted the lieutenant, trying his best to be brief, "to deliver a message in person—even if it meant waking the Admiral up."

"You'll just have to tell me," scolded the ensign. "I'll see that he gets it."

"But— "

"I have my orders, Lieutenant."

"So do I, Ensign."

"Mine come from the Admiral."

A few minutes later, after once more proving to himself the hopelessness of combating female logic with appeals to mere reason, the lieutenant gave it up.

"All right," he snapped, "have it your way."

The look of haughty triumph in the ensign's eyes almost convinced him to start the battle over again, but the sensitive nature of the message made arguing over protocol a useless formality. And if he couldn't trust to the discretion of the Admiral's personal aide—well, even if he didn't really trust anybody these days, there were some he'd trust less than others.

"Tell the Admiral that Girshoona has fallen. The message from the Planet is that they met no resistance in the sky. Enemy ground forces aren't giving up the fight for the planet's surface, but we've seized or destroyed all major cities and industrial centers. So, the bottom line is that the planet is ours—and without a real fight.

"Got that?"

The ensign nodded. The look of confusion that washed over her face convinced Phillips that he was dealing with a brainless bluebird, the type the men called the Full-Crested Flake. And so he repeated the message and left, hoping that something had registered in her vacant little head. He prayed that he wouldn't be called on the carpet for leaving his mission in the hands of an empty-headed twit.

As the door closed with a rush of air, the ensign leaned back against a nearby wall. She took a long, deep breath before starting down the hallway leading to the dining room. She well knew what the drooling, post-pubescent courier was too dim-witted to realize: there had been no order given to advance on the planet. Not by Fleet Command, and certainly not by the Admiral. There would be hell to pay, she thought to herself as she neared the dining room's access panel. And she hoped that her commander wouldn't confuse the messenger for the message. In her short time as a staff officer she'd seen enough of Medwick to know his strengths and weaknesses as a commander. His ability to react to the unexpected was not one of his strengths.

Pressing the button on the access panel, she stepped into the dining room, where the Admiral was having his breakfast of coffee, toast, and reconstituted eggs.

"Admiral Medwick," she said, standing at attention by the door, awaiting the command to advance. As she stood, she exchanged a cold stare with Mrs. Medwick, who'd arrived unexpectedly the previous day in order to surprise her husband.

"Yes, Ensign. What is it?" the Admiral said stiffly, his eyes wandering warmly, as if welcoming the interruption. He had no idea that his mood was about to change abruptly.

* * *

THE TERRAN FLEET drew nearer to the Great Cloud, drawn toward a low-frequency pulse emanating from the crescent shaped formation that filled the skies near the star the Crutchtans called *Ling'tari*.

Realizing at once that they were in terrible danger, the Crutchtan fleet quickly abandoned its advance on the *Ling'tari* Crescent and moved into the clear skies just beyond the heliosphere at *Shuno'lashi*. As the Terrans neared, the forces of His Worthiness scrambled into position, drawing into a massive defensive crescent comprising nearly ten thousand warships. The Terrans inched closer, forming three attack wedges. Each wedge carried two thousand frigates, cruisers, and starships, and anxious crews on the approaching ships could see the Crutchtan formation with the naked eye. Soon both sides saw their enemy stretching endlessly in the vastness of space, countless points of light flickering brightly against the reddish glow of the Cloud.

Then the advance stopped, and the opposing fleets floated in the void. Each waited and watched for the slightest movement, the slightest sign of weakness or fear in the other. Only the Crutchtan's ceaseless jamming of all subspace frequencies broke the stillness of space, but their frantic effort to stop the enemy fleet from speaking to its most potent weapon made their own communications clumsy and difficult. As the Crutchtan commanders tried desperately to devise a plan of attack, the Terrans, safely out of range, wondered among themselves how they had let themselves be drawn into such a predicament.

Suddenly, from far behind the Crutchtan formation, came a low-frequency signal, cutting through the fog of interference like a beacon. Clear as a church bell, the signal was so strong that everyone on both sides knew at once that Cook had transferred all his power into the ship's transmitter—all to send them a signal.

As the Terrans waited and listened, the message came through as clear as the signal.

One long pulse of twenty seconds duration—followed by five shorter ones, of five seconds each.

Over and over... one long, five short; one long, five short.

The Terran call to attack.

Soon the Terran battle wings started moving forward as inevitably as the approach of night. They crept closer and closer to the Crutchtan lines, sending the enemy ships into a flurry of desperation.

"BUT MY LORD!" pleaded Dra'Tanglos, the First Assistant of Tactics, the favorite nephew of Dra'Lengish, and the One Designated to speak in his absence.

"Silence, Fool! You have my Command. Your duty is obedience!"

"But— "

"One full attack squadron—no, make it three! Follow the source of the transmission. And there is to be no escaping this time. I want him dead. I shall have the head of anyone who fails me."

"But Lordship—we cannot spare them!" screamed Tanglos.

"Guards— !"

As the Ordermasters dragged off the unhappy officer who dared to question the Lord Commander, Ga'Glish turned his eyes to the approaching threat from the West. The Terrans were outnumbered, but mere numbers would not decide the battle. It was crucial to know the exact deployment of their dreaded death ships: that, more than mere numbers, would decide their Fate.

Though sensing the terror of those around him, Ga'Glish was surprised to find himself as calm as a summer breeze. Their peril had only heightened his senses, and he felt an spirit of exhilaration that he could not understand. It was as if a cloud had lifted, letting him glide serenely over the danger, unaffected by the fear of those around him. It let him at last see the Terrans for the clumsy apes that they were.

All the Terrans but one.

But that one would be dealt with soon enough, Ga'Glish smiled darkly.

"All remaining ships keep Battle Formation Twelve," thundered Ga'Glish. "Ships forward, to the attack."

Beneath his feet, he felt the Flagship's engines fire and strain, as the pilot maneuvered into position to guide the rest of the Fleet into battle against the Terrans. Ga'Glish turned his eyes toward the rear viewer, to watch the rear guard move away from the main body of the fleet, toward the Beast and his infernal signal.

With all his being, Ga'Glish wished to be going with them. For now, he could only wish them well; his duties were with the main Fleet. Through the dire straits into which Fate had brought them, the Fleet needed their Commander at the helm.

"The Terrans are advancing, Lord Commander. One-quarter astronomical unit and closing. All our ships report themselves eager to do battle, my Lord."

"Hear me now—all ships to battle stations," screamed Ga'Glish, a lust for revenge dripping from his voice. "All ships stay at the ready—to attack on my command!"

LUNGING UNEXPECTEDLY toward the very center of the Terran battle line, the main body of the Crutchtan fleet advanced quickly. Through a ceaseless fusillade of Terran guns, the Crutchtans pushed forward until they had nearly split the middle third of the Terran fleet, winning the early initiative and taking the battle directly to the enemy. With their starships scattered on either flank, the Terran center suddenly found its communications disrupted, and their first instinct was to withdraw until they could regroup. As the Crutchtans pressed the battle, pursuing the two bedraggled halves of the enemy forces with a fierceness born of desperation, the Terran flanks pivoted to position themselves for a counterattack along either side. But as the battle raged in the center, with the deathfires of hundreds of ships obscuring the ebb and flow of battle, the Terran commanders soon confronted diversionary attacks along both sides of the battle zone. So long as the Crutchtans kept the flanks pinned, there was nothing the Terrans could do to relieve the overmatched forces holding the center of their line.

Minutes passed, and death flamed across the skies. The Crutchtans found themselves believing in miracles for the first time since the early days of the war. As they carried the tide of battle against the longnoses, an unfamiliar thought slowly rose throughout the fleet: victory—an unthinkable concept, one that seemed almost alien to Crutchtan experience of late.

But as they fought what at the time seemed destined to be the decisive battle of the war, victory—at long last, victory—appeared to be within their grasp.

* * *

PACING NERVOUSLY about the Communications Center, Admiral Medwick had worked himself into a froth. The veins on his thick neck pulsed furiously, and his portly face was red as wine. Turning on the hapless lieutenant commander who'd been on duty in the control room when the message first arrived, he shoved his face almost into the young blueshirt's nose and sprayed his fury all over her face.

"I said I want answers!" he demanded. "Answers—not goddamn mush-mouthed drivel! I want to know what goddamn bastard ordered the fleet to sail, and I want to know what goddamn bastard told them to storm the planet! That operation's been in the planning stage for weeks—*weeks*, mind you. And they could have thrown it away in a matter of hours by some crazy-ass, disorganized attack. Now you tell me that someone sent three fucking starships against the planet—and the rest sailing off into the middle of goddamn nowhere?"

"Yes—yes, sir?"

"Shut up, Commander! Shut up—and don't be getting smart with me. You try that and I'll make you the lowest, most miserable little cunt in the whole damn fleet. I'll have you saluting goddamn *liberty girls*! Are you reading me, Missy?"

"Ye—ye—ye— "

"I asked if you're reading me, you miserable, dimwitted slut!"

"Yes, sir," she whispered, her face burning a deep crimson. The rest of her command stood silently at attention, terrified that the Admiral would turn on them to vent his rage, yet so embarrassed for their watch supervisor that each one, to a man, would later feel deeply ashamed for not standing up for her.

"Now who?! I want to know who!"

"I—I didn't take the message myself, Admiral."

"Who!—I asked who?—you goddamn little tart! Are you just plain stupid, or is there someone you're trying to protect?"

"Commodore Cook," she said softly, her watering eyes cast down toward the floor as she tried her best to stand at attention.

"Who!?"

"I—I heard that the order came directly from Commodore Cook."

A malevolent glower flashed over Medwick's face, and his eyes filled with a vengeful hate.

"Cook," Medwick snorted derisively, his narrowed eyes still fixed menacingly on the young bluebird struggling to maintain her composure. But his face soon softened and the scowl vanished, replaced by the barest shadow of amusement and triumph.

"I should have known," he smiled humorlessly. "I should have known."

Relieving the humiliated young officer of her duties, Medwick ordered the second-in-command to begin work clearing a security channel to Central Command in Covington, gruffly telling him to make less of a hash of things than his predecessor. One task complete, the admiral waddled out of the communications center. His mind, until recently consumed by worry over the upcoming invasion of the now-vanquished planet, had stopped worrying over tides of distant battles that were out of his control. Storming into the main corridor, ignoring the salutes of passing subordinates, his mind was filling with more important matters.

As he neared the moving sidewalk that would take him the hundred yards or so to his office, he was already savoring the prospect of telling the Chief of Staff that he could start the ball rolling. They could, if Admiral Weatherlee saw fit, begin the paperwork for a general court-martial in what promised to be the trial of the century.

"SQUADRON BLUE—Squadron Blue? Are you there?"

"You cannot lose us that easily, One Called Del'Ashan. We are still behind you. But I have instructed my ships to move eastward, into position for our approach to the interior of the system. We do not wish to leave the Hated One a clear avenue of escape, do we Ashan? And how better to catch him than to use those shoals to screen our presence, and trap him before he reaches the clear skies behind us?"

Del'Ashan smiled grimly. Of all the groupleaders in his command, Bra'Challah was the ablest—the finest pilot he knew, with the sharpest sense of tactics and the best head for navigation within his circle of knowledge. The Brahanashi's squadron had come through peril after peril nearly unscathed, and he had said a prayer of thanks upon hearing that Challah and his squadron would be included among the detachment sent to dispatch the Beast. Not only that, but Challah was a noble companion and a fine friend. The two had shared much in the days before the War, "From food, to wines, to concubines," as in the ancient song of fellowship. Now that each had proven himself in battle, it was only natural that they watch over each other as brothers.

Yet as they neared, he felt a gnawing sense of disquiet grow with each passing moment. The signal they were following had not altered so much as an atom's width in the time it had taken them to approach. Though its fading strength could be explained by the energy drain upon the Terran's engines, it was odd that the Beast would hold his position steady in the face of an approaching enemy. It was very odd, indeed. Something told Ashan that they needed to be careful.

As if anyone nearing a battle with the One Called *Khu'ukh* would be careless. Or, if they were to be truly rational in the first place, anything other than terrified beyond words.

"Groupcommander Del'Ashan?" A tense voice called over the speaker, his worried tone slicing through the subspace interference of the Great Cloud. "Ashan, answer me quickly. Quickly— "

"This is Del'Ashan," said the commander. "I am listening, Altern."

"I am close enough to take readings from the Terran," said the voice of Gra'Lanna, a young lord from the distant planet *Rahadan*. "But my instruments show no Terran ship in the vicinity. It is a probe—a marker, nothing more—broadcasting a signal to the surrounding heavens. But I see nothing of the Beast!"

"Lanna?" Ashan called into his microphone. "It is a trick. Be on your guard."

"Ash—" The return broadcast was severed in mid-sentence, dissolving into a spattering of interstellar static.

"Lanna? Do you hear what I am saying?"

Receiving no response from any of the ships on his point, Ashan switched to his rear sensors, just in time to see the fading embers of Bra'Challah's ship glowing against the blackness of space. Nothing was left of his command; only the faintest hint of dying ashes lit the skies where the rearmost squadron had sailed only moments earlier. As the glow from their death fires dimmed into nothingness, the dying light cast shadows against the shoals where they had hoped to trap their deadliest enemy.

For what seemed Eternity, a terrified Del'Ashan stared, the memory frozen forever in his mind as he glimpsed the specter of death. In the blackness loomed the gray outline of a shadowy disc, moving away from the rocks where it had hidden, waiting to spring a trap of its own. Now slicing serenely through the heavens in a great flash of light it fired its engines and departed into the distance, on its way to join the desperate battle raging to the East. For the only time in his life, he saw it—he saw the death ship of the One Called *Khu'ukh* as it slipped past him on its way to work destruction on the Forces of His Worthiness. In that instant, in one moment of stunning and profoundly disturbing insight, he realized how hopeless his mission had been, and just how closely he had strayed toward the shadows of nonexistence.

It seemed like an eternity passing. But the chronometer told him it was a only a matter of a few heartbeats before he was broadcasting his warning to the Flagship, and regretting that death had not claimed him along with his fallen comrades.

* * *

"THE LIZARDS are pummeling our flanks."

The radio officer's tense voice matched the mood on the *Corona's* bridge. Chandler, the ranking officer for the entire battle group—and the one whose head would be on the chopping bloc if they ever got out of this mess—turned to face her, expecting the worst.

"Detwiler reports they've almost broken through Battle Group Red. We're caught in the middle. If they turn the far flank...."

Chandler didn't need to hear any more. The lizards were frenzied. He'd rarely seen them fight so fiercely, and never so well. Not since the First Battle of Lagrush had they mounted such an onslaught against massed starships. Now enemy ships pressed upon them from all sides; the lizards were fighting as if the smell of victory was filling their nostrils.

He looked at the tactical monitors. Each showed the same scene: the Terrans were in retreat everywhere, fighting against the full fury of the Crutchtan fleet. He struggled to maintain his composure. Panic wouldn't help them, and he needed a clear head to salvage a draw out of the disaster looming around him. If only they could regroup, and join forces to mount a counterattack.

"Signal B Wing to pivot east—and to drive toward our present position."

"Sorry, Captain, the lizards are jamming the hell out of all our normal channels. All I get is static, up and down the line. Unless we get a ship to break free—move into the open skies to the North or South—we're stuck talking to our own wing. And if they penetrate the center...."

Even as he spoke, the Terran center bowed and gave way. Soon, Crutchtan battleships poured through the breach, splitting A Wing in two and sending ships scattering in panic. It looked hopeless, and their position was getting worse by the minute. All that was left was to sound retreat—the throbbing double pulse on the low-frequency band would penetrate even the densest enemy jamming.

Even then, without effective communications there would be no orderly withdrawal. If disorder spread from the battle line to his whole wing, he'd create a panic; if it spread from Center Wing to the whole fleet, he could turn the defeat into a rout. But when the alternative was to stay and get slaughtered—well, he thought, even a bad choice was still a choice.

He was about to give the command when the override control on the communications desk began sounding loudly, signaling an incoming priority message, beaming clearly to all ships on the general frequency channel. When the radio officer transferred the signal to audio, it trumpeted a call to general quarters—the blaring, buzzing pulse that commanded everyone's instant attention, and called all hands to battle stations.

"Tracing the signal," said the radio officer. She scanned the skies, tracking the broadcast to a rapidly approaching point of light calling from the clear skies of due north.

The systems officer displayed his sensor readings onto a tactical overlay of the northern skies. Immediately, all hands recognized the approaching object as a starship.

Seconds later, the *Corona* received another signal, this one from the exuberant commander of a nearby ship.

"Switch to Security Channel Forty-four," exulted Westheimer, the captain of the *Augustus*. The broad smile on his face buoyed the spirits of the *Corona's* entire bridge; when they heard the news, it came as a surprise to no one.

"It's Cook!" he shouted, grinning from ear to ear. "He's just coming into visual range, broadcasting from clear skies and issuing battle orders."

* * *

FROM HIS station, far to the side of the main viewer, fa'Shenali sensed a tidal shift in emotions washing through the command center. He could feel a rising gloom in the minds of his comrades, as the monitors displayed the changing course of battle. All watched in amazement as the Terrans stirred from their torpor as if awakened by a wizard's spell.

The moment the Beast appeared on the screen Ga'Glish ordered a detachment of warships to intercept and destroy him—and decreed a renewed assault upon the weakening Terran flank. The command room watched in amazement as the enemy flank pivoted suddenly, letting some few squadrons of *g'Khruushtani* ships race past them into the breach, only to thrust quickly and mercilessly into the center of the oncoming battalions, sending the onrushing *g'Khruushtani* reeling in a dozen directions, crumbling their lines and communications, pushing the remnants of Al'Nadra's forces toward the Terran center.

Ordering Gal'Reyna to press toward the Terran center, trying to take the battle right to the heart of the Terran forces, Ga'Glish paled to see—even as the words were forming on his lips—the Terrans preempt his movement by mounting a furious attack against Lord Reyna's assembling divisions. Without warning, the Terrans had hurled half of their available forces against the right flank of the *g'Khruushtani*, catching the entire battle quadrant by surprise and opening a vulnerable hole in the center of their own lines, causing all in the command center to wonder if the Beast possessed the power to read their minds.

Enraged by the sudden turn in their fortunes, Ga'Glish commanded a general assault by the remainder of his forces upon the weakened

Terran center, exhorting them to crush the enemy like insects under their feet. As the main body of the fleet neared the Terrans, a growing sense of anticipation gripped those present at the command center. Everyone was united in praying for victory, and all thrilled at the thought of breaking the Terran fleet in two.

But just as the first wave of *g'Khruushtani* ships engaged the Terran advance positions, a shout of alarm arose from the central monitor. The attention of all shifted from the central focus of the battle to the rapidly approaching point of light streaming toward the battle.

Leaving behind the fading death fires of the forces dispatched to destroy him—with guns fully charged and blazing before his approach, and shields primed and strong as a mountain looming high above the plains—the Beast raced toward the center of battle, where his own countrymen were in greatest peril, and where the full force of the *g'Khruushtani* fleet was threatening to bring destruction to the invaders. Alone and at top speed, the Beast skimmed the northern edge of the battle line like a great bird of prey, daring his hunters to take to the skies in pursuit. Into the periphery of the *g'Khruushtani* lines he dashed, visiting death and fire to all who stood their ground—only to retreat in long, arching spirals before returning, deeper and deadlier than ever, streaking deeper and deeper into the heart of the fleet, taunting his enemies and hurling destruction with every deadly change of motion, every breath of fire from his guns.

Fa'Shenali's chest thundered with each passing heartbeat. It seemed Fate had decreed that the war would be decided here; and as events all around him screamed for attention, he found himself drawn to the screen showing the Beast—alone and defiant—toying with his enemies like a demon of death, sowing terror and chaos throughout the *g'Khruushtani*. Yet fa'Shenali suddenly realized that they had it within their power to vanquish the Terrans: he knew it in the very core of his being, and could see it with his eyes. It was less a thought than a consuming emotion that raised him to the pinnacle of elation. With all the power at their command, the longnoses were nothing without the Beast; the dimness of their wits and the clumsiness of their maneuverings held all the might of their machines for nothing. So long as their own superior numbers kept the Beast at bay—and they of the *g'Khruushtani* did not succumb to the panic of the moment—they could regroup and destroy the Terran forces. It seemed so simple, and it was all but inevitable: their numbers and superior positioning decreed it, and for all his ferocity and cunning, not even the Beast could change it. All they needed was time. Time and patience. One by one, the Terran positions would crumple like the withering leaves of autumn, and they could turn this brush with annihilation into the first rout of the Invaders since the early days of the war. They needed only to keep the Beast from rejoining his fleet; and they needed to keep pounding at the center of the Terran positions as fiercely and mercilessly as they could until their lines buckled and cracked.

Suddenly his ears plunged him into despair.

"Left flank," rasped the voice of the Lord Commander, his throat dry and cracking. "Order all ships along the Left Flank to turn and attack the Beast—*now!*"

With a roar of approval, the Command Center echoed with a thirst for red Terran blood. Soon, to his horror, fa'Shenali saw the ships of Al'Nadra pivot, moving into position to advance against the Beast.

Summoning all his energy, and all of this remaining strength, the young subaltern fought his way through the crowd, up the latter, and into the presence of Dra'Lengish.

"This is madness!" hissed fa'Shenali. "Utter madness!"

"Watch your tongue, Young One," warned the old man, pulling him aside, dragging him into the small corridor between the two main batteries of computers that dominated the walkway leading up to the Command Tower. "Your career teeters over the rocks already. Do not send yourself plummeting— "

"But we can beat them!" cried fa'Shenali. "We have them! If we just continue to hamper their transmissions—and concentrate our attack—"

"Silence!" hissed the Chief Tactician. The young one's agony registered immediately on his face; it convinced the old one that his own doubts were not lacking in merit.

"But— "

"*Silence!*" Dra'Lengish commanded. "Do you wish to be banished again? Or worse, clapped in fetters for the rest of the war?"

Crestfallen, fa'Shenali struggled against the tears that were trying to flood his eyes. Feeling utterly defeated, he sank to the floor, burying his face in his hands.

"Dra'Lengish," he said, his voice little more than a whimper. "My Lord...."

"I agree with you, Subaltern."

Fa'Shenali looked up, his tear-stained cheeks casting shadows against the wall.

"We are squandering our best, and perhaps our last chance for victory. But taste this thirst for blood hanging in the air, Young One. Dissension will be taken as treason. And we cannot serve the Imperator from a detention cell, can we?"

"But...."

"Compose yourself, Subaltern," Lord Lengish said gently. "Compose yourself, and let us both forget this incident. But do not really forget it. And recall it, at the appropriate time."

"I do not understand."

"You will," Dra'Lengish smiled sadly. Yet, fa'Shenali felt a great wave of sadness wash over the Elder's soul. "At the appropriate time."

With that, Dra'Lengish departed, leaving the young man alone with his thoughts, giving him the privacy he needed to restore him to control over his feelings.

And leaving him to wonder what changes were stirring with the wind.

GA'GLISH WATCHED the viewing screen eagerly as a *g'Khruushtani* wave swept toward the solitary point of life that stood for all that was Terran, all that was evil in the Universe. Though he could not trace the source, he felt the secret doubts of some around him, and his heart surged with fury against those treasonous thoughts. For now, he could do nothing. He could not even pause to identify the traitors. But once the battle was won....

Suddenly, the Beast moved, charging like a madman directly toward the surging *g'Khruushtani* lines.

"We have him," whispered the Lord Commander. "We have him at last."

AS THE Terran ship glided forward, fa'Shenali stepped from between the battery of computers. Shielding his eyes at first from the lights, he stepped onto the metal grating that lifted the High Staff above the monitors and technicians that worked the machinery of command.

Watching the Beast surge toward certain death, fa'Shenali felt his chest pounding wildly. It was as if *Khu'ukh* had determined that the time had come to die, and that he would carry off as many brave *g'Khruushtani* with him as he could. It seemed so out of character, the young subaltern thought. Yet staring across the abyss of Death made some wild with fear, others wild with rage. Until one's own time came, he mused, none could foresee his own reaction.

In heartbeat, fa'Shenali was breathless with alarm. Pulling short and racing before the leading edge of the approaching *g'Khruushtani* lines, the Beast pummeled their pursuit force—then turned almost on his heels, at the last moment cutting the sharp but graceful turn that only he was able to master, retreating just beyond the reach of their guns. Desperate to destroy him, the pursuers raced after him, all the while pulling further and further away from the main body of the Terran forces. Young fa'Shenali cried in anguish, for now he understood: suicide was not the Beast's plan at all. But the cunning Terran was quite willing to dangle his own life as bait, drawing the *g'Khruushtani* away from the crumbling Terran battle lines—and giving the longnoses another chance to turn the tide of battle.

"No!—*no*!!!!" he screamed at the top of his voice, causing eyes to turn, and almost calling the vengeance of Ga'Glish himself upon him.

At that very moment—as if on signal—the trapped Terran central brigade pressed a furious assault upon the weakened *g'Khruushtani* lines, bowing the front ominously and fighting with a fury born of desperation. As a confused and disoriented Lord Commander barked contradictory orders and commands to his underlings, a darkening gloom once again gripped the Command Center.

And as the Beast streaked toward the Terran flank, trailing pursuers in his wake, the suddenly rejuvenated Terrans pushed the battle past him all along the flank. It seemed that Death had been mocking them all the time, using his Chosen One, the One Called *Khu'ukh*, as his demon to dash their last hope for salvation. When finally the Beast slipped past the sorry rear guard of the Left Flank—dispatching the half-dozen *g'Khruushtani* warships sent to stop him with an easy grace that seemed to carry the blessings of Evil—it seemed clear that Death would soon visit all of them.

And that he would carry away many good and brave souls into the fire with him.

THE *D'ARTAGNAN* DREW into the temporary safety of the Terran right flank, her blackened sides showing the scars of battle and the bearing the stains of every enemy gun that had come within firing range. The Terrans quickly closed ranks and moved to attack the advancing Crutchtans. Their new commander came about with a vengeance, and sent his ship rising high above the plane of battle. Soon, in a continuing boom of low-frequency pulsing, the *d'Artagnan* was transmitting an uncompromising order to attack up and down the line.

All along the front, charged to exhilaration by the presence of their new Wing Commander, the Terrans responded with a furious charge against the enemy lines, finding them soft and yielding. In a brutal series of quick and deadly advances, the Terrans battered the Crutchtans up and down the line of battle, each advance building upon the last—pushing, ever pushing the enemy back toward the wispy claws of the Great Cloud. On the left flank, under the merciless urging of the One Called Cook, the Terrans sent the Crutchtans into a panic, their disorderly retreat threatening a collapse of the entire front. Reinforcements poured desperately from the Crutchtan center, seeking to shore up the flank to prevent a full-scale rout.

Suddenly, without warning, the Terran center surged with deadly fury. Ignoring the Crutchtan flank now retreating in panic, Cook turned both Terran flanks toward the center. Within seconds the maneuvar sent shock waves of terror through the Crutchtan lines and cut the main body of the Crutchtan fleet neatly in two.

Caught between onrushing forces, their communications now a hopeless jumble of contradictory readings and false enemy signals, the Crutchtans struggled valiantly. But relentlessly, with the inevitability of death, the Terrans pushed them back—back toward the Cloud, where the deadly storms raged furiously as ever, and interstellar lightening flashed every bit as deadly as the flash of the Terran guns.

And as the order to retreat sounded—calling all Crutchtan ships to fall back, as orderly as possible, to take up defensive positions for a counterattack—nearly half the Crutchtan fleet had already fallen, or were dying in flames, cut off from hope and rescue, in the cold blackness of space.

THE COMMAND CENTER was madness—all madness.

Throughout the cavernous facility, officers and menials scurried about, each trying to do a dozen things at once, each trying his best to keep the instinct to panic from spreading.

Over the dizzied, chaotic buzzing, the booming voice of the Lord Commander sounded, calling his forces to battle, urging them to resist unto death itself. But few were listening. All energies were directed toward massing their ships for defense, and stopping the Terrans from forcing the Imperial Fleet back toward the Cloud.

"Fa'Shenali!"

At the sound of his name, the subaltern came to attention, searching around for the voice that called him.

"Fa'Shenali—here!"

Following the sound, Shenali looked to see Dra'Lengish beckon him toward the ramp leading to the Top Echelon. There, on the raised platform, the command staff controlled not only the Flagship, but the whole Fleet as well.

At once, the young man bounded toward the walkway, meeting the Old One at the bottom of the ramp.

"A retreat through the Cloud," gasped Dra'Lengish. "It is possible? That is my question—I want an answer."

"I—well, that is— "

"Come now, Subaltern. Do you not have the casualty figures from our transit?"

"Yes, my Lord. They are in the augmentorial records. But— "

"There is no time to argue, fa'Shenali—get me an answer. You have a hundred heartbeats, no longer. We must make a decision soon, before the Terrans break through our remaining perimeter. Otherwise—"

"I understand," interrupted the Young One, and he sped on his way.

"And do not use the Central Augmentor," called Dra'Lengish at the subaltern's receding figure. "Tap in through an open terminal! And use your own personal security clearance!"

Fa'Shenali waved his hand as he ran, acknowledging his instructions. Dra'Lengish took a deep breath and tried to compose himself as he ascended the walkway. He was certain what the young subaltern would find; and it was, he felt in his very bones, their only means of escape. But he would need facts to convince his own Commander. Facts to demonstrate the logic of such a course.

He was not at all sure that facts would matter anymore. Perhaps with the Ga'Glish of old—a man of reason and enlightenment. But not with the ranting stranger who was barking commands like a puppetmaster gone mad.

Now was not the time for dissension. Not with the Fleet in such mortal danger.

Not with the Fate of the Empire dangling over the abyss by a thread.

HIS CHEST pounding furiously, fa'Shenali entered his personal code into the first computer access terminal he found. Before he had time to wonder why Lord Lengish did not want him to use the central records augmentor, the information appeared upon the screen. The report was ominous: more than one-fourth of the ships entering the cloud had been destroyed. But those losses seemed inconsequential, compared to those they faced at the hands of the Terrans.

Transferring the data onto a printing sheet, fa'Shenali ripped the report from the output terminal and dashed back to the walkway. As he neared, he saw all heads suddenly turn to the main viewer, and felt a wave of horror wash over the entire Command Center. Even Dra'Lengish seemed no longer interested in the errand of the moment; his eyes, too, were fixed on the viewer, widening in fear.

Fa'Shenali arrived at the walkway, panting and out of breath. Lifting his eyes toward the giant visual monitor screen, he saw it as well.

Staring in dumb amazement, fa'Shenali found himself transfixed; like the others, the sight left him frozen in place, unable to move. It had come without warning, silent as a shadow. The young subaltern arrived just in time to see the quick and deadly fire of the starship's mighty main batteries, lighting the skies with each flash of its powerful guns.

For the first and last time in his life, fa'Shenali saw the monster with his own eyes: it was the Beast.

The great ship loomed in the heavens like a ghost. Scars of battle darkened its bow, ugly black streaks stretching halfway to its stern. Slicing through the sky, the monstrous Terran machine floated through the blackness, raining death with every passing moment, casting destruction in all directions.

Turning slightly to bring fire to bear on three small ships just to its left, the ship glowed under the harsh light of death, dispatching the fleeing *g'Khruushtani* vessels with an easy grace at once compelling and terrible. As it danced alone and silent through the unending darkness, the flash of guns and deathfires filled the silent skies, killing everything in its reach.

Serenely, with the gathering chill of a thundercloud in the wind, the Terran ship turned again. As it started its effortless approach toward the Flagship, fa'Shenali felt his legs go numb and his heart rise until it thundered in his brain. He was cold as the winter, helpless as a baby abandoned to the elements. His mouth was dry as ashes.

He had never before felt the crushing weight of total paralysis. He had never been so painfully aware of the fragility of existence. And never again would he feel such stark, unsullied terror.

"FULL POWER to weapons!"

The shrill voice of the Lord Commander called his minions to action. As underlings scurried about around him Ga'Glish smiled darkly, a cauldron of emotion. He had found the Beast at last, thought Ga'Glish; after all this time, they would clash again.

Only this time, the outcome would be different.

This time, Ga'Glish told himself, there would be no escape for the Evil One.

"Ready, my Lord!"

"Hold for my command!" thundered Ga'Glish. Hatred had left him a bitter thirst, a thirst for the Terran's blood. He watched the Beast near, relishing every moment of the Evil One's approach as a dying man savors the setting sun. At five battleunits, the Terran shields suddenly shifted inexplicably to the left, and power drained from the Beast's forward guns. It made no sense until....

"Yes," hissed Ga'Glish—that must be it. The Wicked One planned to swing around the Flagship, trying to catch him off guard.

But he would be ready; he had awaited the moment for too long, had suffered too much sorrow, not to be ready.

"Prepare for Enemy Transverse," he shouted. "Charge Gun Battery Four and await my signal."

"I hear, my Lord!"

Ga'Glish could feel the panic of others quivering around him. But he kept his own mind focused on the detestable monster on that abominable ship. He screened out the treasonous doubts and cowardly apprehensions that infested his subordinates.

"Two units, my Lord."

Ga'Glish felt himself soar as from the crest of a great mountain. His whole being raged with thoughts of revenge and hunger for self-atonement.

"Set your targets," he hissed at his Chief of Weaponry, his eyes riveted on the screen. At the final moment, his heart and voice each screamed with undying hate.

"All guns—blast him into oblivion!"

The Flagship began to shudder under the weight of discharge, just as the Terran ship darted slightly below and to the right, deflecting the full force of the Crutchtan blast every so slightly. In the same instant, the Beast summoned his reserve power to his ship's shields, focusing all of his weaponry into a lone, forward blaster. As the two ships fired simultaneously, the tactical screens showed the Terran shields bending—bending, until the burning force of the full *g'Khruushtani* barrage charred its outer tiles—bending until its hull glowed from the impact of a hundred small suns—yet holding until the end.

But on the Flagship....

The pride of the *g'Khruushtani* fleet shook and convulsed under the impact of the Terran salvo. The Terran blaster caught a seam in the Flagship's defenses and its shields shattered like glass. The engines on the great ship lost all of their strength, power draining like water poured into a bottomless well. The ship shook helplessly—violently—buffeting men and equipment from side to side like a great storm tossed leaves and branches. By the time the convulsions had ceased, and the survivors among the Command Staff had recovered their wits, the Terran starship was completing a leisurely turn and gliding into position for another pass. This time, with all guns charged.

The Lord Commander raged impotently at the viewing screen. His Chief Tactician, the gill slits on his throat as pale as mountain snow, quickly summoned every available aide and assistant, desperately trying to recharge the Flagship's engines.

"Route all emergency batteries into the power drive," Dra'Lengish commanded. "Charge on my signal."

The technicians struggled to breath life into their dying ship. Fa'Shenali numbly watched the approach of the One Called *Khu'ukh*, his horror at the nearness of Death having sucked all feeling from his senses.

"I have something in Engine Battery Four," cried a technician, his eyes wide with fright. "Shall I route it into the shields?"

"Do it!" screamed Dra'Lengish. "Do it now!"

The ship stirred reluctantly, like a wounded animal struggling to regain its feet. It swayed gently, as power surged through the ship's circuits, and fa'Shenali found himself staggering like a drunkard. He even sensed the growing hope welling in the breasts of his comrades. It ended in a stark terror that swept the ship as the overloaded circuits burst into sparks, leaving the vessel without power and defenseless. The last, haggard remnants of their shields collapsed, and the great ship listed helplessly in the cold, unforgiving sky.

Amid the screams of his companions, fa'Shenali resolved to meet his end as bravely as his fragile nerves could manage. He closed his eyes—he took a deep breath....

And when, to his astonishment, he found himself running out of air, he opened his eyes. Panting like a fool, he stood dumbly, his mouth wide open, staring at the retreating image of the Terran ship as it streaked away and disappeared into the blackness.

Ordering the technicians to keep working on the engines, Dra'Lengish fought through the silent crowd until he stood beside the young subaltern.

"Why?" asked the old man.

For a long moment, fa'Shenali said nothing. All he could do was stare into the empty skies into which the Beast had vanished. The lurch of the engines springing back to life jolted the young man from his reverie.

"I am sorry?"

"Why did he spare us?"

Fa'Shenali searched for an answer, but could think of nothing.

"I do not know, Lord Lengish. Unless...."

"Yes."

"No, that could not be," fa'Shenali declared abruptly, banishing the thought at once from his mind. "That is no explanation."

"What is not an explanation?"

"It is unimportant. To spare us, when we would have eagerly killed him? It is senseless. There can be no explanation for it."

LOOSE PAPERS rained down toward the floor. The *d'Artagnan's* bridge still rang with the sound of the Weaponry Tech Manual thumping against the main viewer. Janet closed her eyes and took a deep breath. Near tears herself, she could tell by the look of torment in his eyes that he was in agony. Jeremy's death had affected everybody on the bridge, but Cook's homicidal rage had terrified all of them. His daring had always before been tempered by his own sense of mortality; stripped of any fear of death he'd nearly killed them all, and brought the Fleet to the brink of disaster. Only his strength of will, and the instinctive brilliance of his tactics had saved them from disaster, leaving the enemy routed and panic-stricken.

And now this.

None of them knew what to expect.

Cook stared hatefully at the screen, his mind raging furiously against every aspect of his existence—furious at himself for being weak—for letting the syrup of sentiment stand in his way and keep him from claiming the final measure of revenge for his best friend.

He felt everything welling up inside him. He could taste the hatred still filling his throat. He hated himself for killing his friend—for he had no doubt that he was responsible. And he hated himself for being so soft, so flabby with emotion—for being so foolishly weak that he couldn't kill off the last of his enemies. He was a coward—the thought rang in his brain. A coward with a foppish sense of honor. His throat started aching, and his head begin to throb. He could have killed them, he told himself; he could have killed them all. Every last one of them; he could have sent them all to burn in Hell. If he weren't a coward; if he were man enough to shut out the nagging doubts that kept ringing in his head. His chest hammered away, pounding until he could feel it in his brain—echoing, echoing more loudly than ever. The weight of exhaustion started pressing down upon him, and each beat of his heart cried more angrily than ever. Closing his eyes, he swallowed hard, and turned to face the rest of his crew.

"The battle is over," he said, his voice almost a whisper. "We're no longer needed. Move the ship to safety, and take her home for repairs." Without saying another word, he left the bridge, leaving his crew in stunned silence.

By instinct, Janet rose from her station. She wanted to run after him; she knew he was in agony. She wanted to do something to ease his pain—and to bury her own in a strong pair of arms.

But as soon as she had started, she thought better of it. She had other duties, other responsibilities, and all of them took precedence. Quietly, she stepped away from her station and sat down in the captain's chair. Beckoning Ensign Baker to the helm, she wiped the tears from her eyes and cleared her throat.

"Ease us back to our own lines," she said. "Heading 727."

"Enemy ships are starting to retreat into the Cloud," announced Dexter. "The bulk of their fleet is heading due east. Looks like they're following the first wave right into the teeth of the Cloud."

"I'm getting a call from C-Wing," began Mary, turning away from the communications console to face the Command Seat.

"Tell C-Wing to disengage and head around the far bend in the Cloud," said Janet. "We want to cut off the enemy's last avenue of retreat. That will force them either to surrender, or continue into the next arm of the Cloud."

"Janet?"

Janet looked Mary squarely in the eyes.

"Is he all right?" Mary asked.

Janet cast her glance around the room. The same stunned look was in the everyone's eyes. There had been no time during the battle for anyone to think of anything but duty. Now they were all worried.

She leaned back in the Chair and felt the ship lean into a starboard arc. As they sailed westward, she could see the bulk of the fleet heading east, pursuing the beaten enemy with a hateful vengeance that left her feeling nothing but emptiness.

"I don't know," she said, slowly shaking her head. "I just don't know."

Chapter 30

STARING NUMBLY INTO the empty screen before her, Suzie Yang was growing angrier by the minute. The glare from the hot, summer sun, shining through the slats in the west window, made it hard enough to work. Now, the Neanderthals in the copy room were whooping it up like a bunch of college freshmen, making it impossible to think. She was already mad enough at Ben Brewster for her current assignment. Outlining the upcoming Senate debate over the procurement budget was going to be hard enough, with Boros and Loomis likely to do little more than ogle as she begged them to concentrate on more than her own chest. Now Ben wasn't even taking the time to keep the boys and boors from turning the newsroom into a college frat house.

The dull thud of a book careening against her door made her start with fright, an instant before anger overcame her. She'd told herself that she wouldn't leave her office until she had a first draft of the story, but enough was enough.

Flinging open the door, she was amazed to see Brewster—Benjamin Brewster, of all people; Mr. Down-to-Earth himself—casting papers and trays into the air, and whooping as loudly as the rest. Her first glance confirmed that every man on the floor had lost his mind. Still, as a woman of some experience she knew that men tended toward exuberance like children tend toward mischief, though they usually reserved such outpourings of feeling for special occasions, like a weekend sporting event. It seemed surreal in a place of business. But a moment's reflection convinced her that this was different—the exuberance was genuine, impassioned. And that could only mean....

Quickly, the sounds of shouts and cheers ringing in her ears, she stepped from her office to the giant telex terminal that stretched along the east wall. Among the routine press releases and wire service messages was a Code Red report, dateline Looking Glass. As she read it, she allowed herself to believe that it might actually be true—that the war was really coming to an end.

/UMN/r/LOOKINGGLASS/23Nov2455-01537covstd/cc:144-4141.3:
LOOKINGGLASS
FLASH—
> THOUGH EASTERN FLT HQ DECLINES TO CONFIRM, RUMORS
> ABOUND THAT WAR'S DECISIVE ENGAGEMENT MAY BE OVER.
> HIGHLY-PLACED SOURCES IN LOOKING GLASS COMMAND STAFF
> SAY ENEMY FLEET HAS BEEN THOROUGHLY ROUTED IN SKIES
> OFF GIRSHOONA, AND FORCED INTO DISORGANIZED RETREAT
> THROUGH PERILOUS ARM OF THE CRUTCHTAN CLOUD. SAME
> SOURCES SAY ENEMY FLEET MAY BE FINISHED AS AN
> EFFECTIVE FIGHTING FORCE; AT THE LEAST, ENEMY WILL NEED
> SIGNIFICANT TIME TO REGROUP AND RECOVER. DETAILS
> SKETCHY; MORE TO FOLLOW.
> -- FLASH/30/

Suzie closed her eyes and let out a loud cry of delight. It had been a long time coming, she thought, and it couldn't come a moment too soon. Even this far away from the front, she still had nightmares about the fighting—the torn bodies she'd seen, brought to Looking Glass from the fighting on the ground; the pictures of ships disappearing in silent flames in the darkness; the screams of death crackling over the subspace radio. Now it looked to be all but over.

Suddenly, the printing board sprang to life, and she read the follow-up transmission live as it came over the wire—exactly as it appeared in newsrooms across Terra. All around her, the bodies pressed against each other, as everyone pushed and strained for a look.

/UMN/r/LOOKINGGLASS/23Nov2455-01537covstd/cc:144-4141.3:
LOOKINGGLASS
FLASH—
> FOLLOW TO LEAD, THIS DATE: BATTLE OF GIRSHOONA:
>   HEAVY ENEMY LOSSES FROM INTERSTELLAR BATTLE ARE
> THOUGHT TO EXCEED 50% OF ENTIRE ENEMY FLEET. FIRST
> REPORTS COUNT MORE THAN 2,000 ENEMY WARSHIPS
> CAPTURED, EQUAL OR GREATER NUMBER DESTROYED. BATTLE
> APPEARS PART OF TERRAN MOVE AGAINST PLANET GIRSHOO-
> NA, NOW REPORTED UNDER TERRAN CONTROL DESPITE
> CONTINUED HEAVY FIGHTING ON THE GROUND. GIVEN

ADVANCING TERRAN FLEET, LACK OF ENEMY STAR FORCE STRONG ENOUGH TO OPPOSE THEM, AND LOSS OF VITAL STRATEGIC OUTPOST OF GIRSHOONA, SEVERAL HIGH COMMAND OFFICERS BELIEVE THAT ENEMY'S NEXT COURSE WILL BE TO ASK FOR ARMISTICE.

BATTLE DETAILS SKETCHY, BUT IT APPEARS THAT SURPRISE ATTACK CAUGHT ENEMY FLEET OFF GUARD. ONE HIGH COMMAND SOURCE TOLD WRITER THAT TERRAN COMMANDER WAS COMMODORE COOK; WHEN ASKED DIRECTLY, SPOKESMAN FOR EASTERN FLEET HQ DECLINED COMMENT. MORE TO FOLLOW.

-- FLASH/30/

The cheers of her friends exploded in her ears. Suzie shook her head, wondering how she could doubt that Cook would be in on the kill. She caught herself grinning broadly, for the first time in ages. She froze momentarily when Brewster spun her around and kissed her full on the mouth; she broke out laughing when he passed her to Kennedy from the City Desk—and then moved on to the next female within reach, nearly starting a stampede among the men, each eager to join the party. And she laughed when the boys from Composing began dousing everyone with beer. Champagne was too expensive, they all claimed—and they had plenty of beer left over from last week's birthday party for Mark Fishman. As the beer dripped down her head and into her face, she felt her sides start to ache. But she didn't care; none of them cared. At last the end seemed in sight.

Before long, the celebration poured out into the street, where they joined half of Covington. For the rest of the day, few people in the city would feel much like working.

HE TRIED not to squint; he was honestly trying his best. But as the afternoon sun peeked past the fourth floor overhang and through the gap in the curtains, the light shined directly into his eyes.

As it was, it seemed that the Admiral was barely paying attention. Though that was ominous in its own way, at least the young lieutenant didn't have to worry about his post.

Not today, anyway—though why his boss wasn't doing handstands of glee was positively beyond him.

From across the room, Winthrop Weatherlee, the shine hardly gone from his new epaulets, glowered harshly at his inept young staff aide. The sorry fool was the husband of Senator Hollenbach's niece, so getting rid of him was out of the question. But having the young idiot around at a time like this was too much to bear. Shaking his head, Weatherlee plopped down in the soft leather chair behind the desk.

The chair just below the Seal of the Cosmic Guard.

The chair that belonged to its new Chief of Staff.

It was his now—his, and nobody else's. And once again, he intended to put it to use.

"Dismissed, Lieutenant," he scowled.

"Yes, Admiral. At once, Admiral." Reflexively, the hapless young officer bowed as he backed toward the door, turning just in time to miss Weatherlee's sneer of disdain.

Pressing the summons buzzer on his intercom, Weatherlee narrowed his eyes hatefully. He'd written the communiqué a hundred times, in his head. Each time, events had pushed him back.

Well, he thought—no more. This time it would be different, and there would be nobody to pull the Isitian's candied ass out of the fire. A surge of triumph filled him. He slammed a fist onto his desk just as Atley, his secretary, come through the door.

"Gracious—such a greeting!" exclaimed Atley, his eyes widening in mock horror, before dissolving into an easy grin. Striding to his place, he took the seat in front of the desk

"Shut up and take a message," laughed Weatherlee, leaning back in his chair, his eyes filling with the sweet glee of revenge. It had been a long time coming, he thought. That would make it all the more satisfying when it finally came to be.

"To Admiral Jonathon Medwick, Commander, Task Force Bravo," he began.

"Task Force—Bra-vo!" repeated Atley, finishing his stroke with a flourish.

* * *

"THE END of the fog is approaching," announced fo'Rendish, the senior monitor. As the young one's fingers sought to focus the blurred images onto the viewing screen, Dra'Lengish turned his eyes to look upon the exhausted, overworked menials who had labored to guide the Flagship through the Great Cloud. Despite the lack of food or rest for the past two days, he had yet to hear a complaint from any of them.

"Any reports from the advance party?"

"No, Lord Lengish," replied Rendish, his eyes never leaving his viewing screen. "But the fog is densest at this end, you may recall." He turned to face Dra'Lengish, his eyes calm with the serenity of one who has lost his fear of death.

"We have lost a great many ships in transit, my Lord. The death fires registered clearly on our instruments, never more clearly than in the last hour."

"I know, Monitor."

Fo'Rendish returned to his screen. Dra'Lengish could sense the young man's soul-fires burning, the anger growing like flames through a drought-parched forest. The old man had felt many such embers in the hearts of those around him. But true to their duties, none said a word in protest, and Dra'Lengish had never felt prouder of anyone in his life. He prayed that they would emerge from the Cloud to find enough strength among the shattered remnants of their Fleet to continue the fight. And he fought to suppress the fears that whispered the darkness of doubt into his own ear.

"Your thoughts are as subtle as thunder, Young One," Dra'Lengish whispered to the young aide. Feeling the monitor sink into a chasm of fear, the Chief Tactician reassured him with a gentle pat on the shoulder. "Be strong," he smiled. "*G'Khruushte* needs all her sons to be strong."

Dra'Lengish strode toward the middle of the control tower to let the young man recover control of his emotions in private. They would be leaving the Cloud at any moment. Dra'Lengish wished to lose no time regrouping whatever remnants of the Fleet had survived the passage. As the last wisps of fog faded from their forward screens, he came to stand beneath the Central Monitors, hoping that the scene might give them cause to hope. At that moment, the attention of all was seized by a dreaded call to alarm.

"Terrans!" cried fo'Rendish, his voice ringing with hatred. At once, the monitor sent the image from his viewing screen to Display Screen Number Six.

Casting his glace to Number Six, Dra'Lengish felt himself miss a pulse. There, like demons of the night, was a full battalion of Terran warships, pouring around the far bend in the Cloud, moving into position to trap them in *Fruseniti* Clearing, the broad wedge separating the two local arms of the Great Cloud. They had trapped the Beast there earlier—only to see him escape by plunging headlong into the swirling eddies of the Cloud.

Now that their positions had reversed their course seemed obvious. With the Terrans moving to block the only lanes of egress, they could surrender, fight, or flee: the first course was unthinkable; and in their current weakened state, the second would be suicide.

"Command Order to all ships!" thundered Dra'Lengish. "Move through the Clearing into the eastern cloudbank. We shall meet on the far side of the Cloud. Engines, move east at quarter-speed; we shall maintain this position until the last moment, to guide any stragglers to the point of regroupment."

As the call went out over all channels the old man could sense the renewed apprehension of all in the Command Center. Traversing the interstellar fog was not a happy prospect. But menials and their officers turned to their duties with grimness. Not one of them indulged even a passing thought of failure. Yet as the Fleet began easing toward the eastern rim of the Cloud, Dra'Lengish sensed an intrusive anger pressing upon his consciousness. He lifted his eyes toward the control tower. At the railing, an angry presence glowered down at him like a wrathful god stirring storm clouds in the heavens.

"How dare you?" thundered Ga'Glish.

"How dare I do what, Lordship?" Dra'Lengish replied calmly, careful to give his superior no further cause for anger.

"You have misused the Access channels, open only to pronouncements of the Lord Commander!"

"I was unaware of your presence, Lordship," Dra'Lengish dissembled and bowed deferentially, his swelling pride kept under tight control. He was, of course, fully aware of the Lord Commander's presence on the Tower. But the Ga'Glish he had once known would never put pride before duty, and this imposter's wildly swinging emotions could not be trusted.

"I apologize for the oversight, my Lord."

"And your order was the order of a coward!" screamed Ga'Glish, "One who runs at the sight of the enemy."

As the Lord Commander lashed at him mercilessly, Dra'Lengish stood stiffly in his place, accepting whatever correction his superior chose to inflict, retreating into an emotional shell to keep from surrendering his feelings to anger or despair. He could sense the horror of his companions, as they recoiled from the torrent of abuse hurled upon the One whom they all regarded as their Second Commander.

When the correction was over, Dra'Lengish bowed properly and excused himself. He strode down the hallway leading to the Western corridor, heading toward the sanctity of his personal chambers. He was thankful that by diverting the Lord Commander's attention onto himself, he had kept Ga'Glish from countermanding the order of continued retreat.

As he entered the confines of his own room, a wave of anger and indignation swept over him. Picking up the nearest object, a small statuette of his long-deceased mate, he hurled it across the room, where it shattered into dozens of small pieces and left a gash in the wall.

Something had to be done, Dra'Lengish told himself again and again.

The Lord Commander was losing control of his emotions. Hatred was seizing his entire being. Ga'Glish was surrendering his mind to the instincts of anger and revenge. Something had to be done.

Ga'Glish was leading them all to destruction, the old man thought. And there was no one to stop him.

* * *

"BASE COMING up on the main screen," announced Dexter. As the looming figure of Liberty Base 223, temporary headquarters for the Third Fleet Command, appeared on the forward viewer, he checked the guidance beacons for a positional sounding. He fixed on the outer pulse of light, then on the innermost, taking the average for the approximate distance.

"Range, one hundred astrokilometers."

"Helm—slow thrusters to one-third."

"Yes, ma'am," said the young ensign sitting in the helmsman's seat. "Are we steady from here, or don't you trust me on manual?"

Janet smiled wearily. Almost lost amid the oversized cushions of the captain's chair, she started to lean forward to peer over the Apprentice Helmsman's shoulders to get a reading on the helm controls, before remembering about the variable monitors on the captain's armrest.

"No offense," she said, once the readings appeared on the undersized sidescreen. "But I don't think I want to take the chance. We're limping enough already, and Skipper would never forgive us if we rammed the base on approach. We'll let the computers take it from here."

Baker nodded his head and signaled the base to activate its tractor beam. Once he felt the ship pass from his control, he breathed deeply and turned to face the Chair.

"I don't blame you, Commander," he said, shaking his head. "She's feeling sluggish. Awfully sluggish. And I get a definite list to starboard."

"The hit from the lizard flagship," said Gerlach. "It fritzed out our portside guns. I doubt it did the engines any good, either."

"Incoming message," said Mary, holding her earpiece in place. A wide, surprised grin flashed across her face, and her eyes widened with pleased amusement.

"Well—I'll tell them," she giggled, her face turning a bright crimson. Then, turning to face her colleagues, she burst out laughing—and found that despite her best efforts, she couldn't stop.

"They—they—they said—" she kept repeating, causing her comrades no small measure of impatience.

"Well, Mathison," Gerlach said impatiently. "Are we getting a heroes' welcome, or do we have to settle for a night club act?"

For some reason, that just made Mary laugh all the harder, much to the consternation of the rest of the bridge crew.

But Janet wasn't paying much attention. Her mind was elsewhere, and with the ship passing out of their hands, she felt out of place on the bridge. Rising from the Captain's Chair, she stepped toward the ramp leading to the Conning Deck corridor.

And to the side exit, leading toward Captain's Office.

"Dexter, take the Chair," she said over her shoulder. "I'll be right back."

Before long she found herself standing inside the small foyer separating Cook's study from his sleeping quarters. Over her shoulder, she felt the soft glow of the security light; the dim lights cast tenuous shadows onto the door leading into his bedroom. Janet felt awkward; the Skipper was taking Jeremy's death hard. In the days after the battle he hadn't been out of his office. The untouched food trays just piled up outside his door, where they would wait until a redshirt came to fetch them for the yeoman who ran the mess detail. She longed to be able to do something—anything, to bring him back. The ship's doctor had even prescribed some medication, a mild sedative, and some nutritional supplements. At first, he refused even to open the door; when she and the doctor had insisted, he'd taken the pills without uttering a word—and that was the last anyone had seen of him.

But that was two days ago. With their arrival at the liberty base less than an hour away he simply had to snap out of it.

"Skipper?" she whispered into the intercom box.

She hated to think of him in such pain. He seemed so sad, so hopeless. And there was little she could do, except reach out to him. He was so lost, so alone. To withdraw into himself so completely simply wasn't healthy. If word ever got out....

She shuddered and shook her head. She hated to think of the consequences. With the list of enemies he'd made among the top brass, it could keep him from returning to the Front for quite a while. It could even cost him his command.

"Skipper— ?"

Janet took a determined breath. She could be just as stubborn as the Skipper, she told herself. And she would keep at it, until....

"Go away."

Even masked by the intercom, Janet was sure she could sense the pain in his voice. She pressed the speaker button again.

"Skipper—it's me," she said gently. "May I— "

"Go away."

"If I could just..."

"Leave me alone, Commander."

"But if— "

"Leave me the hell alone."

Janet closed her eyes, struggling with her own emotions. Her feelings were already bruised by Cook's callous manners. The past they carried with them were never been far from her mind. But as it often did, his brusqueness swept away what remained of her defenses. Her own grief at the loss of a friend suddenly hit with full force, and she felt crushed by an overwhelming sense of helplessness. Her eyes filled with tears, and she stepped away from the doorway. She was determined to reach her own quarters before losing what little remained of her self-respect.

As Janet hurried away from his cabin, on the other side of the door Cook leaned against the wall, the images of sleep still freshly burning in his brain. His eyelids heavy with the weight of exhaustion, he fought the urge to sleep with the savagery of desperation. In the end, too tired to fight any longer, he found himself stepping drearily toward his bed, his head as foggy as the Cloud, too tired to cry any longer.

* * *

"SILLY BASTARDS."

Yeoman First Class Nathaniel Hawkes thought he'd seen it all.

All manner of foolishness, that is.

From the greentails at the training station at Demeter to the dustbrained spacers back from the ore runs, from young fools who'd rather spend their hard-earned money on a louse-infested space whore instead of good honest whiskey to dotty oldtimers so far past their prime they couldn't even remember the year, he'd seen more of Mankind than he cared to admit. And quite a bit more downright stupidity than most men thought possible. But this—this was just sop-headed gawking, that's what it was.

"Tower to docks, how do you read?" came the signal over his headphones.

"Dockside control," he answered. "We've got her well in hand, Tony. Easing her into the lane right now, heading her toward Number Twelve. Hope the boys are ready for her."

"Hangar Bay Twelve reports all clear," Tony's voice responded.

"Wish I could say the same for the Concourse. Looks like Kiddies' Day at the Zoo over there."

Tony laughed rougishly. "Take her in easy, Nate. Don't want to rough her up any. Not this one, anyway. Tower over."

"Roger, Tony. Over and out."

Hawkes looked toward the viewing window. It was like a zoo, all right, only he didn't know whether he was looking at the chimps or the children. Half the base had turned out; pressing their noses against the glass, they'd fog up the window for everyone if they weren't careful. Gaping like a gaggle of schoolgirls—and for what? They'd had hundreds of ships dock here before, all without incident. The fools never came to watch any of them, and he doubted they'd come for any others.

But even as he scoffed at the gawkers craning their necks to get a glimpse of the great ship as she eased into port, Hawkes couldn't help feeling proud as a lording bull mutluk himself. He was more than a witness to history. Son of a simple Earthborn farmer, here he was, helping to make it. He couldn't help smiling at the thought that when the war was just a dim memory, and the Guard had brought peace to the skies again, he'd be able to tell his grandchildren about the day—right after the Battle of Girshoona—that he brought Commodore Cook's ship safely to harbor.

Still smiling, he overlooked the quickening approach of the massive vessel and forgot to shift the controls to close approach. Or activate the emergency auto-override. Suddenly realizing that CosGuard's most famous ship was in danger of ramming one of its least-known docks, Hawkes shifted the tractor controls to full manual and throttled the beam to dead stop, hoping to bring the ship to a halt before it reached the bay. As the ship slowed he eased up on the controls, turning the near disaster into a smoothly modulated approach.

Fool! he told himself. Machines could do a great deal, but they couldn't overcome human stupidity.

The ship glided past the observation platforms, gently floating toward Number Twelve, the only hangar bay on the base with a dry dock big enough to service a starship. She wore her scars like large black patches, reminders of the great battle she'd just seen. Dwarfing dozens of smaller stains, one wide swatch ran from fore halfway to aft along her portside; two more, narrower and deeper, ran the length of her keel. Together, they showed just how close the enemy had come to finishing her off—scorching her outer tiles black, coming within an eyelash of searing through the hull and sending all aboard to a death of flame and ash. Soon the locks closed around the Grand Old Girl, battlescarred but defiant, and still the pride of the fleet.

His work done, Hawkes suddenly found himself grinning like a lovesick codger. It was the luck of the draw that brought Cook's ship to Liberty Base 223 on his watch. Just yesterday, Tommy Olsen had promised him an extra day off to swap shifts. Poor Tommy O would crap in his drawers to find out what he'd missed, Hawkes laughed out loud.

"Dockside control to Number Twelve," he said into his speaker. "Secure the moorings, and stand by the clearing lights. Let's do ourselves proud, Laddies—and move it with a will. They'll want to disembark as soon as they can, and we don't want them thinking that Old 223 has greentails running the docks."

Soon, thunderous cheers filled the concourse, near the intake gates, all but drowning out the dull monotone that carried the message half the base could see with its own eyes—and yet could not hear, over the delirium of celebration.

"Starship *d'Artagnan* disembarking at Hangar Bay Twelve; Security Team Thirteen report to Mr. Withers....Starship *d'Artagnan* disembarking at Hangar Bay Twelve; Security Team Thirteen, report to Mr. Withers."

Most who listened heard only half the message; those few who heard the rest kept it to themselves.

The scent of blood stained the air and screams of the damned lapped like thirsty flames. Higher and higher they rose, exploding into undying death and eternal damnation.

As he crawled up the side of the pit, the embers seared his flesh until he wanted to scream. But he knew that the sound of his voice would rise into the chorus of lost souls and drag him screaming into the depths. Seconds passed like eons, each pouring into the next like oceans of eternity, his flesh burning until he could no longer stand it.

Looking down, he saw the flames rising toward him, dancing as they assumed a human form—a laughing human form. He wanted to scream but didn't dare. He looked again and saw arms of flame reach toward him like an endless army. And the faces—the faces!!—laughing through tormented tears as their fiery arms crept toward his leg. All the faces of the dead and dying hissed his name with an acid that burned his flesh and made him ache to scream in torment. But he dared not speak.

Then there was a voice—forcing open his eyes with an irresistible sound, prying them open to stare into a glowing pit filled with the laughing, screaming faces of the damned. He recognized the voice!—but he did not know how, and he dared not remember. He wanted to look, but he was terrified of what he would see. An arm of roaring fire grabbed his leg, and he felt himself being dragged down. His charred hands clawed at the burning sides of the pit while he struggled in silence, daring not to utter a sound.

The voice—the voice called again, forcing his head to look at the monster dragging him into the cavernous pit—laughing as it dragged him into the pit.

It was Jeremy Ashton—laughing like a demon, his eyes burning with the fires of Hell....

AWAKENING WITH a scream, Cook found his heart beating with the fury of a starving predator in the middle of a kill. He struggled to calm himself, to tell himself that it was, after all, just a dream. But this time, his mind ached with a searing pain. He found himself unable to think, unable to do anything but shiver and sweat.

Soon, his pulse slowed to normal and the pain faded, as he'd come to know it would. Alone in the dark with his thoughts, he found himself frightened beyond anything he had ever known. Frightened of something dark and sinister, something that was about to swallow him.

As the minutes passed, he came to feel less and less fearful. Before long the panic that had gripped him was only a memory.

But the memory made him lose any interest in sleeping.

* * *

THE ROUGH sounds of laughter mingled with the clinking of beer steins. Through the dim lights, Crewman First Class Tom Sullivan peered across the narrow pathway separating the tables from the bar. The tables, sturdy and made to resemble wood, ringed the central bar like orbiting debris. Along the walls liberty girls clustered in groups of twos and threes, occasionally stepping to the bar through the crowd of patrons to fetch something for themselves.

"It's a zoo, Timmy, a goddamn zoo."

"Aye on that, Sully," said Crewman Apprentice Tim McBride, polishing his unit badge to make sure the word "*d'Artagnan*" was plainly visible to all lookers. "The laddies are full of spirit tonight. Too bad the lassies ain't quite up to trim."

"Well, they're only Standard Issue, ye know," laughed Sully. "And if they look to be a wee bit haggard—well, the lads here should take it as a bit of a compliment, don't you think?"

Winding their way through Shonkwiler's Pub, the two redshirts paused every few steps to receive a slap on the back from the locals, who were still hailing every member of *d'Artagnan's* crew as if he were the Skipper himself. Sully and McBride ambled over to the bar and ordered themselves each a pint of beer, which the bartender promptly informed them were on the house. Ignoring the smiles of two local hostesses, they retreated toward the far corner of the room, hoping the hunting would be better further down.

"It's not like I'm particular," McBride said, when they found an empty spot to stand.

"Particular, my ass. Those two are like to give you change in Demmy rot. And—well, dammit—I mean, we're supposed to be heroes."

"Well, we're not officers, after all, Sully."

"Ahh—bosh!"

"Well, can you deny it?"

"Once—just once, before we go tasting the flames ourselves—I'd like to taste something a wee bit sweeter than stale whore sweat. And if the girlies hold a man's uniform against him when they won't even be seeing it when it really counts—well, then they're even stupider than I thought."

McBride was about to reply when he spotted a familiar face at a table two rows down.

"Chief!" he cried, clapping Sullivan hard on the shoulder. "It's Chief Connors! Look lively, Sully—the classy tarts take a greenshirt almost for an officer. Maybe the Chief will let us tag along."

"For all the good it'll do."

"Well, it certainly couldn't hurt."

"Not as much as the cure for Demmy rot, anyway."

"And it's a far sight better than standing around feeling sorry for ourselves. At the very worst, we'll have some drinking company. And then it won't much matter which lass we wind up with, now will it?"

"Bloody nonsense."

Despite his misgivings, Sully followed sullenly along as McBride made his way through the crowd. Truth to tell, he had to admit that the young Ceresian might be on to something. As they neared Chief Connors' table, Sully actually found himself thinking that the night mightn't be a total loss. His spirits were rising as they fought their way through the crowd, pulled up a couple of chair, and sat themselves down. He was unprepared for what greeted them.

"Hey, Chief...," began Sully, only to cut himself short. Lifting his bloodshot eyes to greet them, Connors looked like he hadn't slept in weeks. His face, careworn from his years of service, creaked with every inch of his age. His mouth, so used to twitching with humor or grimacing with the practiced outrage of a yeoman about to lower the boom on some hapless redshirt, hung like an aging hound left alone to whimper. Misery was written all over him. And as the Chief struggled to manage a smile of greeting, Sully thought, for the fleetingest of moments, that he saw the watery traces of tears in the old spacer's eyes.

"Chief," said Sully, grasping Connors' arm in friendship and alarm. "Chief—what's the matter?"

Connors shook his head and stared ahead into his pitcher of beer.

"They're going to cut his nuts off," mumbled Connors.

"What?"

Connors closed his eyes and shook his head.

"Forget it," he said, managing a weak, humorless smile. "Let's just hope to God he's wrong."

But as he stared glumly into the pitcher—his second of the session, and by no means the last—he found his numbed brain struggling to focus. Perhaps old Kevin Ward was wrong after all, he told himself. But he knew that it was no likelier than finding the girl of his dreams working the pubs of a liberty base. Ward had seen the dispatch himself. And, Connors sighed, the changes in the top brass they'd heard about since reaching port gave him a sickening sense of clairvoyance.

"Just hope to God he's wrong," he whispered again, too heartsick to care if his shipmates were listening.

Chapter 31

THE BLAST FROM the enemy laser cannon shook the ground on the overlook above them as Shl'Lanasha heard the soul-splitting scream from behind. Turning to look, he saw them—dozens of the ugly, monstrous things, their body armor colored to blend with the foliage, streaming down from the hilltop, pouring over the pocked surface of the hill. His revulsion was instant and unwavering, filling him with so much hate that his instincts told him to turn and attack. It was only the clear signal for retreat, sounding from the Command Bunker, that froze him in his tracks and restored the coolness of sanity to his head.

"Shen—come," he clapped his bunkermate on the shoulder. "We must depart."

"Run?" spat ls'Shen, turning upon his friend with the fire of indignation in his eyes. "From these foul-smelling savages?" He raised his weapon and fired at one of the longnoses, who fell and tumbled halfway down the hillside. More numerous with every heartbeat, the Terrans kept coming, pouring over the summit like a swarm of carrion ants. The valley shrieked with the deafening sound of weapons. The stench of death and the ominous sounds of approaching Terran airships filled the sky.

"Come!" thundered Lanash, wrenching his companion from the ground and pushing him along the trench, toward the transit ramp a few steps away. Moments later, what had been their position was laid waste by a blast from a longnose hand-cannon. Rocks and sand blew high into the air above them, and debris rained from the sky.

Through the vents in his helmet Lanash could hear the wild, animal sounds of longnoses cheering themselves on toward the *g'Khruustani* fortifications. Scrambling up the steps, he ran with dozens of his comrades across the open field leading toward the next skirmish line. With the Terrans attacking from two directions, all was chaos.

G'Khruushtani soldiers were dashing about wildly, many in the wrong direction, many more falling for the last time as the Terrans opened fire, pressing their advantage to the fullest.

Forcing himself to remain calm, Lanash ran as quickly as he could through the clearing, toward the defensive perimeter at the edge of the forest. On all sides, misguided blasts from Terran handweapons raised the dirt, pocking the ground from one side of the clearing to the other. Everywhere friends and comrades were falling, and he heard the sounds of enemy fire whizzing past his head. Suddenly, the ground beneath him shook—and the fortification before him disappeared in a cataclysm of fire and dirt. A single blast from a Terran airship had destroyed their sanctuary, leaving them leaderless and without shelter.

Like everyone around him, Lanash dove for the ground, letting debris from the explosion fall harmlessly onto his back. An instant later he was on his feet—tugging at Shen's arm, begging him to rise to his feet before the Terran infantry resumed its pursuit.

"Quickly—quickly! There is no time to lose."

"We are lost already," ls'Shen shook his head. "Lanash— "

"On your feet, Small One!" hissed Lanash, pulling his younger comrade to his feet, pushing him toward the forest, now a few dozen paces to the west. "Only cowards surrender at the sight of Death. It takes courage to keep fighting."

Running with the energy born of panic, the *g'Khruustani* soldiers scattered as they tried to escape the Terran onslaught. From the hillside, the advancing enemy resumed their fire, each passing moment sending scores of *g'Khruushtani* to the ground, dead or writhing in pain, their screams of agony filling the air. Racing toward the cover of the nearby forest, his legs numbed from the exertion and his heart about to burst, Lanash dove past a flowering gashashbush just ahead of a stream of enemy laser fire. Lying there, his brain shouting with the exuberance of survival, he heard a cry of pain from the other side of the bush—just before Shen crashed through the branches, howling wildly, his face riven with torment.

Clasping his friend in his arms, Lanash saw at once the cause of it: Shen's still-smoldering back was burned black by the fire of enemy guns, his left arm dangling limply at his side. The scent of seared flesh was suffocating, and Lanash felt the urge to vomit. But survival hinged upon his ability to function, and he realized at once what he must do. Hoisting

Shen onto his shoulders, ignoring his friend's ear-splitting scream of pain, Lanash bounded off towards the woods. Cursing his own selfishness, he prayed that the longnoses would be so busy slaughtering his comrades in the field that they would not follow. Yet he was so naive as to stake his life upon such fond hopes.

Onward he trudged, past tree trunks and branches, thickets and hollows, his lungs heaving in his chest. Coming to a small stream, Lanash placed his friend in the shade of a tall fernwood tree and paused to rest. Shen, already in shock, had lost all color from his gill slits and hands, and his breathing had become labored. The hot sun, kept at bay by the towering canopy of the forest, fell in gentle speckles along the moist ground; this would be a good place for them to rest, thought Lanash. But, hearing the sounds of approaching footsteps, he heaved Shen onto his back once more and plodded, quickly as his load permitted, deeper and deeper into the forest.

Before long, the woods became wilder and denser. Lanash knew that he could not keep up his pace forever. His strength was already starting to fade and would not last much longer. They both needed sustenance and rest if they were to survive. Besides, it was the rainy season. They would need protection from the nightly downpour that would soon drench the forest.

Coming over a ridge, he noticed a line of rocks pushing through the forest floor, leading toward the top of a gentle slope. Pushing onward, he reached the summit, and found a large hollow amid the stones. The small cave offered protection from the wind and a hiding place from unfriendly eyes. Placing his friend inside, Lanash scoured the surrounding area for branches and brush, fashioning a crude covering for their small refuge. He returned with an array of nuts and berries to supplement the meager rations in his survival pack.

Soon, darkness crept into the forest, and the sounds of day quieted into the stillness of night. Through the rustling branches of the trees, Lanash could hear the shallows of the nearby river. Off in the distance, the sounds of Terran artillery rumbled through the valley, mingling with the approaching thunder from the evening storms.

The next day would bring its troubles soon enough, Lanash told himself. The forest had many dangers, and with his unit all but obliterated he dreaded the task of finding a new battle group in the denseness of the Shunian wilds. For the moment, he had worries enough to last the coming night. Starting a small fire, Lanash stoked it with the driest brush he could find, until it heated the entire hollow. He knew the fire would never last the night; he hoped it would last long enough. He would be unable to get more wood until morning.

He turned toward his sleeping friend. Shen was shivering from the coolness of nightfall. Though the bleeding had stopped, Shen was deathly pale, and his chest rattled with every breath. Lanash removed his own body armor, and placed it around his friend. Aside from making him groggy and sluggish, the night air posed no danger to himself. But unless Shen's body stopped losing heat, he would die before the next light of day. Dressing the wounds as best he could, Lanash curled himself up beside his friend, hoping to lend some of his own body warmth to the task of keeping Shen alive until morning.

A few heartbeats later, unaware that he was exhausted, Lanash was asleep. He never heard the rain start dripping from the rocky overhang that gave them cover from the elements. No crack of thunder was loud enough to bid him stir, or rise to admire the rough handiwork that kept both of them dry, and his friend alive, through the long, chilly night.

THE FINAL Report was even more ominous than he expected.

Walking down the Main Corridor of the Imperial Flagship, Dra'Lengish could not erase the information from his brain. The engagement with the Terran fleet had brought them to the brink of ruination. *G'Khruushtani* losses from the battle alone were disastrous. Their losses from the engagement and retreat together exceeded half of the entire fleet. It was an unmitigated disaster, all the more so because it had been so pointless, so unnecessary—and because they had come so close. So very close, indeed.

Dra'Lengish stopped walking and leaned against the wall. Tears of sorrow filled his eyes. After all their suffering and devastation, it had come to this: the barbarians were growing stronger with each day, and the Imperial Fleet had squandered its best chance at victory. He struggled against the tide of emotion rising within him, against the thought that such struggles would soon become meaningless. They were already approaching the Grand Bend; by this time tomorrow, the Fleet would pass the eastern terminus of the Great Cloud. The whole Empire would soon stretch before them, naked before the eyes of aliens and now all but defenseless. Once the Terrans passed the Bend—once their detestable *shtarsh'ieps* obliterated the last remaining defenses and found themselves with open skies on all sides—their Cause would be hopeless. Civilization, the Civilization they had known for countless millennia, would crumble like dried leaves under the hooves of stampeding beasts. All they had known or loved would be destroyed forever.

Suddenly, cries of alarm sounded down the corridor, snapping the Old One from the reveries of self-pity.

"My Lord!—Lord Lengish!" cried dra'Khranda, his own personal menial, and a favorite of the family.

"What is it, Khranda?" Dra'Lengish said sternly, regaining his dignity with the speed of a lightening bolt. He stepped out from the shadows proudly, his eyes merciless and demanding.

"Oh, Lord Lengish—the Terrans! The Terrans are coming! The Command Room has been looking for you for the past half-hour. It's a lunatic bin, your Lordship, that's what it is. They're coming for us—they're coming."

"The enemy fleet? That's impossible."

"No, no, your Lordship. The patrols—the Terran patrols. Terran patrols are on the screens right now. And you know what that means!"

Dra'Lengish smiled patiently, his affection for his old servant dispelling his sense of grief and hopelessness. Khranda had not the slightest idea of what any of it meant, but would never admit it. The Terran patrols presented no immediate problem: they were but a harbinger of the larger fleet lurking in the darkness, well beyond the bend in the Cloud. They were coming, thought Dra'Lengish; there was never a question about that. The One Called *Khu'ukh* would never fail to press an advantage. The Fleet would have to make a stand—here, before the terminus. Perhaps they could delay the Terran advance, and summon whatever reinforcements were available for the battle. But they could retreat no further: here was where they would have to draw the Final Line.

And if he could not convince the Lord Commander of this—well, the pot would simply have to be brought to a boil. One way or another. Sanity had to be restored to the Effort, or all would be lost.

If it were not lost already.

"All right, Khranda," Dra'Lengish said at last, trying not to let the grimness of his thoughts displace the gratitude he felt toward his old companion for dispelling the darkness, if only for a time. "Let us both return to our duties."

The menial nodded enthusiastically, then followed along in his master's wake. As they trod down the corridor, Dra'Lengish found his mind wandering back to the simpler times, and longing for the companionship of another, the Softer One of his heart, now lost to the fog of time and memory.

She had died many cycles past, he mused as they walked past the scrambling of laborers and the bustling of technical aides, all intent on their duties. In the summer of her youth she had left, with so little warning that the fragility of life was not even a worry for them at the time. Yet he still treasured the fleeting moments of the Aftertime, when the immature boy of his youth last touched her soul and bid her farewell. He had caught himself remembering his one and only mate's passing with greater frequency of late. The thought of rejoining her was becoming ever more pleasant to contemplate.

* * *

"But it makes no sense!"

"Sorry, Commander, but I have my orders."

"*Yaahh-ee!*" Janet shrieked loudly. The tall, strapping CSO guard who was blocking the entrance into the Commandant's office, winced visibly. He was surprised by the sudden change in tactics, and slowly coming to the conclusion that his training would not be enough to cope with a bluebird who refused to be rational. But he stood his ground; and no matter how much she tried, Janet knew that her powers of reasoning would never compensate for her lack of upper body strength. Tanshirts weren't chosen for brains, she thought. It was the one muscle the CosGuard Security Office wasn't concerned with, and this one looked like he spent most of his off-hours doing pushups. But time was running out, and she was getting more desperate by the minute. And so she refused to give up. Not until she made some sense out of what was happening.

Not until she could find out what was really going on.

"I'm sick of hearing about orders—do you understand me, Sergeant? Sick—*sick*—*sick*!"

"Yes, ma'am."

"I've got to see him—do you hear me? I have an urgent message for Commodore Cook! Do you understand:—*I have to see him!*"

"I'm sorry, ma'am," said the guard, again reciting the litany he had been given. "But he is occupied—he is being debriefed—and he cannot be disturbed for any reason."

"For any reason, indeed," huffed Janet, trying to calm herself. Try explaining to this brainless oaf how things were getting out of hand on the ship: basehoppers skittering through the ship. All but trying to take over, from stern side forward. With the order to sail putting everyone into an ionic dither—well, if Skipper told them it was all right to go ahead, it would go a long way toward calming everybody's nerves.

But it was obvious that the nitwit blocking her way could not be expected to understand such things. She'd just have to change her approach, Janet thought. Find a flank to turn, somewhere up the line. And it would have to be fast: castoff was just an hour away. If Skipper wanted it changed, she'd need time to hack her way through the paperpushers to get the orders signed. She turned snitfully, about to make a great show of leaving the muscle-headed buffoon in her wake when she noticed something. Something on his sleeve. Something that brought chills to her spine.

On each shoulder, just below the space black CSO patch marking him as a ground soldier—a blighter, in CosGuard vernacular—was a thin yellow swatch, a lightening bolt bearing the initials of the CosGuard Security Office, a unit designation that easily passed unnoticed.

The oaf was no oaf, Janet gulped, and her eyes widened in horror. A look at the campaign badges on his sleeve confirmed it. He was no common blighter—and no ordinary, brain-deadened non-com. He was a ThunderCat, a sergeant in the elite division of shock troops that CosGuard used for its most dangerous, perilous raids into enemy territory. She'd almost missed it: the insignia was too subtle to see at a glance, and without the scarlet beret they used as a garrison cap when on the ground they were nearly indistinguishable from any other unit in the Security Forces.

"What," she whispered, her eyes widening as she spoke, "what—what is a 'Cat doing standing guard over this door?"

"Ma'am...."

The young sergeant reddened, shifting uncomfortably on his feet.

"Any tanshirted ape can guard a door, Sergeant," she said, her voice becoming shrill and demanding. "The Brass doesn't use Commandos just to screen visitors. You're specially assigned to this detail, aren't you? You and whoever else is with you, behind that door. Why all the fuss? Why is the Security Office so interested in Commodore Cook?"

"I'm not at liberty to say, ma'am."

Janet felt herself growing physically sick, as realization began to set in. Her anger grew with each passing moment, and she felt helplessness wash over her. Her eyes started watering with fury and rage.

"He's under arrest, is that it?"

"I have orders not to discuss the Commodore's status, ma'am," came the awkward reply.

"Is he free to leave, then?"

Blushing uncontrollably, the young sergeant tried to avert his eyes. But Janet was almost on top of him. Her voice seething, she refused to leave him alone.

"If he tries to leave, what are your orders then?" she demanded, moving to stay in front of each turn of the young soldier's face. "He's a hero, Sergeant. The biggest hero you'll see in your life and the bravest man you'll ever hope to meet. Or are you too dim-witted to remember everything he's done? For all of us?"

The young man took a deep breath, and lifted his gaze. For the first time, Janet noticed his cold blue eyes showing some emotion.

"I'm sorry, ma'am—I'm truly sorry. But I can't—it would mean my stripes."

"Listen to me, Sergeant," she said, pressing the opening with all the intensity her own frazzled emotions gave her. "If I got word to him that his ship was about to sail—*sail without him*, Sergeant. Sail now, before repairs are complete, with the whole bloody ship crawling with base-hoppers nosing about every nook and cranny—if I got word to him and he tried to come out to rejoin his ship...."

"He can't come out," the young man said, struggling not to show the pain in his voice. "Now—please, ma'am—I can't say anything more about it."

But he didn't have to say anything more. Janet sank to the floor, a look of dazed bewilderment across her face. What was going on, she wondered. And how could they treat him like that? Without warning, the magnitude of what was happening struck her fully a-broadside—and the thought of what to do about it made her call out audibly.

"Ma'am?"

What could she do, she wondered. How could she possibly do it in time? And what would she ever do without him?

"Ma'am?"

It was several seconds before he realized that the young non-com was kneeling beside her. It was only then, as she buried her face in the young man's chest, that she realized that she was sobbing uncontrollably.

RAPPING HIS fingers on his desk, a smile of jowly complacency turning up the corners of his mouth, Admiral Medwick could not help feeling smugly content. His guest, he was sure, would be so thoroughly defeated by the turn of events that further resistance would be out of the question. His own crafty interrogation was going to be the icing on the cake. It would make things so hopeless for the poor fool that the man would be forced to throw himself on the mercy of his superiors. Adding to the sweetness of Justice, Medwick smiled to himself, was the fact that he—Jonathon Stanton Medwick, son of a dock worker and looked down upon by most of his graduating class—was going to administer the final blow. And if he had anything to say about it, Central Command would throw the Book at the obnoxious misfit.

"So when you broadcast—or, shall we say, issued your...orders, for lack of a better word," he said mysteriously, arching his eyebrows in the crafty manner he had practiced for the past few days, "you acknowledge that your actual intention—or motivation, or reason—for acting in the manner that you did, was to...supplant all or any of the duly-constituted authority over the ships with your own personal command, for your own personal reasons or purposes?"

Coming right out of the CosGuard Regulations Book, the question reeked of the Advocate General's Office. Cook squinted in disbelief, losing what little patience he had left. Something was happening, that much was certain. From the looks of things, he knew it was something he wouldn't like. But having to listen to a nitwit was bad enough; being patronized by this particular nitwit was more than he could bear.

"With all due respect, Admiral," Cook said acerbically, "if it were up to me personally, I really wouldn't care enough to get out of bed. But as long as we're at war, it did seem to me that some actual fighting might be called for, once in a while.

"Besides," Cook smirked, his eyes narrowing with contempt for the squat little bureaucrat whom some brass-assed idiot thought could replace Miriam Wright, "I was never relieved of my command over any attack wing. And upon my return—at least to the best of my knowledge—you still have not issued any order to the contrary."

Watching Medwick's jowls begin to flap with anger, Cook seethed with rage. The Crutchtan fleet half-destroyed, half on the run—despite the ineptitude of fools like the dolt sitting across the way. Fitz dead, Jeremy dead. The entire command staff changed beyond recognition—Cook was confused and angry. As sick as he felt over the loss of his friends, he was in no mood to put up with any more nitpicking. Leaning forward over the table, he glared defiantly into Medwick's eyes.

"I don't know what you're up to, Admiral," he said. "But I'm no fool, and I won't be treated like one. You don't need Security around, just to talk to one of your line commanders," he motioned with his head to the CSO lieutenant standing at the door. "And you don't seem particularly interested in anything I learned on my mission."

Medwick's face reddened. He hadn't expected this show of resolve and was determined to strike back at the earliest opportunity. He opened his mouth to speak, only to be cut off by his adversary's cold fury.

"Now then," Cook continued, his voice calm, his eyes burning with rage, "before I say another word, I am going to know why I'm being detained—why you won't let me contact my ship—and why I have to sit here, answering all these stupid questions. If you like, you can keep me here until you fools blunder your way into losing the war. You see, Admiral—I just don't care anymore."

His jaw twitching nervously, Medwick wondered just how much he should let Cook know. The Chief of Staff had been quite explicit about keeping the Isitian in the dark, and Admiral Weatherlee was not prone to forgiving mistakes. Still, Medwick thought, it was obvious that he'd gotten as much as he could out of the man. If he was to get anything more he'd have to tip his hand—though just a little, he told himself, for he still considered the session to be going quite smoothly. And one of the cardinal rules of interrogation was never to let the prisoner turn the tables and start directing the course of questioning.

Besides, he smiled, the look on Cook's face promised to be worth the minor breach of his instructions. Anyway, somehow the Isitian seemed to have pieced things together on his own. The answer to his last question all but proved it.

"All right, Commodore," Medwick smiled smugly, leaning back in his chair like a chessmaster making a game-clinching move. "The fact of the matter is that you are under arrest."

Cook continued his icy stare. His unflinching face made Medwick nervous. Casting a quick glance toward the door, taking reassurance from the presence of the tanshirt officer, Medwick decided to press the attack.

"The charge, Commodore...," he paused, trying to maximize the effect, "is mutiny."

Cook's cold stare went on unabated. Already angry at the brash daisy-sniffer for his inexcusable cockiness, Medwick decided to lower the boom.

"And you will be taken to the base at Demeter Command—for a general court martial, on charges and specifications to be filed under General Order Forty-four."

Cook stood, his upright frame now towering over the seated Medwick. Looking down, the commodore's eyes filled with contempt, and his lips curved into a smile of grim self-satisfaction.

"Thank you, Admiral," he said at last. "Now if the kind Lieutenant could escort me to my quarters, I've had a long day."

"But— "

As Cook started toward the door, he exchanged a brief glance with the guard, closing his eyes and shaking his head scornfully. The lieutenant, taken aback, was at a loss for what to do next. Medwick's instructions had been strangely murky, and extended no further attending the interview. Nobody said anything about escorting a prisoner anyplace. Especially a prisoner like this. His uneasiness only worsened when Medwick rose from his chair to speak.

"Cook!" he shouted at the commodore's back. Cook turned slowly to face him.

"You're a menace and a disgrace," Medwick bellowed. "For all your reputation, you're rude, you're insubordinate, and you're an insult to every decent officer in the Guard. It will be a pleasure cutting you down to your proper size.

"Lieutenant," he continued, pointing to the closed door with a flourish, "take him to his quarters in the Detention Wing."

"Aye, sir," said the young officer, trying to conceal how sick he felt. The lieutenant pressed the button to open the locked door, and motioned for Cook to proceed ahead of him.

"You know something, Lieutenant," the commodore said in a firm, clear voice. He turned to wait for his escort on the other side of the open door, his merciless gaze focusing on the beady brown eyes of his erstwhile interrogator. "I've always wondered why the guys most obsessed with everyone's proper size so often turn out to be dickless."

As the door closed on a red-faced and sputtering Admiral, the tanshirt caught himself laughing. He was glad to be out of Medwick's portly presence. With all the posturing and relentless preening, the Admiral made the young officer nervous. Smiling nervously at his charge, the enormity of what just happened struck the lieutenant like a cannon. His eyes widened, and a hole opened in the pit of his stomach. After several false starts, he finally managed to force the words out of his throat.

"Commodore, " he began haltingly, "I just want you to know that—"

"Thank you, Lieutenant," came the reply, before he even got the words out. "I appreciate the sentiment. Perhaps now more than ever."

Cook glanced down at the nameplate on the young man's breast pocket, then clapped him on the shoulder and motioned ahead, down the corridor. "And don't worry, Mr. Stokley—I never fault anyone for following orders. I won't do anything to make this tougher on you than it is already."

Nodding silently, the lieutenant coughed to relieve the tightness in his throat. "After you, sir," he said after a deep breath.

"And thank you, Commodore. Thank you very much."

"Acch— "

* * *

THE SUN beat down through a clearing in the forest canopy. A southerly breeze rustled the treetops, like the gentle shake of a morning drum. His shoulders weary under the weight of his friend, Lanash could push himself no further without rest.

It was as good a place to stop as any, he thought. The rise in the land gave them a good vantage of the valley to the north, and the rocks would give them cover from any unwelcome guests. Laying ls'Shen down in the shade of an arching datefern tree, Lanash dropped to his knees and flopped onto his back. Lying in the full sunlight, he felt the healing rays soothe his aching muscles. He pulled his field map from his belt pocket. Breathing deeply, he used it to shade his eyes.

Scanning the map once again, he felt reassured. There was an encampment—if it still existed; if the Terrans had not tracked it down and annihilated it, as they had so many others—some three days journey to the south, just off the river. Perhaps four or five, given the load he had to carry. And the forest teemed with berries this time of year. If they were careful to stay hidden, they should be able to reach it.

He looked at the unconscious body of his friend; Shen's chest heaved mightily, as if laboring under a heavy weight. At least, thought Lanash, he could reach it by himself. With each passing hour, he was becoming more and more fearful for his friend. Shen's wounds no longer bled, but each time Lanash changed the bandage the damage seemed more severe, the wound blacker and uglier. A doctor could save him; but here, far away from civilization, Shen's chances lessened with each sunset.

Suddenly, a hush fell over the forest, and Lanash sensed a presence around him. Quickly, he rose to a crouch. The creatures of the forest had grown ominously silent; in their unreasoning wisdom, they rarely did so without cause. A predator of some sort was nearby, he concluded Purging himself of all conscious thought, he could feel the danger himself.

Slowly, he rose to his feet. He made sure that his friend was comfortable before retrieving his weapon and easing his way down the river.

Lanash knew that the woods were filled with predators. Most of them would keep their distance. If it were a hunting cat or a fanged bear, it would see them as little more than meat for its dinner, and if hungry enough it would attack them. But the wind told him that the predator he was stalking was not a native one. It came from a far land, wearing a hideous face. And it was far more dangerous than any other animal in the forest.

Looking at his compass, Lanash noted his heading. There was a large rocky crag a few hundred paces to the north, overlooking a small waterfall where the river widened and slowed. As he paused to burn the surrounding landscape into his memory, the wind shifted to the north, and he caught the scent: foul and unmistakable it was, like the smell of rotting meat and stale urine.

"Terrans," he whispered, his voice lost in the rustling of the trees.

Inching his way northward, careful to make not a sound, he reached the rocks. Silently, he crawled onto an overhang, high above the river. Concealing himself from view behind a scruff of brush, he peered down on the shallows below. And there he saw them.

There were six of them—four wading in the water, two along the shore, all of them stripped to the waist. Dozens of large, heavy barrels were nearby, some on the ground, a few neatly stacked on a raised platform behind a transport of some sort. The transport had large wheels and a compartment for passengers at the fore. It looked to Lanash as if the Terrans were busy taking water from the river and loading it into the barrels for cartage to their own encampment.

He raised his weapon and took aim at the one closest, a large, broad-shouldered beast with a grotesque growth of fur hanging from its face. As his finger began pressing against the trigger, he let his body relax and lowered his weapon.

He would wait until two of them had left, he decided—or stepped off, away from the others. He was certain he could kill four before the last had a chance to react; with six, the likelihood of one surviving to sound an alarm was too great to justify the risk.

As he waited for two of the ugly creatures to depart, he thought of his son—safe for now on a distant world, whom he might never see again. And he thought of his stricken friend, lying helpless in the woods. Ls'Shen would die without help, Lanash reminded himself. And die alone if he bungled the ambush and let the Terrans kill him.

But he quickly dismissed such thoughts as the meanderings of a woman. Hatred burned in his brain, and Lanash banished the weakness of sentiment from his brain. Killing longnoses was all that mattered—now, and until the Terran menace was destroyed. If two g'Khruushtani had to die in order to kill four Terrans, it would be a fair bargain.

"GODDAMN MISERABLE little— "

Sergeant Peter Simmons looked over his shoulder toward the water. Flailing wildly in the air, one of his men came within inches of decking the blighter next to him. Simmons laughed aloud; the bloodgnats were getting on everyone's nerves, and the little buggers seemed to like this particular soldier better than anyone else on the planet.

"Watch it, Nick!" he called. "The lizards are bad enough. We don't want to lose any men to the gnats."

"Well, hell-fire, Sarge," drawled the soldier beside him, a tall, gangly Earther named Ike. Simmons thought this one could stretch the shortest thoughts into the longest string of sound he ever heard. "If we keep to swattin' bugs every ten seconds, how do we ever get anythin' done?"

"You think we got problems, soldier? Men are swatting the air all over this damn jungle. It's the same in every goddamn jungle across the goddamn universe—bloodgnats, mosquitoes, cherryticks. They only exist to make us feel like shit. Between the lizards and the heat, this is as close as you're likely to come to hell in your lifetime."

"Think this is hell, Sarge?" piped Nick. "When the wind comes from the South, the mess tent back at the base is downwind from the latrine."

"Might actually make the chow more appetizing," laughed a handsome young draftee from New Babylon, stopping to splash water on his face. The sun had warmed the shallow water until it gave little relief from the beastly heat, and the humidity was enough to mildew his armpits. But if there was no escape from the heat, at least he could keep the sweat from stinging his eyes. And soon, he was back to work, filling the water casks, trying not to think about how wretched the heat was.

"Actually," laughed the sergeant, "you grunts don't know how easy you have it."

"Easy?" scoffed the kid from New Bablyon. "If we're not trying to keep from dying from the heat, we're trying to keep from dying of boredom."

"Clancy's right, Sarge," said Nick. "If we're not fetching water, we're digging latrines—or ditches—or trying to get the supply trucks running again. I mean, support troops get to see damn little action."

"Action?" laughed Simmons. "Well, I guess there's always the lizard women—if we ever find any on this steampot they call a planet. And if lizard tail isn't the kind of action you want, just talk to Colonel LaSalle about it. They always need grunts on the front lines. And I'm sure he'd be happy to oblige."

"Aw, Sarge...."

But Simmons wasn't really paying attention. Pulling out his wallet for the tenth time that morning, he looked at the picture his wife had sent of their newborn baby daughter. Sarah, she'd named her. All wrinkled and red, she looked more like a Ceresian potato than the little princess she was. With the new offensive, it looked like he wouldn't be getting home any time soon to say hello. He'd been lucky enough just to have gotten his furlough for the important part, he smiled.

He looked up at the sky. It was almost noon; the mess tent would soon be teeming with men, and the last water cask at camp was nearly empty. Mess detail was bad enough, he thought. He didn't want to expose the kitchen staff to the prospect of a food riot.

"Clancy, get in the truck. You and I are going to take the first batch of water jugs back to the base. The rest of you keep working. We'll be back in half an hour."

"Sure thing, Sarge," said Clancy. The young man bounded out of the water and over to the oversized groundrover they'd pressed into service as a supply truck. It was a rough ride, but took less power than the hovercraft they used to skim the treetops. And for transporting supplies along the ground, and mashing anything that got in their way, it was tough to beat.

"Hold it—Nick, you go along with him. You're getting eaten alive out here. I hope that teaches you what happens when you forget to douse yourself with bug spray before setting out. Get some glop sloshed on you, and bring back an extra bottle for the rest of us. We should have things pretty well wrapped up by the time you get back."

"Thanks, Sarge."

As the groundrover roared to life, Simmons found himself swatting the air, as furiously as Nick ever did. Miserable insects, he fumed to himself. Just like those back home. Another of those universal constants, he thought. Most of them were a universal pain in the ass. He watched the truck bounce and grind its way over a stand of brush and onto the supply road they'd cut through the trees leading back to camp.

"Hey, Sarge," Ike called from the middle of the stream. "Really now—when are they gonna send some girls down here? I mean, it's getting downright depressing."

"When?" answered Simmons still looking down the road. "When you grunts get cleaned off enough not to send them screaming back up to the ships because of the stench. That's when."

The private's laugh was cut short by a burst of strange whirring sounds that Simmons couldn't quite place. Hearing an unexpected splash in the water, he spun around quickly, his training taking him into a low crouch. He saw two bodies, face down in the water—and Ike, reeling and collapsing onto the ground near the shore.

Too late, he realized what was happening.

Lizards!! his mind screamed in terror. Horror froze his limbs in place, paralyzing him with fear.

He barely felt the laser blast searing his chest. Though it sent his mind spinning, it seemed no more than a strong gust of wind on a blustery day. As he briefly stirred from an enveloping cloud to find himself lying face down in the sand, unable to breathe, his last conscious thoughts cursed the indignity of dying on such a miserable, bug-infested planet. And he cried over his mind's fading image of the wrinkled little girl he would never hold in his arms.

HIS MUSCLES straining with his load, Lanash stopped to rest in the shade of an arching fern. The aching in his legs was becoming unbearable, and he could push himself no longer. He sensed no Terrans approaching from the north, though he trusted the birds and forest animals to alert him to their presence more than he trusted his own instincts. But he did sense a sadder presence, pressing its way onto the weakening body of his friend.

Looking about for a soft patch of moss, he placed Shen down in the shade, making his own pack into a pillow for his friend's head. Shen's breathing grew more labored with each passing moment, and he wheezed thickly with every breath he took. Lanash could sense his friend's mind filling with weariness and despair.

Shen winced with fear at the thought of Death. Frightened as he was, he had no desire to be a burden any longer. Summoning all his strength, and drawing a deep, painful breath, he managed to speak, his voice faint and cracking.

"Go—go ahead, my Final Friend," he whispered. "You can do nothing for me here. The Terrans— "

"They are well to the North," Lanash interrupted, stroking Shen's forehead like a mother stroking her infant child. "We will rest here for as long as you like."

"Leave me. On your own, you may yet find the Regiment and continue the fight."

"We shall always fight them together, you and I." Lanash took Shen's limp, trembling hand in his own, squeezing it as if to restore the warmth of Life. "Side by side, through the darkness and the mist. I will not leave you, my friend. I am by your side, always and forever."

Too weak to speak any longer, his body writhing in its final agonies, Shen managed a brief smile. Lanash soon sensed his friend's welling panic of doubt and terror, the sense of falling, headlong and alone into a bottomless pit. Shen was fading, faster and faster...fading toward the unknown.

In the timeless manner of the *g'Khruushtani* through countless generations, Lanash squeezed Shen's lifeless hand, projecting his own strength and affection through the shadows. Briefly joining with his dying friend, he felt his own calming presence guiding them both as if soaring through a warm, endless sky, bearing them on wings through the mists of eternity. A moment later Shen was gone, leaving Lanash his final thoughts of farewell and eternal gratitude, gently washing his friend's soul with shimmering echoes of joy and peace.

Finally free to give vent to his emotions, Lanash found himself weeping like an infant. As he began digging with his hands, thoughts of the Terrans kept their distance. He appeared to have the luxury of time, and would not have his friend's memory sullied by the vileness of hate. The sun would set in a few hours. After he had buried his friend, the safety of darkness would be upon him. He would set out again tomorrow, a new lust for vengeance in his heart.

* * *

"Commodore?"

Returning from the seclusion of his own thoughts and lifting his gaze from the tiled floor, Cook was surprised to find himself several paces beyond his escort. They'd stopped just at the Westbay viewing window, overlooking the space docks along the western face of the starbase.

"I thought we'd stop here for a few minutes, sir," said Stokley, the tanshirt lieutenant.

"Just to rest," added Sloan, his sergeant.

Cook shrugged and began walking back toward the guards when he saw it. Instantly, he headed to the observation window, his eyes drawn irresistibly to the immense gray disc coming into view. Slipping out of the near berth, it glided out into the blackness.

It was the *d'Artagnan*.

Stained and scarred by the rigors of battle, her markings obscured by a black streak running halfway across her keel, she listed slightly toward starboard and wobbled clumsily as the bridge crew tried to execute a final salute to their commander. But it didn't matter to Cook; all he saw was the glistening, silvery girl he'd fallen in love with so long ago, when they were both younger and war just a nightmare of madmen past. His throat aching with swallowed tears, he stood and watched his ship sailing off without him, his thoughts drifting into space along beside her.

It was several moments before he stirred enough to realize that he was not alone, and found himself standing next to Janet, surrounding her with his arms as she stood crying softly, with her head on his shoulder. The gratitude she owed his guards for their complicity in bringing him to her had stripped her of any remaining shreds of dignity. All the hurt he'd caused her, the pain and the doubt and the suffering of self-pity, were washed away with the tears that streamed down her reddened cheeks. All that remained was love.

She said nothing at first, for there was nothing to say. She could almost touch her Skipper's hurt and anger, and felt helpless because she could do nothing to ease the pain. The moments passed, and their ship became a fading speck of light lost amid the stars. Finally, it was Cook who broke the silence, kissing her tenderly, again and again, then lifting her gaze to meet his.

"I thought you didn't believe in coincidences."

"Stokley and Sloan—I told them I'd meet you here. I thought you'd want to say goodbye to the ship. I told Dexter to take her off proudly for you. I guess he—everyone, really—couldn't match your style."

"Why aren't you— "

"I forged your signature. Before they relieved you—officially, I mean. Before they came to the ship with the order relieving you—I signed your name to a backdated document. Assigning me as your personal aide for the duration."

Cook smiled. "The duration of what?"

Janet blushed, and shrugged her shoulders.

"Well," he said softly, "this time, I guess it really is for keeps."

He held her tightly, wanting to bring her inside of him, and never wishing to let go. Then he kissed her like he did long ago, before war and death came to dominate their lives. Arm in arm they walked, under the discreetly watchful eyes of the guards, off toward his quarters. They each hoped that Life and Fate would never separate them again. Yet both of them knew that the times were proving as treacherous as rocks in the heavens, and love could be as cruel as fate.

COMMAND MEMORANDUM

CC: 144-4744.8
FROM: CSO Major A.J.Whiting
Acting Commander, Camp Girshoona North
TO: Executive Liaison Committee
SUBJECT: *Establishment of Second Labor Facility on Planet Girshoona*

Arrived this date to find nothing in place: no equipment, no facilities, no preliminary excavation work done to ready base for implementation of Plan 7, and nothing accomplished in the way of proper training for the assembled camp population.

To remedy this deficiency I have conscripted a work detail from Girshoona South, consisting of 50 CSO troops and officers, and 250 trained enemy nationals. Pending their arrival, I have determined that the location cannot be secured. The base command staff, consisting of 13 officers and 250 enlisted, cannot effectively supervise the camp's current work force, which the prior command permitted to reach five times normal guidelines. Accordingly, I have undertaken to neutralize the existing population and start over from scratch.

Given the expected arrival of a trained labor force, and to minimize future labor problems, I have also suspended the standard labor selection process to give emphasis to discipline in culling the camp rolls. This should avoid the management problems that many facilities encountered on Greloosh while still providing meaningful incentives for the residents. Given the numbers of enemy prisoners arriving daily, we should be able to remedy any temporary deficiency in numbers or skills within a short period of time. In addition, the exercise should help instill a proper attitude on the part of those enemy nationals allowed to remain, as well as restoring an appropriate level of objectivity to our own people—which, as we know, the previous command permitted to atrophy.

Per Directive of 144-4670, I will continue to make weekly reports of progress until we rectify the problems outlined in that document. At this point, however, it is too early to make any recommendations concerning necessary personnel changes. That recommendation will come as a separate report, as soon as I finish my investigation. Once again, however, I recommend that you come to a prompt decision concerning the replacement for Captain Burdick, even before his court-martial. This facility requires a full-time commander, and I cannot defer my responsibilities at the Main Facility indefinitely.

CSO Maj. A.J.Whitting
Commander, Girshoona South
Acting Commander, Girshoona North

Chapter 32

THE ROAR OF the ventilator engines nearly drowned out all else. Dra'Lengish and the underling he had summoned had to shout to make themselves heard. The rushing air chilled them enough to make their muscles ache, and they stood nearly chin-to-chin, for the mid-level grid in the crawlway gave them little room to turn about. It was, all in all, an unpleasant place to meet, but for one such as Dra'Lengish, for whom secrecy was a necessity more pressing than water, it was a boon from the gods.

"You are certain of this?" shouted the old man, his arms wrapped tightly about himself to conserve his diminishing store of body heat.

"I am positive," answered fa'Shenali. "He is nothing if not tenacious. Were he the current Terran commander we would not be discussing the matter, for he would have attacked long before this."

"So the mere fact that they have halted their advance— "

"I am certain of this much," interrupted the subaltern, clapping his sides to stimulate his circulation. "*Khu'ukh* is not one to waste an advantage, nor surrender the initiative. There may be more at work here than we realize. And we may very well awaken one day to find ourselves facing him elsewhere. I hesitate to say more than the facts warrant, my Lord, but that is my opinion. Either he is absent or, if he remains in the vicinity, someone else is directing their movements."

Nodding to himself, Dra'Lengish found himself as one with the opinion of the young commoner, and not for the first time. He smiled inwardly at the irony, for despite the gravity of their circumstances he was not without humor. But as his mind drifted off to contemplate how to use this new piece of information, his young consultant found himself numbed by the cold, and without any grander thoughts to distract his mind from his body's misery.

"A dozen pardons," fa'Shenali bowed deferentially, stomping the metal grating as he tried to recover some feeling in his feet. "You have not volunteered why you wanted my opinion, and I am too discreet to ask. But if you no longer need the noise to mask our voices— "

Dra'Lengish laughed loudly, and motioned the bechilled young one toward the exit.

"A dozen pardons of my own," he said, using the deferential form of address for the first time in fa'Shenali's presence, a fact that did not escape the subaltern's attention. "My preoccupations are no excuse for impoliteness."

"I shall follow— "

"No—warm yourself first. I insist."

"You are too kind."

"No—I am in your debt, One Called fa'Shenali."

"...AND SO we can see that our position solidifies with each passing day that the longnoses do not advance," said Lo'Galifa of *Ma'Shana*. He looked up from his notes to see the somnolent faces of his superiors, gaping at him from behind glazed and stuporous eyes. "It is a tribute to our persistence and dedication," he continued, undaunted. "And it is a testament to the courage of those whom we lead. But most of all—"

Amid the old lord's droning monotone, the door to the Sanctum creaked open. From curiosity or sheer boredom, all eyes quickly turned to the entrance, and saw Dra'Lengish step toward the meeting table.

"...with the leadership of our own Lord Commander.... "

His eyes stern and fixed, a satchel filled with charts and briefing papers in his hands, Dra'Lengish neither met nor acknowledged the glances of those who had arrived on time for the briefing. Taking his seat, he folded his hands on the table and purged his mind of tension. He knew that he would need to keep as calm as the dawning sun to assert his point without seeming to be disrespectful.

"And in conclusion.... "

"We are in your debt, Lord Galifa," said Ga'Glish, seizing the attention of all present. His anger at his senior aide's tardiness registered clearly with all present Dra'Lengish alone seemed unperturbed by his displeasure. "Now that Lord Lengish has seen fit to join us, perhaps we may proceed to more pressing matters."

Bowing in acknowledgment, Lo'Galifa resumed his seat, grateful for the interruption. He was painfully aware of his own limitations, and sensed the growing boredom of his associates. As much as he admired

Dra'Lengish, Lo'Galifa was profoundly relieved to have someone else become the focus of the Lord Commander's attention.

Clapping his hands to activate the projection screen, Ga'Glish rose to his feet. Towering above the seated members of his senior staff, he radiated the drive and power that had held the forces of His Worthiness together through what later historians would call the Dark Times. Speaking forcefully and confidently, he pointed grandly to the star map showing the skies just west of the Grand Bend.

"It is a godsend," he bellowed, his voice ringing in the ears of all present. "Whatever its reason—and the reasoning of longnoses is as alien to us as the cold skies of their home Planet *U'rt*—the halt to the Terran advance is a cause for rejoicing. It gives us time to regroup and reorganize. Most importantly, it gives us time to plan and recover our strength.

"Still, we would be fools to trust our fate to Terran forbearance," he continued, his thundering voice filling those present with the will to fight. "We may expect an attack at any time. We must be prepared to repel it, whatever the cost, whatever our losses."

"Dra'Lengish," said Ga'Glish, glaring fiercely at his tactical commander. Dra'Lengish felt mindless fear surge throughout his being. Riven with panic, he wondered how Ga'Glish had guessed his intentions, and felt certain that his only hope lay in confessing his ambitions, and asking for mercy. But his panic was short-lived, for he was mistaken.

"Kindly tell us," hissed the Lord Commander, contempt for what he perceived to be weakness showing in his scornful smile, "precisely what steps you are taking to provide us with adequate reinforcements."

Taking a moment to calm himself, Dra'Lengish rose and replied in a voice strong and self-assured.

"Such steps are beyond our power," he said, quietly and forcefully. "A single makeshift division that will probably cause us more trouble than the Terrans is departing the Homeland tomorrow. Additional reinforcements will take the better part of a full *g'Khruushtani* cycle, and are being raised by the Central Government. We are all that remains between the Terrans and our homes. This lamentable fact will not change in the foreseeable future."

"That is unacceptable!" thundered Ga'Glish. "That is completely unacceptable!"

"Unfortunately, it is also the truth."

"I cannot believe that we can obtain nothing from other arenas—from other scenes of battles. Reports cross my desk constantly of less pressing fronts of engagement."

"Our forces are already stretched to the limit," said Dra'Lengish. "With the Terrans massing elsewhere, threatening our neighbors and pressing at our flanks, we would be foolish to recall our already inadequate forces from those frontiers."

"They will not be foolish enough to attack their erstwhile benefactors," Ga'Glish scoffed. "And over some trifling trade disagreement?"

"I recall similar observations about the prospects of their attacking us, my Lord. And their ships are always a force to consider. Should such a thing come to pass, our task there will not be victory. It will be merely to hold the line until other races can join the battle in full force. And that, Lordship, may well be our only chance at salvation."

"Silence!" bellowed Ga'Glish. "I will hear no more of such dark thoughts and evil doubts."

"Then perhaps you would care to examine our weaknesses for the upcoming battle," offered Dra'Lengish. "Weaknesses that come from trying to destroy a single foe, rather than the enemy fleet. It has cost us dearly in the past."

"*Silence!*"

"Still, if the Terran commander is conventional enough to focus his attack in a single frontal assault, perhaps we will manage to muddle through."

"*Khu'ukh* is anything but conventional, Dull One. But perhaps you can tell us how to force his ship to the front where we may destroy him!"

"We force him to the front by threatening victory—but if he is already there, then I am afraid we are lost. He will simply outwit us. Among his other dark talents, he knows quite well how to exploit foolishness. And he has already seen how we will sacrifice victory trying to kill him."

"*Impudence!*"

"But our best analysis suggests that he is absent from the front. So planning our defense as if he were present would be the act of fools."

Ga'Glish was livid; his gill slits glowed a deep, angry green, and his eyes bulged in fury. Amid the gasps of all around him, Dra'Lengish sat quietly, holding his gaze steady, trying to keep his own wits about him. On all sides, he felt the wonderment of his companions, but sensed little disagreement. And his own heart knew that what he spoke was true.

Finally, Ga'Glish had calmed himself enough to speak in a controlled manner. But his emotions were barely under control, and his words gave no comfort to any at the table.

"It seems that I have missed the last dispatch from my Uncle," spat Ga'Glish, his words cruelly edged in ridicule. "For I do not recall your appointment to Lord Commander. Or perhaps you are merely longing for a trip to the front lines, though that is already within your own power to arrange."

Bowing in submission, Dra'Lengish raised his eyes to look into the those of his longtime friend.

"I regret any offense," he said. "But a true subordinate owes his Master honesty, when blind obedience would lead to destruction."

"Leave us!" commanded Ga'Glish. "Leave us to plan our defense without this treason you call honesty."

Dra'Lengish rose and bowed respectfully, and turned to depart. Maintaining his dignity as the meeting resumed without him, he strode proudly to the door, which opened with a rush of air as he approached.

As the door closed behind him, he gave vent to his sorrow. Weeping like an infant, he saw his duty come clearly into focus, a duty that he had hoped would never come to pass. For all changes that time and circumstance had brought to his life, it was his affection for the Ga'Glish of old that most grieved him. And it was the happy memory of Glish-Glish the Small One riding on his father's own shoulders that threatened to break his resolve.

* * *

"DEMCOM CONTROL, this is the *H. W. Harrington*, CGE 01245. Ready for approach to dock. Do you copy?"

The pilot of the *Harrington* stared at the sight and couldn't help but smile. Demeter loomed like a sapphire in the darkness, growing larger with each passing minute. But the great, blue planet wasn't what had drawn his attention. Streaming toward them, like a million sparkling diamonds, was an endless strand of lights. The whole planet, it seemed, was coming to greet them. Each small ship, reflecting the sunlight of Mullinberry's Star while gliding through the heavens, was broadcasting a message of welcome. And it was a welcome straight from the heart, broadcast with the spontaneous cheer and simple affection of a public growing weary of slogans and eager to show its appreciation to a real hero. He looked at his young navigator and shook his head.

"Someone sure leaked the word out," he laughed. "To tell you the truth, I doubt you could keep a trip like this a secret."

Both men laughed. They knew—apparently like everyone on the planet—who it was they were ferrying to Demeter. And they knew no more of the real reason for the trip, or the attempt at secrecy, than the approaching Demetrians.

Suddenly, the radio crackled with the awaited reply from the Base traffic controller.

"CGE 01245, Escort *Harrington*, this is DemCom Control. You are cleared for Security Bay, Dock Number 2."

"Roger, DemCom. Request additional escorts. Looks like we've got a party out here."

"Can you blame them? Not every day a planet gets a hero come calling."

"Any word on why he's here, Control? Now that the rabble knows all about it, I can't see the point in keeping it secret."

"Sorry, *Harrington*, the lid's still on. But you're right—only the Service would keep common knowledge a secret."

"About our escorts?"

"Dispatching them right now, Commander. They'll be on your wings in five minutes."

"Roger. I'd hate to start ramming a fleet of civilians, you know. Probably bad for morale. Wouldn't do my reputation any good, either."

"I copy, *Harrington*. We'll do our best. Over and out."

"*Harrington*, out."

The pilot looked out the window and smiled. It was enough to give a grizzled old spacer the chills. Pleasure boats, schooners, shuttles, cargo carriers—as far as the eye could see. It seemed that all of Demeter had turned out for the welcome.

A hero's welcome. And God knew there weren't any more deserving than good old Cookie.

"Makes you proud, doesn't it?" said the navigator, gazing out at the approaching vessels.

"They're not coming to see us, you moron."

"But..."

"Keep to your duties, Lad. No time for us to go a-gawking."

"Now don't go local on me, Charlie."

"Sorry, Laddie—happens every time I come to be nearing the home of me ancestors. But mind you none—it'll bloody well pass like the cosmic winds."

"Those aren't the only winds you've been passing, you know."

"Mind your screens there, Laddie."

"Okay—Pops."

JANET AWOKE gradually from the drifting sleep that lingered in her mind and body. Stretching as far as she could reach, she basked in a glow that she wished would never end. She wanted the moment to stretch as endlessly into time as the blackness outside stretched into space. For the first time in years, she felt needed and loved. Despite herself—despite the guilt that haunted her from hour to hour, making her miserable for finding a blessing for herself in someone else's disasters—she was filled with gratitude and a profound sense of relief. She was torn between singing for herself and crying for the tattered remains of her love's career.

Reaching out, she saw that Cook had already risen. Sitting up, she saw him standing at the observation platform, staring out into space.

It was not the first time he'd done so since they left Liberty Base 223. She was even starting to get used to it again. But there was something in his gaze that caught her attention—an intensity she hadn't seen in quite a while. She was surprised to discover she'd missed it without even noticing it was gone.

Rising from the oversized bed that was theirs for the trip to Demeter, she stepped softly to the window and sidled up beside him. Feeling the comforting warmth of his arm around her, she looked up at him and thrilled to see him smile at her. It wasn't the sad, wistful smile she'd seen since that horrible day they watched the *d'Artagnan* depart without them. In its place was the cocky grin she'd grown to love over the years, brimming with quiet confidence. No matter what was going on around them, she knew that everything would be all right.

Looking out the window, she felt her throat tighten, and tears started blurring her vision.

There, before them, stretching out into the blackness of infinity and guiding them toward the point of brilliant blue that she recognized at once as the Planet Demeter, were ships—thousands of them, large and small, tugs and butterbox shuttles and interstellar sloops, surrounding the ship and blinking their running lights in unison, in a touching gesture of greeting. Some of the nearer ones trailed what appeared to be signs in their wake, signs that, at this distance, were impossible to read. But it didn't matter. She had no doubt what they were saying. Or who they'd come to welcome.

She opened her mouth to say something when the paging of the intercom broke the silence and interrupted their solitude.

"Hate to intrude, Commodore," said a voice over the speaker; Janet recognized the pilot's voice. "You might want to take a watch at the porthole. We seem to have some well-wishers, coming to pay their respects."

"The post's already manned, Commander," Cook replied. "But thanks for the briefing, anyway."

"Isn't it a wonder?" said Janet.

"Life is the wonder," rejoined Cook. "This is just the comic relief—the delicious touch of irony that either make you laugh or cry. If it doesn't drive you crazy first."

"You can't just enjoy the moment?"

Cook laughed wickedly. "These poor fools haven't the foggiest idea of what's going on," he said. "For that matter, I suppose, neither do I. I spend half my life in the clouds, it seems, the other half in a fog. Not that anyone else can tell which is which. But that doesn't mean I don't enjoy it in my own way."

"Why do you talk in riddles?" Janet huffed, her feelings hurt. "Why do you always make me feel like you take me for some brainless idiot?"

Bemused, Cook looked into her eyes and sighed. He'd done it again, he thought. He'd insulted her, and had no idea how he'd done it.

"Sorry," he said softly. Hugging her warmly, he rocked her gently in his arms as they stood watching the ships come to escort them to the planet, and felt her annoyance start to melt in his arms. At least this time she won't go stalking off in a huff, he smiled, keeping his thoughts discreetly to himself. Of course, this time she had no place else to go, so perhaps that was the key to the whole thing. Choices did seem to confuse people: whatever the array of possibilities, most people seemed to guess wrong, anyway. Maybe that was the real reason poets and philosophers spent so much time being miserable or misunderstood, he thought. Or, if they were lucky, smiling as they savored life's ironies.

"What are you laughing at?" asked Janet, a note of suspicion creeping into her voice.

"Nothing. Watch the ships."

"But— "

"The ships—watch the ships."

* * *

A HUNDRED parsecs from the budding celebrations on the Planet Demeter, another officer was facing a less bracing reward for his efforts.

"I didn't ask for explanations, Commodore Steinbrenner," snapped the Chief of Staff. "I want to know exactly who is responsible for this breach of security."

"Yes, Admiral. I'll do my best."

"That's not good enough. I don't want you to do your best—I want you to find me answers. Somebody's going into the burner for this. And if I don't have anyone else's ass to fry, I'll roast yours—either for fucking it up in the first place, or for failing to get to the bottom of it. Do you understand me, Steinbrenner?"

"Yes, sir. I understand you perfectly."

"Dismissed!"

The hapless flag officer turned on his heels and strode out the door, leaving CosGuard's troubled Chief of Staff alone with his two civilian advisors, who were concealed in the alcove overlooking the courtyard of Central Command's headquarter complex. As the door shut with a dull thud, Fleet Admiral Weatherlee slammed the conference table with his fist.

"Damn!"

"Listen to me Weatherlee," called a voice from the shadows.

"We have him. We have him nailed! And I'm still going to do it. So help me, he's not getting away from me this time."

"Don't be an idiot," chuckled the other voice, stepping out into the light. Emerson Hollenbach lighted his cigar, glad to be rid of the candy-ass commodore his partner in the High Command had chosen to trust with such a delicate mission.

"Right," glowered Weatherlee, looking hatefully into the eyes of his Senate Hill ally. "You've been wanting to say that for a long time, haven't you Senator? That's what you've been wanting to call me since Day One."

"Hey," interrupted Nicholas Schiller, the Executive partner of the triumvirate. He stepped past Weatherlee's oversized desk, and took a seat in one of the plush chairs across from the Chief of Staff. "We haven't come this far by sniping at each other. I think we should all just relax and...."

"It doesn't pay to call people idiots," snapped Hollenbach. His steel gray eyes coldly analyzed the new facets now showing in the personality of their man in Central Command. He did not like what he saw. "It pays to keep them from behaving like idiots."

"Now look, you two— "

"All right," gritted Weatherlee. "I've had just about all the flak I'm going to take about this, from you or anybody else. That Isitian prick is mine, now. And I'm not going to let anybody stand in the way of sending him down in flames. You try to stop me— "

"Don't threaten me," Hollenbach said quietly, his eyes betraying as little emotion as his voice, "Not unless you have some way of making it good. Better men than you have tried it," he continued, his lips turning up at the corners, "and their careers or bodies litter every dark closet in the Capital."

"Emerson...."

"I have my own reasons for wanting to see Cook turned on a skewer," Hollenbach smiled darkly, plopping into his chair. "Personal reasons—Schiller and I both, stemming from before the war even started. I'd like nothing better than to see him twisting over the coals. But personal reasons won't lead me to lose my head by being greedy. And I won't risk one jot of power by overplaying my hand."

"So what are you saying?" growled Weatherlee. "That I should simply give it up and let the windy little daisy-sniffer— "

"Politics is the art of the possible, my friend. If I didn't learn that lesson, I wouldn't be part of this Triumvirate. And some other jolly old Earther would probably be helping to guide Terra to her proper place in the galaxy."

"If you're quite through congratulating yourself...."

"And if you're through trying to sink your teeth into ultrynium, you'd try something a little more practical."

"Not on your life, Hollenbach. That little snot is history."

Slowly shaking his head, Hollenbach snorted. How such a fool had risen to command the whole Cosmic Guard was beyond his power to understand. Maybe it had something to do with cosmic radiation frying the brains of the competition; maybe it was just simply that the fact of command always colored military politics, and that civilians didn't have the luxury of sending miscreants to the brig on a whim, or shooting inferiors for insubordination. But like him or not, Hollenbach concluded, for the time being they had to live with this imbecile. If that meant another try at recalibrating their loose cannon, then so be it.

"Why let your lust for revenge limit your horizons?" Hollenbach said at last, winking at Schiller as he spoke.

"*Revenge*," whispered the senator. "That's what you're really after, isn't it? That's what this is really all about."

Weatherlee said nothing. He glowered at the mocking hulk who was leaning over the admiral's polished desk.

Sensing his advantage, Hollenbach pressed the attack.

"Revenge. It's such a useful, flexible tool, you know. It can move mountains if used properly. And it can be the source of infinite satisfaction, savored like the memory of a fine wine, or a fine woman. It's a pity people can't always see past their own noses, so blinded by the urge to crush something under their boot that they loose sight of the far grander possibilities that a little imagination could bring for their enjoyment."

Weatherlee held his tongue. He was starting to wonder whether he had badly underestimated his colleagues.

"You've read the reports from Demeter," Hollenbach continued, his voice low and conspiratorial. "Rallies, parades—welcoming flotillas. Thousands upon thousands of ships and boats of every kind. And every self-dealing Demetrian politician trying to get him to come to town for a visit. They're going crazy. To be honest, I can't blame them. They're just being patriotic. They don't see Cook the way you do, you know. They just see the hero. The biggest hero of the war—and the brightest star in their small, pathetic lives. Heaven help the poor soul who tries to stand in the way of hero worship. You try sticking him with a mutiny charge and the rest of Terra will take you for the biggest fool in the galaxy. The public won't stand for it—they simply will not stand for it. In any contest between a hero and a bureaucrat, it won't be the paper-pusher who comes out on top. And if public opinion starts clamoring for scalps, no politician will risk his ass to cover for a paperpusher."

"So what you're telling me— "

"I'm *telling* you nothing," Hollenbach smirked. He resumed his seat, taking no pains to conceal his smug sense of superiority.

"I'm *suggesting* that if you open your eyes, you'll see that you're not without leverage. You're just a trump or two short of a grand slam. But if you can consider something else besides nailing his ass to the wall on some manufactured charge or other, you might find it just as enjoyable to turn that daisy-sniffer into a puppet on a string—or a dancing girl, dancing to whatever tune you choose to call."

Weatherlee opened his mouth to reply, only to find himself dazzled by the possibilities. His lips curled into a tight smile, and soon he found himself chuckling.

As the rough laughter spread around the room, Hollenbach made a mental note of the incident and filed it away in his head for future reference. He didn't like this Cozzie: Weatherlee was too easily manipulated to be trusted with anything sensitive or important again. But people like Weatherlee had their place in the Universe. Properly controlled, they could prove invaluable. So long as he could keep Weatherlee entertained, the fool might prove useful.

"Make him dance for me," Weatherlee marveled, when he had caught his breath again. "Now that's something I want to think about."

Quite useful indeed, Hollenbach chuckled to himself.

* * *

COMMAND DIRECTIVE 144-4989.4 TO FTADM L.L.BENNING-TON, CHIEF OF STAFF, COSGUARD SECURITY OFFICE: Cancel ComDir 144-4202. Effective immediately, cancel Subject's 1-A security detainee status and scan Eastern Fleet records to sanitize all references to 1-A Detention. Continue Subject's isolation from all visitors, other than security detail. Under no circumstances is he to set foot on Planet Demeter without express authorization from Chief of Staff. Eastern Fleet shall not acknowledge nor confirm Subject's whereabouts; if pressed, defer by reference to reasons of security. You may remind subordinates that failure to conform to security restrictions are grounds for court-martial, and details of operation are to remain classified, for your eyes only.

Once sanitization is complete, you shall personally arrange Subject's secured transportation to Central Command with all available expedition. Mission is Code Blue; log on personal files only, replies are restricted to security channels.

FtAdm WWWeatherlee
Chief of Staff

"ENCRYPTED, SECURITY code Zebra," droned the computer. "Transmitting."

Admiral Weatherlee smiled darkly; his heart racing with excitement. He felt as if he were in the middle of a great battle, fighting and defeating his darkest enemies and surmounting his blackest fears.

Hollenbach had been right, he marveled to himself. The crafty Earther hadn't risen to the heights of power by accident. Politics on Senate Hill might be more circuitous than in the halls of the High Command, but this way was going to be less risky. In the end, it might prove to be a lot more fun.

Interrupted from his musing by the beeping of his intercom, Weatherlee swung around to face the door. "Come," he barked, smiling to see the advancing figure of his top assistant, approaching with further evidence of the admiral's growing power.

"Here is the Final Draft you wanted, Admiral," said Atley, placing four crisply bound sets of official-looking binders on his desk.

"Took long enough to get them back from the printers," Weatherlee scowled. Opening the top binder, he poured over the two-page document, searching mercilessly for any flaws or mistakes in reducing his order to print. The last three drafts he'd sent back were good enough, but they weren't quite perfect.

Narrowing his eyes, Weatherlee reread the document. It was all there, everything he and the others had wanted: The diversion of ships to the borders, to deal with the growing problems with the neutral aliens along the extending Terran flanks; the assignment of ships to the ZarCom sector, in anticipation of action to the West; and the commitment of the High Command to use all available means to meet the "growing menace" along the frontiers—whether coming from human or alien sources. It had taken months to get everyone to sign onto the program, or to replace those who stubbornly resisted what Policy Directive 144-4989 called the "Final Phase" of the war. Taking a little extra time to make sure it read properly might seem a petty indulgence to some. But Weatherlee fancied himself something of a perfectionist.

Raising his head, Weatherlee winked at his favorite aide. "Looks good to me, too," he said, signing all four copies of the document. "Send them next to Mr. Schiller at the Executive Mansion. He'll see that it gets forwarded from there. And tomorrow we'll have to draft letters of thanks to Schiller and the Senator. We owe them a big debt for backing us up on this one."

"Yes, Admiral."

"It's a day to remember, Mr. Atley. A day to savor—a day to celebrate. Just like the day Clay took his big fall."

"Oh yes, Admiral."

* * *

Declassified and unsealed from the Cosmic Guard Archives, 27Jan2606:
POLICY DIRECTIVE 144-4989
TO ALL DEPARTMENT HEADS
Classification Code: Blue
cc: 144-4989.5

Given the success of our Crutchtan initiatives, and the imminent collapse of resistance to the East, the High Command has concluded that it is now detrimental to Terran Security for the containment of Crutchtan aggression to continue enjoying unrestricted priority among our military objectives. Our strategic and tactical position of unchallenged superiority in the East means that we can no longer justify ignoring other threats to our security, from various sources, which now pose greater dangers to Terran interests than the vanquished Crutchtan fleet.

During this Final Phase of the War Effort, it will continue to be the Policy of the Government to resist hostile moves against Terran interests by all appropriate means, including the use of military force. In recent days, such hostile moves have taken increasingly subtle forms, including encroachments upon Terran space by Atkvalo vessels masquerading as merchantmen; confrontations by Glincian vessels with official craft of the Cosmic Guard; and resistance by rebellious elements to the west of Planet Zarathustra to the legitimate territorial aspirations of the Terran Government, such resistance including an unremitting and hostile indifference to the success of the War Effort and a corresponding failure to recognize the pressing Terran needs for supplies, resources, and manpower. With the fall of the Crutchtan Empire secured, the Government can now begin to deal appropriately with such intrusions into Terran zones of interest.

To counter the increasing threat of alien attack from hostile Glincian and Atkvalo forces, and the threat of attack or insurrection from the rear, the High Command has decided upon a wide-scale redeployment of forces. Specifically, the High Command directs:

(1) The withdrawal of surplus forces from the Crutchtan battlefronts, and their reassignment to zones of potential conflict along the Glincian and Atkvalo frontiers.

(2)   The reassignment of existing and uncommitted Central Fleet battle group remnants to the base at Zarathustra Command, and the encouragement of dissident groups on Planet Isis by means of interstellar broadcast.

(3)   The active cultivation of Terran public opinion, to prepare for eventual hostilities in the event that diplomatic means fail to secure our objectives.

(4)   Preparations to seal all borders and points of access, in the event that a military resolution of the relevant issues in any new theater of operations becomes necessary. Along our Glincian and Atkvalo borders, such a move is needed to maintain the security of our preparation; in the Western theater, such a move may render overt military moves unnecessary by playing to native pacifist sentiments, and allowing us to reassert central control over the recalcitrant planet by supplanting the existing government with a more malleable regime.

(5)   The active use of diplomacy to give legitimizing cover to any steps undertaken, now that the sanitization of the senior Foreign Office staff is complete.

All department heads shall review their present operations and commence transition planning immediately. Drafts of initial plans for redeployment shall be forwarded to the High Command from all departments within ten days. All proposed future activity will be reviewed for compliance with this directive.

Adopted January 27, 2556, at Covington, New Babylon
/s/ W.W.Weatherlee,
Chief of Staff, Cosmic Guard
/s/ N.S.Schiller,
Chief of Staff, Office of the President
/s/ E.E.Hollenbach,
Chairman, Senate Governmental Affairs Committee

Chapter 33

NERVOUS DAYS PASSED along the front, where the crippled forces of His Worthiness were all that stood between the *g'Khruushtani* and the forces of barbarism. The last remnants of their battered Fleet stood guard over the approach to the broad expanse that opened into the Homeland. All were painfully aware that they could be overrun and destroyed at any time. From the Great Bend to the Glincian Frontier, damaged ships crawled into orbit around any available port. Those who sailed them viewed their screens with a numbing, draining anxiety. Half-dead with exhaustion, they waited and watched for the first dreadful signs that the Terrans were beginning their final onslaught.

Yet day after day, they saw nothing—nothing but routine military traffic. And from the listening posts near the Terran lines they heard nothing—nothing but the intermittent chatter of military routine.

Finally, the signs came, signs of intense activity. Terran ships were seen massing around known Terran encampments, and the blaring of subspace gibberish indicated the increased transmission of coded messages that could only mean one thing:

Invasion....

As the front stirred with rumors and reports of Terran ship movements, the sinking feeling that the end was near seized the heart of more than one *g'Khruushtani*, and the heavens were alive with words traveling eastward.

Words of farewell to friends and loved ones, filled with love and despair.

Words bereft of hope, yet filled with the longing for deliverance that spanned the ancient Empire as it teetered closer and closer to destruction.

And words filled with the bitter resolve to win a last reprieve for those left behind, and to fight the barbarians to the death.

* * *

"FOR CRYING out loud."

From her seat at the microfile index screen, Suzie Yang turned her head toward the transtelex to see Mark Fishman standing over the machine, reading the copy as it came over the wire. The office cynic, Fishman could find the lint in any pot of gold, though he often said things only to laugh at the reaction. This time he seemed genuinely offended.

"Did you— " he sputtered, only to turn away shaking his head in disgust. "I'll tell you," he said, looking in Suzie's direction. "I'm getting a bit sick of this."

"Sick of what?" asked Suzie.

"Sick of the whole damn thing. All this fuss over one lousy space jockey. Some hero, too—heading safely to the rear while war's ranging all along the front. Day in, day out—and it's still two days before he even gets to New Babylon. It's enough to make you puke."

Suzie had heard enough.

"I suppose you'd find him more admirable if he managed to get himself killed," she shot back. "That's fine talk from one who's spent most of the war helping to keep Cahalan's Tavern safe from the Crutchtans."

"Now just a minute— "

"I'll tell you something," she continued, her voice rising in pitch and the words coming faster and faster. "Heroes are a cheap commodity along the front. Some of them are floating through space as interstellar dust—and I've seen thousands of others with my own eyes, coming back in body bags, boys who never got the chance to grow old enough to be cynical like some punch-drunk reporters I know. Who have nobody to write about them, and only mothers and fathers to cry over their graves. When someone like Roscoe Cook comes along, people sense it. People with an ounce of feeling, that is. He's saved more lives than the whole hospital corps. Every Terran mother with a child facing death along the front says a prayer for Cook every single night. Because of him, the war's almost over—and if CosGuard wants to give him a rest, or if he ever wants to take one himself, then he's earned it. I don't think he needs your permission to do it."

Most of the men she worked with had learned it was useless to argue with her when she started bringing mothers and gravestones into the conversation. Fishman was quite willing to let the matter drop, until Ben Brewster came barging onto the scene to toss a grenade of his own.

"Damnfool brasshats," drawled Brewster, coffee cup in hand, making his way toward the wire service outlet. He peered onto the screen to see if word had reached the wire services yet.

"What's up?" asked Fishman, grateful for the interruption.

"I just had Ellen call up Central Command," drawled the Earther. "You know, to get Cook's itinerary. Tryin' to be responsible and on top of things. When she ran into problems, I took over the job myself."

"So?"

"Well, not only won't the dang fools release his schedule. But now that word of his trip has leaked, they're refusing to confirm that he's coming to New Babylon at all. I tell you, someone at CentCom is plenty miffed. Either that, or they're as sick of all the fuss as everyone else."

Suzie howled in frustration as her colleagues nodded and laughed. Grabbing her purse, she huffed off toward the door.

"I'm going to lunch," she snarled, just before the door closed behind her.

"My, aren't we testy today?" Fishman sniffed, in a low-pitched rendition of Suzie's accent.

"Well, don't worry about her," drawled Brewster. "She's a sport—and a dang fine reporter."

"Just wish she didn't get so..."

"Yeah, well. You know— "

"Right on schedule. I checked."

* * *

IT ARCHED MAJESTICALLY through the skies, ending at the vast stellar desert marking the natural boundary of what Terrans call the Local Arm of the Milky Way. The broad archipelago of *Glincimaterna* stretched eastward, from the narrow gas clouds of the Trillinary Rille to the flat, open skies of what the Glinci called *tril'ne'ge-Lehnseh*—the Homeland, in their Mother Tongue. As tensions crested from the Crutchtan Basin to the Terran capital, the clear, cloudless skies east toward the Galactic center were filling with tensions of a different kind.

"RED ALERT sounding over the security channels, Commander."

His lieutenant commander's bars still shining like new on his epaulet, Mason McGee swivelled his command chair to face his radio officer. Since assuming command of the frigate *Farragut* three weeks earlier, he'd had the feeling that something big was about to happen. The Cozzies didn't turn over warships to gadabout spacers without a bloody good reason. And he was only one of several dozen bounder laddies to get promoted and handed a frigate.

Something was in the works, and he had the feeling they were just about to find out exactly what it was.

"Incoming message."

"Is it cleared for general audiences, Ensign?" Mason asked.

"Aye, sir. In fact... "

The radio officer turned to face his commanding officer, a broad grin flashing across his face. "In fact, Commander, the feeder text says that they want it played for the whole crew."

"Put it on the screen then, Laddie," Mason chuckled. "Let's get to findin out just what we have goin on here." He leaned back in his chair, amazed that the Cozzies would trust him with one of their finest ships, so proud of himself that he wanted to crow.

He hoped to heaven that he was about to hear what he wanted since the day he signed up to wear CosGuard blue. What they'd all been waiting for, if truth be told. When the screen cleared, Mason found himself gaping, his eyes bulging widely.

The forward screen filled with the image of the President himself.

With eyes steadfast and steely, and a jaw set with the determination borne of decades of posing in public and private, President Heathcoate smiled and nodded. In the background, the Terran flag—the gold pentastar on a sky blue field—hung prominently over the President's right shoulder. To his left, a stately bookcase flanked the artificial flames of the stage-prop fireplace that his aides insisted be visible in the background of every official proclamation. Mason gulped and paled; he was not alone in failing to notice that the recorded message was not coming to his ship alone. It was being broadcast across the whole frontier.

"Good day to you all, brave guardians of Terra," Heathcoate said, in his warmest, most velvety voice, " You who are so far away, and yet as close as our hearts and prayers."

After a kindly grin, the president continued, his voice filled with avuncular affection. His eyes were friendly and unthreatening.

"Some time ago," he went on, "I took an oath—much like the oath you took yourselves, in those dark hours when your nation needed you most. Like you, I swore to protect Terra and all her citizens—the weak and the young; the old and the sick. The mothers and children we left at home; the parents for whom the blossom of youth is now just a beautiful memory. All of them depend upon the strength and bravery of Terra's military might to keep them safe and secure in their beds at night, and to keep our children laughing in the innocence of play.

"We have accomplished much in these past few years. The Enemy is no longer pounding at our door, about to destroy everything we've known. The Enemy has been routed and all but vanquished, thanks to the valor and courage of the Cosmic Guard. And on the captive worlds where the Enemy once worked unspeakable acts of barbarism, the Terran army now patrols, keeping the newfound lands safe for uncounted future generations to explore and prosper, bringing the eternal blessings of peace and freedom for all."

His eyes darkening with concern, the President shook his head as if in despair. His brow furrowed with incomprehension, and his face clouded with an inexpressible sadness.

"But now, just as Peace was dawning on the fields of battle, I'm afraid our skies are darkening again. Not from any lack of foresight or bravery on the part of Terra's soldiers or guardians of our heavens. Not even from the last desperate stirrings of our vanquished enemies. The clouds we see now come not from enemies—but from friends. Friends who have chosen not to join us at our table as friends and equals, but who seek to profit by our continuing peril, lunging with knives at our backs when they could be sharing in our celebration of Peace."

Lifting his eyes until they seemed to stare straight into the heart of each of his listeners, the President spoke without bitterness. But his voice carried the subtle hints of eternal wrongs, and the unslakeable thirst for righteous vengeance.

"In the past few days," he continued, "I've seen evidence—undeniable evidence—of massive preparations for war by the same supposedly friendly alien powers who have professed their peaceful intentions for the past five years. The past weeks have seen incursions by Atkvalo vessels into Terran space, the accosting of Terran merchant vessels by ships of the Atkvalo and Glinci, and the massing of alien vessels along the frontiers of both neutral powers. The pattern of harassment can have as its aim only one goal: the Atkvalo and Glinci are testing the Terran will to resist. They are probing to see if our will to fight has been exhausted by our long struggle against the forces of the Crutchtan Empire. And the pattern of alien deployment can have only one meaning. They are massing for an attack, bent on streaming across the border as soon as they are ready—or as soon as we show ourselves so spent by our battles against the Crutchtan aggressors that they perceive we have lost the will, or the ability, to defend ourselves.

"That, my valued friends of the Frontier Fleets, is what they have been waiting for. And that, my brave guardians of everything good and decent in this Universe of ours, is what we shall never show."

Defiance beaming from his face, Heathcoate pounded the desk in front of him, his resolve unambiguous and unbowed, his eyes brimming with the fury of betrayal and the majesty of indignation.

"As a result," he continued, "it falls to us once again to take the battle to our attackers. To be as uncompromising in war as we are magnanimous in victory. A state of war now exists between the Terra and the combined Forces of Evil—a war that we must win, for the survival of all we hold dear. And if it is our duty to stand, tall and strong and proud, for our homes, and our families, and our children, then let us resolve to make History proud of us. And let us ensure that when History takes its final measure of our Time and our Era, she will find, in the words of an Old Earth statesman and historian, that this was our Finest Hour."

As the President's image faded, to be replaced by a security-coded communiqué, Mason let out a whoop. Across the ship, loud cheers filled the corridors. On the bridge, the command officers clapped each other on the shoulders, happy to be part of the battle at last. No more would they be relegated to the status of second-classers, whenever they met with any of the Cozzie regulars. Now it was their war, too. And they'd deck any blowhard who scoffed at their contribution to the effort.

Stepping to the radio station Mason pressed the print button, and called for a printed copy of the communiqué from Headquarters. His eyes widened with delight at the heading; and he felt a surge of power at the crisp, businesslike tone of his orders.

BATTLE ORDERS

To: LtCmdrMMcGee
Commanding Officer, *Farragut*
CGF 9003

cc: 144-5048.2

Effective 144-5048.5, you are ordered to rendezvous with Frigates *Sikorski*, *Ezekial*, and *Dorchester*, and to proceed to rendezvous with Battle Group designated Alpha, current position Ballenger's Star, under command of CGS *Constitution*, Captain LLStark, cmding. You are ordered to maintain radio silence to point of rendezvous, except for standard IFF exchanges. Upon arrival, you will receive further briefing from Alpha Command Staff.

"Mr. Hodges," Mason bellowed, grinning from ear to ear. "Prime all engines; Mr. Masterson, plot a course for Ballenger's Star, on the double. Trim the shields to running strength; prepare to set sail."

As the bridge crew scurried to carry out his orders, Mason strutted to the command chair, prouder than a harem's stallion. As his ship shuddered from the surge of power to the engines, he felt the thrill of battle surging through his veins. After all the slights and humiliations, he thought to himself—after all the slaps and insults from Cozzie regulars, and the petty indignities from the goonybirds across the border— he was finally going to strike back. Goonybirds, lizards—they were all the same now. The war wouldn't pass him by. And nobody was going to accuse Mason McGee of ducking combat when the nation was at war, and aliens were storming the gates.

In his state of giddy exuberance, it never registered that Ballenger's Star was on the other side of the Glincian border.

And in all the excitement, he never quite read the communiqué's second paragraph:

> You are advised that enemy forces are in place, and casualties are expected. Caution is urged at point of rendezvous with Battle Group Alpha.

* * *

Headline story from Trans-Terran Dispatch, 08Mar2456:
COSGUARD REPELS ATTACKS,
LAUNCHES COUNTEROFFENSIVE

Glincian Ambassador, Six Senators Detained in Capital

Covington(UMN) COSGUARD CENTRAL COMMAND REPORTED today that forces of the Cosmic Guard have stemmed sneak attacks along Terra's borders, and have turned the tide of battle against Glincian and Atkvalo invaders with a series of quick counterstrikes. And as the war took a sudden turn along the frontier, allegations of treason and corruption have surfaced on Senate Hill.

The first attack, occurring yesterday along the long boundary with the mysterious Atkvalo empire, is reported to have penetrated nearly ten parsecs into Terran space before a makeshift flotilla, under the command of Commodore Anthony Quackenbush, pushed the invaders back past the frontier. Quackenbush, a recently promoted veteran of past battles under Admiral Medwick, had been on routine patrol in the sector when it came under heavy attack. Sources in Central Command report that only quick action saved the entire sector from being overrun, and credit Quackenbush's forces with turning a near-rout into a classic military victory.

Less than an hour later, along the mist-shrouded border with the Glincimaterna, a battle wing under the command of Captain Lionel L. Stark repelled a massive invasion along a wide front by forces of the Glinci, the race of tall, feathered birdmen who last proclaimed their neutrality only days ago in a statement issued by the Glincian ambassador in Covington. "My country desires Terran friendship above all else," Ambassador Drub'd stated at a news conference on Saturday. "With peace in sight along the Eastern frontier, it would be folly for our peoples to let minor differences interfere with the development of mutual trust and respect." Informed sources say that these differences, including a disputed region of space near the mineral-rich star systems of the Trillinary Rille, had led to increasing tensions in recent weeks, culminating in the Glincian attack upon Captain Stark's forces.

These same sources, noting the absence of previous incidents with the Atkvalo Empire along the anticenter frontier, suggest that the size and timing of the attacks along both fronts indicates a high level of advance planning and coordination by the enemy governments. "We hesitate to rush to judgment," one source said, "but everything points to a joint effort to press an advantage before the opportunity slipped past them."

Asked if this meant that the aliens may have been planning their attack for some time, this source declined to comment. But, he noted, recent Terran victories against the crumbling Crutchtan Empire had all but ended the war in the East. "It was only a matter of time before Terran forces came home," he added. Whether this entered into the alien decision to launch the attack quickly was, in his opinion, a matter of "speculation."

"Just the same," he said, "whatever the cost, we will not let Terra fall to alien aggressors."

Across the Capital, others expressed the same sentiments....

Chapter 34

"THIS IS SENSELESS."

Looking out the porthole, Janet saw the blue seas and wispy clouds of home. For the first time in years, New Babylon hung outside her window. Straining her eyes to make out the contours of the mainland, she found her heart racing as she saw that the skies over Cape Mountbatten were clear as could be. *Home.* She thrilled at the thought.

Mother—father—her brothers—all of them. For the first time in ages, she could see them. Hug them. Hear their voices, and remember the days when she was a little girl. It was like a dream.

"Acch—this makes no sense at all."

Startled from her reverie by the fire in his voice, Janet turned away from the observation window. She saw Cook, floating weightless high above the unmade bed, shaking his head as he pored intently over the day's news. She smiled at the sight, for each turn, of his head sent his body spinning in a different direction. Soon he was rotating quite vigorously, port over starboard and head over heels—yet completely oblivious to the motions of his body until, at last, his head collided with the ceiling.

Cook's eyes flashed indignantly as Janet started to laugh. "Now that will be quite enough of that!" he snapped. But as he careened from one wall toward the next, it only made her laugh all the harder. As Cook fumed quite helplessly overhead, she made her way to the compartment's gravity controls, and gently brought him back to the floor.

"For crying out loud— "

"Just be more careful, next time, Skipper."

"Well, next time don't leave the damn zerograv on. That's the daft part, here. Leaving me floating around the cabin like spilled oatmeal, for Pete's sake. And trim the giggling, Missy. This is no laughing matter."

As Janet melted helplessly onto the floor, Cook took a deep breath and tried to keep from getting angry. She'd been moody enough as they neared the planet. All things considered, it was better to have her laughing rather than scolding him over one silly thing or another.

But that didn't change what was going on around them. He didn't like was he was reading. Not one bit. Until he had things figured out, he was in no mood for distractions.

He looked at the story from the newswire again: the banner headlines announcing the alien attacks and the Terran counterattacks. The story, printed in bold type, detailed how the Terran commanders on the scene had turned a near disaster into a rout.

Of course, none of it made any sense. Nothing in any of his old briefing papers even hinted that either of the alien races along the border had ships with the capacity to challenge the Terran starships, and mounting such an attack without the ability to make it a good fight was madness. But beyond the apparent lunacy of an alien race he didn't understand, there was no reason to have starships in those areas in the first place. None at all. With war raging in the east, frigates were better suited to routine patrol. And as far as he knew, every Terran starship was committed to the war. The thought kept thundering in his head until he thought it would drive him crazy.

Then he saw it.

And he thought the blood was going to freeze in his veins.

He nearly missed it, he would think later, buried at the bottom of the business page with a headline no bigger than some obscure announcement of management reshuffling at some medium-sized firm from eastern Terra. If his eyes hadn't caught the mention of his home planet in the story's lead paragraph, it would have escaped his notice entirely.

GRAIN SHIPMENTS THREATENED

Covington (UMN) The Ministry of Agriculture confirmed today that the supply of Isitian grain promised for the upcoming winter on Earth has run into yet another snag. Sources close to the Ministry say that the current regime on Isis, having declined to approve the necessary permits for commercial shipping, has threatened to cancel all existing contracts unless the Heathcoate Government agrees to let Isitian merchant ships lade and transport the cargo.

Edgar Winters, Deputy Trade Minister, estimates that under the current restrictions proposed by New Alexandria, the cost increase from such a move could exceed 40%. "Given the continuing drought in Earth's northern latitudes," he said....

The instant he saw it, he knew it was a lie: keeping your word was the second lesson every Isitian child learned. Breaking a promise was worse than breaking a window, his father had told him years ago, and nearly as bad as hitting a girl. Isis would never renege on a contract. Not without a compelling reason. Besides, the excuse given was ridiculous: Isis didn't have nearly enough cargo transports to ship a season's worth of grain. It was a matter of simple economics: it made more sense to let the customer risk his own ships to transport a perishable cargo like grain. Surrounded by stormy skies on three sides, Isis had long ago opened its markets to any ship willing to make the run to Zarathustra. And the duty to help feed the rest of Terra was something every Isitian took seriously—far too seriously to sell their birthright for the chance to extort a few meager credits from the starving children of Earth.

Suddenly, other lies started falling into place. And then, he knew.

It was enough to make him sick. But with the stark clarity that all heretics bring with them to the scaffold, he knew.

* * *

STATIC CRACKLED through the speakers with each flash of guns. A battle raged fiercely, beyond the trio of protostars to the east, filling the sky with blinding light. Yet the young stars themselves continued their effortless path through the blackness, and the small, reddish cloud surrounding them raged with fire and interstellar lightening, absorbing the dim lights of the small, mortal struggles raging nearby like an enveloping blanket of night.

"Group Zelda—arc West to 050. We need reinforcements—pronto."

"Zelda Leader acknowledging. Let's go, laddies. Move it—we can't let the goonies push us back. Not when we've come this far. McGee, you take the point; Huslander and Woodhouse take the flank aportside. The rest of you, stay with me to starboard."

"Roger," said Mason, into the security speaker. "Moving into position."

He guided his frigate toward the bright yellow star that was the focus of battle. Ahead of them, on all sides, he saw the death fires of dozens of ships; as they neared the line of battle, he saw that many of them were Terran.

The fighting had been tough, far tougher than he'd expected, and Terran losses were mounting. The gooney skippers were skilled and rugged. It looked like they'd taken the lessons of the lizards to heart. They fought over every inch of space—madly, fiercely, as if possessed by demons. What their ships lacked in speed or hull strength, their skippers made up in pluck and guile.

Still, the goonies were outmatched and hopelessly outnumbered. It would be only a matter of time before the Guard would break the back of the enemy fleet. If he could only live that long, Mason snorted.

"The Guard," he whispered, his lips curling into a wicked grin. He'd lived most of his life cursing the Cozzies and everything they stood for. Now, God save his soul, he was one of them.

As his squadron eased into position, a series of massive explosions dotted the skies around Ballenger's Star. Like any skipper along the front lines, Mason's first instinct was a desperate thirst for information: he had to know what kind of trouble his ship was heading for. Forgetting all about regulations and protocols and security blackouts, he'd even ordered his systems officer to launch a wide range Yankee scan, sending active probes in all directions trying to learn what was happening on the line of battle. Suddenly, the security channel crackled with news, turning his desperation into a raging sense of triumph.

"Attention all ships—the enemy line is breached," came the call from Stark, aboard the *Constitution*. "Enemy forces have broken off, and are retreating from Planet Glan'ra along a broad line."

Loud cheers rang across the *Farragut's* bridge. Mason bellowed a stern command to maintain silence, and riveted his attention on the incoming orders.

"Effective immediately, the Wing is divided into three command groups. Groups Alpha and Omega, consisting of Battle Forces A through D and G through M, shall pursue the enemy from the flanks, under the command of Captain Stewart and myself. Forces E and F, together with all reserve forces, shall comprise Group Beta, under Captain Michaelson. Beta shall secure the planet and provide cover for the Landing Forces. Immediately upon securing the anticenter approach to the system, General von Mueller of the Federal Army will assume command of all landing operations. All ships assigned to Beta shall render any and all assistance he requires during pacification of the planet, until he relinquishes operational command.

"Good fight so far, people. Now let's jam the bastards in the ass, as well. That is all."

"Helm, prepare to come about," Mason shouted over the din of cheering voices, not even waiting for the formal order to come down the line. "Mr. Gleason, lay us a course for Ballenger's Star. The sooner we get there, the sooner we get off mop-up detail. And the sooner we get to go a-huntin goonies."

As if swallowed by the darkness, the whoops quieted, and ship after ship changed course for the planet. As the line of giant troop transport ships eased into their approach—fat, awkward and ugly, five times the size of a starship but with the speed of a glacier and the maneuvering grace of an asteroid—few gave a second thought to the size and power of Terra's machines, or to what they were doing in alien skies. They knew only what their commanders had told them: the Glincians had started whatever trouble had brought them there. And, by God, Terra was going to teach them a lesson.

* * *

From the Trans-Terran Dispatch, 18 March2556:
To the Editor, Trans-Terran Dispatch:

I have read, with more than passing interest, certain remarks attributed to Mr. Nicholas Schiller, currently Chief of Staff to President Heathcoate, apparently concerning, among other things, the testosterone levels of the typical Isitian male.

I can assure him, from personal experience, that he is quite mistaken. As for his comments about our disinclination to join the Terran war effort, I wish to point out that Isis has never shied away from any of her obligations. We do not, however, regard willing complicity in mistakes, misjudgments, and blunders of historic proportions to be part of our obligation under the old Terran Charter. And if he has any lingering doubts about our native abilities to undertake the rigors of military discipline, or suffer hardships for the sake of a cause, I suggest that Commodore Cook could ease his mind greatly on that score, should Mr. Schiller care to inquire about the matter.

IRENE N. McINNIS
Chancellor, Republic of Isis

* * *

"WAIT HERE until you are summoned," said the young lieutenant. Turning smartly, he strutted from the waiting chamber, past the large oaken door and into the marble-trimmed corridor leading to the vast Central Complex.

Turning to view the doorway leading into the spacious Main Auditorium, Cook smiled wryly at the irony. The last time he was here, he recalled, was Graduation Day—the day he left the Academy with an ensign's bar on his shoulders and a head filled with a sense of invincibility. Now, come full circle at last, he stood before the same doorway, no less mindful of his unique gifts but harboring no illusions about the harshness of the Universe or the cruelty of Fate. He had no idea what was waiting for him behind the massive oak doors. For all his talents, his career could come to a flaming end in a matter of minutes, for reasons so trivial as to be the stuff of high comedy were it not for the bitter reality of war. But he found himself oddly indifferent to the outcome, and was surprised to find that he no longer cared about the war, his ship—or even, to his grim satisfaction, his commission. About to face what he sensed would be some sort of tribunal, with his own future hanging in the balance, he smiled to learn that, in the end, there were only two things he really cared about.

He cared about Janet.

And he cared about Home.

Slowly, the door swung open. Straightening to his full height, Cook strode through the entrance. The blue and yellow bunting still draped from the walls, its colors matching the Terra flag. At the base of the great auditorium, he saw three small figures seated behind a dark, massive desk. From his vantage, at the end of the main walkway, all he could see were the heads. As he approached the desk, his footsteps echoing throughout the cavernous room, he was not surprised to find that he recognized the middle head. Drawing nearer, he saw the pure white uniform of a Cosmic Guard admiral with five gold stars on each epaulet.

He didn't know the others; his only clue to their identity was the fact that they weren't wearing uniforms. But the one familiar face told him everything he needed. Cook came to stand at attention six feet in front of the desk.

"Admiral Weatherlee," he said, nodding his head ever so slightly.

"You will address the Tribunal only when invited to do so," Weatherlee replied archly.

"I did not address a Tribunal," Cook retorted, his eyes cold and humorless. "I acknowledged an acquaintance of some long standing—whose presence, like my own, is still unexplained to me."

"Does your mouth ever stop flapping, Cook?"

"From time to time," he said, his own gaze slicing like a knife into his adversary's eyes. "But not very often."

"That is twice that you have spoken, uninvited. You are not getting your defense off to a promising start."

"I would have thought a sullen silence to be ruder, Admiral. I guess rudeness, like beauty, is in the eye of the beholder. In the end, I doubt it will matter very much."

"To my left is Senator Hollenbach, Chairman of the Governmental Affairs Committee of the Terran Senate."

Hollenbach's nodded; Cook smiled coldly and returned the gesture.

"To my right is Counselor Schiller, on behalf of the President. Together, the three of us comprise the Supreme Military Tribunal, charged with examining all cases of insubordination, mutiny, and high treason among the Command Staff of the Cosmic Guard. We are all here today to examine your conduct, Commodore—your conduct during the last days of your command, and what the Guard should do about it."

"According to the press," Cook smirked defiantly, "a medal seems appropriate, don't you think?"

"Be silent!" Weatherlee thundered, slamming his fist onto the desk as his two colleagues tried to hide smiles behind a cough or two.

"Then don't waste my time," Cook hissed. "And kindly tell me what this nonsense is all about."

Weatherlee's nostrils flared, his eyes widened with vengeful delight. "We really didn't have to look very far," he said, his voice hushed and dark. "Let's just see what your own logs have to tell us."

Standing at attention, Cook was determined not to let his adversary see the slightest trace of emotion. The weight of a million deaths clung to his conscience, and he couldn't bring himself to feel outraged by the irony of his present circumstances. But his mind burned with curiosity. He wanted to see what Old Blunderbutt had bouncing around his small, petty mind.

"First charge," Weatherlee said, his lips curled in a tight smile. "Dereliction of Duty in the First Degree—punishment, twenty years in prison."

"What are your specifications?"

"Your own log entries—confirmed, I might add, by interviews with members of your crew—prove that on your recent mission you showed an unexplained and unwarranted hesitancy to attack enemy merchant shipping. Eight times, you waited to permit enemy crews to abandon their ships before destroying them, and you ordered the two ships under your command to do the same. And in one instance, you willingly allowed a major convoy of enemy ships from Girshoona to pass your zone of control. How do you answer the charge?"

"With contempt," Cook replied. "I am a scientist and an explorer. I was a willing policeman, when that was my duty. And I am a reluctant soldier. I am not a murderer."

"Might I remind you, Commodore— "

"My mission," Cook continued, his eyes harsh and unforgiving, "was to establish an effective blockade—which I did. So effective, in fact, that I came to find myself being chased by the entire Crutchtan fleet. I had no cause to kill noncombatants, as long as they posed no threat to my ship, my mission, or myself.

"As for the refugee transports from Girshoona," Cook said defiantly, "I refuse to go down in History as the greatest mass murderer since the Twentieth Century. If this tribunal questions my judgment on the matter, I welcome the chance to air our differences in public. And make no mistake about it, Admiral—our differences will be far more public than any gaggle of paper pushers will ever find comfortable."

From his seat across the table, Emerson Hollenbach looked with fascination upon Terra's most famous warrior. By all rights—stripped of his ship and position, isolated from friends and the flow of events—they should be viewing a man without hope and near despair, as their esteemed colleague had promised. Isitians were just daisy-sniffers, Weatherlee had laughed; and at the first attack, Cook would crumble like a sand castle. Instead, the Isitian's merciless scowl had Weatherlee squirming in his seat.

They should have expected it, Hollenbach reflected grimly: cowards don't win battle after battle. Despite his intentions to the contrary, he found himself coming to like this combative young spacer. The man had backbone—and razor sharp wits, that much they had to give him. Cook was hardly the cardboard legend Weatherlee had described. Hollenbach's doubts about his colleague were growing by the minute.

"The Tribunal will record a response of 'not guilty' to Charge One," Weatherlee continued. "Charge Two—Negligent Homicide in the First Degree."

Cook rolled his eyes impatiently.

"Punishment—twenty years in prison."

"I don't believe this," the commodore muttered in disgust.

"You are charged with homicide in the death of Captain Fitzgerald and unknown others aboard the Starship *Magellan*. Specifically, it is charged that you failed to ensure the prompt and thorough evacuation of the disabled *Magellan*, and ordered your weapons officer to fire upon the ship with full knowledge that Captain Fitzgerald was still on board. How do you answer the charge?"

"I returned to the *Magellan* at considerable risk to myself and my ship, secured the evacuation of several dozen crewmen, and destroyed the ship at the last possible moment to avoid her capture by the enemy. How do I answer that charge? I welcome it. In fact, I dare you to press it, Admiral. It will put your own incompetence on public display."

Silently, from their seats on either side of the CosGuard Chief of Staff, Hollenbach and Schiller exchanged wide-eyed glances. Both knew that Weatherlee was a necessary ally. But both realized that the Isitian's show of resolve threatened to disrupt more than just a sop to someone they needed.

"The Tribunal records a response of 'not guilty,'" thundered Weatherlee, furious at the way this inquiry was proceeding. Cook was doing it to him again, he thought. The very idea of being brought low once more by the Isitian made the admiral angrier by the minute.

"Charge Three—Mutiny and Treason," hissed Weatherlee. "Punishable by death." Under Cook's unwavering gaze, Weatherlee averted his eyes, and then looked to his notes to read the specifications.

"You are charged," he said, pausing to clear his voice, "with seizing command of the fleet at Girshoona and launching a attack on the planet and the enemy fleet, in derogation of all lawful authority."

"After wasting week after week, squandering your chance to move against an undefended enemy planet, you dare to challenge my order to attack?"

"You had no authority— "

"I was the senior wing commander on the scene."

"You were not in command."

"Produce the order relieving me, then," Cook demanded. "And have the wit to acknowledge that my attack destroyed the enemy fleet. The war is over, gentlemen—unless you're too blind to see it, or too greedy to stop. Terra has won the war. And I won it for you."

"I will not tolerate such insolence," spat Weatherlee, slamming his fist onto the desk.

"You mark my words," Cook said coldly, ignoring the outburst. "Terra has the war won—today. But the enemy will keep getting stronger, day by day, week by week. Until peace finally comes, each moment will push victory farther from you and bring it closer to their desperate grasp. Wait long enough and they will rise up to crush you."

"Keep silent!" thundered Weatherlee.

"I don't know when, or how. But crush you they will. It is inevitable."

Weatherlee glowered malevolently. Nothing was going as planned, and Cook was proving more infuriating than ever. Even worse, that damned Isitian smirk was starting up again, darting across the smug, self-satisfied face of his. It made Weatherlee hate him all the more. And it hardened his resolve to teach this particular underling some humility.

"It might interest you to know," Weatherlee said, smiling spitefully, "that our Fleet is already undertaking to finish the task you could not complete yourself."

Hollenbach watched with interest as Cook stared at them—shoulders back, eyes flickering with intelligence and wit. Silent but not subdued, the young commodore seemed to be listening past what was being said, sifting through the spoken words in search of any hidden meaning.

"Even as we speak, the orders have already been given to launch the final phase of the war against the Crutchtans, to annihilate the danger they represent, and to remove all remaining clouds on the horizons."

Cook saw Hollenbach start, and Schiller suddenly turn pale. He surmised that Weatherlee's words revealed more than he intended.

"Those horizons are not, I presume, limited to Crutchtan skies," Cook said bitterly.

"That is none of your concern," Weatherlee snapped. "Not now, and not ever."

"Have you any more charges to level, then? Or do you intend to continue talking in riddles and wasting my time?"

Weatherlee paused for a moment, debating whether to level the final charge. It struck him as the weakest of the four, the only charge they hadn't been able to document with witnesses. If Cook had been sufficiently cowed by the others he'd have simply dropped the matter. But the Isitian's arrogant and self-satisfied arrogant demeanor decided things for him: he'd get in one last shot. If that didn't do any good, he'd keep Cook standing at attention until the arrogant snot begged to be dismissed.

"Charge Four," he said malevolently, his eyes coldly furious. "Dereliction of Duty in the Fourth Degree, punishable by two years imprisonment."

"Specifications?"

"You are charged," Weatherlee hissed, "with improper and indecent fraternization with a direct subordinate, to wit—one Lt. Commander Janet Mendelson, your own Executive Officer. How do you answer the charge?"

This time, to Weatherlee's astonished delight, Cook held his tongue. At once, the admiral sensed that he had drawn blood. Leaning forward in their chairs, his colleagues sensed much the same thing, for their quarry appeared to have lost his edge of defiance.

Lifting his gaze beyond his persecutors, Cook realized how little he cared about the cesspool the Guard had become. He knew little of legalities: they didn't matter outside a courtroom. But he knew at once that they could probably make a case against him, and that he had no stomach for dragging the woman he loved through the mud. He realized as well that his face must have betrayed his thoughts, for he saw Weatherlee's face flare in triumph. He knew that he must make some answer, or be taken by his enemies to be admitting guilt.

"I will defend myself if I must," he said simply. "But I see no dishonor in anything I've done."

Leaning forward in his chair, Hollenbach sensed that Weatherlee had struck the mark this time. The hotshot seemed less confident, less cocky than before. But the senator couldn't believe that Cook would go along with what they had in mind: the commodore simply wasn't the type. Hollenbach cringed to imagine the Isitian calling their bluff: whatever the outcome, dragging Terra's greatest hero through a court martial would be a political disaster. All Terra would take the three of them for fools. And cashiering a hero for dallying with a woman—well, nobody in his right mind would call Cook to account for indulging in a little recreation, even with a subordinate. Certainly, he thought, the Isitian saw this, too. He exchanged a look of apprehension with Schiller, who seemed to have many of the same doubts.

Undaunted, Weatherlee pressed on, oblivious to the pitfalls and dangers that were making the politicians wince.

"Of course, we are not the vindictive sort," the admiral said, his voice filled with a concern so counterfeit that Hollenbach lost any hope that the Isitian would fall for it. "And we'd hate to see anyone tarnished by scandal—you, Commodore, or the Guard. Especially the Guard."

Hollenbach stared intently at the quarry, hoping that their colleague knew what he was doing. He saw Cook's brow furrow intently, as the young commodore appeared to be carefully weighing his options.

But Cook had long since determined what he was going to do. Tactics were all that mattered now: mere details.

"In light of your past service—or, shall we say, what the public perceives to be your service—we are prepared to offer you a graceful way out. A way to retire gracefully from command and still be of some service to your fellow citizens."

"What do you have in mind?" Cook asked, the softness of his voice concealing the direction of his thoughts.

"Our manpower needs are always increasing," Weatherlee continued haughtily. "Those of us with less limited vision know that protecting Terran interests will require a greater commitment, with no lessening of our efforts. And the neutralization process underway in our new theaters of operation will require more spacers to man our ships, more technicians to repair our equipment, and more soldiers to pacify the worlds we encounter."

"Exactly what are you proposing?"

Weatherlee narrowed his eyes hatefully, more certain than ever that he knew Cook's soul. Years of anticipation had gone into the moment. For all his bluster, Cook was small and defeated, standing before them alone in a dimly lit room, with no crowds or toadies to protect him. At long last, smiled Weatherlee, he had the bastard at his mercy. Keeping the little snot under his heel would be the start of the sweetest revenge he could imagine.

"In lieu of a court martial," Weatherlee cooed, his voice dripping with spite, "I will assign you to special operations duty—under my direct, personal control."

The admiral was so busy congratulating himself that he paid little attention to the Isitian's reaction; Cook raised his eyebrows, but made no comment.

"You are finished as a starship commander," Weatherlee continued. "I will see to that personally. But I will permit you to remain in the service, helping the war effort in a manner better suited to your abilities."

Hollenbach stared at Cook intently, hungry for the smallest outward sign of the Isitian's thoughts. Intent on his search, he was taken aback when Cook, sensing the Senator's interest, suddenly turned to look directly into Hollenbach's eyes. Surprised at the unexpected attention, the Senator started. Smiling blandly, Cook returned his gaze to Weatherlee.

His belly suddenly churning like a cauldron, Hollenbach felt a premonition of disaster. He was stunned to discover, for the first time in his life, someone with an equal ability to mask his thoughts.

"Your future duties," Weatherlee said coldly, "will consist of assisting our current and future recruitment drives. You will appear in public to give speeches prepared by my office which you will deliver verbatim. And you will perform any other duties I care to assign you. In exchange for performing this service, all charges will be dropped, and you will not have to stand a trial which would, I am sure, be embarrassing to all concerned."

Looking at Cook's cold, determined eyes, a chill seized Hollenbach's spine. The Isitian showed no sign of surrender, and the senator could almost feel just how little Cook thought of them. He fully expected the Isitian to hurl the offer back in faces; Cook's reply astounded him.

"When would you want me to start?"

Eyes brightening with satisfaction, Weatherlee's lips widened into a broad, beaming grin.

"You leave for Earth in three days."

"Could you please make it a week from today?" Cook asked, pleasantly but without warmth. "I have some personal matters to straighten out, and would be grateful for the time."

"All right," Weatherlee said regally, gloating like a peacock and making a grand show of his beneficence. "But understand, Cook: this is the last concession you can expect for quite a while. You're under a microscope now. Under my personal thumb. Toe the line, or I'll set you spinning in the wind, away from the crowds and the headlines."

Triumphantly, Weatherlee slowly leaned back in his chair. "And that, more than your precious ship or the glory of command, is what you crave most."

Cook smiled. Hollenbach would later recall that it was the coldest smile he'd ever seen.

"I won't make waves, Admiral," said the Isitian.

"See that you don't."

Saluting smartly, Cook turned and strode from the room. Weatherlee turned to his colleagues, triumph on his face. "I knew he'd finally show his true colors," he chortled. "Nothing in the Universe is easier than seducing a whore."

"I'm not so sure," Hollenbach said, shaking his head thoughtfully. His instincts told him that something was dreadfully wrong, but he had no clue what was in the Isitian's heart or head. "You better watch him. You watch him like a hawk."

"Nonsense," crowed Weatherlee, rocking nonchalantly in his chair. He relished the taste of victory, and savored the sweet delight of bending the arrogant Isitian to his will at last. He would long be anticipating the moment when the fallen hero learned the delicious irony about his first assignment—and learned, well after the fact, just where all those the new recruits would be heading, once their training was complete.

"Isitians are a gutless breed," said the admiral. "Cook is no different than the lot of them: lazy, undisciplined, fit for little more than sniffing daisies."

"I hope you're right," said Schiller, breaking his silence at last. "There's a hell of a lot riding on it."

"Believe me, there's not an ounce of backbone on the whole bloody planet. Just watch them crumble when push comes to shove."

Chapter 35

I T WAS SPRINGTIME.

The birds, singing playfully from the trees, filled the air with songs and laughter. Everything was fresh and green; the damp, chilly days of Winter were little more than fading memories, and flowers filled the air with a subtle sweetness, proclaiming the sublime transience of life.

It had been years, Cook thought. It had been years since he'd experienced the wonder of Spring. Perhaps losing his career in the vortex of politics and conquest was no great loss. At least he didn't feel cheated in the exchange.

He walked silently through the open field. Everywhere, New Babylon was alive with budding life. But there were a few chores that still troubled him. He'd ignored them as long as he could, and putting them off had just made things harder. Wordlessly, he kept pace with his companion, a short, balding man of about sixty, whose gait hadn't lost a step in all the years.

"Janet tells me that you're quite a wonder with a spaceship."

"Your daughter is exaggerating, Mr. Mendelson."

"I told you I hate formalities," the older man smiled. "One more time and I'll have to start calling you 'Scooter.'"

"Sorry," Cook laughed nervously. He had no idea how to begin, and he blessed his continuing good fortune when Janet's father broached the subject himself.

"I don't know that I ever liked the thought of my little girl flying about the galaxy on a stream of light. I hate seeing her carted about as bait for some enemy gunner."

Stopping at the crest of a hill, overlooking the park where the women were laying out the picnic table, Grant Mendelson looked over this Great Hero with a sharp, critical eye. The man was a charmer, Mendelson thought—at least when he wanted to be. There was no denying the scope of the commodore's interests, or the sharpness of his wits. But something about this Cook fellow didn't quite add up; there were things the man kept locked inside, like some dark secret. And no daughter of his was going to be left to fend for herself where matters of the heart were concerned. Hero or not, there were some things a father was entitled to know. And if this character wasn't one to be trusted—well, it didn't matter how many friends the man had in high places. Nobody would break his little girl's heart, not as long as he could help it. Mendelson wanted that to be as clear as the New Babylon sky above them.

"I'm grateful to you, Cook. The one thing that's left my sanity intact is knowing that my daughter is in the best of care."

"She's very special to me, too, sir."

"I hope, for her sake, that nothing is in the offing that will change things for the worse. I wouldn't like that, Commodore. Don't think for a minute that I care one whit about power or position. I'll never forgive any man who breaks her heart."

"I've given her too much grief, already," Cook said, his lips tight, his gaze distant and forbidding. "I'd never do anything to hurt her."

"That tells me nothing."

"Sounds like I'm on trial."

"There's a lot of craziness in the air," the older man replied. "A lot of ugliness I want no part of. I know damn well that you're not being completely straight with me. Why?—I have no idea. But if it involves my daughter, I'll damn well get to the bottom of it."

Cook lifted his gaze to look him straight in the eye. Mendelson was caught off guard by Cook's abrupt chance of mood, and stepped back for a moment.

"I'll answer any question you care to put to me," Cook said quietly, his eyes alive with a look of resolve that made Mendelson reluctant to push him any further.

"Just be careful," Cook continued, "not to ask me something unless you really want an honest answer. I'm not in a diplomatic mood. When I'm like this, I don't pull my punches. And there are some things I just won't talk about."

"You're going to be taking Janet back to the war, aren't you?"

"No," Cook shook his head. "That's not in the cards. At least not in the current deck. It might lead to that, though."

"How?"

"Can't say. Sorry."

"What about Janet?"

"She's always in my thoughts—but she can't say either. In fact, she wouldn't even know. She isn't very good at sensing changes. She's always better at tactics than strategy. And she's a bit distracted, right now."

"Her head is in the clouds."

"Mine has been there for years."

"Except that you're going to do what you want, anyway."

"I'm going to do what I think is right. I always do."

"You know, the news services are making your planet out to be some sort of villain."

"Sure seems that way."

"Dammit!" Mendelson snapped, angered by the younger man's habit of turning his answers into riddles. "You're not giving me any straight answers!"

"You're not asking me any straight questions," Cook shot back, his voice calm and controlled.

Mendelson paused for a moment. He never understood Janet's decision to leave home to sail the stars, and hated surrendering his daughter to events beyond his control. All this verbal fencing was getting on his nerves, and he was starting to resent the smug-faced man who held his daughter's heartstrings.

But he'd always wanted her to be happy. And so he waited for his anger to subside. Some people were incredibly stubborn, and Cook could very well be the most stubborn man he'd ever met. But as Mendelson's temper subsided, it dawned on him that Cook was perfectly capable of ignoring him, or fighting back. Yet here he was, calm as ever, waiting patiently for the next question.

Maybe Cook wasn't just being difficult, he thought. The answers, if you could call them that, seemed honest enough as far as they went, though his vagueness was hardly reassuring. And the grudging reluctance to reveal anything was setting off alarm bells in the older man's head. Struggling to give the Great Hero the benefit of the doubt for the sake of his daughter, Mendelson searched his mind for a logical reason for the commodore's evasiveness, and wondered whether Cook might not just be shielding himself from attack. But why? Mendelson thought a moment—and then it hit him. It was so simple, and right before his eyes. No wonder he'd missed it.

"You don't believe any of the stories. About Isis, I mean."

"No, I don't."

"But the proof is in the details. And the details are devastating. Isitians burning their harvest, rather than selling their grain to the starving Earthers. Firing on unarmed merchant ships as they approach the docks, warning them off under pain of destruction. And all the eyewitness accounts—don't forget all that. Somebody's going to a lot of trouble, documenting dates and places. And nobody questions the fact that you Isitians are rather an odd lot of characters. How can you be so sure it's all a lie?"

Cook smiled humorlessly, his eyes flashing with a bitter sadness.

"Suppose you were on Demeter, and the local papers ran stories about New Babylon building a doomsday weapon on their third moon. One which, when finished, would be capable of attacking and destroying planets across the rest of Terra at the touch of a button. The technological fiction aside...would you believe them?"

"New Babylon has no moon."

Smiling distantly, Cook turned his gaze to look down the hill, to where a checkered tablecloth was now spread on the ground. He sniffed the air, and smiled at the scent of barbecued meat as if wafted past them.

"You think the girls have dinner ready?"

Mendelson felt his anger return to a boil. "What does all that have to do— ?"

"I've said too much already," Cook interrupted. "And I think it's time to eat."

As Cook started back down the hill, Mendelson grabbed him by the arm and looked fiercely into the Isitian's distant, impenetrable eyes. "That's my little girl, Cook," he whispered intensely. "I won't have her trifled with."

"She's also the girl I love," replied Cook, returning the glower without the faintest hint of backing down. "Neither will I."

"Just so we understand each other."

"Of course," Cook smiled. "Though it would be nice to say the same about the women in our lives."

Mendelson laughed, though without any real warmth, and the two men started back toward the picnic. As the men neared the food, the ladies smiled and waved, and asked in a mocking tone of voice how they could stray so far from dinner. The men, making some excuse about wanting to stretch their legs, mentioned nothing about their talk.

As they proceeded to feast, Mendelson had the eerie feeling that something big was about to happen. Something that had to do with Cook being here on New Babylon, instead of on the Front where he belonged. And then there were those stories about Cook's planet—and perhaps some other dark secret that was lurking somewhere in the shadows. Mendelson knew he was missing something, and apparently Cook was hardly the type to divulge.

But then, Mendelson thought, such discretion made Cook a rare man these days. And not every daughter brought a legend home to dinner. He'd read enough history to know that her most intriguing characters were often her most mystifying.

* * *

"I HEAR movement."

"They are coming!"

"Silence—all silent. Scouts confirm the approach. All arms take positions. Await my command."

Scuttling to a dense copse of thick, green bushes, Lanash pushed past the prickly thorns that protected the lush blossoms from the ruminants that lived in the forest. He seated himself on a rotting tree stump in the center of the thicket, as sweet fragrances filled his senses. His chest pounded furiously. It seemed like ages since he'd seen a Terran—and back then, the long-noses always seemed to have the advantage. Now, if all went according to the Centurion's plan, they would have a chance for vengeance. They might never drive the Terrans from *Gr'Shuna*; and wherever the longnoses came from, there certainly seemed to be an overabundance. If help did not come from the sky, they would all die trying to free their homeland from the invaders. But whatever the future held for the *g'Khruushtani*, they would make the Terrans' stay as miserable as possible.

He waited in silence under the cover of the bushes. Around them, the sounds of the forest returned, as birds and animals went about their affairs. He felt an irritable prickling in his feet, as instinct told him to flee from the approaching danger. But true to his training and his mission, he held his post. So did the others.

Before long, the birds fell silent again, and the forest was noiseless, except for the sounds of approaching footsteps coming up the trail.

* * *

"DAMN!"

From his position to the rear of the company, the lieutenant came running forward as soon as he heard the enemy laserguns firing up ahead. Rallying his retreating men, he raced toward the sounds of battle, hoping to arrive in time to engage the enemy. His lungs were soon bursting under the strain, but he knew it was already too late for Charlie Squad. Rounding the bend in the trail with the bulk of his company he heard only the rustling of leaves and the whispers of footsteps fading into the jungle.

Stopping to survey the scene, he was depressed to find that he faced it more with boredom than with horror, with impatience rather than anger. It had gotten too familiar to sicken him, too routine to be more than a burdensome annoyance.

Lying in wait along one of the few pathways through the thick underbrush, the lizards had fallen upon his advance team before they knew it. Firing from behind cover, they slaughtered yet another unit, only to disappear into the dense jungle, to reappear whenever the mood struck them.

"Sir?"

The lieutenant turned toward the sound of the voice. It was Buckingham, the unit's radio operator.

"What is it, Corporal?"

"Shall I...."

"Yes—yes," the lieutenant said, shaking his head in disgust. "For all the good it'll do. Radio headquarters and have them send in air cover. Let's level this section of the damn jungle too, for all the good it'll do."

As Buckingham called in the whirlybirds to respond to the ambush, the lieutenant stepped toward one of the bodies, sprawled in the dirt by the side of the trial. Rolling the body over with his boot, the young officer saw the body of Sgt. Pulaski, his face contorted by his agonies of death, his torso blackened by an enemy lasergun.

"What a waste, Tony," he whispered to the lifeless ears of Pulaski, the sergeant he'd known and trusted since the Greloosh campaign. "What a fucking waste."

Soon the roar of aircannons split the air around them, and the surrounding hills were covered with a thick blanket of flame. It was impressive as hell, thought the lieutenant. And it probably gave some measure of satisfaction to the grunts who'd just seen buddies killed before their eyes. But he'd seen too much to think that any of it would be effective.

The jungle was everywhere, it seemed. And the lizards just blended into it. The land was probably riddled with caves and tunnels, and fortified with supplies and ammunition, to boot. Scorching the surface wouldn't do any good, he thought; nothing would do any good. The jungle would grow back in a week. And to pacify the planet, they'd have to hunt down and kill every last lizard on the face of this hot, miserable world. It might have been different on other conquered planets, but the wild stories about prison camps and work farms had spread like a brush fire, even among the enemy. Earlier in the war, the lizards might have let themselves be captured. But on Girshoona, it had been ages since the last lizard was willing to be taken alive.

Waiting for the dust and smoke to clear, the weary lieutenant ordered his men to don their gas masks so the fumes wouldn't overcome them. But he'd long since come to the conclusion that it didn't much matter. Not anymore. It was different in the early days: then, each battle they fought seemed to mean something. They were pushing the lizards away from home. Making the galaxy safe for Terrans everywhere. Now, all the killing just made him numb. He had few hopes of seeing the war through to the end. Just like Pulaski—or Chang before him. Or Benish. Or Mattingly. He was sure he'd wind up sprawled in the mud some day, wheezing his last on some godforsaken patch of ground.

As long as he didn't think about it, he could make it through the day. Then the next day would come, and it would start all over again. So long as a single lizard was alive, they'd see no end to it, he thought. They'd have to kill them all to pacify the damn planet. And the fucking world was too damn hot, anyway.

* * *

"You know," Janet laughed, her voice breathless as the wind rustling through the trees, "I'd forgotten just how blue the sky was."

She stopped a moment to breath the air. The fresh air. It was so—so exhilarating, she thought. She'd forgotten how sweetly the summer blossoms tickled her nose, how the melting dew could make the morning so fresh and new.

"I hate to say this," she continued, closing her eyes and basking her face in the gentle morning sun. "But the chance to see Mom and Dad again—well, it's made me think that even the worst disaster can bring about some good. Sometimes it's more hidden than other times. I'd forgotten just how wonderful home could be."

She paused to listen to the early morning sounds, and giggled to hear a chittersinger, trilling its song of dawn from a distant branch. She used to take walks like this all the time, she recalled. As a girl, she loved sneaking out of the family house in the summer, going up the hill to watch the dawn creep over Cutler's Ridge. The gentleness of nature could be a balm for the soul; she wondered how she'd ever come to leave it.

"Skipper, how long do you think we can stay?" she asked. Her eyes darted about her, greedily drinking in her surroundings. "I worry about where the Brass will send us next. And I do hope they won't send us off too soon. There's still so much to show you—of course, you were here as a student, too, but that's not the same. You have to live in the country to know its moods and its sounds. And we can stay with my parents as long as we like.

"You know, they think the world of you. Especially Daddy. He asked me not to tell you this—and really, you know, your head is big enough already—but he really seems to like you. He admired you for the longest time as a commander. And not just because you were my commander. But he thinks you're the greatest thing I've ever brought home. At least, that's what he told me. Of course," she laughed brightly, "he doesn't know you like I do."

Stopping at the crest of the hill, she turned to tease Cook. She saw at once that he was sad and troubled. It was a mood she'd found did not respond well to teasing—though, like most men, Cook had no scruples about taunting her when she most needed understanding. She stepped to his side and wrapped herself in his embrace, rocking herself gently in his strong arms.

"What's the matter?" she whispered gently.

"I received my orders from Weatherlee this morning," he replied. "It's time for us to go."

Janet's heart sank, and she could feel the tears begin welling in her eyes. "So soon?"

"He's ordered me to Earth. I'm supposed to help dredge up cannon fodder for the Army, and give some speeches about the war effort."

"Earth?"

Suddenly, her spirits started to return. She shook her head, tossing her soft brown hair out of her face.

"Why—Earth isn't so bad. It's only a few parsecs away. We can visit more on our return trip. Or when we get an odd week off."

Cook held her by the shoulders and looked into her eyes. What she saw brought cold shivers to her spine and sent her mind reeling in a panic of doubt. She knew every inch of Cook's face and every one of his moods. She found herself looking into the eyes of a different man than the one who'd started off with her on their walk. His was no longer the kind, warming gaze of a man in love; she saw only the merciless stare of the warrior.

"I'm not going to Earth."

Janet could feel the tears beginning to come. "What do you mean?"

For the longest time, Cook just looked at her. As as the tears kept flowing, Janet suddenly felt quite foolish. But he just stood and stared.

"Something is dreadfully wrong," he said at last. "I don't know exactly what it is. But it's something vicious. Dangerous. Ugly. And I want no part of it."

Taking a deep breath, Cook raised himself to his full height. Janet, feeling quite alone, struggled to say something but the words just wouldn't come.

"I've won their damn war for them," Cook continued, "and that isn't enough. But I've done my part. I'm going home."

"What—home? Where— ?"

"I'm going back to Isis."

Janet could feel herself splitting in two. She felt betrayed and abandoned. She hated him for doing it to her again. And she hated herself for letting it happen.

"And I want you to come with me."

Janet screamed and fell to the ground in tears. "Why are you telling me all this? Just off and leave—you've done it before, you know. I should be used to it by now. Go then! What do I care? What do I ever have to say about anything? Just go and leave me in peace."

"I won't do that."

"Why are you torturing me like this?" she cried.

Cook sat on the ground next to her. Guiding her protesting chin with his finger, he raised her eyes to meet his.

"My orders are to leave tomorrow. I want you to think about it. "

"Think about what?"

"About leaving with me. For home—for Isis."

"Why are you even— "

"I won't leave you. Not until you make up your mind. If not now—if not here—then we'll go to Earth after all, and you can decide there. It'll be a lot harder for us to get away, yet somehow we'll manage. But you have to promise me to decide. Soon."

Janet shook her head free and cast her eyes down to the ground.

"Desertion is a capital offense," she whimpered. "Aren't you afraid I'll turn you in?"

Cook snorted. "Don't be silly."

"My parents— "

"I wanted you to see them again."

"You had this whole thing planned from the start!" Janet fumed, her face flaming with anger. "You planned this whole thing!"

"No, not exactly. At least, not until we got to New Babylon. Not until I saw what this government is becoming."

"What are you saying?"

"I think your father has most of it figured out. Not the details, of course, but the main contours are staring everyone in the face. He doesn't like it any better than I do. I think he knows I'm leaving. And I get the distinct feeling that it's all right with him, if it's all right with you. I have no idea about your mother. All she ever says seems to involve feeding me."

"But why? Why leave at all? And why now, of all times? Just when things are starting to.... "

Cook interrupted her with a bitter laugh. "Oh, things are only starting, that's for sure. The signs are all there, at least unless I'm just looking for ghosts in the shadows. I don't know if dashing off to Isis will do the slightest good either, for myself or anybody else. But I'm sick of war. I'm sick of death. I'm sick of killing. And it's all become such a part of me I can hardly remember anything else."

He paused, and wrapped Janet in his arms, rocking her gently in place as they sat together. The summer wind gusted through the trees, rattling the branches and bringing early signs of an approaching storm. As he spoke, Janet sensed that all of his cold confidence was little more than a facade. He was speaking from his heart, even if he was doing a remarkably poor job of explaining himself.

"Isis is in danger. She's in mortal danger. I can feel it. And I have to go home."

"Danger?" Janet sniffled. "From whom?"

"I just hope I'm not simply going from one war to another. But everything I see around me— "

"Oh, Skipper— " Janet said through her tears, suddenly fighting the urge to laugh, though she knew Cook was being deadly serious. She nestled comfortably into Cook's arms, her head swimming, but certainthat things would turn out for the best. "Maybe you're just being ridiculous, again."

Cook smiled, the twinkle returning to this eyes.

"Well, that just shows the kind of fool you are, sometimes," he said, quietly drawing his hands into attack formation.

"This is being ridiculous."

Suddenly lifting her over his shoulder, Cook pressed a merciless assault on a favorite spot on Janet's bare calves, tickling her as she slapped helplessly against his back and her heartache turned into tears of laughter and love.

* * *

"*AHHHH—* !"

A sudden shift in the warm summer breezes brought the spray from the nearby fountain to the easternmost stone bench in Van Brandwijck Park, in the center of downtown Covington. Springing to her feet, Suzie Yang found her hair soaking wet and her sundress revealing a good deal more of her inner self than she cared to show in public. As she grabbed her brown lunch bag and tried to retreat to a park bench a bit further from the spray, she realized why the bench she'd chosen was the only one unoccupied in the whole park.

"Oh, for crying out loud."

Squishing along the courtyard to a dry spot in the shade, Suzie plopped angrily onto the grass and began trying to squeeze some of the water from her dress. Looking about, she saw birds scrambling madly about, trying to evade the clutches of two small children left to wander the park while their mothers chatted on a nearby bench. Her eyes caught a smile from an elderly man who'd been trying to distribute breadcrumbs to the birds; he looked away, red-faced and embarrassed by his obvious delight at the show she was providing. Taking a deep breath to calm her growing sense of mortification, she tore into her lunch with the subtlety of a starving lioness. She was grateful to have something to help relieve her frustration. Ripping her sandwich apart with her teeth might not be ladylike, she thought. But sitting on the ground, soaking wet with her dress clinging to her like a slobbering blind date didn't make her feel very feminine. She shot an angry glower at the miserable fountain—

And then she saw him—through the spray, walking right across the far side of the courtyard. He carried a small bag in his arms, looking to all creation like a shopper out for an afternoon's stroll. She opened her mouth to shout something after him, nearly gagging on her food in the process.

By the time she stopped coughing, and had recovered her enough of her breath to scramble to her feet, he was out of sight. Leaving the soggy remains of lunch behind on the lawn, she raced the direction of his last known heading.

Of all the times to run across him, she thought to herself as she slogged down the sidewalk. She nearly tripped trying to avoid a convention of baby carriages, only to be caught behind a troupe of feeble old women resting on their canes from the exertion of an outing. Willing herself to remain calm, she was determined to maintain as much composure as the circumstances allowed. She didn't want to scare him off; and if she made a good enough impression—fat chance of that! she kept repeating over and over in her mind—there was no telling how far such a scoop could lead her. She was already thrilling to thoughts of the professional glory an exclusive interview would bring when she realized, to her horror, that she had lost sight of him.

He was nowhere to be found.

As she stopped for a crossing light, the sickening realization of defeat settled on her. She shook her head, angrily berating herself for daydreaming instead of concentrating on the job at hand. Turning briskly to leave, she ran smack into the arm of her target, himself standing calmly beside her, apparently lost in daydreams of his own.

The light changed, and the waiting people started to cross the street. Lagging behind, staying near her target to let the mob clear, Suzie waited until the crowd had passed well beyond earshot before turning to face her quarry.

"Commodore Cook?" she whispered.

Ignoring the greeting as if it were meant for someone else, Cook kept walking until he was nearly past her. Surprised by his reaction, Suzie tugged at his sleeve as he passed, following him to the opposite side of the street.

"Commodore Cook?" she said, her voice more insistent than before. As they reached the curb, he turned on his heels; Suzie took a step backwards, taken aback by the fire in his eyes.

"What do you want?" he said with quiet intensity. His stern eyes quickly took their measure of this rude intruder, and his broad shoulders and commanding presence proclaimed that he was not one to be crossed.

"And what do you mean, grabbing my arm like that? Didn't your mother teach you any manners? Or don't civilians go in for such things, these days?"

"I'm Suzie Yang," she blurted reflexively, surprised at how awkward and defenseless she felt, all of a sudden. "I'm a reporter for UMN—for United Med— "

"I know who you are. I've seen you often enough on the monitors. That wasn't my question."

"I'd like to speak to you. That is—if it's convenient. Or, if not now, then perhaps— "

"I don't talk to reporters," Cook snapped. He turned and began to walk away.

Flabbergasted by his brusque manners, it took a moment for Suzie to recover her wits. Trotting behind him, her short legs strained to keep up with his brisk military stride. It took a few seconds to overtake him.

"Call me a journalist, then."

Without slowing in the least, Cook turned and smiled wryly.

"I don't talk to their snooty relatives, either."

"But— "

"By and large, your attention spans are too limited to see past the next deadline. I don't have time to waste explaining things to you."

Undeterred, and knowing that she'd never get another chance, Suzie pressed on, trying to a semblance of dignity as she trotted beside him.

"Commodore—what are you doing here? Why in the world are you still on New Babylon? From all accounts, there's a major battle forming in the East. Don't you think.... "

"I'm a simple soldier," he said, without breaking stride. "If you want answers, ask the Brass."

"Hey— ! " she said, surprised at the annoyance in her voice, but too angry not to let it show. "I'm trying to *get* some answers."

"Try a different well, Missy. This one's dry."

"Don't you think your buddies deserve better? I mean—you lurking around back here, when they're fighting and dying at the Front?"

"Strolling through downtown Covington in broad daylight is hardly lurking," Cook shot back. "But it's still a free country, and you're entitled to load your own verbs. That's another reason I don't like reporters."

Suzie looked at Cook's clothing—blue twill pants, and a tattered brown work shirt. Plain ordinary civilian work clothes. It suddenly dawned on her that he wasn't in uniform. She stopped to consider what it might mean.

"You certainly aren't advertising your presence," she said.

"I like advertisers less than reporters," Cook called back, keeping his brisk pace toward the center of town.

"So this is it," she shouted after him. "I work the whole war—front lines to back, all the sweat and worry, kissing up to paper pushers from Demeter to points East only to get shoved into the back with the others. And in the end, this is my interview with the great Commodore Cook? Insults and non-answers? This is what every reporter's been dreaming about for the last four years?"

"Afraid so."

"Thanks a lot, Commodore," she called bitterly. "Talking with you is great for morale. I can see why you're such a hit with the troops."

"You're welcome, Missy," he called back as he walked. "For the rest—keep your eyes front and your sides clear, though you might want to trim the tone of voice a bit."

He turned around to face her for a moment, slowing his stride to a slow backwards step. She saw belligerence in his penetrating gaze, and felt the blood rushing to her face.

"You might also try changing clothes the next time you go swimming," he smirked. "And if you want the real story in all this death and destruction, try moving your butt instead of wiggling it."

Cook turned sharply, resuming his pace. Incensed, Suzie picked up a rock to hurl at the retreating figure. Quickly thinking better of it, she threw the rock to the ground and kicked at it with her foot—only to miss, sending a full broadside into the nearest light post and nearly breaking her foot in the process. As she limped back toward her office, she wondered how heroes could be such miserable human beings, and why men were so contemptibly arrogant.

* * *

"H EY, DARLIN '—I'll help fill your cabin, if'n you're gettin' lonely."

Coarse laughter filled the loading dock, and Janet felt her face turning six shades of red. It was bad enough at the start—ogling looks from a dock full of rough spacers always made her feel dirty and abused. Now their taunts were getting too loud to pretend she couldn't hear them. She resolved to remember this moment the next time Skipper suggested meeting him someplace.

Especially when "someplace" was anywhere near a spaceport.

Glancing toward the docks, she snapped her head back toward the walkway when the leader of the stevedores, a short, balding man of about fifty, with a pock-marked face and badly discolored teeth, puckered his lips at her.

Cook was too easily distracted, she thought angrily. Once he's made landfall, he's as likely to wander off, or spend his time talking to an interesting old groundtoad, as to keep his mind on anything in particular. And he needed a nanny to remind him of the time. How anyone like that could run a starship was inconceivable.

She was so busy reminding herself of all the things she was going to tell him that she failed to notice the approach of a tattered, bearded spacer. He strolled up the walkway toward her, carrying an overstuffed sack on his back. As he opened his mouth to speak, Janet nearly jumped out of her skin. Her mind exploded with every story she'd ever heard about frontier women dragged off by strangers, never to be seen again.

"So, what do you think?" asked the bearded spacer with the unusual accent and comfortingly familiar voice.

Bending over to take several deep breaths to calm her jaggled nerves, Janet was livid.

"You're late!" she growled at last. "You're always late!"

"Sorry. I needed the time to finish rearranging CentCom's computers. It's rather hard to do, you know, when they've taken away your security clearance. Still and all— "

"Do you have any idea—?" Janet began.

She lifted her head to glower at the man who'd caused all her grief. When she finally had a good look she found herself laughing, despite all intentions to the contrary.

"What's so funny?" Cook asked, his tone of voice hinting that Janet was being difficult again.

Janet tried looking away, but the moment she turned to face him again, her giggling fits returned. His scruffy clothing and oversized boots gave him the look of a tramp from the poorer section of New Chicago. The scraggly brown swatches on his face looked passably like a beard, she supposed. But the poor job he'd done pasting it to his cheeks and chin made it look like he was shedding his skin. All in all, it would have been enough to make her own skin itch if he hadn't looked so ridiculous.

"I suppose you want me to say that the beard makes you look mature?"

"Actually," he said, looking at his reflection in the walkway window, "I rather enjoyed acting as a boy. Did quite well in the school play, as a matter of fact. I just hope desertion doesn't take all the fun out of it."

"What took you so long?"

"Well," Cook began, wondering just how he could phrase it to place himself in a better light. "I ran into a few—let's call them complications, for lack of a better word."

"Oh no! You mean to say— "

"No, I finally found someone willing to take our tickets to Earth. Which I booked via Athena, with a week's layover in Gaea. Since CentCom insisted that I travel under assumed name, as long as that nice young couple stays hidden, as they promised—and, well, given that they're getting their fare almost for free and without paying any transfer fee to the starliner company, I suppose they aren't likely to risk getting caught themselves. At least, that was my reasoning. We're just lucky that Admiral Weatherlee thought it would be an insult to make us ride coach, rather than having us take a military transport. But in any event—"

"Skipper...if we could just focus at bit?"

"Anyway, CentCom won't know we're gone until they can't find us when the ship arrives at Port Jupiter. And I did manage to log us into the transport here. As passengers."

"Oh—then— "

"Well, sort of. And we're not going Coach."

"That's a relief. Tourist accommodations are so much nicer."

"Actually, Tourist was booked."

"Skipper— ! You better not have— "

"No, no, no. Booking us as Baggage was just a joke."

"Well then— "

"The only thing left was First Class."

"What!!"

"It'll be fun."

"Do you have any idea how much— "

"Granted, going First Class might be more fun if we dared to leave the cabin. Although, now that I think of it— "

"Where did you get— "

"And you can't imagine how fussy those Starliner computers are. Especially when you keep feeding them the wrong credit account numbers."

"We're going to be shot....."

"No, I fixed that. At least I think I did. Of course, I guess we won't really know until we try to disembark at Zarathustra. But you know... for a fellow with an invalid Security Clearance— "

"Skipper—just what kind of trouble have you gotten us— ?"

"Oh, by the way...did you know that CentCom has never actually terminated Jeremy's access code."

"What!"

"Well, mine's gone. Completely, so it seems. And I thought yours would be too easy to trace—although, that's how I managed to get in there in the first place. You know, once you're in the system, it's easy enough to yield access. And that's where poor Jeremy comes in. Once I finally figured out how to cancel the security alarm— "

"That's enough, Skipper. That's quite enough."

"Well," Cook said sheepishly, "it doesn't get any better."

"I don't want to hear any more of this."

Nodding his head mildly, Cook marveled at his continuing good luck. He was actually quite confident he'd covered their tracks. The Security Office would spend the next few weeks looking for him from Earth to Gaea to Ceres. But at least Janet hadn't forced him to admit the real reason for his tardiness. Maps, it seemed, were not placed intelligently in the Capital. At least they weren't placed anyplace someone without a map could find them. He'd spent the better part of the day wandering aimlessly around the streets of Covington, lost as a moose at a glass-blower's convention. He'd probably still be there if he hadn't happened to overhear one young woman telling another how to get to the downtown spaceport transfer deck—which wasn't downtown at all anymore, it turned out, but several miles outside the City and quite impossible to see from ground level unless you were almost on top of it. In the meantime, he'd spent all afternoon walking around downtown, cursing every idiotic city planner and teleportation engineer he'd ever met.

He was relieved to let the subject drop without having to answer any more of Janet's silly questions.

Taking her by the arm, he started walking toward the loading ramp. The ship's captain, a gruff-looking old spacer, stood by the gate, checking his passengers against the manifest. Cook reached inside his vest pocket, and pulled out a travel pouch. He'd taken hours to forge their travel documents, but try as he might, he couldn't counterfeit the precise grade of paper Covington used for their official documents. If they didn't pass muster, it could cost them. And if this flinty old skipper proved too honest to be bribed, it could cost them dearly. Bending toward Janet as they walked, he whispered into her ear.

"Just follow my lead."

Janet nodded. Her eyes darted nervously from crewman to crewman. She wondered whether they could really pull this off, and why she always put such blind faith in the idiot standing beside her. But she couldn't bring herself to regret the day she fell in love.

"Don't do anything to call attention to ourselves," he added.

Standing in line, waiting for clearance to board, Cook felt a wild, exhilarating pounding in his chest. He'd known the feeling often enough, the anxious crescendo leading to the onset of battle. But as he came face to face with the first hurdle along their escape route, and handed over their tickets and identification papers, he realized that this current anxiety had very little to do the with the danger that faced them. It was, he discovered to his amusement, a simple case of stage fright.

"I'm Captain Harriman, skipper of the *Melinda Rose*," said their host, glancing at their travel documents. "You'll be with us all the way to Zarathustra, I see."

"Aye, Cap'n—that we be," said Cook, speaking with an Ishtarian brogue thick enough to stop a laserblast. His tension vanished as he focused on the task at hand.

"The woman hare be taken ill at the thought o'leavin fer parts unknown without takin leave o'her only brother left aloyive—Gawd carse his mis'rable ne'er-do-well hoyide. An' me bein the gentle man I be...."

Janet felt tears welling in her eyes as she strained to keep from laughing.

"Thund'ration, woman!" Cook bellowed, shoving her roughly down the gangplank. "I be seein enough o'your bloody blubb'rin on the ship out from Ceres! I'll be seein no mare of it, or I'll thrash ye from top to bottom—unless ye be givin me the arge to go a-startin just for the bloody fun of it!"

"You'll be in Suite 26-Z," called the Captain after them.

"Thankee, Cap'n, " Cook called over his shoulder. "Just have the cabin boy be slippin our food under the door. We'll not be wantin to be distarbed. At any rate, not for the farst week out."

As the passengers disappeared through the hatch and into the bowels of the ship, the Captain smiled and shook his head.

"A rum weird lot, them Ishtaris," offered the next in line, a portly oldtimer with a spacer's walk and a bosun's scowl. He handed the Captain his papers and smiled nervously: "Isaiah Jones," read the name on the passport; "Occupation: Professor of Literature, Covington University." The Captain eyed him harshly, and bade him pass.

"All in order, Professor Jones," he winked at the young deck hand beside him, a strapping lad in his teens, with the wispy beginnings of a beard and a knowing smile on his face. The young man checked the name off, and motioned for the next passenger to step forward.

"Secrets aplenty with this bunch," the lad whispered. "Like the run over by Portsmouth way, eh? Not a straight shooter in the lot."

The Captain grinned and took the papers from the next one, a young couple with a baby in tow and another one apparently on the way. He passed the couple, winking wryly at the young lady as her load started slipping inside her dress.

"Eyes front, Mr. Phelps," he said, his twinkling eyes mocking the sternness of his tone. "There's the Spacer's Code to maintain. Prying noses are for groundtoads. Just leave the questions where you find them. Someone will surely come along soon enough to pick them up, without any help from the two of us. And if not—well, it's none of our business in the first place."

* * *

"Merciful protectors of Light."

At first, all fa'Shenali heard was the single hushed whisper. But panic quickly spread throughout Control. As he turned to face the overhead monitor screen, he heard himself gasping as well.

They were coming at last.

Spreading across the skies in wide, arching ribbons of death, the Terrans were racing toward the Imperial defensive positions with incredible speed.

Rushing to sound the alarm, fa'Shenali soon felt himself trembling, his heart pulsing in unison with the call to arms. Glancing at the monitors, he realized that the single division of reinforcements upon which their hopes were resting were too far distant to be of help. Truth being told, it looked as if the Terrans had detected the approaching Imperial fleet, and launched their offensive to ensure that they caught the *g'Khruushtani* in weakness. Their meager reinforcements would not arrive in sufficient numbers to render assistance for another six days; the Terrans would arrive in less than two. They would have to make do with what little they had, the young subaltern realized, and wondered how they could ever survive the assault. Retreat was out of the question: they already stood at the perimeter of the Great Basin. Retreating a single astronomical unit would open a half dozen settled planets to Terran atrocities. And if they lost the chance to head off the longnoses before they rounded the Grand Bend, all would be lost.

He was too frightened to think of what might await them. That was a burden for others to bear. His task was only to help ready the Command Tower for the coming battle, he reassured himself. Others would decide the outcome.

Chapter 36

D RA'LENGISH FELT HIS pounding heart ache, even as his rushing blood warmed his soul to murder. Yet this meeting was little different than any other of recent memory, and the words of Ga'Glish only hardened his resolve. The Lord Commander had learned nothing; his mind was frozen in the past. With a final peril looming in the West, there was no time left for inaction.

"He will come at us in one of three ways."

With the intensity of one possessed, the darkened voice of Ga'Glish spoke in the hushed tones of conspiracy. As images of destruction raced through his brain, the Lord Commander pointed a light cursor at the large map of the heavens projected from the domed ceiling.

"He will come through *Kalagicha* Pass; through the *in'Tevisha* star cluster; or here...."

Ga'Glish circled his point of light around a large, empty clearing in the skies.

"Across the *Meduchi* Void, near the Denlubi Vortex. That is where he will attack us. That is where we must face him, and that is where we will destroy him. The tide of battle has turned against us too many times. It will not turn in our favor—Fate herself will not smile upon us—until we have destroyed him."

Dra'Lengish rose from his place at the briefing table unbidden, in challenge to the wisdom and authority of the assembly's acknowledged leader. Around him, he sensed a collective gasp; not a single member of the Command Staff had it in his heart to rise with him, or to join his challenge. But he felt not a single member rebel at the thought. He hoped that Ga'Glish, whose senses were even more acute than his own, would realize just how perilous his hold on command was at this moment. Looking into the eyes of his commander, he suppressed all thoughts of fear and affection for the target of his rebellion.

"As I loved your father, my Lord, you have my undying affection," he began. "But loyalty to our cause requires me to speak my mind, whatever the cost to myself."

"Speak whatever words you dare," Ga'Glish hissed, his mind flaming with rage at the challenge. Dra'Lengish stepped away from the table, toward the center of the room, stopping a few steps away. From their posts by the doorway, the guards readied their weapons in case the challenge escalated out of control.

"Your obsession with the Beast has blinded you to opportunity as well as danger," Dra'Lengish said, circling warily around the leader. "Your mindless hatred has cost us thousands of ships, and millions of lives. You have made it abundantly clear that you will not rest until you have personally extinguished the Beast."

"He is a menace!" thundered Ga'Glish.

"He is but one of many!" countered Dra'Lengish, his hand slowly reaching for the dagger concealed in a fold in his belt. "And he uses your obsession against us all. You are blind to the dangers you create. And you are no longer fit to command us."

"Traitor!!" screamed Ga'Glish. "A traitor from a family of traitors!"

"Forgive me, my Lord," shouted Dra'Lengish, lunging at Ga'Glish with a lost agility born of necessity and plunging the dagger home with all the strength he could muster. The old man's thrust was stopped by the merciless blast from the guard's sidearms, which sent Dra'Lengish half-way across the room to sprawl limply on the floor. Ga'Glish, his old friend's dagger still imbedded in his side, dropped to the floor as well. He was quickly surrounded by a ring of attendants, each eager to attend to their leader now that the danger had passed.

Stirring dimly, Ga'Glish looked at his wound; just wide of the path to his heart, the daggerhead was lost in a pulsing sea of his blood. Numbed by the onset of shock, he felt his head growing dizzy, and he was groggy from the lack of sensation in the rest of his body. But as sensation began to return, he realized what had happened. Though the dagger had missed its mark, the attack had struck a target far more important.

"I will be all right," he whispered to those around him. "Tend to Lord Lengish." A guard knelt beside him, shaking his head.

"He is dying, my Lord."

The word struck Ga'Glish more grievously than the thrust at his heart. With the assistance of his aides, he staggered over to the side of his old friend. Kneeling beside him, Ga'Glish called for a pillow to prop up the head of his stricken Chief of Tactics. Dra'Lengish, looking up at the face of his old master's son, winced from the pain of his internal hemorrhages.

"You were so light on my shoulders as a boy," the old man smiled wanly. "Such an inquisitive mind—and a kinder, gentler little one none could ever hope to see."

"What have I done?" Ga'Glish wondered, emotion flooding his eyes with tears. "What have I done to make you hate me so?"

"I could never hate you," panted Dra'Lengish, struggling against the pain. "And you have spared me the trouble of taking my own life, Little One. I could never live with the knowledge that I had harmed you, whatever the cause."

"Lengish— "

"I pray that you remember—the old Dra'Lengish. Fom the good times...before the war."

"Lengish— "

"Oh— " His head swimming from the effects of shock, Dra'Lengish's eyes fluttered briefly, and he fainted. Moments later, he was gone; and almost at the moment of his death, the alarm bells sounded.

It was the start of the Terran attack.

"Take the body of Lord Lengish," commanded Ga'Glish, "and prepare it for the highest honors of state."

"But—a traitor?" ventured Dr'Bushni, and until that time a serious contender for rank of Chief of Tactics. "Surely, Your Lordship...."

"I will decree the death of any who call him a traitor," thundered Ga'Glish, struggling to his feet. "The fault was entirely mine. I forced Dra'Lengish to choose between opposing duties, and I alone am responsible for his death. His family will know no dishonor. And none here shall speak of this. Ever."

"As you wish," came the reply, from the rest of the command staff.

"Now," commanded Ga'Glish, his voice regal and dominant once again, "to the Control Tower. We have a battle to win."

As he spoke, the lights flickered and dimmed for a moment. As the light returned, the assembly was greeted by the terrified face of a junior aide, frantically pressing the release button on the doorway.

"The power drain—! " the young one whimpered. "The doors—the elevators—!! "

No power would come to open the doors; there was no way out.

"Summon the accursed technicians! We must get to the Tower!" stormed Ga'Glish, desperately trying to keep his growing sense of panic from infecting the others.

But he need not have struggled so valiantly. The others were panicking quite nicely on their own, without the need for encouragement from the Lord Commander.

* * *

"THE TERRANS have passed the *Denlubi* vortex," the monitor for Sector Six said, his voice nervous, his eyes on the edge of tears. "They are halfway through the Void, and we have yet to move against them."

As the flashing lights from the display screens dotted his face, Fa'Shenali's mouth was parched as a barren desert. The only officer on the Command Tower, left behind while the others were off deciding how to repel the long-anticipated enemy attack, he had never felt so isolated. The Terrans would soon be upon them, and yet the command staff remained trapped in the Conference Room, two decks below. The power failure was a transient, a freak accident caused by too many systems demanding too much power simultaneously. It was a fine time to learn that the engineering staff had worried about such an occurrence for many months, he thought, as if concern would undo the damage to their defenses. They were certainly quick with assurances that everything would be back to normal soon, and that they had nearly burned through the reinforced door and that help would arrive momentarily. But it would be too late. The Imperial fleet could wait no longer.

Striding toward the Command Tower, fa'Shenali leaped over the handrail and scaled the entry ramp. His belly knotted with fear, he pushed aside the dithering monitors and technicians and elbowed his way to the central screen. There, the sensors showed the contending forces, opposed in blue and green. Traveling at brisk speeds across the interstellar clearing, the Terran advance was a daunting sight: an endless sea of blue reached out at them from the west like a host of groping, angry animals. Yet something about their lines seemed out of place to the young subaltern. It was not until another voiced an opinion that fa'Shenali realized what it was.

"So now we are left to face the Beast alone," said fo'Rendish, the young technician from *Gr'Lusshe*. "Even our commanders do not dare to oppose him."

"It is not the Beast," fa'Shenali said, surprised by the ring of authority in his own voice. "The enemy force is arrayed too conventionally. Note the *shtarsh'ieps* deployed within each enemy division? The Beast prefers to mass his best ships in the center, where they give a sharper point to his attack. And the advance is too slow, too lethargic."

"Lethargic?" scoffed the monitor. "It looks rather adventuresome to me." The murmurings of the other monitors showed that his view commanded widespread agreement among the menials.

"Their commander is another," fa'Shenali continued, barely hearing the subordinate's differing opinion. "Let us hope that such a blunder will prove to be our salvation."

As he spoke, a large force from the Terran center broke from the main body of the fleet, rushing toward the static *g'Khruushtani* defensive line. Across the Command Tower, voices whimpered in alarm as all resigned themselves to meeting their end within the day.

Numb with despair, the monitor depressed the advance button and looked to the senior officer—the only officer on the Tower.

"All is prepared for the order to counter the Terran thrust, Subaltern," Rendish said, as he had done countless times in the past. "Which division shall lead the advance?"

All eyes turned to fa'Shenali.

Through the numbness of his own fear, a clear voice in his brain called to the young subaltern; to his astonishment, it spoke through the voice of an alien. An enemy alien. All that he had learned, all that he had studied about his adversary—the reason he could sense no pattern, even the reason none could predict the Beast's movements or tactics—in the panic of need, all of this came into clear focus in the young man's mind. Among all the lessons of battle, the great Terran commander had mastered the greatest of all: in battle, as in life, nothing is so terrifying as the unknown. To exploit this fear, one need only do what is unexpected; and to guard against it, simply expect the enemy to do his worst. With self-doubts echoing in his head, and misgivings pounding furiously in his chest, fa'Shenali was surprised to hear his voice rising like a thunderclap in the midst of the general despair.

"No!" he shouted, drawing himself up to his full height, his eyes narrowing in fierce concentration. "Upon my command, Divisions Ten through Fifteen will retreat three hundred transits, directly eastward from the center of the line. Divisions Five through Nine shall prepare to mass along the left flank; Sixteen through Twenty are to mass along the right.

Reserve Divisions One through Twelve will advance to the front lines upon my signal. Ready all to deploy when I give the word!"

Ignoring the looks of astonishment around him as he walked the length of the Command Tower, fa'Shenali refused to surrender to his own sense of inadequacy. In truth, he had no idea if his idea would work: the forces of the *g'Khruushtani* were weak and exhausted. They could shatter like glass at any moment., and could never withstand a direct frontal attack by the Terrans. He knew only that the Beast had lured the forces of *Gr'Lusshe* to destruction by setting a similar, if less clumsy trap. And he reasoned that the Terrans would be just as hungry for victory as the defenders of that lost planet, and could well destroy themselves if given the chance to become reckless. He would later tell his friends and subordinates of his profound gratitude upon finding them too well-trained to think about questioning his orders.

THROUGH THE blackness the Terran lines charged, their neat columns surging toward the churning Crutchtan formations. From his vantage, well to the rear, the Terran commander sensed a great victory in the offing. The confusion behind the enemy lines was evident. And past the outnumbered enemy fleet, he could already see the vast expanse of the great Crutchtan Basin, where the clouds suddenly stopped, and the local wing of the galaxy opened up into the endless, bejeweled skies of the enemy homeland. Once beyond this last turn in the Crutchtan Cloud, nothing could stop them. After they crushed the last remnants of the enemy fleet, all of Crutchta would lay at their feet. For Jefferson McKinley Jones, now the admiral in charge of Terra's great Eastern Fleet, it would be his grandest victory. And, in many ways, it would be his most gratifying, for it would be the first he could enjoy without the second-guessing or one-upmanship of the infernal Isitian.

A wave of excitement gripped the Terrans as the center of the Crutchtan line broke, and then fell back in retreat. They could all see what lay ahead; anyone who could read a starmap knew exactly how close they were to destroying the enemy. And the lowliest crewman on the lowliest ship in the Terran fleet knew that the Crutchtan fleet was near collapse. They could almost smell the blood of their enemy through the great void, and could all but taste the victory that was within their grasp. As they sliced through the skies in pursuit of the retreating defenders, their only worry was keeping friendly ships out of the line of fire.

Suddenly, like trap doors swinging on a hinge, the two prongs of the Crutchtan counterattack plunged into the fight along both Terran flanks. Battling fiercely to cut the Terran attackers off from the main body of their fleet, knowing that they carried the fate of their people with them, the pincers sliced through the distended Terran column and joined to sever the vital communications link between the Terran commander and the foremost half of his fleet. The Crutchtan center then surged forward to attack the trapped Terrans, and along the entire front the Crutchtans pressed the attack toward the crumbling center of the Terran lines. Suddenly beset on all sides, the foremost Terran positions swayed and bowed, each side pressing the fight with inhuman ferocity, each side inflamed to madness by the knowledge that the fate of Crutchta was dangling over a precipice.

* * *

"BATTLEGROUP A is to push the attack toward the left flank—and send a squadron of communications ships to Sector Seven. We need a clear line into the teeth of the battle."

"Yes, fa'Shenali."

Slowly ascending the ramp to the Control Tower, Ga'Glish was amazed at what he saw and heard. Everywhere, the monitors and technicians were scurrying about their duties. The display screens, bright with the lights of battle, cast shadows through the room. And on the Tower—his Tower—the young subaltern stood, a look of horror frozen on his face, steadfastly directing the course of the great battle. Nearly a full feasting hour had been the delay, one that Ga'Glish was certain would spell the doom of his people. Now, seeing the movements on the screens, and sensing the hushed excitement and growing confidence of those directing the operation, he smiled at his own conceit and allowed himself to wonder if the delay might not prove to be their redemption, instead. As his great heart warmed with satisfaction, subordinates on the Tower sensed his return and stood aside to await his bidding.

All except the young subaltern, who stood transfixed by the images on the screen and gripped by the ebb and flow of the battle. Taking no notice of the Lord Commander's return, fa'Shenali continued issuing directives and watching the results return with painful slowness on the monitors around him.

"Welcome, my Lord," said an aide, bowing in deference to their returning commander.

"Lordship," suggested Va'Nazze, another pretender to the rank of Dra'Lengish. "Your forces await. Are you ready to resume command of the Fleet?"

Looking at the young one poised on the Tower, Ga'Glish turned to Va'Nazze and smiled. "It seems to me that the Fleet is in good hands already," he said softly.

Va'Nazze's dismay registered on his face, as well as in his belly. "But surely—surely, you cannot mean— "

"Besides," Ga'Glish continued. "My side is beginning to hurt."

"But he is a mere subaltern," hissed Va'Nazze, his voice thin with panic. "And a commoner! How can one such as he command the allegiance of the Fleet?"

"The Fleet will not care who gives the orders," answered the Lord Commander, "so long as they lead to victory. And from the looks of it, he will not be a subaltern for much longer."

Even as they spoke, the shattered remnants of the Terran fleet were disintegrating before their eyes, fighting desperately to escape from the death trap of fa'Shenali. Soon, the Terran lines crumbled into a slow retreat, and the g'Khruushtani forces began a tentative advance to press their advantage. It was their first advance since the early days of the war.

As Ga'Glish left the Tower, his heart bleeding for the loss of his friend, he vowed that the death of Dra'Lengish would not be in vain. He cried with the pain he knew he had forced upon his old friend, and nearly wept at the thought that Dra'Lengish had to give his life to restore Ga'Glish to his senses. He promised—he pledged to himself an oath of blood—that the future would find him wiser and humbler. Yet his aching soul laughed at the merciless irony, that his own hate had blinded him to hope; and that the means of rescuing his people might have lurked in the shadows forever, emerging into sunshine only by the winds of fate and the bitterness of tragedy.

Chapter 37

THE BLACK SKIES looked the same across the Universe, mused Janet. The stars hung silently in the same eternal night, and the glow of a nearby sun still filled the heavens with life-giving warmth. But gazing out the Observation Deck on Planet Zarathustra's Port Babylon station, she could tell that something was wrong.

Dreadfully wrong.

Since their arrival the day before, she'd sensed tension throughout the station. Now she knew why, and looking out into space sent shivers through her spine. As far as she could see, warships of the Cosmic Guard were streaming through the skies, heading around the planet and toward the giant starbase known as ZarCom, home port of the Western Fleet. Routine maneuvers, according to CosGuard's public relations office—that's all it was. Just routine maneuvers. But she didn't believe it: there were no pirates to bother about in the western skies. And with war still raging in the East, there was no reason under Heaven to mass so many ships so far to the west. Judging from the civilian broadcasts she'd heard from the planet, nobody else believed it, either.

Chilling as the sight of Terran warships might be, nothing prepared her for the announcement that came over the station's public address. Janet had to listen to the message twice, before it registered. Even then, for a small eternity, she was too numb with disbelief to move.

"This is an official bulletin from the Zarathustran Government," came the voice, solid and sonorous over the Port Babylon loudspeaker. "Cos-Guard Central Command has announced the immediate suspension of all interstellar traffic between the Planet Zarathustra and points west. Until further notice, no ships will be permitted into the space west of the Zolahari star system."

* * *

"GRANDPA?"

Seated on a small dockside stool, beside the mooring leading out to his sloop, Will Schroeder put his face in his hands and took a deep breath. The trip to Zarathustra had been hard enough on his nerves. He didn't want to seem worried. At least, not in front of the children.

Everyone told him he was out of his mind, and everyone had been right. But he couldn't stand the thought of his own grandchildren stranded so far from home, through no fault of their own—even if the starliner company that had misplaced their tickets did agree to put them up for free for the duration of the crisis. Even though the wildest rumors were filling every nook and cranny back home, he'd been sure he could make the dash from home to Zarathustra and back again before anything happened. Two weeks there—two weeks back. And then, if the rest of the family wanted, they could chide him for being a foolish old man. They all thought the kids were safer where they were, and wouldn't hear of their father sailing off into the heavens again, like some star-struck boy of twenty. But bitter times were coming; and if they couldn't avoid it, it was best that they faced it together. Leaving the youngsters alone on a strange planet just didn't seem right.

Still and all, he had to admit that they all had a point. It was a thin reed, and close to dotty, the whole thing was. But he hadn't really believed the war talk—all the talk of invasions and such. He thought it so much nonsense from a bunch of dim-witted alarmists. And climbing behind the controls for the first time in nearly a decade—well, it made him come alive again. If he'd turned back after the hour he promised, he knew he'd never have the courage to press on. The trip brought back the sense of adventure he thought he'd lost years ago. And he would have made it, he thought bitterly, if he hadn't been so damn impatient. If he hadn't been so thrilled at the prospect of reaching port two days ahead of schedule that he wound up smashing into a mooring dock. Putting a hole the size of his fist into the hull and scrambling his engines like Sunday's leftovers. Three weeks, it had cost them, and now the borders were closing around them. Seeing the Terry buildup for himself—more warships than he'd seen in a lifetime of sailing—had made a believer out of him. War was coming, he now knew. Coming sooner than even the alarmists dreamed possible.

Foolish old man, he kept telling himself. Dotty as a potter, he was. Now the three of them were stranded—alone, the Universe going mad all around them, and no way to get home. No matter how he wracked his brain, there was no way out. Even if they did get the ship running, they'd have to run the blockade to get home, and his small sloop was no match for the Cosmic Guard.

"Grandpa?"

Schroeder raised his eyes to see his grandchildren—twelve-year old Willie, and little Rachel. Rachel came running up and gave him a big hug, unmindful of the events unfolding around them. It wasn't until he saw Willie standing before him, his eyes wide with fear, that the awesome weight of what they were facing made itself felt.

"Grandpa— " Willie began.

"I heard," replied Schroeder.

"What do we— "

"We'll talk later." Schroeder motioned to the little one, too busy giving her grandfather a hug to notice the worry on the faces of her relatives. "We have a lot to talk about."

Nodding silently, Willie felt his heart come as close to breaking as he could remember. For the last three months, all the time he was stuck on Ceres, visiting this old aunt or that old uncle, he'd wanted nothing so much as to see home again. Now, with the war threatening to come even to Isis, he doubted that he ever would.

"Hey," called his grandfather, reaching over to cuff Willie gently on the cheek. "It'll be all right, I promise. Everything will be all right."

Willie tried his best to smile. But he realized his grandfather was simply being brave. For himself, it was all Willie could do to keep from crying.

* * *

COOK STILL MISSING EN ROUTE TO BATTLE

"*ACHHH*—REPORTERS!" Cook spat in disgust, mumbling to himself. "Hate mysteries, don't believe in facts. They obviously don't have nearly enough to do."

He scratched his beard, now full and his own, and speckled with a few flecks of gray. Scanning stories from three different local news services, he learned that he was spotted either on Earth, or Demeter, or Gaea, and in the company either of uniformed home guardsmen, commando units of the StarHawks, or a gaggle of scruffy-looking anti-war protesters. The broadcast reports were even worse, though Cook found their accounts contemptible more for showing his graduation picture from the Academy than for their inane speculation about his whereabouts. He was ready to chuck the whole mess into oblivion when a small headline near the bottom of the Trans-Terran Dispatch caught his eye: "SETBACK AT DENLUBI" it read. Scanning it further, he found plenty to stroke the petty needs of his own wounded ego.

Jones had finally gotten his comeuppance, it seemed: a full scale rout at the edge of the Crutchtan Basin by an enemy force half the size of his own. From what he could glean from the account, Jones had done it again—split his starships and led with his chin. Only this time, the Crutchtans finally did something smart: suckered him into overextending his middle, then cut it off, wrapped it around his neck, and chased him ten parsecs back along the Cloud. Even the sanitized account released well after the fact made it look like a colossal blunder, and a major victory for the enemy.

Enemy, Cook chuckled, grimly. He shook his head in amusement, realizing that he no longer considered the Crutchtans to be enemies at all. In fact, before too much longer the enemy's face might well be indistinguishable from his own. Glancing at the byline, he smiled to discover he knew the author, one S.L. Yang, whom he suspected harbored no pleasant memories of their own brief encounter. But he was pleasantly surprised by the quality of her writing, and was about to continue the article when a familiar voice seized his attention.

"Skipper!" Janet shouted, running as fast as she could across the concourse. Cook smiled as she approached.

"Hello," he said warmly. "You won't believe what those idiots are doing at the front."

"Skipper!" Janet panted, gasping for breath. "They—they've closed the border. The announcement just came over the speakers. What—what do you think it means?"

"They're going to attack Isis," Cook shrugged. "I've been saying that for weeks. Not that anybody around here listens to me, of course, but—"

"Skipper—stop it!" Janet snapped. "You've been playing know-it-all ever since we left New Babylon, and it's wearing a bit thin, don't you think?"

Cook shook his head, trying not to seem patronizing. When she was in one of her moods, he'd discovered, it was useless to reason with her. On the other hand, if he was going to be in trouble no matter what he did, perhaps the thing to do was just press on and say what he thought, anyway.

"Well, you've seen all the frigates," he sighed. "All the supply ships streaming in. You've seen the maneuvers. And you've heard me go on and on about the lies and misinformation in the papers. What do you think is behind it all?"

"You really think that's why they closed the border?"

"I sure hope so," said Cook, looking over his shoulder toward the big observation window that stretched the length of the shopping mall. "Otherwise, they did it to try to catch me. And though I'd be flattered by the attention, it would be terribly disappointing to know that they'd figured out where we are after I took such pains to cover our tracks.

"Of course," he continued, "our ultimate destination should be obvious, even to an imbecile like Weatherlee. So it seems to me— "

"Me, me, me!" Janet stormed, her patience as frazzled as her nerves. "Some people sure think a lot of themselves, don't they? Well, what do we do now, Mr. Roscoe Andrew I-Told-You-So? Stuck out in the middle of nowhere—no way to get out—no way to go back— "

"I'll think of something," Cook smiled blandly, and returned to his reading. Sensing that Janet was about to have at him again, he immediately changed the subject.

"There's more news from the front," he said, furrowing his brow as he continued the account of the battle. "Looks like the Crutchtans have found a new commander. Someone named Fashenali."

"Is he any good?"

"Quite an improvement, actually," Cook said, scrolling through the article. "At least, according to this account."

"Well, what do you know."

"Of course, I'd still cut him to ribbons," Cook added absently.

"Oh—*of course!*" Janet snapped.

Cook just smiled.

"Seems like your folks' slice of New Babylon is having another spot of wet weather. Says here a rash of thunderstorms hit the northern plains two days ago...."

* * *

AS UNSEEN and unknown events unfolded under distant stars, the first tremors of hope crackled through the ancient skies of the *g'Khruushtani*.

The words were barely discernible through the static. Terran jammers could mask all but the most powerful signals, but this message was broadcast with all the power the forces of His Worthiness could muster, from every corner of the Empire and on every channel along the subspace spectrum. Huddling around the fire, shielded from Terran sensors by the walls of the cavern hideaway, Lanash felt a surge of hope for the first time in ages.

"Terran forces are regrouping for a counterattack, and are expected to make their next move somewhere along the broad front stretching from the Great Cloud to the Yulangi star cluster. But momentum as well as rightness now belong to the Imperator's Forces. All Sons of the g'Khruushtani must remain true to our cause and not lose their faith. We are moving relentlessly forward. We will lose many more of us before the dawn, and the oppressor is still strong and dangerous. But the time of deliverance is coming.

"Do not despair, Sons of the g'Khruushtani. The Imperial Fleet is coming to your rescue, bringing Victory in its wake. Wherever you are, whatever your situation, resist the Enemy whenever you can, and never surrender to hopelessness."

As the words of Gal'Shenga faded into background static, a messenger poked his head around the turn in the cave. On orders from his master, he had waited until the announcement was over before beginning to summon the troops.

"Lanash—Dralen—everyone! Come to the command tent. Our scouts report another Terran encampment over the next ridge. Lord Glishek has drawn plans for another raid. He plans to lead the attack himself."

As they rose, Lanash could feel the cleansing elation of his comrades, and the surging of his own heart at the prospect of battle. Suddenly, he realized how small it had been to be fighting for hatred or mere survival, as they had done these many days before. With the tides changing in the skies above, they were now fighting for their freedom and their families. For such a prize, the prospect of death seemed insignificant. They thrilled to think that each Terran they killed brought them a step closer to victory.

* * *

HE WANDERED the corridors and concourses of Port Babylon for hours, or so it seemed. Lost in thought, hardly mindful of the time or the wary looks of the passersby, Schroeder shuffled his way from one end of the huge base to the other, and back again. Past marble fountains and statues of local politicians long dead, each step he took told him that it was even more hopeless than he'd thought. As he looked up to see the signs point the way back to the mooring docks, he'd finally convinced himself that he was as addled and absentminded as everyone told him. It wasn't the act of a rational man to sail through space in the first place. And if the universe around them was going insane, it was better to spend the little time he had left with those who loved him. If it were in his power to return, he'd do it in a minute. But as he neared the dock where his sloop lay moored, it all came into focus again: the children needed help; they'd have needed help whether he stayed home or not. And if help was his to give, how could he stay behind when part of the family was lost and alone so far from home?

Now, he had a different decision to face. Stranded and alone on a strange planet, what was waiting for them back on Isis? A land gripped by fear of invasion—some waiting stoically to be blasted from the sky; others squawking to maintain their independence at all costs; still others clamoring in the streets for capitulation to Terry threats...until they remembered that capitulation would mean a quick trip to the battlefront for most of the young men on the planet. Squabbling with each other had always been the Isitian way, he thought. It was the reason he'd always hated politics: it was a profession for liars, fools, and incompetents. But now that he'd seen enough of the universe to know better, nobody wanted to listen. Perhaps they were better off staying on Zarathustra. But wasn't that the way for cowards? For if the end were truly coming, he wanted to be with those he loved; but did he have the right to decide such a fate for his grandchildren? It might well be better for them to wait out the crisis here, in relative safety, rather than rushing off on another mad dash, this time leading to destruction at the hands of the CosGuard blockade.

As he struggled to decide what was right, he turned the corner leading to his dock. Suddenly every hair on his body tingled with alarm.

He'd left young Willie in charge, but they were no longer alone.

Willie was busy, just as he'd left him—tinkering with the ship.

But now, there was a stranger on their part of the dock.

A bearded stranger, poking about the insides of their only hope for home.

"What's going on here?" Schroeder demanded, his suspicions rising. The last thing they needed was some scruffy-looking outlander nosing around their ship. If they were going to stay put, they needed no interference. But if the Government was trying to round up all the Isitians it could find, they'd need no more excuse than catching them in the act of trying to return home.

"Who is this?"

The stranger turned to face his interrogator. Something about him seemed familiar, Schroeder thought; something about the eyes. But he dismissed the thought as soon as he heard the stranger's accent.

"I'm a friend," said the stranger, speaking in a Northlander accent too pat to be other than contrived.

"A friend, eh? What's your name, friend?"

"Can't say."

"Where are you from?"

"Can't say that, either. Sorry"

Sensing that things were going badly for his new friend, young Willie stepped forward to speak.

"He knows a lot about ships. Grandpa. A whole lot. He says he can fix the engines, and we're halfway done already. We'll be ready to leave in another day or two, he says."

"We don't need any help," Schroeder said, staring coldly into the stranger's impenetrable eyes.

"Oh, yes you do," the stranger said, a tight smile crossing his lips. "You don't have the tools to reconfigure an engine. And I doubt you have the know-how to recalibrate your subspace accelerator from scratch."

"We might just surprise you."

"Meanwhile, you need to get home, and I need to come with you."

"Not interested," Schroeder snapped. "Now if you'll just excuse us...."

"Then I'll buy your ship," the stranger replied calmly. "How much to you want for it?"

"It's not for sale."

"But Grandpa— "

"That's enough, William."

"*Grandpa—!*"

"That's enough!" Schroeder said angrily. "We don't know who he is, or what he wants."

"We want to go to Isis," the stranger interjected, "my fiancée and I."

An uncomfortable young woman stepped out of the shadows, smiling nervously and holding little Rachel by the hand.

"She's real nice too, Grandpa," volunteered Rachel.

"Who are they?" Schroeder demanded of his young grandson. "Who are they, that you'd have us risk prison on the chance they aren't federal agents?"

The boy looked down and said nothing.

"And who said anything about going to Isis?" the elder Schroeder snapped at the stranger. "The border is closed. Or haven't you heard?"

"Seems obvious enough to me," the stranger shrugged. "Your ship markings are Isitian. The charts I've seen inside are of Isitian skies. Even your accents are Isitian."

"And yours?"

"It's genuine," the stranger smiled. "A little watered down over the years, perhaps, but real enough."

"No, you're too easy with the answers. And I'll have nothing to do with anything—anything—that will put my family in danger."

"You'll be putting them in danger if you try to run the blockade," came the grim reply. "As for my answers, I'm only telling the truth. Or, so much of the truth as it's safe for you to know, just now."

Angrily, Schroeder glared into the stranger's stubborn, unshakable eyes.

"And you just want to help. You can guarantee our passage, to wherever we want to go."

"I can guarantee nothing, except that your chances of getting home are better with me than without me. Much better."

Struggling to maintain his composure, Schroeder mulled over their prospects. The stranger did have a point, he thought: they could try to run the blockade, but Schroeder knew they'd never make it. In his younger days, perhaps. But now his eyesight was too dim, his reflexes too slow.

"Then tell me who you are," he said at last, staring defiantly into the stranger's eyes. "So I can run a check to satisfy myself that you're not a federal agent."

The stranger smiled sadly, but shook his head. "My friends call me 'Skipper.' Beyond that—I can't, and I won't. It would place you in too much danger if we're caught before we leave, and I won't risk it."

"So it's for our own good that you won't tell us anything?"

"That's right."

"The answer is no."

"Grandpa— "

"You're making a mistake, Old Timer," the stranger said gravely.

"Maybe," Schroeder shot back. "But you look me in the eye and tell me I'm being a fool." Much to his surprise, the stranger actually paused to consider the point, furrowing his brows for a moment as he mulled the problem over. Soon, the edge returned to his eyes, and the stranger returned Schroeder's steady gaze.

"I can't honestly say that," came the reply. "But you're still making a mistake."

"And if our situations were reversed—if you were the one with the ship, and we were trying to hitch a ride—I suppose you'd open your door to us in a minute."

The stranger paused once more; this time, Schroeder found the reply astounding.

"Actually, if our situations were reversed I'd be in no position to offer you a ride."

"*What!*" exclaimed the young lady beside him, her eyes flaring in genuine outrage. "Have you lost your mind—*again?* What are you saying? And just what do you think you're doing?"

Exasperated, the stranger turned to face the sputtering woman. "This is no time for dishonesty, Janet," he said. "And my mother didn't raise her son to lie to his elders." When his gaze returned to the older man, Schroeder could feel the stranger's eyes penetrating into the inner reaches of his mind.

"Besides," the man continued solemnly, "if our situations were reversed, our moral dilemmas would be considerably different."

Schroeder felt his eyes widening. A cold chill ran the length of his spine as everything fell into place: the mysterious press reports, the stranger's half-hidden secrets—even the Northlander accent. All at once he knew exactly who was standing before him, searching for a ride and desperately needing his help.

Suddenly, the old man knew that he'd move heaven and earth if he could, to get the stranger home.

Or he would die trying.

* * *

TWO DAYS later, a scruffy-looking spacer walked toward a postal kiosk, trying his best to look nonchalant.

Checking to make sure nobody was watching, and feeling very much like a spy in one of those Old Earth thrillers, Cook took a piece of paper from his vest pocket. He wanted to read it once more before sending it off; mostly, he didn't want to embarrass himself by sloppy spelling.

cc:144-6136.8
S.L.Yang
United Media Network
UMN Building
Covington, New Babylon

Dear Miss Yang:

Enclosed is the key to a mystery you may find intriguing. It will open a locker in Concourse C on the Port Babylon Station circling the Planet Zarathustra. I hope you choose to come and get it yourself, for the contents are too bulky to take with me, and it would be a shame if they fell into the wrong hands.

If I have judged you correctly, and you have the wit to guess my identity, I wish to apologize for my rudeness when we met some time ago. I hope you never learn how disillusionment can make you cynical, nor stop trying to discern truth from the chaff of human existence.

Sincerely,

one who chooses to remain anonymous, but who would gladly

Replace his Anger with Civility, if he could undo the past.

PS—Because I set the timelock on the locker not to open for a solar year (for reasons that should be apparent if you ever come to open it), I have paid for the locker through the end of the next year. If you come later than that, the manager won't release the contents unless you pay him any past due rental. Come to think of it, I wouldn't be surprised if he attempts to double his fee, and tries to charge you anyway. Whether you choose to pay him is up to you, of course, but I think it would be silly to come all this way only to go home empty-handed. Should you insist on pressing the matter, we can settle our accounts if we ever meet again.

In any event, I trust to your discretion and judgment in deciding what to do with the materials you will find. And I apologize in advance, if you find that they become a burden, rather than a source of enlightenment.

Cook placed the key inside and sealed the envelope. He checked one last time to make sure he'd placed enough wrong delivery codes to keep the letter shuffling around the whole of Terra for the foreseeable future. And then he placed Fourth Class postage on the package and slipped it into the "Surface Mail" delivery slot. Stepping away from the mailbox, he continued down the corridor, heading back toward the docks.

Actually, it should get there in about a year, he smiled to himself. If it's a good year for the Post Office. In any event, it should give him plenty of time. Still and all he was, to put it bluntly, being muddled. Muddled and self-righteous. And, he had to admit, insufferably egotistical. But he was sure that any attack on Isis would come long before then. If the reporter lacked the curiosity to come—well, they wouldn't have room to store it all on the *Lucky Lady*, anyway, and he hated the thought of destroying a career's worth of log entries and memorabilia. Especially the last entry, detailing what had happened to him since losing his command. Better to try giving them to someone who'd know how to use them. Besides, he thought, it would be fun to think about all the mischief he'd be causing. Rounding the corner, he grinned widely to see Janet, her arms stuffed with packages and foodstuffs for the trip, still waiting for him and impatient as ever.

"You're being foolish, Skipper."

"*Achhh*—I don't put stock in the short-sighted approach, Missy. It's not very Isitian."

" 'Not very Isitian.' You say that whenever you're trying to justify doing something silly."

Laughing softly, Cook took her by the arm and led her toward the dock where the Schroeders were busy trimming their ship to set sail.

"You know," he said, "someday you may just get the hang of living on Isis, after all."

"I suppose helping a lady with her arms full isn't very Isitian, either."

"Oh—right. Sorry."

//!!/COMMAND ALERT:
  cc: 144-6140.5/
  TO: CommandingOfficers-WesternFleet/
  FROM: CosGuardSecurityOffice, CentCom/
  SUBJECT: Classified, Code 019XJ23ZZ6/
  SECURITY CodeBlue/
  PREFIX: Need-to-Know,Eyes-Only/
  FLAGS: red1;red2;red3/
CSO suspects Subject on or en route to Planet Zarathustra, bound for renegade Planet. Best guess is that Subject will arrive Zarathustra circa

144-6145, at Port America or Port Babylon stations. Given near certainty that Subject is traveling with forged documents, all entry points are cautioned to check travel records carefully.

Given current state of WF preparations for offensive action, and Subject's known sympathies for the renegades, it is imperative that Subject not reach Isis. All commanders in the vicinity are ordered to intercept and interdict all unauthorized ship movements in the direction of Planet Isis, without exception and at all costs.

Commanders are further directed not to accept Subject's surrender, once he passes beyond civilian jurisdiction. Subject fled to escape court martial for treason; due to likely effect on civilian morale, CSO CentCom strongly advises that his apprehension and trial are not in the national interest.
ENCRYPT/TRANSMIT//

Chapter 38

HEADING EAST FROM Port Babylon, a small convoy consisting of ten merchant freighters and a half-dozen sloops and schooners started a leisurely sail toward the Planet Earth, passing from ZarCom's traffic control zone on cc:144-6144.2. Two days later, one small sloop began lagging behind the others; and on the third day, the rest of the party lost sensor contact. A CosGuard frigate, dispatched to investigate and assist, combed the vicinity for two whole days to no avail, before reporting the ship lost. The next day, ZarCom logged the *Lucky Lady* out of Westport as lost in transit and presumed destroyed in the asteroid field six parsecs east of Zarathustra. The incident would have passed without further notice if a sharp-witted young lieutenant in the CosGuard Security Office, specially assigned by the Chief of Staff to watch for just such an occurrence, hadn't remembered that Westport was one of the three civilian spaceports circling the Planet Isis.

Scoffing at the young officer's speculations, ZarCom's veteran commander declined to scramble his ships just to hunt for one missing sloop. He told the young lieutenant in no uncertain terms that the safety of the entire sector was more important than a single ship. After all, they needed the frigates to maintain the blockade and respond to real emergencies. And so the ambitious lieutenant reported his findings through the Security Office chain of command.

The next day, the commodore's replacement gave the necessary orders, and the entire Western Fleet was deployed to find the *Lucky Lady* that same day. Two days later, a phantom blip on a subspace radar screen briefly showed the barest trace of westward movement near the Donnelly Shoals before fading into the background static, and the six Terran warships patrolling the sector quickly moved to converge.

THE BRIDGE of a sloop was small by CosGuard standards. Twelve feet long, and about twenty feet across, consoles and monitors stretched from

one side of the ship to the other and along the sides. until they met over
the archway leading back to the hold and the living compartments
beyond. The critical screens were all arrayed in a small semicircle around
a central chair, where the pilot could see his surroundings, position, and
heading—as well as the ship's vital signs—all at a glance.

On the *Lucky Lady*, two ragged sofas lined the sides aft of the
command chair, a concession that Will Schroeder had made to creature
comforts during his sailing days. They would have formed a comfortable
sitting area, except for the fact that they hadn't been cleaned in ten years.
With the sofas and the collapsible stools from the cabins, there was room
for everyone on board to gather on the bridge during the long passage
between stars. And once Cook put everyone to work bringing the bridge
to proper trim—scouring the control panels and dusting the monitor
screens, clearing the desktops of clutter, and polishing the wooden hand
rails and walkway molding—the charm that the ship had once known
began to shine through once again.

Janet wasn't used to seeing Cook take such an interest in appearances.
She still had to pick up his discarded clothing from the floor of the cabin
they shared, and he seemed congenitally incapable of putting anything
away by himself. But a ship was, after all, a ship; and once a Skipper,
always a Skipper. She did not, of course, give him any less grief about his
personal sloppiness, but resolved to try not to take his failings personally.

"Still no sign of the Terries, Willie?"

"None, Grandpa. Sky's clear as crystal."

"Keep a close watch, now. We don't know where they'll be coming
from. And we don't want to be taken by surprise."

Lounging on one of the newly cleaned sofas, luxuriating in the fact that
the helm was not her responsibility, Janet smiled at the sight of Schroeder
and his grandson taking their duties so seriously. Outside, the stars hung
like jeweled lanterns lighting the heavens, and the bright ribbon of the
Milky Way stretched across Creation. But with their eyes glued to the
screens, the Schroeders were fretting like a pair of mother hens over
matters quite beyond their control. She decided it was time to help them
relax. Besides, she was curious about the world to which the Skipper was
taking her.

"What's it like?" she asked. Schroeder turned, confusion in his eyes.

"What's what like?"

"You know," Janet laughed. "Isis. Skipper's mentioned it often enough but he's never told me anything about it. I mean, nothing that makes the slightest bit of sense."

Schroeder shrugged. "Same as any other place, I guess," he said at last. "People squabble like they do anywhere else. Kids sass their parents, young couples fall in love. Right now, everyone is scared to death of the Terries."

"It's very green," volunteered young Willie. "With mountains and fields and seashores. And miles of sandy beaches. And in the outcountry— "

"The outcountry?"

"The unsettled continents."

"*William!*"

"Unsettled continents? I don't understand."

"We call it Virgin Isis," Schroeder explained. "And we don't talk about it much. At least not to outsiders."

"But— "

Schroeder sighed, then turned his chair to face the pretty young Outworlder. She'd soon be one of them, he thought, and she'd learn soon enough.

"We've settled only one of our six continents," he continued, "only New America. The rest we've left as wilderness—except for isolated settlements, mostly for research or scientific exploration."

"One! I'd heard you'd left a lot of it alone. But what in the world—"

"It's a big planet," he interrupted. "At least, it seems that way when you're walking around on it. And Isis doesn't have very many people. We don't need much room for ourselves. We consider ourselves guests on the Planet—trustees, if you prefer. We don't like to waste what we have. That's the mistake Earth made and you can see what's become of her. We take no more than we need and try not to need more than we can replace. And we can't think of a single reason to disturb the wilderness any more than we have to."

"We don't want to disturb the Ancients."

"William!"

"The Ancients?" Janet whispered. She had nearly forgotten the tales of the artifacts and ruins that dotted Terra's westernmost planet.

"Well, we still use some of the ancient constructions as our underground transportation network. And it will make a fine shelter, if the Terries actually do come for us. As for the rest...well, legends abound, including one that holds that the Ancients are still with us, in one form or another. But that's mostly for the children."

"*Grandpa—!*"

The edge of panic in Willie's voice could only mean trouble. At once, Janet was on her feet and staring at the controls.

"Starships!" Willie shouted. "Starships abaft to starboard."

"Those are frigates," Janet said, her eyes narrowing in alarm. They were on an intercept course, heading at flank speed right for the *Lucky Lady.* Janet knew at once they were in for the run of their lives.

"Well, I think they're starships!" Willie protested. "Six of them."

Janet turned to Schroeder; she could see the fear in his eyes, and could feel his anguish at subjecting his grandchildren to such danger.

"Fetch the Skipper," she said.

"And don't worry," she added, with more confidence than she actually felt. "He'll get us through."

* * *

"BOGEY HEADING 790, north twenty degrees. Number Two, do you copy?"

"I copy, Red Leader. Looks like a merchant ship. Schooner or a sloop, I'd say. On that heading, she's definitely trying to skirt the blockade."

"You guys think it's him, too?"

"Can the chatter, Number Six. We're not to discuss it."

"Bogey's speed and heading are constant. I don't think they've spotted us yet."

"Three and Four, break off and circle round her left flank. The rest of you follow me."

"Roger."

"— roger and out."

"RIGHT THERE! Starships!"

Cook glanced at the screen and shook his head.

"Frigates," he corrected.

"Why do you two keep saying that? How can anybody tell—"

"Practice, Willie," Cook smiled. "Years of practice."

Wiping the soap from his freshly shaved face, Cook dropped the towel onto the floor and glanced out the viewport. This was not the stretch of space he'd have chosen to make his dash for it, he thought, but there was no use griping about it. They were five parsecs from the nearest decent-sized bank of clouds, and the surrounding skies were disturbingly clear of shoals and other debris. If they were going to escape, they couldn't try to lose their pursuers; they'd have to outmaneuver them.

And outwit them.

"All right," Cook said, the firmness in his voice admitting no room for debate. "Let's get this ship on alert footing. Rachel—get to your quarters and stay there. Pretend that we're on a giant roller coaster ride. That's just what it's going to feel like.

"Willie, you stay here on the bridge with me. We may need a gofer between here and engineering."

"Engineering?"

"Well, the engine room," Cook said impatiently. "Mr. Schroeder, your station is in—in the engine room. I rewired the ship to pump more power into the shields, but everything must be done manually. Cut power from the weapons now, and stand by to cut from navigation to shields, and back again, precisely on my command. Timing will be critical, and I'll alert you as best I can. But do things exactly as you're told, and as precisely as you can manage."

"You're crazy!" hollered Schroeder, agitated and on the edge of panic, and more than a little bit aggravated at having his ship taken from him so effortlessly. "No weapons? We're facing six friggin' frigates and you want to turn off our weapons?"

Cook's voice was stern and dispassionate. "We can't outgun a service ship, and we can't outrun them," he said coldly. "We can outmaneuver them, if we somehow manage to stay alive. The way to do that is to boost the shields.

"Now—Aft, Mister!"

Sullenly, reluctant to admit defeat but painfully aware that there was nothing he could do about it, Schroeder began stepping slowly toward the stern. "I sure hope the hull can take the stress," he muttered. "It's not built for fancy sailing, you know."

"Well, then that's just the way it goes, Old Timer," Cook shot back. "In the meantime, you have your assignment."

Schroeder shook his head. "I still don't see— "

"Janet!" Cook interjected. "Take him astern—and then stand aft. Stand on top of him, if you have to, but I need that extra edge. I want you there in case I need more work done on the engines. And I need you to keep all the dials and gauges in the safety zone."

"I'm not an engineer, Skipper," she protested. "Anyway, I belong on the bridge."

"Just what we need. Another prima donna."

"Well—just who's the helmsman here, anyway?"

"Aft!"

"Skipper! You steer like a—a *navigator!*"

"Aft!!"

"*Skipper*—!!"

"Aft, *Missy!*" Cook snapped angrily.

Her eyes bulging with rage at being relegated to babysitting duty, Janet stormed toward the engine room. Shaken by the exchange, Schroeder tagged along behind, finally catching up to her at the hatchway.

"What's that mean?"

"It means he's being a jerk," Janet snarled.

"But what does he mean, 'that's the way it goes'?"

Mindful that the old man was not used to the stark realities of combat, Janet would later wince at her harsh words. For the moment, she was too angry with Cook to play diplomat for him.

"Well," she whispered impatiently, "if the ship falls apart, then that's the way it goes."

"But that would mean— "

A sudden chill of cold fear seized Schroeder's spine. Seeing the look of terror in his grandson's eyes as the boy looked down the corridor after him, it was all the old man could do to keep from crying himself.

"Yes," Janet said coldly, opening the hatch and standing to one side. "That would simply be the way it goes. Now, after you, if you don't mind. The Skipper will have us both growing new hides if we dawdle out here any longer."

"SO WHAT do you think, Larry?"

"I think I don't want to discuss it."

Lt. Commander Larry Sadler looked at his control panel. They must have seen them by now, he thought, but the sloop hadn't varied its course one whit. Its pilot was either crazy, or one cagey rascal. And the numbness in his stomach was betting that the pilot wasn't crazy.

"I think it's him," said the navigator. "I really do."

"You're not listening to me, Ken."

"Well—the blockade itself sent the fear of God into the 'Sissies, and this is the first one trying to make the run to Isis since then. On his own, yet. You draw your own conclusions, if you want, but— "

"Ken, shut up."

"Aye, sir."

Fidgeting nervously in the comfortable, contoured command seat, Larry gazed silently at the screens, but was paying little attention to the white blip on the monitor—nor to the bluish tertiary system off to port, nor to small binary system they were approaching off to starboard. He knew his job well enough to perform it without a second thought. That's what all those years of training were for, he told himself.

But still he kept hoping against hope—hoping that the dispatch was a hoax; that he would awake within minutes, with a delicious liberty girl by his side. Mostly, he hoped that the pilot they were chasing wasn't Cook, after all.

He had admired Cook for years—from his own first days at the CosGuard Academy, when he'd seen all the ribbons and medals and plaques bearing Cook's name, to the days when Cook was unstoppable along the battlefront, claiming victory after victory, in battle after battle. The Commodore was a gifted man, Larry thought. Gifted and irreplaceable. Though sworn to do his duty, Larry hated the thought that he would be the one to bring the commodore down. And Larry clung stubbornly to the thought that maybe—just maybe—this was all a mirage; that Cook wasn't a traitor, after all; and that all of this was just a drill.

But in his heart he knew just how real everything was. A dream, even a nightmare, wouldn't have the sweat and exhilaration of a real pursuit. And a voice kept telling him that there was, after all, only one Isitian who would dare to pit a small sloop against a Cozzie blockade.

The readings on the subspace radar screen blipped routinely, showing that their target was still keeping a steady heading. Suddenly, a voice sounded over the ship-to-ship speaker. "Red Leader, this is Red-5, over."

"Go ahead, Number Five."

"We're coming into position. Do you copy? We are coming into position. Over."

"I copy, Red-5. All ships, this is Red Leader. Assume battle formation. Prepare to attack on my command. We're going in for the kill."

"...TO UNIDENTIFIED craft heading 790 over 20. You are ordered to come about immediately. Repeat, you are ordered to come about immediately."

Squirming uncomfortably in his seat, Willie felt beads of sweat forming on his forehead. Frightened as he was, he was amazed to find that now that the Terries were actually bearing down on them, he was less afraid of dying than he was terrified by the unknown. If he ever lived through it all, he marveled, he could honestly say that staring through space into the eyes of death was the most exciting experience of his life.

Of course, he thought, it wasn't the sort of thing he wanted to do every day. But just the same....

"CosGuard Frigate *Valpariso* to unidentified craft heading 790 over 20— "

Willie's voice was breathless and shallow. The unremitting broadcast from the Terrans was beginning to get on his nerves. "Shouldn't we do something about the message?"

Sighing harshly, Cook reached over and switched off the subspace radio.

Willie was astounded. "Shouldn't you—I mean, don't you want to respond, Skipper? I mean—we don't want to make them mad, do we?"

"They're already mad."

"But— "

"Eyes front, and quiet on the bridge."

Cook eased back on the throttle, and started edging slightly toward starboard. He expected a ship or two along his port flank, and reasoned that they wouldn't expect him to dart right into the thick of things.

"Watch the power display for signs that they're sending a charge to their weapons," said Cook. "That's very important, but that's all you have to do. On these screens, the charging frigate will register as a yellow light, becoming redder and redder as the charge gets stronger. I've already programmed your ship's computer to signal with a beep when they start the discharge sequence. But I don't like putting my life in the hands of a machine that I haven't tested. So if you see a yellow light, let me know at once."

Willie nodded. "I'll try."

"No," Cook snapped. "Don't try—do it."

Cook checked his portside monitor: there were two frigates, appearing just as expected. He opened the intercom to the engine room.

"Janet? Can you hear me?"

"Loud and clear."

"Stand by, down there."

"Try not to bounce us off the walls, Skipper," Janet replied tartly. "It's bad for morale—mine included."

Cook chuckled grimly. "No promises, Missy. Just keep the line open, and hold the chatter back there to a minimum. No telling what I may need, and I want you two paying attention when I need you."

"Yeah, right."

"And stow the moodiness, Engineering. We've got a spot of rough bother coming ahead. I don't need any malcontents on board."

* * *

AS THE six larger craft converged on their small quarry, the first of the many rocky shoals littering the skies on the way to Isis started coming into view, far in the distance. Irregular in shape, all were formed of the same rocks that menaced navigation, and the same ices and gasses that fouled sensors and made peering through the hazards a physical impossibility. As the small sloop sliced through the heavens, her pilot found himself winding his way through the same obstacles that had amused him as a young boy steering his grandfather's ship by sight and touch and instinct. The sensations of youth flodded his memories as he returned to the skies of his childhood.

But this time, the villains were real.

And so were their guns.

WITH THE first sound of the warning buzzer ringing in his ears, Cook cut the throttle sharply. He didn't notice the tardy sound of Willie's voice warning him of the impending attack. With less than a second to complete his maneuver, he fired the ship's starboard maneuvering thrusters, coming about sharply as far as the ship would take them. Sensing that the lead frigate's guns were about to discharge, he fired the throttle amain and darted off, having changed his heading by nearly forty degrees. The frigate's blast registered harmlessly in the blackness of space. Racing the shock waves from the salvo, the *Lucky Lady* veered off, heading toward the nearby binary system looming off to starboard.

"Where's the warning shot?" asked Willie. His mouth was bone dry, and his voice quivered timidly. "Aren't they supposed to fire a warning shot?"

With the next blast from the warning buzzer, Cook swung the sloop directly across the line of fire, trusting the engines to carry them out of danger before the frigates could fire. As the blaster fire caused shock waves astern, Cook raced the sloop westward, toward home.

"They're trying to kill us!"

"Civilians," Cook sighed, and shook his head. He didn't want to repeat a maneuver. Not just yet, anyway. And he was too busy to say anything else.

"*Oouch!*"

"Mr. Schroeder..."

"Is he—*ow!*—crazy?"

Pulling until her arms ached, Janet strained to right herself, struggling to get back to the engine room control panel. Just as she reached it, the ship swung violently, sending her careening toward the floor. She cracked her chin against a table leg that was bolted to the deck.

Schroeder screamed in terror, his back pressing against the floor.

Janet opened her mouth to say something, but stopped when she felt herself lift off the floor and saw the ceiling coming directly at her.

"Fasten yourself down!" she hollered, bracing to cushion the impact.

"How the hell do we do that?" Schroeder shot back, joining her on the ceiling.

"Hold onto the safety cord!"

"The what— ?"

Suddenly, all was calm again—and the two floated gently toward the floor.

"He's cut the gravity— !" Janet shouted. "Watch out for another—"

She never finished her sentence. With a single visceral scream, the two slammed into the starboard wall with a dull thud.

"Shit!"

"Can the chatter, Number Two"

"He's a demon, Larry. A fucking demon."

"Can it! All ships come about. Attack formation. Let's not get fancy. She's just a lone sloop. We've got her outgunned and outmatched. Spread out and fire at will."

"Anybody have any doubts— ?"

"I said—can it!"

"All power to shields, " Cook shouted into the intercom, veering the ship sharply to port. "*Now!*"

Without warning, Willie felt his body slam into the side of the ship, as

Cook cut the engines completely and they absorbed a glancing blast from the guns of one of their pursuers. Firing all maneuvering thrusters to come violently about, and throttling the engines up to their maximum once again, Cook sent the ship spiraling inside its own course until the *Lucky Lady* had completely reversed its course, defying most principles of navigation still being taught in the service acadamies.

Willie felt his body slam against the side of the ship, and he sagged limply to the deck, stunned and groggy. Regaining his senses, dragging himself back to his seat, he looked to see that they had just slipped past the trailing frigate, leaving a trail of enemy fire just past the stern. Racing to the aft porthole, he looked to see a blast of guns lighting the skies, as the Terries' tardy gun blasts fell well behind them. Smiling, he took a deep breath and started to relax.

"How did you do that?" he asked.

"Professional secret," Cook grinned in return. "I'll explain it to you—someday. If we get out of this mess alive."

Seconds later, lifting his gaze, Willie suddenly found himself sick to his stomach. His eyes were transfixed on the six racing points of light. The frigates were beginning a broad, arcing maneuver to come about. It wasn't over, he realized; it wasn't nearly over.

"BANDIT COMING into range—now!"

"Fire!"

"What the— "

"Dammit!"

"Welcome to the club, Red Leader."

"Oh, shut up."

"Don't you want to come about, Larry?"

"You shut up too, Ken."

"ARE YOU trying to kill us?" Schroeder was white as table linen, his hands were trembling uncontrollably. He staggered down the corridor, heading toward the bridge.

"Schroeder!" Cook commanded. "Back to the Engine Room! *Now!*"

"Just what do think you're doing, bouncing us every which way like that?"

"Mr. Schroeder...," said Janet, sticking her head outside the engine room hatch. "Please, Mr. Schroeder."

Cook glanced at his screens. Gunning the engines, he raced away from the westernmost frigate. From the way his last reversal had tangled the frigates, he guessed he had about three minutes before they regrouped for another attack. Engaging the autopilot, he turned the chair slowly about, and glowered mercilessly at the frightened old man.

"I have no time to argue," Cook said coldly. "Either get back where you belong, or I'll bind and gag you myself, and stow you with the baggage."

"It's all right, Skipper," Janet said, scampering to Schroeder's side. "I'm sorry." Taking him by the arm, she led him back toward the open hatch, trying her best to calm him.

Angrily turning back toward the screens, Cook scanned the skies, trying to decide his next move. He knew he couldn't keep it up forever. Sooner or later, he'd make a mistake or the frigates would get lucky. Or some other ships would join the pursuit. Or he'd just exhaust himself. He had to do something to get them off his back. Suddenly, it struck him: he raised his eyes to look out the viewing bay, and there it was, just as he remembered.

Laying ahead of them, just off to starboard.

Burcaw's Binary.

He checked his heading against the frigates and smiled to himself, thanking the stars for his continued good fortune. Everything was lining up perfectly; and with a little more luck....

He gunned the throttle and changed course for the binary star system, all the while wondering why he never got these grand ideas in time to avoid turning everything into a crisis. Without taking his eyes off the skies in front of them, he nudged the rib cage of the boy sitting at the navigator's station. "What kind of auto-destruct system do we have on this ship?" he asked brusquely.

Willie felt his head swimming. He gulped in alarm, trying hard not to faint.

"— AND HE'S swung centerside of that tiny gas pocket. Look's like he's heading toward that red double-dwarf star system off to the East."

"What's his heading, Number Four?"

"About ten degrees north of heading 850."

"Why head off in the wrong direction like that? Think he's lost his bearings, Larry?"

"I doubt it. He's never been lost in his life. Come to heading 850, and fan out. But play it careful, people. We're in his skies, now—and I'm sure he has more than a few tricks left. Charge your guns now. Let's take nothing for granted."

JANET WAS TRYING her best not to lose her temper. Her head and body ached from her continuing interactions with the equipment and walls of the engine room. She paid no attention to the gauges and dials, which the Skipper's dartings about were sending into the red zones as far as the eye could see. Nothing she could do was likely to change that. She had her hands full trying to keep Schroeder from falling over the edge.

She looked at him again—pale as a sheet and huddled in a corner, his eyes filled with tears. He was mumbling over and over how they never should have left Port Babylon. It took all her patience not to explode in rage. She knew it wouldn't do the slightest good, and would only frighten the old timer even more. But it wasn't the old man who was the source of her anger. Taxing as he was, he couldn't help himself, and getting mad at him wouldn't help one whit.

No, that wouldn't do at all. She was saving the fullness of her fury for Cook.

"Now, just try to relax," she cooed, in her most soothing voice. "Take deep breaths, and try not to think of what's going on outside."

"We're going to die," came the tearful reply. "We're all going to die."

"No we won't. You'll see. Skipper will pull us through. He always does."

The mulish jerk, she stormed in silence. Always takes over everything and grinds everyone under his thumb. Then he bulls his way along, not giving Thought One to anyone else. How typically male, she fumed. And she knew just how scared she was: Skipper or no Skipper, she could feel death closing around her. But civilians didn't have the training to steel themselves against the creeping paralysis of panic. She could just imagine the effect of all this on someone going through it for the first time.

Her anger was broken by a familiar voice coming over the intercom.

"Engineering?" The voice was crisp and commanding; in times of danger, it always was.

"Here," she replied instinctively. Much to her surprise, her resentment was gone.

"I'm sending the boy back there to help you two drag something heavy to the air lock. How long will it take you to program a twenty-second time delay?"

Taken aback, Janet looked around. The engine room was littered with spare wires and connectors and coupling fuses, scattered randomly on the floor. She hoped she could find whatever she needed, but given the size of the clutter she was sure she could find something.

"A minute or so. If I can find an activation switch and a few scraps of basic electronics. Why?"

"Get started—right now. Then start rigging a transfer pipe from auxiliary life support, venting out through the auxiliary thrusters. You've got about five minutes to get everything ready."

"But why— "

"Just start looking. There's no time to explain it right now. Tell Schroeder to start dragging everything we don't need—clothes, papers, leftover food, and anything we can spare that's made of ultrynium—back toward the airlock. Having something to do might keep his mind busy. And get Rachel from her cabin. Maybe she can help, too."

"Can't you leave the poor child alone? She's probably scared to death by this time."

"*Acccb*—so far, she's been the best trouper of the lot."

"You know, Skipper—just once, I wish you'd try getting these bright ideas in time to avoid turning everything into a crisis."

"Stow it, Missy," Cook snapped curtly. "This isn't the time for grousing. It's time to get to work."

"Aye aye, Skipper."

PURSUING FROM the west, the frigates quickly closed on the small sloop. As they neared the twin red stars, Larry sensed that they were closing for the kill. Opening the command channel, he hailed his party with the attack orders. Lost in the thrill of battle, and the excitement of fighting against the very best, was the last trace of doubt about what they'd been ordered to do.

"All ships," he announced, "prepare to attack. Four, five and six, head off to 750, and swing centerside of the system; the rest of you, follow me. If we catch him in the pincer, we've got him."

His eyes fixed on the sensor screen, Larry watched the sloop slicing through the blackness, cutting first one way, then another, desperately trying to keep ahead of the frigates' powerful guns. Pushing aside any pity for the overmatched ship, Larry felt a sudden surge of pride in himself and his men: they were about to do what a whole fleet of lizards could never manage. Whatever else might be said about the cruelty of life among the stars, at least he would have his one moment of glory.

Plunging through the system's heliosphere from the north, Larry could see the glowing stars, distended in the middle as they whirled about each other in a frenzied orbit, flares erupting from each sun in an unending display that made their radar pulse wildly with random static. Nearing their quarry, each half of the pincer approached from the opposite end of the system. Larry watched the sloop cut her power as it flattened her trajectory and darted behind a small planet, about two thousand miles across and spilling rapidly around its dense core of nickel and iron. Suddenly, he gasped in admiration. Too late to do anything but feel the fool, he realized what Cook was up to: rounding the airless world, the sloop would shoot through space like a comet. The planet's gravity would hurl it like a sling, heaving the sloop from the grip of the closing pincers and shooting her again towards Isis, leaving the frigates behind to admire her pilot's cunning and daring, forcing them to give chase once more.

"Code One, this is Red Leader— "

He was about to give the order to cut speed and prepare to come about—when, without warning, he saw the blast of a great explosion, which took several chunks of the rocky world with it, careening off into the darkness of space and tumbling slowly against the dull red light of the nearby suns.

* * *

"S-17 REPORTING."

"Go ahead, Seventeen.

"Nothing, Commander. Just rocks and debris from the planet. Nothing more. No trace of an energy trail, and no signs of life anywhere. I think they crashed."

Larry leaned back in his chair and took a deep breath. The commodore always sailed on the edge of the possible, he told himself. As clever as Cook was, maybe he did cut it a bit too closely this time. But this was just the kind of ploy Cook would try. And this mission, Larry knew, was his personal responsibility; he wasn't about to give up the search unless he found something more substantial than a ship that simply vanished into the darkness.

"Keep scanning," he radioed back. "We're going to keep at it until we find something to confirm the kill."

"But Commander..."

"Sorry people—but I don't trust him."

"Oh, come on, Larry."

"That's enough, Number Two. We'll rotate the scouting teams, and send out another party when they get tired. I don't care how long it takes. As long as it's my neck on the chopping block, we'll take the time to do it right."

"For crying out loud."

"Until we find some trace of that sloop, I'm not calling off the hunt. Now keep scanning."

"Aye aye— "

"— yeah, right."

"   — and suck ultrynium."

"I didn't quite hear that, Number Six."

"Nothing, Commander. Just some subspace static."

"Any more static like that and somebody's going to lose his ship."

"Yes, sir."

SLOWLY, MINUTES turned into hours. After two days of searching, a scouting team sent to investigate the planet's surface detected shards of metals and incinerated clothing, together with traces of foodstuffs and other organic matter near the crater that marked the epicenter of the explosion. The mass was a little low, the scouts reported, but most of it was obliterated in the blast. Satisfied at last, Larry radioed a terse message to ZarCom—a cryptic "Sadler to Base: Mission accomplished"—and ordered his ships to withdraw.

But as his own ship circled the planet for the last time before accelerating out of orbit, Larry found himself gazing sadly at the pockmarked surface where a legend had passed from flesh and blood into the realm of myth, wondering how Central Command was going to deal with the news of Cook's death and reflecting bitterly on the cruel indifference of the Universe and fate. Soon, the frigates had moved on, leaving the empty hours to pass in silence with no shadows of movement, no stirrings of life, nothing but the sterility of barren worlds and lifeless rocks.

* * *

HOURS PASSED. And then days.

Amid the blackness and the dust, nothing moved among the crags, and there were no stirrings or whispers of life—except inside a small, dark cylinder, floating freely through space toward the lesser twin of the system's dominant star.

"WELL?"

"Patience, Old Timer."

"Can't we at least turn another light on?"

"We've been through this before. No nonessential power. Use the other flashlight."

"I can't find it."

"That's just as well. It's probably dead anyway."

"It's been three days!"

"And it'll be three more—and three more—and maybe three more after that—before we move out of here."

"This is crazy. Absolutely crazy."

"Perhaps. But I'd have posted a scout. Maybe two. If the Terrans did that, I want them as bored as we are. Unless we see something approaching from ZarCom, I'm in no particular hurry to move."

"The batteries won't even give me a reading from the navigation computer! For all we know, it may be wiped clean!"

"If I have to, I can get us home from here blindfolded. Now turn off the controls."

"This is my ship, for crying out loud!"

"You'll get it back when we're out of danger. Until then, you'll do as you're told."

THE NEXT day, a single scout fired its engines and departed to the east, toward the base at Zarathustra Command. Four days later, a low-wave subspace signal filled the long-range channels, and a second scout headed eastward. Ten days after the second scout passed out of sensor range, a solitary ship began the journey home—slowly at first, edging out of the rocky heliosphere of the binary system and venturing tentatively into interstellar space. After inching its way through the heavens for several days, at last the small ship fired its engines for subspace travel and slowly began to head westward.

Toward the angry red clouds looming in the distance.

Toward the raging storms guarding the narrow channel that was the only passage through the thick, churning nebulae.

Toward a land struggling with a crisis of conscience, and frightened out of its wits by the dangers that lurked in the east.

Toward Isis and home.

Chapter 39

"I T'S CHECK-IN TIME again, out there," the voice crackled over the speaker, startling Lt. Christopher Barnes so much that he inhaled a large swallow of lemonade and nearly choked trying to clear his throat. "What do you have to report?"

"Outpost 11 reporting all clear."

"All right, OP-11. On the Cosmic Clock it's...it's...oh, just a second. Well, it's about 2200 hours local time. We'll check in again in another four hours or so. Out and over."

"Roger. Over and out."

Rocking slowly in his chair, Barnes stared at the ceiling of his makeshift monitor station and let out a slow groan. The sterile monotony of the beige walls was enough to make him scream, he thought, just for the change of pace. He hated his assignment. For the last two months, he'd hated every second of every minute he'd been cooped up in this tinderbox of steel and ultrynium. He'd even come to hate every book and piece of music he'd brought with him, now that he could recite every word and recall every note by heart. Most of all, he felt cheated. Cheated by Life and by Fate, by everything and everybody.

It wasn't so much the prospect of spending another Solstice Day alone, he thought—though spending the holidays on a forlorn hunk of metal surrounded by blackness and dust was just one of the things not mentioned in the Home Reserves recruitment brochure four years ago when he was trying to figure out a way to get his engineering degree for free. The Recruiting Officer had stressed the tax-free tuition and stipend. That and the Midnight Blue uniforms, which the sergeant claimed the girls simply couldn't resist. That was what Reserve Duty was all about, he'd been told. But that was before....

Before....

That was before things had changed. Now, Isis needed twenty times the number of reservists on hand to man her Navy. And they couldn't spare any of them. Not with the Terries massing at ZarCom and spreading their lies from one end of Terra to the other. Whatever the cost, they couldn't afford to drop their guard for an instant, and in his head Barnes knew all of this. But the holidays were upon them, and he hated the thought of spending the last Solstice Time any of them might ever know away from his family, staring into the darkness, watching the approach from the East and waiting helplessly for the first sign of the coming invasion.

He slammed his fist onto the console table and rose to his feet. Pacing might not keep the Terries at bay, he thought, but at least it helped pass the time. And it was as useful as anything else the Government had him doing. The attack could come at any time, but after nearly a year of preparation, nothing was ready and nothing had changed. There was the same pointless bickering among the politicians back home; the same squabbling among what was passing for a fleet. There was fear in the eyes of everyone he saw, and in every voice he heard. And, the last indignity of all saw him stuck alone for the holidays with just a computer for company. His cursed bitterly whenever he thought about his rotten luck. He was too scared about the future to make any plans beyond the next watch.

Suddenly his heart skipped a beat.

From the far wall, the alarm bell was sounding frantically. Over and over, it sang its brassy song of warning: something was approaching from the East.

Frantically he pulled the emergency transmitter, alerting Home that he'd picked up a signal. His pulse was racing, and his palms started to sweat. His vision darkened around him as he started feeling light-headed. As he focused the incoming signal he began to feel very foolish.

It was not the invasion; from the looks of things, it probably wasn't even Terran. In simpler days, it would have passed without notice, much less caused the near panic now rippling from the tiny monitor station all the way back to Isis.

It was a ship, a single ship, winding its lonely way westward, having just passed through the treacherous clouds and shoals guarding the eastern approach to the Mother Planet.

"How typically Isitian," he muttered in disgust.

Feeling like an idiot, Barnes opened the hailing channel to Home Command. He had to pass the word along sooner or later. There was no way he'd come out of this without looking like a fool, of course, but at least he could spare the folks back home a few extra moments of grief. He was unprepared for the reaction back home to this latest bit of news.

* * *

"...AND YOU are directed to make visual contact with the unidentified vessel."

"Visual...?"

"In addition, you are to ascertain its purpose and intention, and make a positive identification of everyone on board before authorizing it to pass your station. With the border sealed from the other end, the Ministry is taking no chances. Naval Intelligence reports increased activity by the Terran fleet at ZarCom. Since this ship managed to evade detection by all our listening posts on the other side of the Nakahashi Clouds, they believe it may be an advance scout, trying to penetrate our defenses as a prelude to an all-out attack. Keep your communication line active, transmitting all information to Intelligence as you receive it. And broadcast on a secure channel. We're arranging for it right now. We'll make any necessary decisions on this end."

Barnes took a deep breath and smiled wanly at the image on his communications screen, a young lady in her early twenties, whose pretty face had brightened many of his days in recent weeks. Today, her face was somber and businesslike. And her angelic blue eyes spoke a sadness that he found unsettling.

"I understand," he sighed. "Anything else?"

"One more thing, OP-11," the young communications officer said softly, lowering her gaze as she tried to avoid looking into his eyes.

"The Minister himself has authorized the use of force to repel the ship, if it proves to be hostile. He's ordered the fleet to be at the ready in ten minutes or less."

"Fat chance of that," scoffed Barnes. "A ten-minute scramble? They won't be ready in ten months. Or ten years, for that matter."

"But in that case," the girl continued, trying her best to maintain her composure, and to convey her message as gently as possible, "you should know that the Department considers your position—your base, and its personnel—to be expendable."

Barnes visibly stiffened, but made no reply.

"Oh, Chris," said the girl on the screen, "I'm so, so sorry."

"Thank you, Mary Beth," he said at last. "I guess it's better to know where you stand." Actually, he thought, he didn't feel that way at all, but he wasn't about to admit it. Not now. And not to her.

"Outpost 11, signing off."

"Over and out," came the reply.

"Hope to see you around," he smiled grimly as her image faded into darkness on his screen.

They were right of course, he thought to himself. He watched the approaching ship leave the Western Channel further and further astern, moving closer and closer to his defenseless position. Slowly, he tuned the subspace radio to the normal hailing frequencies. As the ship passed into range for visual contact, he took a deep breath and turned on the broadcast signal. There was simply no other way, he told himself. Even if it meant revealing his position, Isis had to know what was coming. And if it was Terry, finally come to call—well, he didn't even want to think about it.

"Unidentified ship bearing 750," he called, his voice brusque and cold. "This is the Isitian Interstellar Navy. You are ordered to slow immediately to C-2."

Immediately, the craft slowed to the required speed. Barnes took it as a good sign until he realized that an approaching enemy would be unlikely to attack until they'd focused on his broadcast signal.

"You are ordered to identify yourself."

To his surprise, the image of a teenager came onto the screen. This is what all the fuss is about, Barnes thought to himself. A joyriding adolescent?

"This is the sloop *Lucky Lady* out of Westport, Isis," said the boy, his eyes brimming with excitement. "We've just run the blockade and— "

"Wait until you are asked," Barnes said gruffly. He'd gotten himself and everyone all worked up, he thought—ready to face death, destruction, and the whole Cosmic Guard—and for what? For some goof-ball kid with nothing better to do than gad about the skies playing pirate. He compared the audio identification with the ship's configuration and entered whole mess into the outpost's mainframe, which confirmed the ship as Isitian.

"Ship status confirmed," he said coldly. "You are William Peter Schroeder, of Crescent Harbor?

"He's my grandfather. He's asleep now. And so are all the rest of—"
"Please identify yourself."
"I'm William Robert Schroeder. We've just had one time of it— "
"Just a moment."
Barnes entered the name on computer, which confirmed William Robert Schroeder, age twelve, as an Isitian.
"Are there any others on board?"
"Are there? Just wait until— "
"Do you have any other relatives on board?"
Young Willie was getting impatient. "Yes, but— "
"Names of other relatives on board?"
"My sister Rachel."
"Any other relatives?"
The boy shook his head.
"Any other Isitian nationals? And any foreign nationals?"
"Yes—one. Isitian, I mean. And he's brought his fiancée with him. She's from New Babylon."
Barnes grunted skeptically, his face darkened by a disapproving scowl. It wasn't enough being cooped up here, day after day. Now, he had to deal with pubescent jabbermongers, running on at the mouth. And the fools on the ship were like rats: particularly dim-witted rats, clamoring to board a sinking ship. The rank stupidity made him all the more bitter.
"Fiancée, eh?" Barnes scoffed irritably. "What kind of prat-head brings his bride to a doomed planet, about to be blasted to kingdom come? Third-class moron, if you ask me."
From the control deck of the tiny sloop, the lad's back stiffened and his eyes hardened. He was only twelve, he thought, but already he knew enough to spot a fool. He wondered how many grownups could say the same.
"It's Commodore Cook," he replied angrily.
Staring into the face of innocent hurt and anger, Barnes' face reddened. He realized at once what an ass he'd been, blubbering over his petty troubles while all around him were enduring their own private hell. Tears welled in his eyes. He thought of his parents, consumed with worry, and his grandparents, looking back on a lifetime of work only to find the threat of invasion waiting for them at the end of it all. Now, this tiny ship was struggling bravely to return home with a cargo that everyone back home had dreamed about for the last year, but nobody dared to mention

out loud. And he had nothing better to do than feel sorry for himself, so consumed by self-pity that he was numb to everything and everyone around him, and quite blind to the quiet heroism that passed for everyday life on Isis.

"I'll relay the message," he said, his voice thickening. "And—well, we've all been under a lot of strain, here. I didn't really— "

"Just guide us home," the boy smiled wearily. "It's been a long trip, and we're all very tired."

* * *

THE FIRE crackled and swirled, filling the small den with a cozy warmth. Outside, the wind gusted angrily, snapping at homes and trees and buildings. Curled on the couch, nestling beside her sleeping husband, Irene McInnis listened to the ancient melodies, telling their sweet tales of peace and goodwill. On holidays past, she'd found serenity and warmth in the tidings of Year's End. This year she found it overwhelming. It made their plight nearly unbearable.

Closing her eyes, she tried to let the music lift her spirits, but all she could feel was the beating of her own heart. The whole universe seemed to be crashing down on top of her, its sheer weight crushing her spirit. Ever since the Crisis began, ever since the dreadful day when the Terrans first delivered their ultimatums and began spreading their lies throughout the Terran press, she'd lived under a mountain of worry. It felt so good to wrap herself in her husband's arms, to lose herself in his gentle strength and tenderness. It was hard pretending to be strong when everything around her was madness. Yet she knew that if the Chancellor surrendered to hopelessness, then their cause was lost. An epidemic of despair already gripped the countryside, and the approaching holidays only made things worse. She doubted that Isis could find anyone else with the stomach, or the bull-headed stubbornness, to take her place.

Suddenly, she was startled by the ringing of the emergency pager. Her face ashen, she fought to stay calm. Easing out of her sleeping husband's embrace, she ran to the videophone and turned on the receiver. When the image cleared, she found herself staring into the stunned and distant eyes of George McKenzie, the Minister of Defense and head of their new Interstellar Navy. She felt a gnawing in the pit of her stomach, and steeled herself for the worst. Silently, he motioned for her to cut the speaker, and she picked up the hand-receiver.

"Yes, George?"

"The Line's secure at this end, Irene. If you could make sure nobody can overhear on yours."

"My husband's sound asleep and we're quite alone. What's the problem?"

"I've cut communications between ground and sky."

"What is it? What's wrong?" She suddenly remembered the bulletin from their outpost, and felt as if she were falling into a dark cavern. Was it time already? She hated to think the end could come so soon, so suddenly. But George didn't exactly look upset. His eyes were red and moist, but he seemed more baffled than worried, and a curious smile, half-hidden by his lips, made him look almost amused.

"Wrong? Oh, nothing's wrong, precisely. In fact, nothing may be wrong at all."

"Then stop this riddling nonsense at once! You've already given me quite a fright."

"I thought you should know that—well, there's a rumor, all buzzing around the skies about now. And what with the holidays approaching and all. And with everything else too, you know. Well, I just thought it would be rather...well, rather demoralizing if it turned out to be—well, just a rumor, after all."

"What is it?" the Chancellor demanded. "What are you babbling about?"

"We have confirmed—for a fact, you understand—that there actually is a ship approaching from the east," McKenzie said absently. "Apparently ran the Terry blockade and all. Actually, from what I gather, they had quite a time of it, too. A real loller of a chase, to hear the boys tell it in the galley."

"That's what's causing all this fuss? One fool daredevil in one fool ship finally ran the damn blockade?"

"No, no, no—of course not. It's just the rumor, that's the thing."

"If you don't give me a straight answer— "

"The rumor—oh, bother, how to begin?"

"*George* !!"

"Just out with it, I guess. That's the first-class ticket, here. But I warn you, it's all terribly unconfirmed."

"I'm warning *you*, George McKenzie!"

A loud sigh came over the receiver.

"The rumor," the Minister said at last, his eyes glistening as he looked into the troubled face of his old friend, "is that Roscoe Cook is on board that ship."

McInnis felt her throat tighten, and her own eyes began to weaken. For several moments, nothing but silence passed on the line.

"Madam Chancellor?"

"You were right to cut communications, George," McInnis said at last, her voice soft and halting. "A rumor like that would be devastating, if it proved false. You are attempting to— "

"Confirm it?" The sound of hearty cheer coursed over the phone lines; the Chancellor could felt her spirits lifting with each bellow of George's deep, rich laughter.

"There are several hundred ships screaming through space right now, Irene, trying to do precisely that. We couldn't stop them with the whole Terry fleet—and to tell you the truth, I'd to be off with them myself if I could manage it. Of course, it's like to scare the poor soul to Kingdom Come if our lads all come upon him at once. But nobody on the damn ship will wake him, and this isn't the sort of thing we're about to take on hearsay. We're just praying like hell that they don't crash into each other out there. That would be a jot of bad luck about now, wouldn't it?"

The two of them laughed brightly. It was the first time in weeks McInnis had heard her old friend joking. And for the first time in ages, she found comfort and reassurance in his voice.

"We're doing all we can, Irene. And I promise I'll call you, one way or the other, just as soon as I get the word."

"Thanks, George. I can't begin to tell you....," McInnis said, her voice trailing off into a whisper.

"Does put rather a ruddy spin on things, doesn't it?"

"It certainly does."

"Happy Solstice, Irene—and merry on to Christmas."

Putting down the receiver, the Chancellor walked to the window, to look at the streets below. The wind was blowing lustily, sending fallen leaves cascading through the streets. The winter clouds loomed overhead, bringing the cold rains with them. But for the first time in more than a year she felt a mammoth burden lifting off her shoulders. Somehow, she was sure, everything would be all right. Somehow, they would find a way to get through this; and in the end, somehow, they would find a way to survive.

"Irene?"

Hearing her husband's voice, she was startled to find that she was crying. Quietly, she stepped to the couch to nestle in his arms.

"What's wrong?"

"Nothing."

"But— ?"

"Nothing's wrong," she whispered, her tears dampening her husband's soft nightshirt. "Nothing at all."

* * *

HIGH ABOVE the sleeping planet, the small ship eased into orbit, beginning its approach to a waiting bay in a dock on the shining space station just below the distant horizon. Beneath the ship, lightning danced between the high clouds of a storm near the terminator line, where night became day and the darkness faded into the breathless blue of a warm, gentle ocean. For the first time in her life, Janet gazed down on the Planet Isis, whose playful clouds and peaceful seas seemed a universe away from the war she had left behind. On all sides were hundreds of ships that had come to welcome them. As one small ship, and then another, and another, passed close enough to see inside, she waved from the bridge to the beautifully foolish people who had come to greet them.

But she knew that she was not the one they all hoped to see: he was in the darkened observation room in the 'tweendeck, alone with his thoughts and his own private torment.

Leaving the Schroeders on the bridge, Janet stepped through the hatch and into the housing that contained the observation window. The unlit room was black as night. In the reflected light of his homeland she saw Cook, staring quietly onto the warm blue seas and green, fertile shores of the land he'd left when still a boy. Without a word, she went to his side, nestling herself snugly in his arms. She pretended not to notice the tears streaming down his cheeks.

SAILING OVER the planet, time itself had little meaning. A warm blanket of air sheltered the tiny world from the bitter cold of space and bathed the planet in life, as it had for uncounted eons. Above the swirling air masses and wispy clouds, the eternal black skies stretched to a boundless infinity, and the mighty guns that loomed so large in the finite minds of the age were but grains of sand on a distant shore.

It had been twenty years, thought Cook. Twenty years since he'd walked the land of his childhood and smelled the sweet Isitian air. She hadn't changed at all: her oceans were still blue as an angel's eyes, her clouds were still the purest white. She looked like any of a hundred worlds he'd seen in his travels. But none had been home. No other would ever be home.

The warrior had returned to his native land. As he gazed on the face of Isis the tears flowed warmly from his eyes, as he thought about lost time, about lost youth and innocence, and about the mortal danger facing everything and everyone he loved.

Coming next...the saga concludes in

The Guardians of Peace

ABOUT THE AUTHOR

JEFFREY CAMINSKY, a life-long resident of Planet Earth, lives in Michigan with his wife and family. His books include a book about soccer officiating, *The Referee's Survival Guide*, and *The Sonnets of William Shakespeare*, a guide to Elizabethan poetry. In an alternate reality, he is a retired public prosecutor in Detroit.

His book *Clouds of Darkness* is the third volume in the *Guardians of Peace* adventure series.

www.ingramcontent.com/pod-product-compliance
Lightning Source LLC
Chambersburg PA
CBHW020826030726
47496CB00001B/117